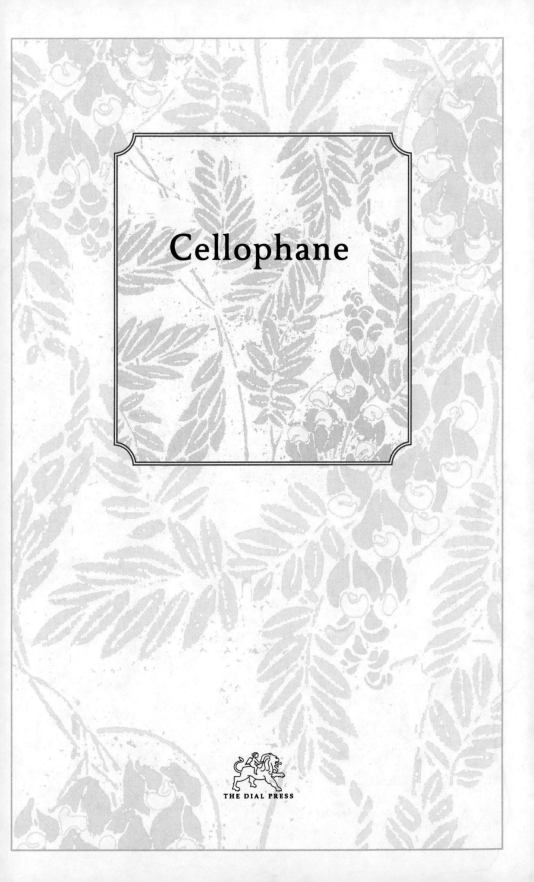

Cellophane

THE DIAL PRESS

Also by Marie Arana

American Chica: Two Worlds, One Childhood

The Writing Life: Writers on How They Think and Work

Cellophane

A Novel

———

MARIE ARANA

The Dial Press

Acknowledgments

I will never be able to repay the kindness and generosity extended to me by the late Loren McIntyre—photographer, explorer, discoverer of the headwaters of the Amazon—who gave me his maps, his books, his vision, and most valuable of all, his friendship.

I am also indebted more than I can say to my father, Jorge Enrique Arana Cisneros, for his gift of inspiration; to my mother, Marie Elverine Clapp Arana, for a half-century of devotion; to Susan Kamil, for keen editorial guidance; to Amanda Urban, for unwavering loyalty; and to my children, Lalo and Adam, for their companionship and love.

CELLOPHANE
A Dial Press Book / July 2006

Published by The Dial Press
A Division of Random House, Inc.
New York, New York

Book design by Virginia Norey

Library of Congress Cataloging-in-Publication Data
Arana, Marie.
Cellophane : a novel / Marie Arana
p. cm.
ISBN-13: 978-0-385-33664-2
ISBN-10: 0-385-33664-0
1. Engineers—Fiction. 2. Papermakers—Fiction. 3. Rain forests—Peru—Fiction. I. Title.
PS3601.R345 C46 2006
813'.6 22
2006040204

Printed in the United States of America
Published simultaneously in Canada

www.dialpress.com

BVG 10 9 8 7 6 5 4 3 2 1

Beware of the man
who says he can see
the truth of your life clearly.

His eyes cannot see
the heart of your heart
for all the light of the Sun.

—*Inca proverb*

For Jon,
who sees the heart of my heart

Cellophane

Prologue

D on Victor Sobrevilla Paniagua always knew that he would die as he was born: in a bustling metropolis, surrounded by doting women, far from his paper, the trees, and the rush of a great, dark river. He had come into the world on an arid coast in the prosperous city of Trujillo and he would leave it on the same coast, in Lima, the teeming capital of the Spanish American continent, but his days would spool out in a greener place, in an uncharted corner of the universe, in a life marked by chance and destiny. How could his mother have guessed—when she sent him from one city to another to pursue an education—that he would go on to spend the better part of his life in the Amazon jungle? Even as a child, in the grip of a vivid imagination, he had not dreamed of so far-fetched a possibility. It wasn't until his eighteenth year, as he waited for a streetcar to take him down Avenida Tacna to Lima's School of Engineers, that he recognized his fate in the window of the SKF Company sales office.

The display was simple, showing the full range of the product for which the SKF Company was famous. Three trays lined in icy blue satin cradled the highly polished spheres in graduated sizes, ranging in neat rows from left to right—from the first, which was the diameter of a walnut, to the last, no larger than the head of a fruit fly. A metal plaque, painted blue and white, made the following assurances: *SKF. Swedish ball bearings. For the discriminating engineer.*

Victor had always wanted to be an engineer: a builder of mills, a virtuoso of machinery, a maestro of paper. Even as a child, he had carefully snipped bits of paper from family letters, gathered up litter from city streets, tucked his loot into his pockets, feeling the nap with his fingers. He began to delight in making paper—cooking it in his mother's kitchen, rolling it into sheets in the servants' quarters, hanging it in the bathrooms to dry. For as long as he could remember, he had been fascinated by the stuff. He had come to the School of Engineers in Lima with all the appetite of an obsessive, and now he was learning the science of it: the chemistry of parchment; the physics of its manufacture; the design and production of machines, down to the tiniest of components. *Swedish ball bearings.*

Each morning, Victor would hurry from his room on the fourth floor of a student hostel to arrive early for the streetcar so that he could study the smooth steel orbs, laid out like glittering moonstones. From time to time the old sales agent, whose name—RODRIGO URRUTIA, INGENIERO— was inscribed on the window, would lift his owlish eyes and register the boy: tall, gangly, sallow, a mass of untended curls like an amber halo, a sharp jaw with a scattering of unshaven hair. As weeks passed, the old man would set out other inducements: replicas of bridges, puzzles of pyramids, brochures of engineering feats in faraway places, fanciful inventions. One such invention became the object of considerable fascination for Victor, who had little to occupy him save his books, his studies, and Señor Urrutia's displays. The miraculous device appeared one morning in the window, flanked by two panels of cardboard, with a sign printed in neat calligraphy: URRUTIA'S PERPETUAL-MOTION MACHINE.

It consisted of a tiny train track—the sort sold in toy shops alongside railroad cars made by Gilbert or Hornsby or Marklin, imported miniatures for rich men with mechanical fancies. The track was set out in a perfect circle, a catena of curved segments on a pitched rectangle of wood. A Ping-Pong ball painted silver sped around it, skimming the rail. Around and around the track it went—in the morning, as Victor awaited the streetcar, and into the night, as he slouched home under the weight of his books. Day after day, week after week, Victor stood in front of that office on the Avenida Garcilaso de la Vega and pondered how a ball could travel in circles with nothing to secure or propel it. He would make a point of coming at odd times—on Sundays, when the office was closed—but the ball was always in motion. Once, he slipped out of his hostel at two in the morning, thinking he would take it by surprise, but there it was, even at that hour, riding an infinite circuit.

One day, as he peered through the SKF window, his eyes fell on the engineer at the worktable. Hunched over a precision scale, pincers poised, Señor Urrutia was weighing the tiniest of his steel balls and placing them carefully into marked boxes. Just then, a fat fly lifted off his shoulder, circled his bald head, bounced off the gooseneck lamp, and made straight for the window. But a most extraordinary thing happened. As it flew over the old man's invention, the fly suddenly spun off course and reeled into quick retreat. What caused that radical change of direction? Victor stepped to the right of the window and then to the left, pressing his head against the glass, trying to see behind the panels that flanked the track. All at once, he understood Señor Urrutia's genius. The racing ball wasn't self-propelled at all—that was the brilliance of the illusion. Behind the left panel, just beyond view, sat a fan. Victor couldn't picture it, couldn't see it, but he knew it was there. A rush of air was driving the ball, and the fly had flown into the current. The physics was elementary: What had applied to the fly in an instant was meant to apply endlessly to the ball. The pitch of the platform, the vector of wind, the velocity of flow, were such that the ball was pushed with enough momentum to loop the full length of the track.

The young man snorted with satisfaction. He put his hands on his hips and surveyed the shop, looking for Señor Urrutia, but his eyes fixed on something else, every bit as compelling as the bug and the ball. A large poster loomed over the old man's worktable, pinned flat against the wall by four shiny tacks. It was the black-and-white photograph of a massive house fashioned entirely from metal. The iron structure rose from the dirt so that the gleaming columns and bolted walls seemed to jut from nature. A veranda ran the full length of the second floor, girding the house like an ornate bracelet. Standing in front of that monument to modernity was a rain forest Indian, naked in all essentials except for the feathers that sprang from his head and the paint that ribboned his chest. From his wrists, knees, and ankles hung little fringes of straw. Beneath the photograph was a caption, printed in bold block letters: AFTER THE SUCCESS OF HIS FAMOUS TOWER, GUSTAVE EIFFEL DESIGNED AND CONSTRUCTED THIS IRON HOUSE FOR THE 1898 PARIS EXHIBITION. TODAY, IT GRACES THE CAPITAL OF THE AMAZON. And in smaller print, barely legible at that distance: *If Paris can come to Iquitos, so can you, intrepid voyager!*

Victor had never really studied the inside of the shop, so fascinated had he been by its window, but now he found himself transfixed by the poster, as streetcars rushed past behind him, as the fat fly paced the veranda of Monsieur Eiffel's magnificent construction like a haughty, impatient guest. He wondered at the audacity of it: How could that iron behemoth have been built in a primitive jungle? How could technology have penetrated that distant beyond?

As he stood there, lost in contemplation, Señor Urrutia appeared before him, rapped his bony knuckles on the glass, and startled the youth from his reverie. The old engineer pointed sharply toward the avenue. At least a dozen trolleys had rattled by on Garcilaso de la Vega, headed for his school and the Plaza de San Martín. Victor smiled politely and nodded, then took a deep breath, puffed out his cheeks, blew, and pointed to the perpetual-motion machine. Señor Urrutia seemed surprised—even offended—drawing himself to his full height and clutching the lapels of his suit. But then the old man's features softened. He put a finger to his lips and winked.

Victor Sobrevilla Paniagua returned to that window in the following days, not to study the ball's barely perceptible variations of speed as it whirled around the track, but to look at the photograph of Eiffel's triumph in the Amazon. There was something about the way the house fastened to land—something about the Indian's shining eyes that made the three-story structure behind him magical. He came again and again, barely glancing at the ball, even after Señor Urrutia had replaced it with another invention: a mechanical robot that plucked steel balls from a box labeled CANNON FODDER and dropped them, one by one, onto a miniature roller coaster. The balls slid up and down, around and around the delicate bearings until they came clacking back again. A neatly printed sign in front of the new display read NAPOLEON'S ARMORY. But, as much as that gadget might have inspired other fantasies, it did not engage Victor's imagination. He returned day after day to reread the words on the wall—*iron house, capital of the Amazon, intrepid voyager*—until, one morning, Señor Urrutia became so irritated at Victor's lack of interest in Napoleon's armory that, as the boy mounted the steps of the streetcar, the old man yanked the poster from the wall, tacks flying. "Insufferable boy!" he yelled. When Victor walked past the shop on his way home that night, he saw Eiffel's palace in a rumpled heap in the corner.

It didn't matter. By then, Victor had learned all he could about the Iron House in the library at the School of Engineers. Its history had been well documented. Anselmo del Aguila, a rubber baron in the Peruvian interior who wanted to flaunt his new wealth, had bought it from Eiffel himself before the turn of the century. He had had it dismantled, every wall plate and crossbeam crated with corresponding nuts and bolts, packed with detailed drawings, and shipped on a slow boat to Lisbon. From there, the boat had crossed the Atlantic and navigated into the mouth of the Rio Amazonas, past Brazil's Ilha Grande de Gurupa, toward the great jungle city of Manaus. Reloaded onto three barges, for its weight was prodigious, the metal house had crossed into Peruvian territory and pressed on toward Iquitos, where it was reconstructed on cleared land in the heart of the Amazon forest. The rain forest Indians had never seen land free of trees, much less anything like that three-thousand-ton structure. How could they appreciate the generations of science that had built it? Even Victor, who had studied under Peru's distinguished engineers for more than a year now, struggled to understand the magnitude of such a feat.

In his single-minded pursuit of that understanding, Victor Sobrevilla Paniagua learned a good deal about the Amazon: The river was the heart and blood of the jungle. There were no roads, no rails—water was the only byway, and the dense green walls of the rain forest the only landscape a navigator could see. Under that towering canopy, man was just another animal. Tapping the jungle's treasures demanded ingenuity. Surviving the jungle's perils was a bold game of chance.

He wanted to go there. More than his obligation to return to his family in Trujillo, the allure of the Amazon, the notion that to build there was to best any engineer in Paris, began to consume him. Eventually, he found the initiative to stride into Señor Urrutia's sales office and offer to buy the crumpled poster. But the old engineer scratched his head, shrugged his shoulders, and said, "Too late, boy. The ragman already relieved me of it." He pointed to a photograph of a black Model T unveiled at the St. Louis Exhibition. Although Victor admired Henry Ford's automobile, it could not erase the image of the house. He longed to stand in a place untouched by man—more remote than Iquitos—and, despite all adversity, raise leviathans out of the earth.

His professors encouraged him. Doctor Laroza, an engineer who had studied in Paris and designed a factory in Marseilles, began guiding him to miracles of construction erected in the most merciless of environments: The Inca fortress at Sacsayhuaman, made of one-hundred-ton boulders that had been transported—no one knew how—across the cordillera of the Andes, then cut and fit perfectly, with no evidence of mortar. Egypt's Great Pyramid of Khufu, a tower of stone perched on acres and acres of treacherous sand. Nebuchadnezzar's spectacular gate of Ishtar, built on the ashes of Assyrian plunder. The Rajputana dam in the pastoral fields of India, the first of its size, constructed entirely of marble.

Little by little, Victor Sobrevilla Paniagua began to realize that he could merge dreams with ambition—combine his passion for paper with a desire to build marvels in the jungle. "Why not?" his teachers exclaimed when the student expressed his idea tentatively. "Of course paper can be milled in the jungle!" "There's water, isn't there? And trees!" "There's no challenge on earth a well-trained engineer can't overcome!"

The idea seemed so logical. The Amazon was rich in cellulose, possibly the only land on the planet so extravagantly endowed with botanical possibility. He began to read everything he could on the subject: from the colonial diaries of Padre Abad to the travelogues of adventurers who had combed its tributaries, hunting cannibals. Victor had listened to any anecdote a professor might offer, pored over rude maps published in travel journals, scoured museums for any mention of the river's extremities—the Ucayali, Urubamba, and Palcazu.

Four years later, in 1913, when he graduated from the School of Engineers, the genial young man secured an apprenticeship with Emilio

Calderón, a papermaker with a factory just north of Lima's port of Callao, where he saw, for the first time, the concrete realities of his destiny: the grinders and threshers that broke down the fiber, the boilers that dissolved the wood into pulp, the beaters that whipped that paste into a fine pudding, the metal screens, the Fourdrinier shakers, the felt belts, and the cylindrical calenders that ironed the wet mass into crisp, dry sheets. As it happened, Emilio Calderón told him, his cousin Gabriel ran a modest paper establishment in the interior. By the time the warm season was over and the *garua* slipped into Lima, choking the capital with a thick gray fog, Victor was making his way to Quillabamba, a highland town on the brow of the jungle.

Scraping together the money he had earned, and with a small stipend from Gabriel Calderón, he took a boat from the port of Callao to Mollendo. He walked the rough rock of those southern beaches for a day, marveling at the dense clouds of migratory gulls that cast long, melancholy shadows on the sea. There was nothing to tempt him save a clutch of drunken hags who serenaded him from the porch of a tumbledown whorehouse as if they were mermaids beckoning Ulysses. He waved at them and grinned, but turned his back and rode the rails to Arequipa, stopping for an afternoon before he boarded the rails to Cusco. He lurched along in the company of noisy villagers, gripping his seat as the iron snake coiled across the spine of the Andes. By the second morning he could see the snowcapped peak of Nevado Ampato in the distance, piercing the turquoise sky. The train took a sharp turn at Lake Titicaca and, as it roared past, Andean geese skittered away in alarm, stippling the calm water with their feet.

For the first time in his life, Victor encountered serranos, tiny Indians with huge barrel chests who swarmed on at every station, peddling their boiled corn, peanut candies, skewered meats—tugging his sleeve and pressing their goods on him with such heartrending sweetness that he hardly noticed how many coins he was giving them. By the time he reached Cusco, he barely had money for a bed in an inn and a mule for the remainder of the journey. After a sleepless night on a fetid mattress, thinking his heart would burst from the altitude, the innkeeper, a kindly Aymara, took pity and waived the fee. He accompanied Victor through the cobblestone streets, held his elbow to steady him, and pointed the way to a hovel with a corral, where a mule driver was feeding his animals. By the end of the following day, Victor Sobrevilla Paniagua had made the one-hundred-kilometer descent from the Andes to the Amazon on the back of an ancient donkey—marking the trajectory of snow as it melts, then rushes, from the hyaline of the nevada to the warm, damp gills of the jungle.

In Quillabamba, Victor mastered the paper trade. By the time he was twenty-two, he was chief engineer of Gabriel Calderón's factory. By the time he was twenty-three, Victor Sobrevilla was standing before an altar exchanging vows with Mariana Francisco Paredes. She was long-legged, large-breasted, with a pretty face and a striking secret deformity. That same year she delivered their first child. The baby was obstinate and ornery, flinging one arm into the birth canal, refusing to move her head into position. Although, in the midst of that crisis, Mariana had the Christian fortitude to pull out her rosary and her prayer cards, the midwife called for a rain forest medicine man to help with the labor. The witchman took one look at the failing mother and immediately understood the situation. He pushed a smooth gray stone into her vagina until it touched the baby's fingers, then mumbled a prayer to the owl spirit who governs all matters of the head. Within an hour, the child responded. She pushed out the stone, making it roll from her mother's labia as cunningly as any ball in Señor Urrutia's shop window. The next thing they saw was a plump little fist, followed by an arm, and then the round dome of her head, launching toward life like a warrior.

The witchman was all happiness, crying out with the mother as she flung her arms wide to praise the sainted Virgin. That was when he saw the accumulation of flesh that dangled from Doña Mariana's underarm—a strange growth that looked for all the world like a hand with five fingers, except that it had no bone. The medicine man pointed to the monstrosity, his face twisted in terror, but she only shook it at him and grinned as if it were a fringe on a mantilla. When he took his magic stone and ran off, chattering incomprehensibly, Victor and Mariana Sobrevilla could only laugh, so delighted were they at the sight of their magnificent daughter, who gazed back with intelligent eyes. Victor suggested they name her Belén, because the word meant

Bethlehem as well as bedlam and therefore captured the spirit of the moment. Mariana smiled radiantly and agreed.

Their second child was born two years later, just as Victor, who had transformed the Calderón factory into a model of efficiency, was offered an opportunity to realize his dream. The grandson of an American railroad tycoon, a jolly, rum-loving playboy named William Randolph Meiggs, had decided on a hunch to grow sugar in the Amazon and ship it downriver to Brazil. Hearing about the brisk production of the factory in Quillabamba, which was making paper out of hemp and sugar cane, and about the young engineer who had made a name there, he decided to call on Victor Sobrevilla Paniagua in person. Meiggs explained to Victor that he was looking for an adventuresome man willing to oversee the construction of a sugar factory in Pucallpa, a town on the banks of the Ucayali River he knew someday would be the terminus of a highway from Lima. As Victor and Mariana sat with the bibulous American on their sunny patio and raised a third glass of añejo, her water broke. She ran to the bedroom, calling for the maid to go fetch the midwife, and Meiggs tottered giddily away—but not before shaking Victor's hand and handing him a fat wad of cash.

Another female child was born that night, presenting her own complications. The baby was perched on her mother's cervix, pressing her head against the maternal heart. The midwife was helpless to do anything about it. Needing no further motivation, Victor went running for the witchman. He found him standing in front of his hut, hacking a long green arm from a giant sansevieria plant. Recalling the woman with the growth on her underarm, the Indian refused to come at first, but the young father seemed so distraught that he relented, bringing a sprig of *uña de gato* to ward off the evil eye.

The medicine man danced at the foot of the mother's bed and rattled a gourd strung with eight beaded skeins that symbolized the eight legs of a spider. When the child pushed into life, she came hips first, and two lemony limbs flopped from her mother's gates so nimbly that the midwife was able to use them as tidy handles. The shaman brimmed with joy, leaping up and down like a cat, proclaiming the baby a natural-born dancer. Mariana, weary by now of the Indian's antics, and feeling that the pressure of the girl's head had taken a toll on her heart, drew herself up and leaned her head on her husband's chest. When he looked into her face and said, "Such an agile child, *querida,* should be given a graceful name," she sighed and whispered, "Graciela!"

The births of Belén and Graciela taught Victor Sobrevilla Paniagua something about rain forest magic. He was sure that the little gray stone and the gourd with eight legs had eased his wife's labors, although he couldn't see how. Perhaps, as with Señor Urrutia's perpetual-motion machine, an explanation lurked in the wings. Events only seemed miraculous—one had to look for the science behind them. The witch-man's medicine worked. Unruly babies were born. An unaided ball flew impossibly around a track. Someday he would trace all these circuits and see the truth of the world clearly.

Their third and youngest child was born six years later, when the little family had already settled in Pucallpa. Mariana braced herself for a difficult labor and, because she continued to be a good Christian, because she put no faith in rain forest medicine, she took out her prayer cards again and propped them on the bed table so that the saints could see her through the ordeal. She climbed into her big brass bed, a hulking piece of furniture Victor himself had designed. (The metalworker had adorned it with such a multitude of shiny knobs that it looked, for all the world, like a monument to ball bearings.) When Mariana announced she was ready to deliver, Victor rushed down the road, elbows swinging, to look for both midwife and witchman. He came back with the first, but not the second, which relieved his wife but launched him on a long chain of worry. When a boy was born easily— headfirst and smiling—Victor understood that good fortune came not only with stones and skeins but with the prayers of Christian believers. The magic might be a saint's card, it might be an object proffered by a witchman, but from that day forward, he thought of all grace as one.

The child was handsome, a thatch of black hair on his large, proud head. He exited his mother easily, slipping into mortality like a well-oiled fish. His umbilical cord was looped around his ankles so that when he slid into the midwife's hands he brought his afterbirth with him as swiftly as a freight train, with a little caboose behind. When Maruca the Gypsy heard of it—for Graciela, her dance pupil, was six by then and a gossipy little girl—the gypsy joggled her bangles and proclaimed Jaime destined to escape a difficult fortune: A baby who left no trace in his mother's belly would grow into a man who could fool the gods.

Victor and Mariana named him after the sturdy saint who was said to be the brother of Jesus. Jaime's sunny good humor so pleased his father that he hardly noticed the physical change in his wife. Mariana often said she hoped to rival Victor's mother by bringing eleven strong lives into the world, but, for all the connubial joy in their big brass bed, the boy with the ready smile was its last filial consequence. She would bear no more children.

Mariana Francisco Paredes de Sobrevilla made up for it. She invested the mothering of eleven children into her population of three. And just as surely as she raised a fine, God-fearing family in the wild splendor of the jungle, her husband raised a metal behemoth from the bare earth of Pucallpa. He fulfilled the brash vision inspired at Señor Urrutia's window; he brought technology to the distant beyond. And he satisfied William Randolph Meiggs's every whim.

By the time Jaime was four and Graciela and Belén were ten and twelve respectively, the factory in Pucallpa was a whirling fount of sugar, shipping its sweetness as far away as Arequipa. But his dream of building a paper factory in the jungle persisted. By the time Jaime was five, Don Victor built a separate structure that made paper from cetico, a slender tree whose roots had the power to purify rainwater. The people of Pucallpa were stunned to see a tree they revered emerge from the other end of his factory in dry rolls of paper. Victor Sobrevilla Paniagua became known along the Ucayali as "the shapechanger," a man who could transform one earthly substance into another.

When Jaime turned six, a great depression ripped through America, and William Randolph Meiggs, now bankrupt, drifted out on his yacht from a port in Rhode Island and drove a steel bullet into his brain. Shortly thereafter, the shapechanger, who answered now only to God and dreams of the impossible, decided to take the orphaned factory downriver, deeper into the jungle—to somewhere between Pucallpa and Iquitos, to an uncharted place where the caoba, the stately mahogany trees, grew in proliferation. He dismantled all of Mr. Meiggs's machinery—the threshers, the washers, the Detroit dryers and Hamburg spoolers—loaded it onto three barges, and sent the whole factory, like Gustave Eiffel's iron marvel, down the black water to a patch of earth his men had cleared in preparation. His wife packed up the big brass bed and all the possessions they had accumulated and, along with thirty other rain forest families one cloudless day in October, boarded a batelon that would take them two hundred and fifty kilometers to their destination. Wending their way down the Ucayali, they encountered no less than fifteen different tribes of Amazon Indians: the Shipibo, the Machiguenga, the Huitoto, the Bora... The gentle ones waved them along, or stared openly at the barges with their monumental cargo. The belligerents rained arrows into the surrounding water, rowed up, and demanded bribes. Little by little, the Sobrevillas learned about the nomads who called that waterway "the blood of the universe," and, little by little, the river tribes learned about them.

A year later, the Sobrevillas had settled onto a four-hundred-hectare clearing, built a three-story mansion with a caoba staircase, a village of thirty shacks, and a factory—all of it blessed by a witchman who lived in a hut on a grassy turn of the river. The shapechanger's hacienda was unlike anything the jungle had ever known. It grew hemp, made paper, and, with time, he christened it Floralinda, "beautiful flowering," in tribute to marvels that spring from a man's imagination.

"If Paris can come to the Amazon, intrepid traveler," Don Victor would say to his wife across the dining-room table, "so can you, darling. So can you."

Imagine if you will that point where the great river begins its race to the sea. Imagine it somewhere between Señor Urrutia's shop and Eiffel's colossus that, to this day, vaults from the mud of Iquitos. Imagine Floralinda as it was: a whirring miracle in the heart of the jungle, a glimmer of a new day. Imagine its creator: a student of science, believer in saints, disciple of witchmen. As rain forest Indians like to say: A man steps into the universe because he is summoned. The spirits call. Motion begins. Fate ravels. Once he is in, there is no turning back: He is the spark between not being and being, between vacuum and life—between the silence and the story.

PART ONE

*A Plague
of Tongues*

1

M any years later, when the wise men gathered with their pierced faces and carved gourds to purify the streets of Floralinda, they agreed they should have known a run of plagues would curse this town. There had been signs, they muttered, sprinkling the hard earth with river water. There was the coughing dog. The blue-skinned boy.

The little white terrier, Basadre, a normally mild, unexcitable creature, had spun through Don Victor Sobrevilla's house whining and frenzied, chasing his tail in perfect circles. There was a madness to his movements—out of control, yet full of grace—a four-legged tango marked by perfect concatenations of the figure eight.

The children laughed, following the dog through the corridors of the mansion, humming, spinning, somersaulting behind him, crashing against furniture until the air clattered with the sounds of the family silver. It began on the top floor of the house, when Basadre came to the doorway of the schoolroom, issued one last bark—a high, strident little cry—then twirled down the stairs to the second floor with its narrow passageways, cavernous bedrooms, and faded mirrors. The five children, age four to ten, sprang from their chairs, so delighted by the sight of the dancing dog that their teacher, Señorita Marcela, didn't have the heart to stop them. They followed the animal, shrieking and bumping along walls so that lizards leapt out and scurried under the carpets in terror. By the time they reached the ground floor, they had chased the little dog over the black-and-white tiles of the foyer, in and out of the portrait-hung sala, around the vast mahogany table in the dining room, and stampeded toward the sacred sanctuary of their aunt Belén's library. The din from Don Victor's grandchildren was so resounding that Boruba, the chief ama of the house, leaned out from the kitchen and with one earsplitting bellow—"*Cállense!*"—dispersed them and sent the ill-fated creature staggering out into the patio, where he sank to the floor and began the terrible business of his coughing. It was a cough such as no one in the Sobrevilla house had ever heard before— dead-dry and brittle, like the rat-tat-tat of a dull hatchet against the trunk of a caoba tree. Basadre coughed and coughed, his white hair matted with sweat, his eyes flat as two desert stones.

Don Victor emerged from his workshop, waving his arms and shouting that he couldn't work with all the racket. "*Que barbaridad!*" he cried. "Here I am putting the last touch of solder on the machine that will bring this misery of a lizard town to glory, and I have to listen to the endless hacking of a demon mutt?" He held a goosenecked pincer in one hand, a ball of wire in the other, and it was clear that he had been in his workshop far too long, for he had that frazzled look—thin hair sprouting skyward, cravat all askew.

Doña Mariana swept downstairs when she heard her husband shouting on the patio. "I'm coming, *querido*! Coming!" Her long silvery hair streamed along her shoulders, as it always did during the hour of the siesta, and her dress was unhooked from underarm to hip. Struggling to tuck her ample bosom into place, she secured one or two hooks and called to Pedro the gardener to move the poor animal out of the sun and into a cool place under the potted cherimoya tree. Pedro had grown to love Basadre and wanted to make him more comfortable, but try as he might, he couldn't lift the poor animal; it was as if Basadre had attached himself to the floor, sent roots into the tilework.

They all came after that: four generations of family members, one by one, registering their concern with varying degrees of dismay. The villagers, in clusters of two and three, came winding up the long path and peered over the brick barricade that had been erected to keep dangerous reptiles from slithering in when the mighty Ucayali overflowed its banks. A barricade without a dog was pointless, and the people of

Floralinda knew it. Dogs were invaluable in the jungle. Don Victor had purchased the terrier on a visit to Pucallpa twelve years before and named him after Federico Basadre, Peru's minister of roads, who had built the highway from Lima to Pucallpa. Just as Basadre, the man, had felt the call to open the Amazon to the world, Basadre, the dog, felt the call to keep it from spilling into his master's house. He could sense a poisonous reptile before a human could, unearth nests of destructive soldier ants, smell wildmen as they moved swiftly along the rim of trees, waiting to raid the cornfields. The villagers filed past the sick animal, clucking their tongues. Basadre was small, but he had been fierce.

Graciela was the first of Don Victor's children to come out to the patio, lavishing the creature with all the attention she would have given her own son or daughter. She had pleaded with Boruba to bring the honey pot from the kitchen, crush the manzanilla flowers, fashion a little nozzle out of a thick rubber leaf, from which she might drip tea onto the tongue of the heaving dog.

Graciela had grown into a magnificent woman, thirty-four years old, with grainy, dark circles that ringed her eyes and gave her a melancholy air that made young men sigh. La Bella Morada, the men at Chincho's bar called her—beautiful purple one—and then they'd hitch their trousers at the thought. She had been a lively child, and those embers still brightened her eyes, her walk, her rare moments of vivacity. There was no one in all of Floralinda who could sing and dance like Graciela. She had lived up to the promise of being a graceful child. When she donned the gold flamenco shoes her tío Alejandro had sent from Trujillo, and when she stamped her long, thin feet the way she had been taught by the old gypsy Maruca, she could bring the whole Sobrevilla household streaming down the caoba stair, eager to see her move.

Graciela lived in the mansion with only her two small children, Pablo and Silvia. La Bella's husband had disappeared suddenly, angrily, five years before, vanishing into the Alto Amazonas like a cobra out of the hot sun. For a while, Nestor Sotomarino had been sighted nearby, in the company of renegade sailors. Some said he had become a rebel guerrillero; others said he was getting rich on coca leaf; but the last he had been seen was by the men down at Chincho's bar, marching off alone with no more than a week's supply of food on his back.

Graciela was the delicately wired antenna of the Sobrevillas. It was she who tasted the sweetness of things to come, felt the ill winds, saw ghosts in the night air. It was she who, on the second day of Basadre's ordeal, tenderly held his dry snout in her hands and realized the cough was no ordinary affliction. It was too otherworldly. Her father had been right to use the word *demon*. There was some witchery at work.

Her older sister, Belén, too, knew that the dog's malady signaled something amiss. Being a person ruled by the head, Belén listened carefully and concluded that it was more complicated than a pulmonary spasm. She put down the book she was reading and began to scour her library shelves for something that would explain the phenomenon. She stood on her toes, stretched a long neck toward her wall of books, and wrinkled her freckled nose. But she couldn't find it. She remembered, however, in lightning concordance between learning and tenderness, a scene from Alexandre Dumas's *La Dame aux Camellias,* in which the heroine's cough is soothed by poetry. Snatching a volume of sonnets by Dante, Belén strode resolutely to the patio, knelt before the animal, and began reading aloud.

"I greet you in Love's name, hoping you will escape that pain so great even the farthest stars flinch, that even the sky drains itself of planet, moon, cloud, as if the end of the world marched on us, as if what I'm about to say were the words that set ablaze each soul, each fear, like a field of dried-out grain!"

The dog gasped and held his breath, leading her to conclude what she'd always suspected, that words could fix everything—she had only to read to the end of the volume to cure their beloved Basadre. But by the third line of the stanza, he was hacking again, with a frenzy that brought tears to her eyes.

If her sister, Graciela, had inherited her mother's heart with something more—a healthy regard for the supernatural—Belén had inherited her father's head with something less—a staunch rejection of jungle sorcery. No matter how often Don Victor told Belén about the witchman, the stone, and her triumphant entry into the world, she refused to think of it as anything but a coincidence. Had she borne children of her own she might have allowed that reproduction was in itself miraculous and that there was scant difference between the roles that a prayer or a stone might play in it. But at the age of thirty-six, she was childless and logical. She regarded rain forest cures as primitive, unenlightened. She disapproved heartily of her father's visits to his feathered shamans. She kept journals, sewn from her father's paper, in which she wrote lists upon lists of random information: the botanical name of each new plant she encountered; amusing aphorisms; foreign words gleaned from books, and their definitions; the title of every novel she had read and its most memorable character.

Her library was a model of organization, every volume in place according to subject and nationality of the author. Her father had built the room twenty years before, when she was only sixteen, worried that his bookish daughter would be lured by his old aunt's standing invitation to come live in Trujillo. He oversaw its construction with infinite care, ordering shelves cut from dense mahogany, seeing that the *urucú* was applied evenly and burnished to a deep red glow. At first, there hadn't been much to shelve, but Don Victor made sure every bagmaker in Pucallpa and every printer in Iquitos knew that he expected books as part of the payment. "Literature!" he'd shout from the dock, as their barges drifted off into black water. "You bring it, you hear me? Bring me Cervantes! Ricardo Palma! El Inca Garcilaso de la Vega! Don't bring me dogshit. I'll charge you more if you do!"

First came the printed matter no one wanted to read—census reports from the military, discarded lesson books, socialist pamphlets about working conditions in Arequipa. But eventually, the collection grew to a laudable diversity: manuals on the navigable waters of the Amazon, dictionaries translating Spanish into a dozen languages, Turgenev's letters, Blake's poetry reinterpreted by Neruda, José Martí's recollections of Manhattan, all of Chekhov's plays. Within twenty years, the room housed more than two thousand volumes. Belén had read them all—some, a number of times—and although she had not chosen to avail herself of the Trujillo invitation, her great-aunt, Tía Esther, had been her library's most beneficent donor, sending books through Tío Alejandro's regular shipments from the coast. And so it was that Tía Esther, from so far away, began to furnish Belén's imagination. If it wasn't with weekly letters written in a bold hand, relaying the news of the day in her bustling city, it was in books, bought at estate auctions by the cartons, inscribed with tender dedications to her grandniece.

There was no question: Books were Belén's faith, her foil against the wilderness. She loved drawing each one from its shelf, handling its spine, dusting away the mites that had been brought to her library from God knew where. She loved that split-second transcendence when reading would carry her off to a realm in which truth reigned, mysteries were explained, and paths unfurled before her—shining and absolute. Reading had made her serious and learned. No, she could not believe a witchman and his stones could make a difference between life and death. Looking down now at Basadre in his misery, Belén wished she could have faith in myths and magic. Hard evidence told her the dog would die.

Elsa, Jaime's wife and the mother of his three children, was next to visit the ailing animal. In mid-morning, after Jaime had departed on one of his weekly trips upriver, she came down, an ivory mantilla hugging her shoulders and a scowl twisting her face. She stood in the frame of the house's carved portals, a good distance from the hacking dog, and yelled, "Stop it, you flea-ridden beast! You're driving me crazy!" But crazy she already was, and the whole household knew it.

Elsa was a parched bird of a woman, as arid as the dunes of Chan Chan. She had come to live with the Sobrevillas after her marriage to Jaime in Trujillo, where he had been sent to attend school. She arrived in Floralinda with a pedigree that proved totally useless in the jungle. Elsa was a Márquez y Márquez, the daughter of the powerful sugar baron whose vast cane fields rimmed the Pacific, between Trujillo and Chiclayo. The Márquezes had built palaces along Peru's rugged shoreline, dug an empire into the desert, filled their shelves with treasures from ancient graves. To meet the growing appetite for sugar in America, the family had sent their agents into the highlands to lend money to the poor freely, but months later they would return to collect what was owed them: in trucks, with whips and shackles, forcing debtors into the cane fields. Elsa had been raised wanting nothing. She wore clothes her father had imported from Paris. She boasted about her education from a French tutor who had been brought all the way from St. Cyr. She was imperious, frigid, self-absorbed. No one in Floralinda could imagine why Jaime had fallen in love with her.

She hadn't always been that way. When Jaime had first met her, she was a clever young woman with a pretty face, a lovely figure, and a socialite's taste for frivolity. The face and figure didn't change. But Elsa's condition had erupted shortly after her arrival in the jungle: a psychosis so acute that Jaime awoke one night to find her shaking uncontrollably. Having been raised along the Ucayali, he assumed she was experiencing an attack of Taki Onqoy, an invasion of microscopic worms that travel the bloodstream, lodge in the brain, and cause convulsions. It was a curse—well known—that jungle Indians inflicted on trespassers. Jaime did what his father would have done: He immediately sent word to a shaman. But as soon as the curandero appeared at the door with bones piercing his nose and a gourd of animal blood in his hands, Elsa jumped on her bed, yipped like a river seal, and refused to allow him to come in.

After the tremors subsided, she began to produce gruesome canvases that featured green men with shriveled teats, lurking in trees. Even as she painted them, she was overheard directing them to keep their distance. More than once, Doña Mariana marched into her room and pleaded with her to paint them over or, at the very least, turn them around so that they faced the wall. She didn't want her grandchildren born with scales and bulging eyes, consequences she was sure would follow if Elsa pursued the theme. On these occasions, Doña Mariana would open her blouse and show Elsa the vestigial fingers that dangled from her underarm. "See this?" She shook her deformity in her daughter-in-law's face and lied, "My mother dreamt of the devil when she carried me, and if you continue to paint those monstrosities, your babies will be born with wings and a tail!" She didn't add that there was a more important reason she had been born with that curse. But this was years before a plague of truth descended on Floralinda.

Jaime tried to save Elsa as she slipped into her dark universe. He spoke to her gently, brought soothing teas to her at bedtime, even complimented her jungle scenes. He followed Don Victor's advice when his father took him aside, handed him a glass of sherry, and said, "Son, a nervous woman is like a nervous cat. Give her a few children, an occasional dish of cream, and you'll see her calm down. Mark my words." But Elsa grew worse when Rosita was born. The girl was beautiful; when Jaime first held her, he thought he would burst with joy. But Elsa took every opportunity to hand the child off to the servants. She began sequestering herself in their bedroom, writing endless missives to her cousins, folding them neatly, taking them down to the river, where she would drop them into the water and watch them float briskly away. When Marco was born two years later with a coat of chestnut down covering his body, she was convinced she had given birth to a bat. "What is that *tail*!" she screamed, pointing at the baby's penis. "Take this creature away before it grows wings!" Jaime was flustered, confused, but undaunted. He doted over his children, worried about the resentment he was beginning to harbor against his wife, but he put on a brave face and made a point to tell her how pretty she was; remembering his father's words, he held her close in their bed. By the time Jorge, their youngest, was born, Elsa was a phantom of her former self, a full-fledged termagant. She berated her amas for raising her children like wild macaques. She screeched at her two sisters-in-law until they skulked out of the room. But the worst of it was this: She no longer spoke to her husband, no longer wanted his caresses.

The odd part was that in a social setting Elsa seemed perfectly normal. She chattered gaily with guests and was fashionably attired in dresses and gloves imported from Trujillo. When the couture was back in her closet, however, her conviviality was stashed with it, and the illness surfaced again: She heaped abuse on the servants, neglected her children, and demanded more attention than anyone else under that roof. Until, that is, Basadre began his infernal coughing. Standing at the portal and glaring out at the wretched animal, Elsa wondered how it had come to pass in that mud hole that a sick beast was ruling the house.

By the third day of Basadre's misfortune, all Floralinda had heard the interminable coughing. They glanced up at the house on their way to the factory and tipped their straw hats in sympathy. On the fourth day, Jaime returned from his travels and heard word of the affliction from one of the workers on the dock. He ran up the path to the patio and put his arms around the helpless dog. "What's wrong, old friend?

Come on, now!" He had raised Basadre, taught him everything he knew, whispered to him every night about adventures they would have together the next morning. But no whispered comforts, no ruby promises, could calm the rattle in the canine throat now.

On the fifth day, Graciela's foreboding came to pass. Monkeys came swinging out of the *jebe* trees, timidly at first, peering about to see if there were some larger predator lurking around the dog. Then they descended in droves, lining the brick barricade like monks along a cathedral pew—chattering, hopping, rocking nervously from haunch to haunch as Basadre's cough worsened, until Don Victor stuck his head out the workshop door to scream, "Will someone, for Jesus, José, and Santa María's sake, please shoot that insane beast!" But, of course, being a lover of animals, Don Victor knew, and everyone in his house understood, that no one would dare do anything of the kind.

Just as the sun was beginning to fade, one of the monkeys began to mimic Basadre's voice with such subtlety and genius—*pac-hac-hac*—that the entire ring of simians turned to look. There was a hoot or two, a clacking of teeth, and soon every beast in the circle was doing it: *pac-hac-hac! pac-hac-hac!* By the eighth day, it seemed the whole jungle, from the four-hundred-hectare clearing of Floralinda downriver to Santa Isabel, was pulsing with that noise. Crimson-feathered papagayos cackled, crickets chirped, and every tribesman from Witoto to Shipibo rattled his arrows, wondering what would follow.

Stranger things had happened in that jungle. Ants had chewed through whole villages in the course of an hour. Alligators had appropriated the workers' shacks. The river had heaved up in one wave and left creatures wriggling in the trees. Snakes sped through the forest singing like birds. What was an epidemic of coughing in the grand scheme of things? Resigned to the din as only the residents of that wild and capricious place could resign themselves, the people of Floralinda plugged their ears with pima cotton, strips of tree latex, and wads of dried hemp wrapped in snippets of woven cloth. Don Victor, revered in the province of Ucayali as its most ingenious citizen, devised a marvelous apparatus: a brace of tin cups, stuffed with shreds of discarded paper from the floor of his factory, then clamped to his head by a stalk of bamboo that circled from one ear to another, fastened under his chin, and could be opened or closed with the quick flip of a metal flange.

In that surrounding cacophony, and with the attendant challenges of having to live on—to eat, sleep, make conversation and love—with strange devices strapped to their heads, few in the Sobrevilla household noticed when the boy came out to the patio, slid his back down the wall, and stayed there, staring at Basadre with eyes that glowed like embers.

At fifteen, the chief ama's only daughter, Tomasina, had birthed the boy after a drunken coupling with a coca-leaf hauler. The man had shuffled through Floralinda on his way to the trading post with a basket on his back, a jug of *chicha* in hand, and an irresistible itch for a woman. After the baby was born and the poor, frightened girl could run without bleeding, she disappeared upriver with a Cashibo hunter, never to be seen again.

Six years old now, Miguelito was remarkably intelligent, quick to learn how to count and read, clever with his hands, agile as a cat. But he was an angry child—given to biting and scratching—filled with such venom that the women of Floralinda pushed their little ones behind them when they saw him coming. *El feroz* they called him—the savage one—and they would cross themselves when he passed.

He was wiry and sullen, the polar opposite of his grandmother Boruba, whose large person always bustled about the house happily, and whose culinary fare and tender mercies filled the Sobrevillas' table and lives. Whereas she was a mix of Shipibo brown and Barbadian black, a crown of nappy hair framing a large moon face, Miguelito was wan and yellow, with a small head, and hair cut tight against his scalp. But his eyes were his most striking feature: narrow and burning, with a remarkable ability to focus on one object at a time. That night, so intense was his focus on the miserable Basadre that when the monkeys sprang down to cough in his face, he did not register them at all.

Before long, he, too, started coughing—*pac-hac-hac*—filling the monkeys with such joy that they swarmed around him, tweaking his ears with their leathery fingers. It was a light cough, befitting the narrow parameters of his chest. But soon enough, it crescendoed so hideously that the rest of the forest was spurred into a thundering free-for-all. That roar—so overpowering that no earplug could mask it—caused all seventeen members of the Sobrevilla household to fly out of their rooms and onto the patio to confirm this new turn of events.

The Sobrevillas stood paralyzed, taking in the pandemonium: the spectacle of the crazed child, whose eyes seemed to glow with a strange light; the stillness of the dog against the frantic dance of monkeys. Don Victor had come out holding a beaker of fine Spanish sherry, and with his evening's drink poised in one hand and his tin-cup device dangling from his neck, he felt a sharp stab of alarm.

Everything happened quickly after that: Boruba came running out of the kitchen. Graciela touched Basadre's chest and felt the stillness of his heart. Miguelito stopped coughing and toppled over, lifeless. And then, like celluloid images spooling through a projector in reverse, the monkeys shot back into the trees, the birds into the night, the deafening roar ceased, and there was silence. When the Sobrevillas looked back at the boy, he was a bright azulene.

That night, Miguelito's body was laid out on the threshing table, between the house and the cotton field, and three shamans and a jungle embalmer were called to observe the preternatural shade of his skin. He was bright as a fish—a taut, shimmery blue—not as if death had transfigured him, but as if nature had made him that way. When they opened him up, his heart was as black as a stone.

The dog, made light by death, was taken from the patio in a hammock. Pedro the gardener rolled him onto it tenderly and carried it out to where the casuarina bloomed by the roadside. There, in full view of the laborers hunched over their *chicha* at the rickety tables in Chincho's bar, he lifted the furry corpse out of the osier, lowered it into a grave filled with tinder, then lit a fire and watched it burn. He remembered how the little dog had loved to scamper ahead of him through the hemp fields, clearing the paths of snakes.

Pedro sat as the gaslights went out one by one in the village. He sat as the drunken laborers made their way home to their shacks. When nothing was left of Basadre but a fine gray ash, it was almost dawn. Pedro's impulse was to cast the remains onto the river to travel the intestines of fellow creatures into eternal life—but he did as the priest Bernardo had taught him. He made a quick sign of the cross with one hand and covered the cinders with dirt. When he was finished, he could see the first light of day breaking through trees across the river. Knowing that dawn would bring the burial of Miguelito, he set out to find Boruba.

She was with the body of her grandson. The boy lay serenely on the wooden slab, his throat sewn shut and tied with a coarse knot above the collar of his crisp white shirt, his face scrubbed so that the blue skin shone. Her head was bowed, as if all the blackbirds of death were perched upon it. The Sobrevilla women were filing past, one by one: Graciela, with a black mantilla pulled tight around her ears; Belén, her gray eyes glistening. Forgetting all the times the boy had sunk sharp teeth into their arms and legs, they reached out to stroke the flat little forehead. When she saw Boruba's face covered with tears, Graciela threw her arms around her and wept.

Pedro kicked off his sandals. Being the son of a curandero and wise about funeral rituals, he could not stand before the dead without feeling the earth beneath his feet. Had he been among his people, he would have expected to find the boy's bones burned down to a fine powder, stirred into a tart white mash of fermented tubers, and passed around in a gourd for all the tribe to drink. Boruba, too, a Shipibo and member of the greater nation of Nahua, might have drunk her grandson's ashes so that he could glide from her head to her chest, where he could stay forever cradled in her heart. But there they were, in a white man's hacienda, and so much had changed along the Ucayali. Pedro approached Boruba, touched the back of her head lightly, then squatted alongside to help his friend keep her sad vigil. It would take time for the boy's spirit to lift from his navel and ride its way to the stars.

As the jungle emerged from the mist and the sun threw a pearly haze over Floralinda, the townspeople came to pay their respects, Don Victor and Doña Mariana among them. Don Victor strode directly to the bier without hesitation, but Doña Mariana hung back, catching her breath and absorbing the sad scene before her. Don Victor looked down with a face that was haggard and worn. He brought his cupped hands over the child's corpse, and then dropped... what? Something filmy—the slenderest wisp of stuff. It looked like fabric but seemed to be lighter than air. As the paper wafted down and lit on the boy's white shirt, it opened, caught the dawn, and shimmered, capturing the glow of the sun, the blue of the dead, the rose of Graciela's lips, the gray in Belén's gaze, the green of new hemp, the ocher of skin. It was a transitory thing—a flash of light, snatched and spun into a fleeting kaleidoscope. When Don Victor took the boy's hand and opened his fingers one by one, the mourners did not imagine that one day they would be asked to remember precisely what followed next. They would have no trouble recalling it. The shapechanger—they would say in their testimonies— *opened Miguelito's hand; I saw it myself. He took the gleaming thing from his little belly, held it high above the table so that it winked with a hundred eyes, then brought it down, pressed it into the boy's palm, and closed his fingers into a fist.* There was little more to mark that transforming dawn, except a rush of wind—as if something had cleared an aperture and flown into the humid morning. Then, clear as the horn at the Annunciation, the cock began to crow. The ripple of color, the luminous paper, the sharp wind rising, and then, *cu-cu-ru-cu-cu!* Everyone would remember it that way.

Even Father Bernardo, trudging along the path toward the crop fields, his sandals flapping against his heels, would say that when he looked toward the boy's makeshift mortuary, he saw an uncommon radiance.

In truth, the floor of Don Victor's workshop was littered with that paper. He had been laboring over it for months, grinding pastes with a mortar and pestle, cooking them carefully in German beakers, stretching moist layers over a delicate netting to dry with the aid of a whirring fan. Whereas the factory he had built in Floralinda spun stiff brown paper out of the hemp that grew copiously in his fields, this new discovery was fragile, pellucid, mysterious: a tissue as beguiling as glass.

He had chanced upon the idea for it on the pages of a lapsed engineering journal, *Novedades de ingeniería*. Every month, when the barge pulled in from Pucallpa, a jumble of the necessary and the ridiculous— from tinned butter to used corsets, from machine parts to moldy magazines—would arrive from Don Victor's ancestral house in Trujillo, now presided over by his younger brother, Don Alejandro. Established, wealthy, with a mansion on the main square of the most aristocratic of Peruvian cities, Don Alejandro would never have guessed as a boy that someday his older brother would leave everything behind to pursue a paper fortune in the jungle. How could Victor have forfeited the comforts of the coast—cavernous salons with portraits that confirmed a pedigree, white-gloved butlers wielding the family silver, crystal flutes brimming with vintage pisco? Alejandro was no prodigal and would never have given up one ounce of the luxury about him, but out of an acute sense of family responsibility and the Catholic notion that a man is ultimately responsible for a brother who wanders from good fortune to bad, every three months Alejandro would box up his household refuse—outmoded shoes, broken toys, old radios, half-used canisters of propane—and have one of his minions truck the entire collection to Lima and up the new road to Pucallpa, where it would be loaded onto barges and shipped downriver. Months later, the boxes of Trujillo rubbish would be cast onto the muddy banks of the Ucayali, and the jungle Sobrevillas' window on the world would flick open, onto the modern day.

It was in that way that Graciela's two children, Pablito and Silvia, learned about Papa Noel, from a broken doll with aquamarine eyes, carnelian cheeks, and a bell around his neck. It was in that way that Doña Mariana acquired her deceased mother-in-law's Italian leather boots—the first article of clothing she slipped into in the morning and the last she removed at night. And it was in that way Don Victor discovered that if you added acetic acid to a mash of fiber and sulfites, if you forced it quickly and evenly through a long line of tiny nozzles, if you allowed it to land gently on a net and dry, the result was cellophane.

Don Victor had pored over his brother's discarded journals, sketching out ideas on leftover graph paper, measuring chemicals from beaker to beaker in the solitude of his workshop, emerging only when a factory worker came running to report that a machine part had gone flying or that a monkey had fallen into the thresher or that a Mayoruna passing through had consumed too much *chicha* and reeled into the acid vat. The making of cellophane obsessed him, seeped into every recess of his imagination. Not since he had set foot on the riverbank and christened the land Floralinda had he sensed that he was on the verge of something significant, that he was—as the witchman who birthed his daughters had told him—being summoned into the universe. Beware of wanting too much, the witchman had quickly added, for greed always ends in privation. But Don Victor didn't remember those warnings; he wanted, more than anything, the grand total of muchness. He felt as if he were standing on the threshold of Eiffel's magnificent palace, ready to best the master. To erect an iron house in the Amazon had been spectacular. To produce cellophane in quantities would be a miracle. Was there, in all the engineering annals of the world, a feat more marvelous than making extravagant paper in the wilderness?

He had been in his workshop for twenty-seven days in a row, applying himself with rigorous concentration, when Basadre had begun the miserable business of his coughing. Even as Don Victor perfected the balance of the compounds and the temperature at which the fiber had to be cooked—testing in turns with cane, hemp, and cotton—he could hear the crescendo outside. What god of synchronicity, what node in the fabric of fate, was tying his progress to that distraction? The strangest coincidence was that just as the noise reached a climax, just as the clamor was summoning him to the door, the first sliver of transparent paper slid from his improvised mill.

When Don Victor had been a boy in Trujillo, his godmother, Tía Esther, had told him stories about mortals who overreached their God-given circumstances. There was King Midas and his ill-fated daughter. Or the fox that was greedy for more cheese. Or the besotted lion that fell in love with the terrified girl, begged for her hand, and wanted her so much that he agreed to give up his teeth—and then lost all power to demand the marriage. But the story that impressed him most was the one about the Chinese weaver.

A hard blight had poisoned the weaver's mulberry grove, and he awoke one morning to find his whole silkworm population curled into inert husks, his livelihood finished. Spurned as a vector of bad luck, the man contemplated suicide. He considered drowning his children in a secluded twist of the Pearl River and leaping, with his obedient wife, into the swirling deep waters. But one day a tall foreigner with sea-green eyes, a thick black beard, and thigh-high boots appeared and urged him to come away to America, to make his fortune. There, the stranger said, you will start again, build your business, grow wealthy. There is gold in the bowels of Peru.

The weaver began to spin dreams of a new life in that faraway setting, where no one would know of his failures—where trees were not poisoned and a silkworm might flourish. He imagined a country that was longing for fine cloth, for Chinese ingenuity; he fantasized all the ways he could ride the bearded man's ship to glory. He began wanting—more than anything—to go. He decided to borrow the money for the journey, persuading his sisters to sell two cows and three goats in order to finance his passage. With a few coins, he bought twenty silkworms. He took the rest of the money, consoled his beleaguered wife, patted his children on their heads, and promised that when he was settled he would send for them.

He was given the first signal that things were not right on the plank that led to the ship's deck: There and then, the captain with the green eyes insisted on taking his money. Three sailors tossed the box of silkworms overboard and led him not to a comfortable pallet, as he had been promised, but to the mildewed hold, where there were many like him, scrubbed clean in pigtails and cloth shoes, crammed in so they hardly could breathe. Half of them died on the hundred-day voyage, chattering in the dark about how rich they would be in America. When the ones who survived that trip arrived at the promised land, they were dispatched to the Chincha Islands, shackled to posts, fed opium by night, and, by day, made to mine the great, stinking hills of guano for a company that exported fertilizer. "*Chinos perdidos,*" Aunt Esther would say. Poor, lost Chinamen. "*Soñaban con seda y se ahogaron en caca.*" They swam in on silk dreams and drowned in the birdshit. Beware of wanting too much.

Watching the first bit of resplendence drop from the metal onto the net, Don Victor was transported from one memory to another. It was a disorienting condition, an affliction, really, and he had suffered it for as long as he could remember. He could go for months, years, blissfully free of the past, and then the most casual sensation could trigger it—a glimpse of wet bark, the feel of fresh paper. And there he would be, reeling through time, helpless.

So it was that he fell precipitously from paper to paper, from the sight of his first scrap of cellophane to the recollection of a cold, gray morning in Trujillo, nearly a half a century before. It was not long after his twelfth birthday, when Tía Esther had taken him to have his fortune read. She had promised him a piece of paper that would allow him to see into the future. That long-ago morning—after Mass and confession—was the day his adventures began.

Victor and his young aunt had walked across the Plaza de Armas toward the statue of La Libertad, a granite and marble colossus of Peruvian womanhood—breasts draped, a torch held high, and two peculiarly squat legs slightly ajar, as if liberty were just breaking into a run. On Sunday mornings, a gnarled dwarf in a shiny black suit would push a shrouded cart into the plaza and head for the faithful as they poured out of the basilica. When the little man reached the foot of La Libertad, he would snatch away the tattered cloth to reveal a brightly painted cathedral beneath. It was made of intricately carved wood, a facade of many drawers, each in a different color, two imposing towers with soaring golden crosses, and a red door with six ceramic saints on either side. A roughly fashioned sign nailed to the side of the cart read: TU DESTINO. Your fate. On top, in the void between its towers, perched a black macaque. She wore a skirt made of multicolored ribbon, a leather collar stamped with the silver letters *La Negrita,* and on her head, a motheaten beret—methyl orange, satin, tilted coquettishly and secured with an elastic strap under her chin. A persistent case of the mange had eaten its way from the monkey's elbows to her underarms, at which she picked incessantly. From time to time, she would produce a tiny nit, roll it between her fingers, and ponder it soberly before depositing it into her mouth.

Negrita was plucking at her fur, staring out into the square, when she registered the woman and the boy from a distance. Leaping up, eyes glossy as beads, she hopped behind her cathedral, grasped the metal crank that jutted from the back wall, and began turning it furiously. A deep, vibrant sound emerged as the studded cylinder inside the barrel organ engaged the metal phalanges. *A-ma-po-la! Lindisima amapola!*— the melody sang forth, rattling the monkey church, waking its secrets. Negrita looked up and down anxiously, eyeing the couple's progress. When Tía Esther pointed to Victor's head, signaling that he was to be the subject of prognostication, the monkey surrendered the crank to the dwarf and hopped down to the front of her domain. Winding her tail around the tiny black head of San Martín de Porres, she pushed herself forward and studied Victor with care. He had never seen a monkey at such close quarters, even in Trujillo's botanical gardens, and the features of the elfin face before him left him slack with amazement. No bigger than his forearm, she bore an uncanny resemblance to his own mother, a spry, black-eyed woman who bustled about the family mansion as effortlessly as this creature flitted about her church.

The monkey cocked her head, stretched a wrinkled black forefinger toward his brow, then lunged back and began pulling out the brightly colored drawers in the church's facade—no less than a hundred of them, with minuscule brass rings that fit her tiny fingers as if they were forged for them. She leapt from one drawer to another, dancing about, changing her mind, until she finally stopped at a yellow one, jerking it in and out five times before she curled back her lips, flashed her teeth at the boy, and chattered vigorously. Her rapture left no question as to the drawer's importance.

"Ahí está!" There it is, announced the dwarf, thrusting an upturned palm at Tía Esther. *"Cincuenta centavos, señora."*

Tía Esther drew a large coin from her silk purse and dropped it into the dwarf's hand. Seeing her master's fingers close around the money, La Negrita reached into the drawer and extracted a sheet of paper—no bigger than a prayer card, and pale pink, almost transparent, as if it had been rubbed with oil. The lettering on it was broken at the margins, printed in green, smudged.

Victor took the fortune and thanked the monkey, forgetting momentarily that a tree animal, no matter how well trained, did not warrant the social conventions he had been taught so meticulously by the nuns at the Escuela de Santa Clara. Tía Esther patted his shoulder approvingly.

"*Ya, pues*," said his aunt as they hurried to the park bench nearby. "What does it say? Read it to me, Victor."

The paper felt surprisingly sturdy in his hand, although it looked thin and fragile. When he drew it toward his face, it crackled. "There are three words on top," he began. "It says: *Para un Caballero*." For a gentleman.

"That's you, of course," said Esther gaily. "You may be a very young caballero, but you're a caballero all the same. Here," she said, reaching impatiently for the paper as she settled onto the bench, "let me try."

Slowly, in a voice that resonated with portent, she began to read the monkey's prediction.

FOR A GENTLEMAN

Beware! There are those who think you a dreamer. Pay them no mind. They are small-minded people with dubious motives, who would have you doubt your goals. Difficulties will pursue you, for the truth is that you attract them, but rewards will also find you, if you dare to reach high. The way will not be easy, but you are clever and good at heart, and as long as you pray to the Virgin of Copacabana, you will prevail. You will encounter many things during your time on earth, for you have an adventuresome spirit, but there will come a day when you face something dire, for which you cannot prepare. When that hour comes, you have two choices: Fight with all your will; resist all failure. Or fly above it, see its God-given value, surrender to a greater force. Here is advice that will serve you well in that day of reckoning:

The more a man sees, the less he will know.

The more furious the battle, the greater the peace that follows.

Let go, and gain the world.

In the meantime, caballero, sail on. Your destiny awaits you.

You will live many, many years. One hundred is your lucky number.

Esther read these lines with great feeling, for there was little she liked more than a good aphorism. When she was finished, she folded the paper and tucked it into the boy's hand. "Come, Victor," she said, "let's get you a treat from the iceman—mango, lucuma, guava—whatever your heart desires!"

Victor slipped the pink paper into his pocket and took Esther's hand. He glanced over his shoulder as they walked away and saw La Negrita sprawled on the monkey church, flicking a lazy tail. The Virgin of Copacabana, he wondered, who was she? He assumed the nuns at his convent school had taught him all the names of the holymen and -women, but somehow they had neglected this one. The more he thought about it, the more his heart sank. What would his ignorance cost him? How could he pray to a virgin he'd never heard of, a face he'd never seen? And where on earth was Copacabana?

It wasn't surprising he'd never heard of the place. The Sobrevillas were adamantly coastal Peruvians, clinging, generation after generation, to the slender ribbon of land that stretched between Trujillo and Lima. Descended from Juan José Sobrevilla Mezones, whose impressive whiskers dominated a vast portrait in the main hall of Victor's ancestral home on Avenida Orbegozo, the family had never ventured east into the wilds of Peru. There was a rumor that one of Victor's great-uncles, a ne'er-do-well playboy of the first rank, had gambled away his fortunes at the tables of the Palacio de Iturregi and ended up owing someone his house, his belongings, and his inheritance. He had left Trujillo on a horse one night and eventually found refuge in the back hills of Yungai with a ruddy-faced mountain Indian who bore him many children. But the Sobrevillas were more likely found in town, not far from the Plaza de Armas, in rooms that were hung with brocade.

The family came from a long line of aristocrats who hailed from the north of Spain. Tall and erect, they were a taciturn lot, given to cerebral occupations and forbidding moods. Victor's mother, Angélica Paniagua de Sobrevilla, came into that fusty household the way a sparrow flies into a ruin. She was sixteen when she married her husband—an alliance not entirely approved by her solemn in-laws. She was too dark, too short—"*No es una de nosotros,*" her mother-in-law announced bluntly over the pumpkin soup one afternoon at lunch before the wedding. Not our kind.

Victor's father, Carlos Enrique Leon Sobrevilla, was insistent. He was enchanted by Angélica's vivacity, her sharp and adventurous mind. When he would see her at garden parties, her bright little eyes never failed to cheer him. She, in turn, was fascinated by his manner: She had never seen a man strut through the world like that—as if he were emperor and all land beneath him his empire. They began to enjoy conversation, and then, through servants, they began to send each other letters. In time, he began taking her on long carriage rides along the shoreline, with a mysterious chaperone—a heavily shrouded little woman—in the rear. It was clear the two were deeply in love, and Carlos, being the eldest of the Sobrevilla children, was given the benefit of the doubt. The family agreed to let him marry her. But only one or two of Angélica's relatives appeared for the wedding. By the time the next Sobrevilla sibling came around to ask his parents to bless a less than satisfactory union, they had learned a thing or two. They said no, stood their ground, and meant it.

There was much gossip about Angélica Paniagua among the Sobrevillas. She was pretty, yes, in her petite, animated way, but there was something odd in the perfect circle of her face, the flare of her nose, the way her eyes tilted up at the corners in an eternal squint. You could not see the complete orbs of her irises, as you could in every other Sobrevilla.

Doña Angélica's parents, the Paniaguas, knew to leave well enough alone. Sensing they were not welcome in the Sobrevilla house, they stayed out in their farm near Chiclayo, content in the knowledge that their daughter had done so well for herself.

At first, the Sobrevillas' coldness made little impression on Doña Angélica. She was forever fluttering about, pampering her husband, tending to a never-ending parade of household disasters, running about the enormous *casona* as if it were her last day on earth.

She was determined to repair the damage that had been done to the house during the War of the Pacific. In the last years of the war, when Don Carlos had still been a student at the university, the Chileans, enraged that Peru had made a secret pact with Bolivia to mine precious metals near Chile's borders, poured into Trujillo. They kicked in the doors of the rich, strapped them to their mahogany staircases—or, if they struggled, slit their throats—and looted their treasures. Two of

Don Carlos's uncles had been killed. Whole rooms in the Sobrevilla house had been plundered; the walls of the *casona* were still riddled with bullets and bayonet slashes from that terrible morning in 1883.

But in the hands of the future mother of Victor Sobrevilla, everything now seemed to prosper: The house was brought back to its original luster; the big canvas of Juan José Sobrevilla Mezones was mended, dusted, and rehung; the cook was cajoled into preparing sumptuous dishes the likes of which he would never have produced for the sour-faced Sobrevillas; the garden bloomed with bougainvillea and floripondio, mangoes and lucumas; and the elders were persuaded that their son hadn't made such a bad marriage after all.

An extraordinary period of fecundity followed. Angélica was not only responsible for a renaissance of Sobrevilla well-being, she blossomed with child year after year. Her Trujillo neighbors could only gasp at what they assumed to be Don Carlos's manly endowments. The procession of offspring was impressive: First came a large, pompous-looking baby, his chin so full of folds that it confirmed the family prosperity. Next was Victor, whose long, gangly exit from his mother was so sudden and violent that it frightened the doctor and sent the maids crying out into the herb garden. After that came four boys and four girls, all healthy and beautiful. Until, at last, came the eleventh child. And it was that child who revealed the very strain the family feared was coursing through Angélica's bloodline all along. She was unnaturally small for a Sobrevilla baby—nose wide, face flat. Her skin was curiously yellow and her black hair grew low on her forehead, then spread down her temples in a fine down. The baby's doctor, her mother, her aunts, her grandmother, her amas, all looked down at her and could come to no other conclusion. The girl was Chinese.

That clarified things. Chinese. Coolies. Indentured slaves with strange little pigtails, brought over by the boatloads to mine guano. To the aristocratic Sobrevillas, Chinese were the lowest form of human life. At first, the baby's aunts tried to make light of it. *"Chína!"* they called her. *"Ay, pues, que cara más interesante, que lindura!"* What an interesting face, what a beauty! But before long, the Sobrevilla elders, shamed by the evidence of their scion's marriage to a shit shoveler, began spending more time at their hacienda in Huanchaco. The younger in-laws began trickling off to other entertainments, spending less and less time on visits, until one day the children could not remember how long it had been since they'd last seen the members of the extended family. Even Victor's father, the formidable Don Carlos, became exasperated with the household pandemonium and began taking long trips to the capital, explaining that he was at work on behalf of the war hero Andres Avelino Cáceres, who had promised, if elected, to bring *yanqui* ingenuity to Peru. One day, when not one of the Sobrevillas appeared at an elaborate lunch to celebrate the fourth birthday of the girl everyone called Chína, Angélica complained to her husband, demanding to know exactly why his family wanted nothing to do with their eleventh child. She knew perfectly well what was wrong; she simply wanted to hear him acknowledge it. But Don Carlos only held a crisp linen handkerchief to his nose and sneezed.

Little by little, their marriage became more distant. Eventually Don Carlos was found on the front stoop of the house of the infamously insatiable Cecilia Mujica de Ortega, flat on his face with two holes in his back and a bullet against his spine. He had been availing himself of her much lauded capacities for "oyster love"—a ravishing, exhausting sexual practice that involved a good deal of scooping and slurping. All Trujillo knew she was mistress of the technique, and mistressing the technique was not a particularly easy thing to do. There was the lifting of the shell—claimed by many to be the most titillating part of the procedure—then there was the tickle to make sure the creature was living, the condiments, the salty liquor, the infinitely cunning little vibrations of the tongue. She had learned it from a bighearted diplomat. (*"Huitre! Huitre! Huitre!"* the Frenchman would chant, rubbing his hands as he rushed into her bedroom. "Even the word sharpens the tongue!") Oyster love, he had told Cecilia—and all her research confirmed it—was taking the continent by storm.

It seems Cecilia's husband, in a fit of jealousy and suspicion, had come in the side door just as Don Carlos was hurrying downstairs after a romp in Cecilia's oyster bed. By the time Victor's father pulled on his white jacket and stepped onto the threshold, the cuckolded husband had drawn his Beretta from the sideboard. The first shot felled the happy lover. The second one stopped his heart.

Victor, who had just turned thirteen, was at home reading. He had been sitting on the stiff wooden chair in the house's vast foyer, studying Jean-Baptiste Dumas's *A Treatise on the Art of Chemistry,* turning the antique pages, when his father's driver ran up the walk, pounded on the heavy front door, then disclosed every lascivious detail to the *mayordomo.* No, Don Carlos had not been in Lima, campaigning on behalf of the presidential candidate—he was dead on the front stoop of the town hussy, only three blocks away. Turning the corpse over, the driver had noted a flurry of love bites that rose from Don Carlos's collar and mounted toward his ear. The driver went on to say that when he saw the wound through which one of the bullets had exited—a gaping hole in an otherwise immaculate shirt—he noted too that, in his haste, the dead man had failed to button his trousers.

Victor listened, surprised at his own lack of emotion. The servants seemed far more agitated than he was. His father had never been warm toward his children, but over the years he had grown colder. It wasn't that Victor didn't like him; he couldn't say what there was in him to like or not like. And he certainly couldn't grieve over the way he had died. Feeling the responsibility of the moment, Victor decided it had fallen to him to relay the news. Soon he was telling the whole tawdry tale to his mother, who buried her face in the Portuguese eyelet pillows that littered her ebony bed. "In front of that cheap little tart's house, for God's sake!" she wept. "For all the world to see!"

Angélica eventually composed herself, lined up her eleven children and twelve of the household's servants—including gardeners, amas, and cooks—and formally announced the news of her husband's death. He had died by the blade, she said, his noble heart sliced in two by a brute agent of the opposition who had waited for him in the bougainvillea that surrounded General Cáceres's headquarters in Lima. Don Carlos would be buried, with full honor, in the crypt beside his ancestors. She strode up and down the human corridor of children and servants energetically, punching the air with her forefingers, as if she had been born to the task. Don Carlos's children did not cry—they could hardly recall the sound of his voice, except that it had been frightening. Seeing the grave look on her otherwise sunny ama's face, the baby of the family began to whimper, but when Victor patted Chína's lemony arms, she smiled up brightly and laughed.

Although the servants already knew every detail of the story, they didn't dare talk except in whispers about the lies the Sobrevilla patriarch had told his wife or the spellbinding particulars of oyster love. But those in the mansions on either side of them began asking openly why the teeming household had shrunk so dramatically. They recalled the days when the Sobrevilla abode had held forty people. Now it had dwindled to seventeen: one mother, eleven children, five servants. Doña Angélica's maids explained to the amas in the neighboring *casonas* that the house had been too full of children. Who could stand it? Of course the señor's family had decided to move away! And of course the *mayordomo* had stomped off in frustration!

Two months passed, and then one late afternoon in December, when the bougainvillea was in full bloom, the neighbors had new fodder for gossip. A little woman wearing a quilted silk jacket embroidered with dragons appeared at the gate. In one hand she carried a brown leather suitcase. In the other was a small birdcage housing a furry, inert object. Señorita Esther Paniagua moved into one of the sunnier bedrooms, unpacked five cheongsams, and set out her most precious possessions: a carved wooden crucifix and a cage with a hideously shrunken head of a cat. She was Angélica's younger sister, a determined, plain little woman of thirty who wore her hair in a tidy bun and favored form-fitting Chinese brocade dresses with stand-up collars and high slits. "This is your aunt," Doña Angélica said soberly to all eleven children as they filed into the front hall to meet Tía Esther. "And to you, Victor and Chína, she is especially important. She is your godmother. You will treat her with all the respect a godmother merits."

On the night of her arrival, as Victor perched on the edge of her bed, studying the cage with its ghoulish head no larger than a plum, Esther sat at her dressing table and took down her jet-black hair. Eyeing her godson in the great, carved mirror, she told him the first of her many remarkable tales.

"Once in the long ago past," she began, "there was an old monk who lived in an ancient church that stood at the foot of a mountain. He had a modest room, one of a number of cells in the underground labyrinth of that venerable structure. He was sweeping the nave on a Monday morning, when he saw a seed lodged in a far corner of the floor, between the pulpit and the stair. It was a fragile little germ—with a straw-colored fringe along one side. He contemplated whether he should pluck it out and sweep it away, but there was something about the way it tucked into the wall and peeked out at him. He decided to leave it alone. 'Rest there, seed,' he said. 'One day, if our Father wishes, you will see the bright face of the sun.' "

"But how did the seed get into the church? Who put it there?"

"Hush, Victor. Listen. The monk went away, and the next week, as he was sweeping, he saw that the seed had sprouted a little shoot. He was amazed—touched, really—that a living thing had come to grow in a dark corner of that sunless place. He scooped some holy water from the fount and sprinkled it on the plant, wondering if it were a flower. He reminded himself to bring a little clay pot the next time, so that he could transfer the shoot to the garden. But the monk never returned. He died in his bed with the empty clay pot beside him.

"The seedling grew and grew, although it had had nothing to drink save the few drops of holy water the old monk had fed it. As it matured, it drove roots into the stone joists and rose up along the wall toward the engraved mahogany pulpit. The monks looked on in wonder. How had a seed, with no particular encouragement, with no dirt—"

"With no dirt! That's just what I was thinking!"

"Yes, *mi amor*, that's what the monks found astonishing. How had that plant not only survived but flourished? Months went by. The leaves created a lovely canopy above the pulpit, over the holy men's heads. Before long, the stalk was rising toward the roof, past Jesus, past Mary, past the cherubim, past the lamb of God, which stood in a stained-glass window in the back wall, gazing down in alarm. The mayor of the town—a man who seldom accompanied his wife to Mass—was called in to consider the problem, but by then the plant had developed a trunk, and its circumference seemed to expand by the day. 'It's very simple,' the mayor said, being educated and knowledgeable about such matters. 'This tree will burst through the roof unless you take an ax to it and level it right now.' "

Victor shifted nervously on the bed and Esther smiled at him. "But the monks couldn't bring themselves to kill the tree," she said gently. "They hadn't planted it, they hadn't watered it, and yet there seemed to be something mystical about its visitation. Time passed and a crack appeared in the ceiling of the church where the branches pressed up against it. Some nights later, the monks awoke in their beds to the crash of falling plaster. As they scrambled from their underground cells, they glanced into the dead monk's room and saw the long finger of a root slither across the floor and reach into a tiny clay pot at the foot of his night table. Hurrying up the narrow stair, they witnessed the most marvelous thing of all: The tree was straining toward the sun, which was just peering over the rim of the mountain, and the church walls were as open as a broken eggshell, cleft, and gaping in awe." Esther stopped there and looked at her godson.

"That's all?"

"That's all."

"But what does it mean, Tía?"

"It's your first and most important lesson, Victor. A man-made thing, no matter how sacred we think it is, is nothing compared to a tree. Even a church is a mere structure like any other. In the face of magnificent creation, man's symbols are paltry things."

2

Don Victor carried the monkey fortune for days, fingering the oily paper, worrying it like a rosary, before he put it into a drawer in his father's mahogany desk. Less than a week after Don Carlos's corpse was lifted from the threshold of scandal to be shoved into the family vault, the servants dragged the elaborately carved desk from the second-floor library into Victor's room. His mother insisted on it.

"You are the only scholar in the family," she said as the monstrous piece of wood with its knobbed columns and feet was pulled past the doors of her other children. "Your father would want it this way."

The monkey's prediction was the first possession Victor deposited into one of the cavernous drawers of that family heirloom. He would take out the paper, turn it in his hands, and wonder at the words: *undertow, let go and gain the world,* and, most puzzling of all, *the Virgin of Copacabana.*

"Mama," he had often asked her, "who is the Virgin of Copacabana?"

"*Ay,* for God's sake, child," his mother had answered, "you've asked me a dozen times already! How many times do I have to tell you? It's just a likeness, another name for the same woman—our blessed mother, may she have pity on us in this miserable life."

Tía Esther was more practical. "Just pray to the Virgin of Perpetual Aid, as you always have, Victor. I'm sure the Virgin of Copacabana, whoever she is, will hear every word you say."

But puzzling over the Virgin of Copacabana was only one aspect of his fascination with the pink fortune. It was the feel of it, the smell of it, the way it crackled ever so slightly when he held it to his ear; the way it shone its strange paraffin color in the light of a Trujillo morning. It was the paper. He had always been fascinated by paper.

As years passed, he filled his father's desk with it: A clipping from *La Industria de Trujillo*, reporting the excavation of a new copper mine. Bits of corrugated cardboard he had found strewn along the shipyard. Snippets of blue onionskin from letters written by his mother's relatives. A tinted photograph of his eight-year-old self as a toreador in a school zarzuela. A striped candy wrapper from the old coolie at the corner store. A page of cardboard, on which he had copied out a valse from his mother's stack of sheet music. A nest of shredded rice paper that once cradled his father's favorite sherry glass. A yellowed map of the Inca Empire. A miniature box of strawboard, filled with colorful confetti. A marbled endpaper from his father's worn translation of *Les Fleurs du Mal*, which his mother had dismembered. A sheet of English bond, on which Victor had sketched out the family house, in lateral and bird's-eye views. A gravure of a flying condor, which he had stippled into millboard.

His father's *escritorio* became a veritable museum of paper, until at last the desk was so packed with every variety Victor had encountered that it groaned when he opened the drawers.

He couldn't explain when one of his ten siblings, Maruca-the-fat or Jorge-the-thin, asked him why he collected so much apparent refuse. "*No sé*," he'd tell them. I don't know. And then, almost as an afterthought, "It's the paper, I think. I guess there's no end to it."

"It's because it's made from *trees* and *grass* and *cane* and *rice*," said his tía Esther, pronouncing each word as if it were a cross in a procession of saints. "It's from the earth. It grows. Up, up, and then, *pah-pum*! It's cut, dried, reduced to two dimensions. You love it because it is portable *life*."

Chína was sitting on the floor of her brother's bedroom, playing with the paper dolls he had made for her. Five years old now and Victor's favorite sibling, she was always welcome in his room, where she liked to listen to the older ones talk. She tipped her head when she heard Tía Esther say "portable life," trying to fit in that pronouncement.

"Oye, hermano," Victor's brother Alejandro crowed, "if there's no end to all the paper, you're going to need more than that *escritorio* to hold it all. Why don't you give me the desk and just stack your collection on the floor until you've filled up the room?"

"Don't be a glutton!" snapped Tía Esther. "You won't get so much as a crumb if you covet your brother's things!" Then she proceeded to tell more fables about wanting too much.

Every afternoon, during the lull of the siesta, Victor would pull his father's leather chair up close to the desk, open the drawers, and breathe in the smell of so much portable life. It might smell sweet, with the subtle fragrance of cane—a perfume he had come to know well in that sugar capital of Peru. It might be like the aroma of freshly cut camphor—a rush invading the back of his throat. One by one, he would extract each slip of paper, hold it to his face, feel its distinct texture against his lips, then set it down on the wood plane before him. He did not tire of imagining where each relic had come from. What tree—Amazon or Andes? What field—sugar or rattan? What rag? What bog of rice? What extraordinary miracle of transfiguration had made that living, breathing plant into the supple thing in his hand?

Often, when his mother took the children on family outings to the beach, he would pluck out a reed to smell the sea salt on it, and he would wonder what kind of paper might come of that. What kind of microscopic life would it carry in its pores? What kind of sound might it make against his ear?

Boyhood was a series of forgotten anecdotes, punctuated by his paper chain. Much later, when Victor's three children perched on his knees and begged him to tell them about his youth in Trujillo, he would raise an eyebrow, ponder their entreaties, then shrug his shoulders and sigh. "I can't remember a thing, my darlings, not a single thing. All I recall is the paper. Drawers and drawers of it. Reams and reams of it. Bolts and bolts of it. My life is a long trail of paper. That's all."

* * *

It was true. By the age of sixty, Don Victor could not summon much of the drama of his long, rich life. Perhaps it was because much of it was sad; perhaps it was because it was best forgotten. But from time to time, one image would bring back another, and the past would rush in with all the force of a sharp stick striking between the eyes. The vision of dead little Chína, for instance, which shot back the instant he flung open the workshop door and saw the blue boy slumped on the patio.

After the accident, Chína's mangled little body had been laid out on the massive dining-room table, and it stayed there, under a starched lace tablecloth, defying all rules of decorum, for another two days. Victor sat vigil beside her, his head in his hands. He left once: to bring her a paper doll, which he fashioned with care, brought to her side, raised in the air, and then placed, very delicately, onto her belly. He stood there contemplating his offering, and then tugged back the shroud, took one of her hands, and opened her fingers one by one, pushing the paper into her limp blue fist. He had not imagined his sister could die.

She had been taken from life on a hot afternoon during carnival day, when it seemed all Trujillo was coursing toward the Plaza de Armas, shouting and dancing. The day had started with a parade, organized by the governor of the Departamento de La Libertad and led by a floral float of pretty girls in long fluffy dresses. The marinera dancers followed, in colorful costumes, waving white handkerchiefs. There was a clown on stilts, jumping through hoops; a truculent panther chained to a cart, slinking down the *avenida*, nursing its revenge; bands of montañeros with reed pipes, playing a ghostly music.

It was the appearance of a rogue gypsy caravan that augured the end of Chína. But how could the adults have known it? The gypsies had not been invited. The carnival posters on the adobe walls of the Mercado Indio had said nothing about them. But suddenly there was the caravan, headed toward the Plaza de Armas along with the rest of the crowd.

Esther and Angélica thought they had warned the children about every possible peril. Tía Esther had taken the shrunken head from her birdcage and swung it about on its string. "See this? It was once a big cat, like a panther. Hard to believe—no?—but its mouth might have bitten off your heads!" And Doña Angélica mentioned the possibility that a clown might step on them with his stilts; they would do well to keep their distance. When all eleven children filed out the door with the amas, the mother and aunt felt sure they had mentioned every danger. They repaired confidently to the closed mahogany balcony, which, with its intricate Moorish latticework, allowed a fine view of the square.

The cloth-covered caravan of Maestro El Misterioso seemed harmless at first. Drawn by a pair of burros, it wobbled down Independencia, the Maestro sitting squarely on a cushion, a black cape furled around his shoulders and a crystal ball in his right hand. He was bewhiskered, bespangled, bejeweled, and to this coruscating splendor he had added three papagayo feathers, which sprouted over his dark blue turban as if they had grown there all along. Behind him and slightly to the left stood a girl with golden hair, dirty feet, and a long skirt whose tattered hem fluttered as the caravan rumbled along. She held an extravagantly decorated parasol over the Maestro, and it, too, trembled in the sun, transforming its mirrors, yellow feathers, and cowrie shells into a bird with a thousand eyes. The wagon's wheels were painted in vivid stripes and bristled with metal swords, so that even as it bumped along the cobblestones, it seemed borne on silvery pinwheels.

El Misterioso turned slowly on his cushion and nodded to the townspeople who lined the noisy avenue. From time to time, he would raise a ringed hand and shout in his booming voice, "Compadres! Amigos! Citizens of the great city of Trujillo! Come! Look in my crystal ball! Talk to the dead! El Misterioso knows all! El Misterioso will reveal all! For a few centavos, ferry to another world!"

With China comfortably straddling his hip, Victor made his way to the edge of the curb, two amas scurrying behind. They arrived just in time to see El Misterioso leap down, cape flapping like the wings of a giant murciélago bat. He strode down the avenue in thigh-high boots, a black fringe swinging from his vest, brass bells jangling on his belt. He had tucked the crystal ball under one arm now, and his free hand stroked his mustache, which lay on his face like two stiff banners.

China began wriggling like a fish, thrashing her legs and shoving her elbows into Victor's side to signal that she wanted to get down. She slid to the ground and pushed away his hands. He allowed her to do it, assuming that she simply wanted to stand. He rested one hand on her shoulder. People were surging behind them now, marveling at the spectacle, pumping their arms in the air. They took up the chant "Mae-stro! Mae-stro! Mae-stro!" to the rhythm of the gypsy's stride. The pandemonium around him was so great that Victor didn't see his sister point at one of the burros in the caravan, nor hear her shout, "*Mira!*" Look. There, dangling from the neck of the creature, was a doll-thing, round, furry—no larger than a ball of yarn. But as the burro came closer, Chína was offered a better view. The ball had eyes, beady black, and round ears, a flared nose. It had straight black hair, swinging from side to side. It was a *tsantsa,* a human head—hunted and sold by jungle Indians— shrunk so that it was no bigger than a fist.

"*Mira!*" she shouted again, but nobody heard her. "The head! The *head!* Of Tía Esther's cat!"

She ran out, hands aloft, and at first the amas just laughed and clapped their hands. After that, events unfolded quickly: the startled burros, rearing back, the child pulling at the *tsantsa,* the dragging, the falling. And then a silvery blade swooped around and lifted the child onto its wheel. It was so sudden she hardly made a sound; a look of surprise came over her face as she traveled from sword to sword to sword—to be lanced again and again on the gears of that terrible mill.

God knows memory is a dangerous thing. In the course of a few years, Victor's childhood had become a nightmare. He had watched the Sobrevillas spurn his mother for the color of her ancestor's skin; he had lost his father in a murder too shameful to prosecute; he had seen the sibling he loved more than any other die like a slaughtered lamb. *The more a man sees, the less he will know,* the monkey fortune had told him. By the time he was fourteen, he had decided that when he came of age he would put distance between himself and Trujillo. He would never forget La Chína, stretched out under the lace on the dining-room table, her legs jutting out like a hard little lemon doll's. Better to forge ahead into a virgin future, better to go without a backward glance. *Let go*—he read the words over and over—*and gain the world.*

After they'd slid his sister's casket into the vault alongside her father, Don Victor led a mostly quiet boyhood in Trujillo. Tía Esther noted it and urged him to make some friends; his mother was too grief-stricken to care. Even with the five-year-old proof of his mother's coolie ancestor wiped off the face of the earth and tucked into the city cemetery, he had not scrambled to improve his station among society, as had Alejandro, his brother. Nor was Victor like the other boys in the Escuela de Santa Clara: raised with the expectation that they and the generations after them would live out their days in gargantuan houses, celebrating birthdays in peacock gardens, taking cocktails at the Club Central, ambling down avenues Bolívar himself had walked, reliving it all in endless toasts to his cronies. He was not a ruminative man. But in a hard world that had dealt him so many losses, paper was a solace, and he clung to the beauty of it, the ingenuity of it, the very promise of it, rolled up and waiting to live again.

Portable *life*, of course that was it, precisely. Human death was heartbreaking, ugly, demoralizing, but pass a plant's corpse through a thresher, baptize it in a vat, flagellate it until it was free of all defect, purify it with tinctures, dry it in a warm wind, and you could watch its soul lift into a new incarnation—move toward purpose again.

It was possible to make paper out of any plant, he learned, and like any of God's creations, each had its identity: Paper from roses was fragile, as easy to bruise as a petal; the long, serrulated leaves of a hemp plant—as insubstantial as they looked in the field—made for robust shooting sheets of brown paper. One could make paper from trees: pine, balsam, cetico. And also from jute, corncobs, or grass. Don Victor knew from experience that paper made from dried orange rinds was porous, spongy, shot through with a brisk perfume. Paper from peanut hulls, plentiful in the hill towns of Peru, was crisp and easy to fold. Paper made from the bagasse of sugar cane needed additional ingredients, as if the reeds did not quite believe that their sweet remains could cling to a new life alone. And, of course, paper made from a cotton rag—which in itself was a miracle of transformation—was strongest of all, as if its soul had entered that second metamorphosis knowing it had survived it all perfectly well before.

Throughout Don Victor's long life, paper had been his religion. He no longer attended church. There was, after all, that unspoken Peruvian code by which boys stop going to church at adolescence, leaving them to seek salvation elsewhere, while mothers and wives pray for their souls on their knees. Don Victor had sought truth where he could: in a covenant with paper, in its promise of regeneration, in the thunder and hubbub of factory revivals. And that is where he had found truth—in tangible things.

3

The evening after Miguelito's blue corpse was wrapped in a grass cloth, placed in a corrugated box, and dropped into a plot behind Floralinda's bright white church, Father Bernardo came to pay the Sobrevilla family a visit. He was a square plug of a man with a broad, parched face. His eyes were framed by a lacework of lines, dug not so much by worry or age as by a long apprenticeship in Puno, a cold, desolate city on the rim of Lake Titicaca, where a cheek can be hard as a hoof. Moving through Floralinda in the damp haze of dusk, his cassock might have been taken for a *cushma*, the loose gown of a Machiguenga Indian. But Father Bernardo had not a drop of Machiguenga in him; no Indian either; nor any kind of Peruvian. He was a full-blooded Spaniard, born fifty-three years earlier in a poor fishing village along Spain's craggy east coast. He had come to the rain forest as so many Franciscans had before him: first, out of curiosity; then, with a missionary fervor; and, finally, because he had grown to love the Amazon: its innocents and sinners, lepers and belligerents.

Don Victor had seen Padre Bernardo for the first time on the stinking banks of La Misión, an improbable, four-pig mud hole on Río Chirumbia, not far from Quillabamba, where thirsty tributaries sent their fingers in a hundred directions, up into the Andean snow. Docking briefly on their way to Pucallpa, Don Victor and Doña Mariana had fallen into conversation with the friendly padre, who was then a young man of twenty-five. Father Bernardo had approached when he saw their two small daughters, Belén and Graciela, sitting on the narrow wharf, splashing each other with river water. It wasn't often two pale cherubs in frilly dresses were seen traveling downriver. By way of preamble, Don Victor had mentioned his own Christian education at Trujillo's Escuela de Santa Clara, tossing in for good measure—because he still carried her name in his pocket—the Virgin of Copacabana.

"No me digas!" Father Bernardo exclaimed, his green eyes lit as if an important and heavenly matter were at hand. "They teach you about the Virgin of Copacabana in the gloried halls of Trujillo convents?" Then he threw back one arm to indicate the sadly dilapidated church behind. "You must visit my altar. It's imperative. There is a beautiful, absolutely magnificent copy of the Virgin there."

Sure enough, it was there that Don Victor first laid eyes on the patron saint of his monkey prediction. She was standing on a slab of rough wood at the rear of the one-room shack that served as the priest's house and mission. There was little save the image of the Virgin to indicate to Don Victor that he had entered a church—a crucifix had been nailed to the door frame outside and a second one hung by a jute rope from the thatched ceiling. In the corner was a hammock of vines. Six wooden benches filled the room—three on either side, creating an aisle in the middle—where worshippers could sit and contemplate the Virgin.

There was nothing magnificent about her. Carved from a handsome length of jungle wood, she stood as long and as tawny as a man's arm. Father Bernardo told Don Victor that the original stood in a church on the Copacabana peninsula of Lake Titicaca, hundreds of miles away. The Titicaca Virgin was much taller and more elaborate, carved four hundred years earlier by the nephew of the last undisputed Inca emperor, Huayna Capac, after the man had opened his heart to Jesus.

Don Victor gazed at the wooden woman before him. Her eyes were cast down, impossible to fathom. Her arms stretched down along her sides, palms toward him; her robes touched her toes, which were as bare and splayed as a jacaranda tree climber's. On her head was an angular crown.

As long as you pray to the Virgin of Copacabana, you will prevail. How often had he drawn the faded slip of paper from its fold in his wallet, read its prophecy? He gazed around the shabby church and saw that a vigorous green liana had wound its way in through the window and was growing along the wall. He thought of the story Tía Esther had told him about the seed, the church, and the tree. In the face of God's creation, she had said, man's symbols are paltry things.

Don Victor would never be able to explain why he looked for Father Bernardo up and down that part of the river six years later, once he determined to build his paper paradise, but he knew, somehow, that it had everything to do with symbols. He found him in a leper colony, ministering to the dying. Not only did the priest agree readily to come to Floralinda to be its spiritual shepherd, he arrived with the copy of the Copacabana Virgin under one arm.

The evening after the boy's burial, Father Bernardo bustled into the tiled hall of the Sobrevilla house. "Welcome, welcome! Come this way!" the parrot shrieked as the priest headed for the main sala, where the family had already gathered. Graciela was at the ebony piano, half-heartedly picking out a bolero. Belén was curled into her father's rattan chair, long legs tucked under her, engrossed in a collection of poems by Vallejo. She tugged at the ends of her short chestnut hair as she read, frowning into the pages. Elsa was perched on the carved leather sofa, proclaiming how tired she was of her husband's incessant trips up- and downriver. "Why go himself?" she squealed. "Why couldn't he have sent one the workers?" A ruffle of lace quivered under her chin like the feathers of an *urubu-rei*. Next to her, Doña Mariana worked a pair of knitting needles, tilting her head toward her daughter's music.

The Sobrevilla women stood when the padre entered, greeting him one by one and kissing him on the hand. They chatted gaily until Don Victor walked in, his shirtsleeves flapping about his wrists. *"Querida, por Dios!"* he shouted. "What have the children done with my cuff links! Where do they think we are, in the rotting jungle? And who do they think I am, an orangutan? Gentlemen need their finery!" His wife rose, went to the massive sideboard by the wall, peered into a silver bowl, and drew out a pair of obsidian studs. "Aha!" he said jovially, as she dusted off each one and put them on him, "those little imps are getting more clever by the day." He adjusted his cravat, turned to the priest, and waved him toward a chair.

Father Bernardo settled in, sipped sherry from the glass that Graciela handed him, and looked around at the family. "Well, I see we are recovering from the chaos. Doña Mariana, you're looking especially well. But, tell me, how is your servant, the grandmother of the boy?"

"Ay, well, Father," Doña Mariana answered, her voice almost a whisper. She was afraid that Boruba might be lingering in the hallway. "You can imagine what that poor unfortunate has been through. He was a difficult child—God knows he was difficult!—but she loved him all the same. He was her link to that ungrateful daughter of hers, and that girl, of course, was the link to the only man our Boruba ever loved. God rest his soul."

"She's far better off with that boy dead," Belén snapped, and then blinked furiously.

"Belén!" cried Elsa. "What a horrible thing to say!"

"Horrible?" Belén turned fierce eyes on her sister-in-law. "Horrible? I'll tell you what's horrible—remembering the misery of that little shit's teeth in my arm. *That*'s horrible." Elsa gasped and then broke into a high, nervous giggle, glancing about with her hand over her mouth. A hush fell over the room. Doña Mariana looked up from her knitting, her needles poised in surprise. Belén seldom partook in parlor conversations: She was always there, curled up with a book on her lap, but she far preferred reading to trading in family gossip. Even Don Victor, as boisterous as he could be with a visitor in his parlor, studied his eldest daughter with his mouth slightly ajar.

Graciela, too, was startled. She had suspected the deaths of the boy and the dog were signs, but she had not dared say so. She had held her tongue as the household went about its business, sending spirits into the afterworld. Now, hearing her sister speak in a tone she hardly recognized, Graciela feared her first instinct might have been right. A spell was descending: an enchantment, a bewitchery.

Belén shifted uneasily in her chair. Though her own words had sounded alien to her, she had said exactly what she felt about that wretched boy, and the candor had been strangely satisfying.

"Well, now!" said Padre Bernardo, nodding affably and fiddling with the rope that dangled from his waist. "We have to remember that we are not ourselves tonight. When there is a death in the house, people can become disoriented and say things they may not mean. It's only natural, dears."

"No, Padre!" said Belén, rising. Vallejo's poems slid from her lap and slapped the floor. "I mean every word I said about that boy." She stretched her elegant neck, smoothed the folds in her skirt. Outside, night had fallen, and the air thrummed with the croaking of frogs, the chirring of crickets—the river's nocturnal commotions.

"All right." Don Victor stood and clapped his hands together. "Enough! We're not going to talk about that boy anymore! Belén, my girl, you are reminding me of a woman I used to know in Quillabamba! She was always *zuzz-zuzz-zuzz,* going on in her flat little voice, and then, before you knew it, *pac!* Quick as an emerald tree boa, in went the forked tongue, out came the fangs."

"What woman was that, *querido?*" his wife asked, smiling sweetly as she reached for a new ball of yarn from her basket. Her husband never spoke about anything remotely as interesting as this, and his sudden plunge into the past intrigued her. She searched her memory for such a woman, but she could think of no one in Quillabamba who fit that peculiar description.

"Her name was Vanessa," Don Victor said simply, then went mute and sank back into his chair.

"Vanessa?" His wife swiveled her head up and studied the ceiling. "You mean the Dutch woman who ran the hostel on Pachacuti?"

"I knew a *Dor*-essa once," said Padre Bernardo earnestly, "but she was from farther south. She was an anthropologist from Arequipa who came to study the mountain dancers in Puno. She was interested especially, as I recall, in the *diablada.*"

"*La diablada!*" sang Graciela, springing to her feet, relieved that the conversation had turned to lighter things. Then she rethought her enthusiasm and added, "But, Padre, the *diablada* isn't a real dance. Not really. They just put on those monstrous masks and move their feet back and forth in a shuffle, that's all." She shambled about to show what she meant.

"Yes! That's it exactly!" said Padre Bernardo, pointing at her feet, the color in his cheeks mounting. "That's it! That's it! She was a graceful girl, that Doressa. She knew a lot about religious art. Very clever. Very pretty too. When she came to the cathedral during the feast of the Virgin of Candelaria, I couldn't take my eyes off her. Those long ringlets. That cinnamon skin. She had the loveliest features." Padre Bernardo's story was coming more rapidly now, his voice breathless. "Oh, she had a fine soul too, of course, but the way she moved! The agility! Her hips! *Ay!* I had a hard time disciplining my mind. She was too beautiful! What could I do?" He looked from one startled face to another, palms turned out in supplication. "Eh? What could I do? In the end, I surrendered. I didn't have a choice. We met every night in the *parque* de Huajsapata, behind the white statue of Manco Capac. There was a convenient little grove of trees. We made love in the soft grass, in summer. It was incredible, really, when you think of it: No one noticed! And there we were, in the middle of nature, for all the world to see! In the end, though, I finally put a stop to it. I was afraid God would send us a little demon as punishment. A wild child, like Miguelito." He stopped briefly and glanced around, his green eyes frantic, wet. Then he added, almost inaudibly, "I mean, as a punishment for our sins."

It was outrageous, a bizarre aberration from what was meant to have been a curative evening. Father Bernardo sat back and looked around him. He may have abandoned a cleric's reserve, but he had not lost all his interpersonal faculties. Reading shock in every face, he leapt to his feet and issued a dozen excuses for not being able to stay to dinner. His hosts were too dazed to object. A priest—*their* priest—making love to a woman in a park in Puno?

Graciela understood instantly. Father Bernardo's confession was like Belén's indiscretion: a burst of candor, springing free from a careful mind. But the very idea of the priest making love made her want to laugh. Was she supposed to believe that the pious man she had known for most of her life was capable of such a thing? The padre who tended the workers' festering sores? The soul of patience who got down on his knees to gather paper from the factory floor so that he could teach children how to write? The meek servant of God who swept mud from his church at sunrise, muttering Ave Marias? *That* man had made love to a woman? And he had admitted it openly, artlessly, in the most public room of the house? It was more than she could absorb.

Elsa, however, did not ponder the inconsistencies. She shot out of the carved leather sofa, horrified, lips curled in a picture of disgust. She squared her shoulders, stood glaring at the red-faced padre, then headed for the door, letting her shoes hammer out a verdict—*plick, plack, plick, plack*—as she mounted the caoba stair to her room.

Boruba, who, as it happened, was about to announce dinner just as the priest launched into the part about the soft grass in Huajsapata Park, stood at the door with her hands clutching her apron, the very image of the bloodless statue of Manco Capac. She remained frozen, even as the padre sped past her, flinging his hands in the general direction of her head, making the sign of the cross.

A perceptive student of character might have noticed that one face in that parlor hadn't registered shock at the priest's confession. Doña Mariana lowered her knitting when she heard the words "as a punishment for our sins" and looked at Father Bernardo's face as if she were seeing it for the first time. Not in the way Elsa had, in repugnance; or as Graciela had, in comic disbelief; or even in the way of Belén, who at that moment was studying the padre as if he were molting from one life-form to another and she wanted to remember the details.

Doña Mariana had caught a subtle apprehension in the otherwise bald confession: Father Bernardo's fear that he might have fathered an imperfect child. She knew something about that. She was the child of a priest herself.

No one in the room knew it, save the one person she was almost certain had long put it out of mind.

"Padre Bernardo!" she called out to the departing priest as she scurried across the tile, a hand over her racing heart.

"Padre Ber-*nar*-do! Padre Ber-*nar*-do!" mimicked the house macaw, flapping its wings and chittering at the brown robe and the vexed matriarch in pursuit.

The padre stopped at the door and turned to face the señora.

"Forgive me, Doña Mariana, for allowing myself such liberties, after so many years of keeping that sin locked in my heart . . . I . . . I think I must be going mad."

"No, no, you misunderstand me, Padre," said Doña Mariana, putting a hand on his arm. "I want to confide a secret. My own father was a priest like you."

How odd to divulge the truth so lightly, to a man of the cloth especially, and there in the theater of her front door, for all the maids to hear. It had been a long time since she had said those words out loud. She had been a young woman in Quillabamba when she'd last uttered them. An honorable man had been owed the truth. When Victor Sobrevilla had dropped to one knee, kissed her hands, and asked her to be his wife, the admission had to be made.

Doña Mariana's mother never talked about it herself, so it was from the cruel taunts of neighborhood children that Mariana had learned the facts about her lineage. But Rosa Paredes was no coward, and so, although the entire Christian population of Quillabamba was aware of the woman's disgrace with the padre, she held her head high, taught her daughters good manners, and, in the comfortable abode she had inherited, ran a fine home. The neighbors gossiped openly in the beginning, when they saw Padre Francisco, with his unmistakable copper curls, coming and going so often from her house, and then when they saw Rosa Paredes herself coming and going with a belly bulging under her shawl. Women spat. Men sneered. There was an angry period when boys threw rotting guavas at her house with such regularity and vehemence that orange ooze seemed to spring perpetually from the walls. There was a particular ferocity to the guava onslaught when the first child—Doña Mariana's sister, Ana—was born with the damning evidence: a head covered with russet curls. But because to sin is human, and because Christian hearts understand this, the anger eventually subsided. The boys put down the fruit. The vendors eventually greeted the young mother when she went to market. And the townswomen continued to line the pews of the padre's church. They loved him too much to not forgive him. He was otherwise godly, a true servant of the Lord, and his homilies had the bright ring of poetry. He was known to utter phrases

from the pulpit—or from behind the iron grate of his confessional—
that were thrilling to Quillabamban ears: *"El pecado es leche
avinagrada!"*—Sin is a curdled milk!—and eyes would moisten at the mere
thought of the sour penance that copper-haired Eros would someday be
made to drink, in the sight of God, for the failed struggle against his
manhood. Many was a Sunday that women would come to church
armed with pencil and paper, scribble his words, proof of his goodness,
and carry them home for their husbands to see.

Mariana and her sister bore their indignities bravely, for, although
the adults had made peace with their mother's sin, the children had
not. Each new generation had to ride its own gyre of forgiveness—first
the shock, then the outrage, then the understanding that we are all sinners in the eyes of the Lord.

Because of her early tutelage about the erratic labyrinths of the
human heart, Mariana Francisco grew up strong in the knowledge that
she was loved. Although Doña Rosa understood the gravity of her own
deviance and knew she could never give her daughters the social comforts she once had enjoyed, she succeeded in instilling in Mariana and
Ana a healthy sense of self-respect and the awareness that they were
God's children, nothing more, nothing less.

The nuns at school were especially fond of them. Only when one of
the girls misbehaved did an inevitable critic raise the question of the
shameful bloodline, usually in a sly whisper, *"Ahí, ves? Es la hija del
diablo."* There! See? She's a daughter of the devil. But, all in all, the nuns
were affectionate, courteous to their mother, and committed to giving
the priest every benefit of the doubt. There was good reason for it: A
silver-tongued orator in the backwater of the cordillera was a powerful
tool for the Lord. Who knows how many faithful would cease coming
to church if some well-meaning but inarticulate padre were sent to that
pulpit in his place? The nuns made a tacit agreement: Except for a rare,
quite unstoppable commerce in whispers, they would forgive the priest
his trespasses.

But there came a day that a lone neighborhood boy started chanting, *"No es muy pura, la hija de un cura!"* not to mention something
about souls roasting in hell's fire. Mariana and Ana were playing in their
garden when they heard it. The rhyme tripped something in Mariana's

head. Pure, sure. Fire, friar. From there it was just two hops to the sur-
name the nuns had given the sisters, Francisco. Mariana put it together.
Her name was the name of the holy man himself, and he was coming
and going from their house every day, whispering to her mother and
pulling her into the other room as if she needed a serious exorcism.
Mariana was only nine years old when those pieces fell into place. But
she discussed it with no one, not even her sister.

Padre Francisco clearly loved his daughters. He worried about their
schoolwork. He tended them when they were sick. When they came
running to greet him, calling out "Good day, Father!" tears would
spring to his eyes. Never once did the adults and their two children
acknowledge what they knew to be true. It wasn't the truth that needed
acknowledging. There was something else far more important: the
unspoken compact between them, their shared resolve. If God had
decreed that in the next life they would be damned to roast in hell everlasting, then this life would require compensatory adjustments. It
would require a larger quotient of love.

Mariana did not want for domestic love, having so much from that
eccentric little family. As she grew older, however, and a tall, lanky
stranger from the paper mill started coming to church to stare at the
back of her neck, she began to want love of a different kind. She would
wave to Victor Sobrevilla as he walked out into a Sunday morning,
engage him in conversation on the steps or on the plaza, chat about his
student days in Lima or his dream of building a factory in the jungle.
She liked the low rumble of his voice; the clear, open forehead; the
steady, long drink of his gaze. At first, she thought she should just
ignore him—he would probably spurn her when he learned who her
father was—but she was piqued by the attention, kindled by desire.

When Victor finally dropped to one knee and asked her to marry
him, Mariana knew she had allowed things to go too far. Her mother,
Doña Rosa, was chaperoning from across the garden, so absorbed by
what she was reading that she didn't register the sudden shift in the
young man's kinetics. Nor did she hear his ardent declaration.

Mariana looked at her mother on the distant bench and then back
at her beloved. She would have given anything to be able to tell him yes.
Instead, she took a deep breath and decided to tell him the truth. She

said, "Victor, in all the conversations we've had, and on the many occasions you've called on this house, you've never asked me about my father."

"No," he responded immediately. "Because my own was killed in a terrible scandal. He died with two bullets in his back. I vowed never to count family history as important—for me it has only brought sadness. I suspected there was a reason why there was no father here. Some sadness of your own, perhaps? Is he dead?"

"Not dead," she said, with remarkable evenness, "unavailable. He shouldn't have children. He's a priest."

Victor glanced up at the sky, his brain threshing the news. "I'm sorry, *mi vida,*" he managed finally, "but what does that have to do with us?"

A reasonable question. For two people whose lives had been rocked by scandal, family history didn't matter at all.

The priest standing at Doña Mariana's door nearly forty years later processed the same information but had another reaction entirely. As Padre Bernardo listened to her story, his eyes darkened. She could see that the truth, meant to soothe him, was having an opposite effect. He turned away and, like a burning man seeking deliverance, dove into the blanket of night.

When Doña Mariana returned to the sala, only Don Victor and her two daughters were there. Graciela was still shaking her head in wonder. Belén's face was red; her eruption had left her bewildered. Never in all the thirty-six years of her life had Belén ever said something so malicious about a child. Not that she hadn't longed to. Graciela's children, Pablo and Silvia, were forever stampeding overhead, just when a book had piqued her imagination. She'd a mind to stomp up the stairs and give them a good box on the ears, but she avoided such confrontations by nature and, besides, she loved her little nieces and nephews.

Don Victor, too, was bewildered. He was standing a bit unsteadily, gripping the back of his chair. He hadn't thought about Vanessa in years, and his inexplicable urge to talk about a former lover had made him more than a little dizzy. He'd had to loosen his cravat.

* * *

By morning, when the *guacharos* had flown back to their caves, the *machacuy* had slithered high in the trees, and the tarantulas had rolled into fists under the *chuchuhuasi,* the world seemed a better place. The priest did not make an appearance as he usually did at ten o'clock, bustling into the dining room to throw a blessing over Don Victor. But the day unfolded just the same: All five children—Graciela's two and Jaime's three—were bathed and scrubbed and taken upstairs to their tutorials with Señorita Marcela. And Belén's husband, Ignacio, having returned late the previous evening from his duties as foreman of the factory, went off early to manage a hefty order from a Contamana bag-maker.

It wasn't that they had put their priest's confession out of mind. They didn't know quite where to put it. It seemed by turns tragic and ludicrous, ancient history and scandal. What does one do with information one would rather not have? They tried burying themselves in work but found themselves drawn back to the evening's revelations. Belén sat in her library chair, contemplating her brash words about the feral boy. Doña Mariana totted up the month's paper sales, but her thoughts kept returning to the sorry padre. Graciela leaned back on the piano stool, asking herself what the next round of truth-telling might bring.

Don Victor, as blessed as he was with a skill for forgetting, was having trouble putting the memory of Vanessa into the compost of history. He had been trying to work all morning. Perhaps it was the transparency of cellophane—perhaps it was those thousand shafts of light as he lowered each crystalline specimen into a stack on his butcher's table. Perhaps it was the sweetness of cannabis, still lingering over the tub of cooked hemp, swelling the air with its giddy perfume. Don Victor couldn't say exactly what it was that suddenly sent his mind rambling back into the past again. As he stood in his workshop and pulled sheet after sheet of transparent paper from the netting, Vanessa's pink breasts, with their two generous cherry-hard aureoles, kept rising before him like waves on a coralline sea.

Vanessa. He caught hold of his chair and lowered himself carefully into the leather. Every morning on the way to the paper mill in Quillabamba he would see the yellow-haired Dutchwoman through the doorway of her hostel, La Holandesa. She would flutter her thick fingers at him and he would answer with a tip of his jipijapa hat. She seemed a proper enough gringa, efficient, running her place as if it were a *zimmerhof* somewhere in the Alps, scrubbing it down every day, swabbing the mountain dust from its shelves, filling its garden with armies of red geraniums.

But one day when she was on all fours, scouring the blue floor tiles with particular Teutonic vigor, he couldn't help but spy two stupendous attributes, bobbing spiritedly between her arms. He found himself thinking about them all day. On his way home, he brought her a nosegay of marigolds. She took him upstairs directly.

"I'm not one to play games," she said, shaking the marigolds in his face.

"Neither am I," he answered, flustered, thinking that she would now lecture him on the virtues of Nordic womanhood and that he should never presume to want more from a Dutchwoman than a threshold salutation.

"No games. I like it simple. Me on top. You with your hands on my ass. You can look all you want at my *tetas*. You can lick them with your tongue like a baby. But no hands, no mauling. Understand?"

That was how they began. Every day before her pharmacist husband came home from his little shop on the plaza, Victor Sobrevilla would walk through the double doors of La Holandesa and mount the stairs to the one room she never rented. If she were seated at the school desk in the lobby, she'd shout to the cook to take her place, and then she'd scurry up after him. He would be waiting for her on the bed, naked and ready as an animal, and by the time she had flung off her shift, kicked off her shoes, and lowered one of her breasts into his mouth, so was she.

She smelled like citrus, except for her underarms, which harbored a stench he'd never smelled on a woman. It was potent, jolting as a bomb of pure cumin. She stank. There would be no relief from it, unless he could manage, as she moved over him, to wedge his nose between her neck and her shoulder, which she had slapped mercifully with cologne.

Vanessa: the globed goddess, the harsh-tongued, hard-nippled harridan, who demanded as much as she gave. In the solitude of his workshop,

Victor pressed the back of his head against the hard wooden rim of his leather chair. She hadn't been the only one.

There had been Refinata, the Lima whore, with her cinnamon-scented red lace panties. Nora, the mulatto, with her avid little *mammillas,* as erect as two black beans, begging to be taken between his teeth. Porfiria the Mayoruna, whose impressive title he'd had to give her, because although she was willing to part her sweet mahogany thighs for him, she refused to tell him her name. Female faces, bodies, one after another, peeled through memory, until the effort to parse so much flesh threatened to burst his head. It was foolishness, he told himself. An insane catalog. He'd never experienced anything like it. Fearing something could be gravely wrong with him, he resolved to consult Yorumbo, his curandero upriver. He felt wobbly, unmoored. There was something diabolical about this carousel ride of profligacies. Tomorrow he would have his witchman rid him of those memories for good.

Struggling to keep his mind in the present, he took a mango from the bowl his wife had put on the table that morning. He turned the fruit in his hands and, slowly, irresistibly, it gave him an idea. He set it down firmly and went back to work.

By the end of the day, Don Victor had much to show for his efforts: There were forty-four sheets of cellophane in varying sizes and densities, hanging from clothespins he had strung from the ceiling. Some, he could see, were less perfect than others, flecks of pith marring their surfaces, but, in the glow of his lamp, they seemed uniformly flawless and pearly. They fluttered there in the breeze of an old fan, casting luminous ripples onto the walls.

Cellophane! In all his forty years of making paper and collecting its omniformities, he had not imagined he could make stuff like this. He had seen it in shops in Lima's Hotel Crillon—sealed around cigarettes, furled around chocolates, cinched around flasks of champagne. But here it was, issuing from the improvised Fourdrinier on his worktable, shooting into his copper tub.

He had spent several months in his workshop—a separate building that stood to the side of the mansion—happy to let his son-in-law

Ignacio run the daily operations at the factory. It was a pleasant enough place to spend the days, mixing and remixing proportions of cooked cotton and hemp, stirring the mush in the narrow wood box, and then watching it shoot out the other side. There were only two people allowed into that inner sanctorum: his wife, who would flit in and out from time to time, bringing bowls of ripe fruit and news of the hacienda; and Pedro, the gardener, whose job it was to sweep the floor, which by the end of the day would be littered with cotton lint, hemp fiber, and shreds of paper, torn and flung in frustration.

The shop's huge worktable had once belonged to a butcher in Pucallpa who had used it to debone carcasses. It was thick, strong, and ruddy with the blood of a thousand creatures, and it stood in the center of the room—still ruthless in its new incarnation. Under it, Don Victor kept an assortment of heavy tools, including an extensive collection of rifles and handguns. On one end was his makeshift machinery, on the other, a desk, from which he could ponder the paper process or, if he preferred, tinker with his myriad tools, which were strewn about in strangely logical disorder. From time to time, he would lean back from work, exhausted, stretch his arms toward the ceiling, and focus his eyes on the stuffed condor—his spirit animal—pinned to the workshop's back wall.

It was, despite squat proportions, a well-lit room. Four windows ran along each of its long walls. On a bright day, Don Victor could sit in his chair and look out at the main walkway to the left or the threshing area to the right. He had built it on that very spot with the notion that he could repair there from bed at any hour of the night, propelled by a good idea. But it was also far enough from the factory to prevent him from seeing the workers and disrupting his creative process.

The workers, always curious about his fantastical inventions, would take every chance to peer up from the road at Don Victor's workshop. It was there, after all, that he had earned his reputation as a shapechanger. He had made tissues from live plants. He had built an irrigation system by stringing coconut shells on pulleys. He had made chewing gum from sapodilla. He had cut tools and knives from the barbed roots of the paxiuba. He had made fragrant, wide hats from eucalyptus, a bit of commercial wizardry that drew trade from Shipibo hunters, who rowed up and shouted from their canoes, pointing to their heads. The Shipibos carried away stacks of the cooling, aromatic headgear, and the hacienda fed on porcupine for a week, fresh deliveries slapping the dock every morning.

But if his workshop was a glorified butcher block, strewn with a steady stream of capricious inventions, the shapechanger's factory was a monument to stability: solid, unswerving, immutable. There, along the river, set on a vast, raised concrete foundation that spread from the dock to the southernmost part of Floralinda, was a building made of gleaming white Eternit. Sitting stolidly within it were William Randolph Meiggs's machines—the Fourdrinier from Marseilles; the swift, wire mesh gauze from Ohio; the suction tubes by Nash, transported from a failed factory in Brazil; the shiny steel dryers and calenders with singularly unpronounceable words engraved on the cylinders: IN DEUTSCH-LAND HERGESTELLTER STAHLWERK. Out on the concrete platform were the cleaning vats and the boilers; behind them, suspended on two colossal arms that looked like the elbows of Atlas—the hulking iron ball digester from Chicago. Sucking and spewing the water that was so necessary to paper production, the monstrous digester cooked down whole fields of hemp into a thick pulp before it entered the front door of the factory, and then a formidable string of machines whirred it into thick spindles of brown paper that rolled handily out the back.

The place, like any medulla of industry, churned with seeming chaos but was governed by discipline. Ignacio, as foreman, paced the rigged bamboo gallery that was suspended from the ceiling and ran the length of the mill, from the wet end to the dry finish. Below, a force of a hundred men—all jungle Indians Don Victor had lured from up and down the Ucayali—routed the water, shoveled the hot pulp, lugged wheelbarrows full of it from the digester to the headbox. When paper was being made, there was no mistaking it: A deafening roar issued from Mr. Meiggs's machines and scattered the birds and animals. Thick orange foam squeezed from the shooting pulp, dropped onto metal trays, coiled through a ganglion of rusty pipes, and slid, in a warm ooze, into the gray, green river.

For more than twenty years, since the Sobrevillas and the initial thirty families had settled on that twist of the river, Mr. Meiggs's machines had chewed hemp into paper, and the hacienda had flourished. Floralinda became so well known that the Wycliffe Bible missionaries, an avid group of American evangelicals that owned a fleet of light aircraft, would fly in from time to time, land on the fallow fields, and gape at the factory's machines. "Just like Ohio!" they would crow, and slap Don Victor on the back. But it was Mr. Meiggs's machinery, Mr. Meiggs's paper, and Mr. Meiggs's dream: Don Victor could not consider it otherwise. Cellophane, on the other hand, the stuff it had taken him months to fashion in his workshop—the stuff through which he could see his hands, even the whorls on his fingertips—was his. All his.

In America, he had read, whole factories were dedicated to nothing but cellophane: for wrapping food, preserving tobacco, protecting manufactured goods. Even the army was placing orders. In France, they had been making it for generations. Why not here in Floralinda, by God, in the one-thousand-nine-hundred-and-fifty-second year of the Lord? And yet, and yet: It was truly remarkable that he had been able to produce it, even in tiny quantities. It had taken time to get the pulp thin enough, the chemical baths balanced, the slits in his mock headbox so narrow that they could extrude viscose in delicate sheets. More remarkable, as Don Victor now reckoned it, was that cellophane hadn't occurred to him sooner. He had all the machinery and material to make it: He only needed to reconfigure things, import the necessary alkaline by the barrel.

It had taken the article in Alejandro's old engineering magazine to make him realize such a possibility. When he read that Mr. Du Pont couldn't make cellophane fast enough and a number of other companies had sprouted to fill the demand, Don Victor began looking hard at its botanical possibilities in Floralinda. Being the sort of engineer who—like old Señor Urrutia, with his ball-bearing miracles—had a dramatic flair, he decided not to share his enthusiasm immediately. He would surprise the family with his ingenuity. Secretly, cautiously, he tried handmaking cellophane from dozens of plants that grew between the house and the banks of the Ucayali. The tall slender cetico trees produced a heavy sheet, but the fiber was cumbersome to harvest. Bamboo made hardy, pliable cellophane, but its surface was too riddled with blemishes, and the bagasse was fussy to cook. The tufted gramalote that grew by the river had made the sheerest tissue, but it had been easy to tear, spewing against his walls like bursts of carnival ribbon. But hemp, the very plant he had been mixing with cane and transforming into hefty rolls of sturdy brown paper, had turned out to make the most resilient cellophane of all. With enough cooking and bleaching, he could produce paper as diaphanous as Fata Morgana's veil.

And why not? For centuries, Amazon Indians had mashed plants to fashion their raiments. The great preponderance of jungle residents went about as naked as their mothers had birthed them, but those few who liked to cover themselves—the Machiguenga, for instance—made their robes out of crushed leaves: soaked in water, pounded with smooth rocks, left out to bake in the sun. In just such ways, Don Victor contemplated, he had spent a lifetime making plants into paper: for those who needed it, by hands that revered it, in a laboratory that was a perpetual renascence of green.

He shook his head and focused on the clock on the wall. Six in the evening. He had been working all day. He reached across to the stack of cellophane, took the top sheet, his most delicate specimen, and pulled it toward him. Carefully, he placed the mango in the center of the paper. Gathering the corners with trembling fingers, he encased the fruit and tied it off with a length of string, then sat back and contemplated his work. Through the clear sheath, he could behold the vivid madder of the skin, the dainty moles along its curve. Finally, he rose from his chair and carried his parcel of portable life, like a precious relic, through the front hall of the darkening house, into the sala, and placed it tenderly on the piano.

4

Graciela was the first to see it. She came down the stairs and into the sala trailing a scarf of antique mousseline that her uncle Alejandro had sent from Trujillo. When she spied the mango on the piano, she thought it was made of glass. She struck a match, lit the gas lamp that hung by the window, and stepped toward it to get a better look. The base of the structure was round, a warm shade of orange; the top, a gleaming crystal. Cinched around was a crude jute string. She had some idea of how glass was blown—her father had given dinner-table disquisitions on the work of furnaces and foundries—but she hadn't imagined that the substance could be so intricate, graceful. She marveled at its fragility, the way the gaslight flickered on its hard angles and contours. She stretched out her hand and pressed a finger onto its surface. It crumpled. She jumped back with a little cry.

"Did it bite?" came a voice from behind. She spun around to see the sturdy figure of her brother filling the frame of the door. A bag was slung over one shoulder.

"Jaime! *Dios mío!* You scared me! I didn't know you were home."

He grinned, teeth gleaming from his sunburned face. His sleeves were rolled to the elbow, his shirt unbuttoned so that she could see the hard wall of his chest. He seemed spirited, happy, invigorated by his trip downriver.

"Who put that there?" he said, lowering his bag to the floor and nodding toward the piano.

"I don't know." Graciela turned to look at it again. "I just walked in. Have you ever seen anything like it? Look how it shimmers."

"Silly girl," Jaime said. "Even from here I can see it's fruit wrapped in clear paper. So that's what the old man has been working on in his workshop! Cellophane! Tricky devil."

"*Oye,* Boruba!" Doña Mariana's voice rang out from her second-floor balcony. "Have the children eaten?"

"*Sí, señora!*" came the reply. "They're here in the kitchen now!"

"Come with me, Graciela," said Jaime, cocking his head toward the door. "Let me show you what I brought from Nauta. Come, before they all pour downstairs for dinner."

Graciela followed her brother into the cavernous front hall. She could see that he had not changed clothes in the six days he'd been away. The back of his shirt was streaked with perspiration; its odor was strong. His trousers were caked with mud. But there was a brisk swing in his step, as if important matters were at hand.

The crate was as large as a table. Jaime removed the bamboo pole that secured one side and set it on the floor. Carefully, he lifted the panel and suddenly a huge dog flew into the room—a mastiff with a muscular neck and drooping ears. He was black as a panther, glossy, and when he reached up on his hind legs to lap Graciela's face with a wet, red tongue, she laughed with delight.

Jaime had found the animal in Nauta, onboard the trawler of a Brazilian who called himself O-Gigante. He was a colossus with obsidian skin, a gold tooth, and fried hair that hung down his back in a braid. He offered to sell Jaime thirty burlap bags filled with coca leaf. When Jaime said he wasn't interested, the man drew a scroll from a rag-covered pile and, with a single snap of the wrist, unfurled it to reveal the twenty-foot skin of an anaconda. "Authentic," he assured him. "The best-quality *pellejo* you'll ever find." Jaime declined that too. But when the Brazilian pointed to the dog in the crate, Jaime took interest. It wasn't often you came across a good dog on the river. The negotiation had not been easy. The instant his master opened the crate, the dog had flown out and sunk his teeth into the man's gleaming black arm. The Brazilian had howled and reached for a dagger, but Jaime kicked the man onto his massive haunches, distracted the dog with a strip of dried *charqui,* and so saved the lives of both master and animal. As he took the dog away, the Brazilian could only thank him.

In the four remaining days that it took to wend his way home to Floralinda, Jaime won the mastiff's love. He fed him with his own food, took him ashore to let him bound along the banks, groomed him with a fine-bone comb. By the time they arrived at his father's hacienda, he understood that the dog was a gentle creature, full of heart, and that the scene he had witnessed on the trawler had been an aberration. The animal had not turned against its master. Jaime saw the evidence in raw rings around its legs—O-Gigante had stolen the dog from someone else.

And there was something more: The animal was endowed with a miraculous ability. It could chortle. It could cackle. It could communicate humor with a near-human sound. The dog was able to laugh.

That night, when the Sobrevilla family descended the staircase, they did not go into the sala. They lingered in the hallway, too enchanted by the sight of the exuberant dog to see the glittering omen on the piano. Papu—as Jaime had named him—leapt across the tiles, throwing his big head back and laughing. The children danced up and down, enraptured by Papu's antics: his wide smile, his perfectly enunciated ha-ha, the way he seemed to answer their giggles with hearty guffaws of his own. It was a faculty no one had imagined possible in a dog—laughter. The parrot eyed the mastiff warily from his cage, turned his back, and ranted into the corner.

"Papu!" Jaime called out, throwing his arms wide, as his father was fond of doing. "Welcome to Floralinda! This is your home! You have brought us a soul again!" When Boruba waddled in to see what the fuss was about, Graciela ran to her side and whispered into her ear. It was a gift from heaven, she explained—a sign from God, for which they should be thankful. Boruba nodded, crossed herself, and raised her palms to the ceiling.

* * *

Don Victor couldn't decide whether it was the way Jaime teased him—
"Cellophane! Fresh from your inner sanctum!"—or his throbbing head
that made him so miserable. There was nothing fresh about this paper.
It had been six full days since he had produced the first perfect sliver.
He had confided in no one, thinking he would surprise his family, but
nobody really seemed to care. Here they were, spilling in, laughing and
talking about a dog.

As he brooded over his plate, Marcela, the children's teacher,
appeared in the doorway. He looked up, startled to see her in that perfect frame. She was wearing a navy dress with a cinched waist and a
square bib like a sailor's, and, as she moved with the others, pushing
the black horn-rimmed glasses up her nose, he could see the line of her
hips under the skirt. She was pretty in the way some women can be:
despite all efforts to mask their advantages. The presentation was
severe, but the features were more than pleasing. The bright, black eyes
were big behind the glass barricade. The straight brown hair was thick,
parted in the center, and pulled tight into a low bun on her neck. The
lips were slicked red—but not to the extent of their fullness. Her hands
were folded against her round little breasts, as if she were in the company of penitents. Even so, there was bright promise in the flare of
those hips, in their natural, uninhibited motion. He watched her with
new eyes, with all the alertness of a schoolboy. His wife brushed past,
patting Marcela affectionately on one shoulder, and the young woman
grinned up self-consciously. She lowered herself into her chair, placing
her perfect little rump lightly on the wood, and then nestled in, as if she
were a hen roosting on eggs.

By the time she had pulled her napkin onto her lap, he was ogling
her openly. Sensing this, she blinked, blushed, and flicked a quick
tongue along her upper lip. Suddenly the ghosts of Vanessa, Porfiria,
and Refinata were there too—and a rainbow of luscious tongues. He
pressed the corner of his napkin against a damp temple. It could wait
no longer. He would seek out his witchman the very next morning.

Padre Bernardo lay rock-still in the nave of his church. Arms spread like
wings, fingers stretched toward the transept walls, he could feel the

beating of his heart against the bare wood floor. Outside, a troop of monkeys howled into the rainy night. The chirr of a thousand mantises pulsed the air. In the distance, at the boundary of the jungle, he could make out the gentle sibilance of the forest canopy, like the rustle of jaguars through grass.

He had been there for hours, immobile, before the gaze of his Virgin. Perspiration ran from his temples and dampened the floor under his face. He had prayed for forgiveness, chanted his litany of psalms, and now his head felt drained, hollow, save for a dim perception that marked the thudding in his chest.

What demon had possessed him? The abrupt confession of a sin he had struggled for three decades to redress had come out of nowhere. He had babbled on like some pubescent youth touting his manhood, with all the judgment of a perfect fool.

Doressa had been the folly of a single summer. He had been nineteen at the time, a mere novitiate, and when he had seen her swaying to the high-pitched flutes in the procession of the Candelaria, a boy's desire had blazed through him like a bout of cholera. She had been too willing, too imprudent. So had he.

She had been the reason he left the punishing cold of Puno. Yes, he had feared the possibility that he might father a child with her; and yes, he quaked at the prospect of bitter justice from an angry God; but he had not cut it off with her just to escape retribution. He had confessed his sin to his superiors, paid a stiff penance, suffered the consequences. He had been exiled from Puno, sent into the gantlet of a cruel jungle, consigned to a lifetime of atonement and to gathering new souls to the Church. He may have told the truth in the Sobrevillas' hospitable sala, but the wider realities—the full effect of his wickedness—had gone unsaid.

And what was he to make of Doña Mariana's bald delivery of an equally difficult truth? She had always seemed the essence of propriety, a rock of Christian rectitude. He knew that terrible sins like her father's were common in this unruly country. Priests strayed. Children were fathered. Some men of the cloth turned out to be mere men, imperfect by definition. The Church staggered ahead, did what it could. But why had she spoken of her father's damnation so casually, and, worse, why had she offered it as a salve?

He raised himself to his knees and considered his wooden Virgin. How different she was from the original in Lake Titicaca: She was not carved from a cactus trunk, slathered with gold leaf, set out on a clever pedestal. It was the humility of her figure that so moved him. Plain wood. Simple lines. But he could not see that austerity now. Over the years, the worshippers of Floralinda had draped her in bright fabric, strung her with beads. Red, blue, and yellow papagayo feathers now adorned her hair; beneath her, a crescent of silver; above her, a halo of gold. A Christ doll was pinned to her bosom.

He knelt there, studying his lifetime companion—her gentle demeanor, her unequivocal forgiveness, her perpetual offer of the child. She had not answered him today. He had not felt the warm infusion of inspired understanding. But there was comfort in her image. It was she who had drawn him to Floralinda. When Don Victor had come looking for him so many years later after their first meeting on the bank of La Misión, he had rejoiced in the man's devotion to the Virgin. He had given up everything to minister to the papermaker's hacienda. What he hadn't figured on was losing Don Victor himself.

The papermaker had installed him and the wooden Virgin in a pretty chapel on white stilts and then gone off to worship with heathens—shamans with potions and stones. Don Victor had spent less time at the priest's altar than he had in a witchman's tambo: a hut hung with caged toads, shriveled entrails, dried vines. It was beyond Padre Bernardo's capacity to understand it. But if he had learned anything from thirty-four years in service to his Virgin, it was that she would eventually make things clear. He crossed himself and drew his rosary from his pocket.

Dios te salve, María. Llena eres de gracia. El señor es contigo.... The thrum of nocturnal enterprise surrendered to a radiant stillness. All was quiet now. When Padre Bernardo heard the soft call of the piracuru, he knew that the sun was well into the sky and that he should sweep the steps, dust the altar, and ready the church for matins. He listened to the sound of a door opening and the shuffle of feet behind. By the time he kissed his rosary and turned to see who it was, Graciela Sobrevilla and Boruba were in the last row, their foreheads pressed into their hands.

Don Victor lay rock-still, prone, on a bed of dried bark in a clearing five miles upriver from Floralinda, half a mile into the jungle. Beside him was his witchman, sucking a bamboo pipe and blowing plumes of *mapacho* over Don Victor's long, pale body. The papermaker was naked but for a strip of leather that covered his manhood. His forehead rested against the mat, purged of the devilish pounding. His arms were spread like a condor's wings. He was reaching an apogee, riding the wind.

Yorumbo, the curandero, had not seen the shapechanger in months. Peering through the straw walls of his tambo, he had watched the familiar form push through the undergrowth. As soon as Don Victor reached the yuca patch, he sent out his woman to greet him. She pulled a beaded switch from above the door and shivered a welcome. Don Victor raised both hands.

The woman was naked except for the red string that circled her knees and ankles. She was clearly a new wife, not the old crone who usually greeted him: Her breasts were firm, nipples erect; her belly did not sag from children. Her hairless body shone with fish oil. Around her mouth was a tattooed chain of hatch marks; her nostrils were pierced with sticks. When she smiled, Don Victor saw that she had no front teeth.

Inside the tambo, he greeted the old sumiruna and congratulated him on the new woman, acknowledging her surrender of teeth, a sign of respect from a wife to a shaman. He saw the pile of stones, a shrine for the old woman, and expressed his condolences. And then he went on to describe his affliction. Don Victor did not speak Mayoruna, the language of the old man's tribe, but the two knew Shipibo and so he conveyed that his head was the source of his torment. It was drowning in images of women. They were filling his loins with desire, slowing his work, flooding his head with distant, unwanted memories. Yorumbo understood immediately. There were few in that vale of the Ucayali who did not know that this man's head was a precious vessel. It was there that the shapechanger carried his magic.

His abilities were legendary. He was not like the termite people, the scourge, who hacked their way through the forest, leaving vast, treeless spaces. Not like the serengueros, rubber-tappers, iron-toting marauders, who would just as soon put a plug into a man's chest as walk around him. The shapechanger had only worked his magic in one place down-river. He hadn't been greedy that way.

It had taken Yorumbo time to trust him. In all his years under the forest canopy, he had never seen such a man: tall as a young tree, nose like a beak, hair trembling above his head like the crown on a vulture. And the layers of covering on his body! How could you judge a man if you couldn't see the strength of his shoulders? How could you know him if you couldn't read age on his flanks? But soon after Yorumbo built a tambo in that clearing, the shapechanger began coming regularly. His interest in cures was genuine. He always came with a reason and spoke enough Shipibo to make it plain. It hadn't mattered to Don Victor that his witchman was ruled by a different animal spirit. Yorumbo was a cat? The white man welcomed the news. That meant his teacher would be agile, a dancer, nimble on hard surfaces! How fortunate to be counseled by a cat! Cats are superior creatures, he had said—hard to please, but passionate. Disinterested, but curious. Sedentary, but graceful. "Look at me," the shapechanger had pleaded, "I'm an awkward man, perching on one leg, and then the other. I need a sumiruna like you!" Eventually, Yorumbo grew fond of his patient's peculiarities; he welcomed his vis-its, healed his wounds, purged his stomach, cooled his fevers. And came to understand that his spirit was a bird.

Yorumbo knew what was ailing the shapechanger. He could feel the heat around the man's forehead, see the wings there, aching to fly. But it would take time to release them.

Yorumbo instructed Don Victor to go outside and remove his many layers of decoration—hat, shirt, trousers, necklace—for these would impede the cure. The smoke needed to fall on bare skin. He handed the shapechanger a string with a leather flap. He told him to prepare for the vine. Don Victor knew what to do. He had gone through the ritual before. He would need to consume a tart potion of ayahuasca so that he could cleanse his innards and mount the wind in a purified body. He would need to drink the stones. At the end of it, the memories would be routed from his head, the lust from his loins, and at night, while he slept, the spirit of the enchantment would come in a dream and tell him what to do.

Yorumbo donned his grass cape and tied twine around his knees and ankles. He slipped the balsa-wood disks into the holes in his earlobes. He painted his face and chest with thick, red *urucú*, while his woman boiled two lengths of ayahuasca. When he was done, he sent the woman away and began singing an *icaro* to summon the spirits. He made a bed of bark on the open ground. He took the pot with the bitter brew, fished out the vine, threw it to one side, raised the pot to his lips, and swallowed some of the liquid. Rattling his necklace of shells, he offered the rest to his visitor. The shapechanger drank it down, knelt at the foot of the mat, and waited for the vine's magic. Yorumbo reached into his pouch, pulled out three tiny white stones, and dropped them into a rain-filled gourd.

Don Victor closed his eyes and let the high, sweet melody of the *icaro* enter him. He couldn't tell how long it had been since he had drunk the bitter potion. The taste in his mouth was rank, his stomach a cauldron of fire. Suddenly, he doubled over and vomited. Black liquid hurled forward like a great, dark snake, followed by more, in spasms of mucus and bile. He sprawled on the bark, holding his belly, whimpering like a child. And then the visions came.

He felt a force, as if his forehead were pushing against the wall of a canyon. An explosion of brightness followed, in which his skull seemed to spray in a thousand directions, catching the sun in its shards. Then came the sensation he had been waiting for: an irresistible lightness, rising through his chest and lifting him into the air.

The shapechanger burst into the spirit universe. Flapping enormous wings, he rose up over the jungle, soared higher and higher until the rush of air through his feathers whistled like a hundred flutes. So powerful were his eyes that he could look down and see frogs leaping from stone to stone, iridescent beetles swarming on palm fronds.

He turned north, following the bend in the river, retracing the route he had taken that morning. He saw his canoe moored to a moss-covered log, a strong rope coiled around the nub of a broken branch, just as he'd left it. Across the river was a Huitoto hunter, rubbing his spear with curare; beside him, a round-bellied boy chewing sapodilla. He flew over a large, emerald island and saw an anteater rise onto its back legs and stare up at a flock of birds in wonder, its great claws suspended in air.

Just as the sun mounted to its high point, he saw Floralinda—the white walls of his factory, its steel smokestack thrusting toward him like a beacon. There was Padre Bernardo's church; a procession of leaf-cutting ants crossing the coca field, its cargo aloft—a stream of green sails. He watched Doña Mariana step onto the patio of their home, brush the hair from her eyes. Then came Pedro, a broom in one hand, a strip of cellophane in the other. The paper caught the light, flashed up like a signal lamp. Don Victor had to avert his eyes.

He circled over the treetops. Now Pedro and Boruba were at the kitchen door. Pedro tipped his hat to her, and a dozen butterflies flew out from beneath, fluttering toward the sky—a kaleidoscope of yellow. The cook was smiling and clapping.

Don Victor turned back, feeling the rush of wind in his feathers. As he swooped south, he glimpsed a sullen vulture perched on a stump overhanging the water; he watched it flare its wings and flick its extravagant crop. He heard it shriek. He banked and flew over the vile-smelling bird. The return voyage was quick after that: the feel of the earth rising beneath him; the branches bristling into another dimension, coming alive, stretching out to greet him.

The next thing he heard was the high warble of the curandero. Don Victor raised his head. A string of saliva dribbled to the bark beneath him. His mouth was hot and foul, but his head felt light, clean, as if the caverns of his mind had been flushed with water. The curandero was coming toward him, singing and carrying a gourd.

Yorumbo gestured to him to drink. The sun was in the western sky—it was mid-afternoon. He took in the cool liquid gratefully, and, as it trickled down his fevered throat, three small white stones shifted and tumbled into his mouth. He rolled them on his tongue and spit them back into the bowl, one by one.

"*Catú, catú,*" said Yorumbo, shaking his head.

The witchman reached a fist toward the shapechanger's forehead, grunted, and pulled away what seemed to be a gnarled white knot, hard as bone. He muttered, touched it lightly to his own head, then carried it to a hole he had dug by his tambo. He dropped it in, covered it over.

It was done. The trouble was purged, ripped from his head, and buried. Don Victor drew a deep breath. He untied the string around his hips, removed the leather flap, and began to dress. His body felt limp but his brain was clear. He took his necklace with the image of the Virgin, pulled it over his head. Yorumbo nodded in approval—he had seen that artifact many times before. The rest of the garments followed quickly. When he was fully clothed, Don Victor drew a slender box from his pocket and handed it to the curandero.

Don Victor had to show him how to open it. When the cover was finally lifted, Yorumbo saw what was nestled inside: a shiny film and, beneath it, a weapon. The witchman reached in and the paper slid back into the box, leaving the knife in his hand. The blade was cold steel, its handle carved paxiuba wood—in the shape of a leaping cat.

Belén's favorite image—tipped into one of her books as a frontispiece—was a portrait of one of the great poets of Spanish America, a young nun with a face like a benediction: She was lovely, bow-lipped, clear-eyed. But her expression was as puzzling as a sphinx's. Was it humility? Was it defiance?

The artist had been careful to record the icons: One was an unnaturally long rosary, which she held delicately in one hand. Another was a bold wooden cross, affixed to the rosary and dangling, like Christ's burden, over her shoulder. Her free hand lay over a book. Pinned to her chest was a miniature of her patron saint, Jerome. Behind was a sea of books—shelves upon shelves of them—and, above, a clock with no hands.

She was Sor Juana Ines de la Cruz, and the three relics told of her trials. Sor Juana's essays were profoundly rational, her poems heartbreaking—the most famous her monumental *The Dream*. She wrote doctrinal works about the Virgin Mary, carols for festive performances, sonnets about erotic love, treatises on roses, and volumes upon volumes of verse about human frailties, the sufferings of the heart, the tyranny of the imagination. By the age of sixteen, she had the Spanish viceroyalty's attention—she became one of the most respected scholars of her day. But like Saint Jerome, she was faced with a dilemma: Would she choose God's faith or man's reason? Her bishop—Manuel Fernández de Santa Cruz—did not trust her mind. Either take the book under your hand or the cross on your left shoulder, he said, you cannot have both. She was commanded to give up her learning, her scholarship, her library. The clock in the painting told the rest of the story: It was handless, timeless, now.

Belén closed the door of her library and leaned against it. A fierce pain gripped her brain. She had watched her husband rise from their bed and shuffle sleepily to the bucket behind the screen. As usual, he had emerged yawning, rubbing his eyes. As usual, she had said what she said every morning: "Here it is! Another day."

"What kind of thing is that to say?" Ignacio had snapped at her. "'Here it is, another day'! You think life's not worth it?"

She had struggled to locate her glasses on the night table. Ignacio was a quiet man, not given to outbursts. But his voice seemed a stranger's, the words harsh and impatient. "What do you mean?" she asked him.

"What does it sound like I mean? We speak the same language, don't we?"

She did not reply, stung as she was by his venom. They rarely said much to each other in the morning. She couldn't remember when they had. Usually, she would sit up and mumble the same thing, "Here it is, another day," and he would nod, rise, dress, and leave. By the time she would go downstairs for breakfast, he would be off to the factory. She was wide awake now, the cotton nightshirt damp against her skin. The mosquito netting was pulled to one side, as he had left it. "What are you saying?"

"Nothing you don't already know."

She drew a hand through her short brown hair and ran her tongue along her lips. They were dry. A slight soreness invaded her throat.

"Ignacio, *por Dios,*" she said wearily, "you're speaking in riddles. What are you, the sphinx at Thebes? It's too early to play games. Tell me what you mean by 'you think life's not worth it.' All I said was, 'Another day.' "

He pulled off his nightclothes and flung them on a chair, surprising her with his immodesty. She blinked quickly and, when he reached into his bureau, she studied him openly. The shoulders were square, sturdy, but there was a new roundness to the belly, a softness in the chest. It was no longer the hard torso of a young man. "Belén," he said, his teeth clenched, "you are lecturing me." He paused, then slammed the top of his bureau with his fist. "Jesus! I wish those goddamn frogs would stop their insufferable squalling. It's driving me insane."

"Say what you want to say."

He walked behind the screen and emerged with his overalls—steel blue, sleeves cut away at the shoulder—and spoke to her as he dressed. "The truth. You know the truth, Belén. I know that you do, you just don't want to acknowledge it. You're so smart. You and your 'sphinx at Thebes.' Will you ever pull your head out of a book long enough to see things as they are? Let's have the truth. Are you ready to hear it?"

She nodded tentatively.

"You live in this jungle. You choose it. And yet every minute of every day, you reject it. Why did you marry me? Because I was your father's foreman? Because it was a way to avoid the one thing you really want?" He finished buttoning his overalls and raised his face toward her. The voice and body may have been new, but the face was familiar: the thick black eyebrows, piercing brown eyes, lips as taut and red as a guava. Here was the face she had married fourteen years before, the eyes she saw night after night at the dinner table. His face had always seemed pleasant enough, handsome even, but the expression on it now was forbidding, the eyes cruel.

"Oh? And what do I really want?" she asked.

"Not to be here. To be in some reading room in Trujillo where you wouldn't have to trawl through the same worm-holed books over and over again. Be honest, this marriage is over."

"Over!" she said in a whisper. She searched his face, measuring its resolve. "So you want me to go? Go to Trujillo so that *you* can stay in *my* house. With *my* family?"

"Yes. It's what I want. Go to Trujillo. Go to your tía Esther. Go where there are others as smart as you are, where there are libraries to visit, and a life that interests you more than this one. All you do now is go up and down the stairs, from bed to books to bed. When you come in here you're cold as marble. A monument of stone."

"So you stay here, eh? I go?" She was almost screaming now. "Our marriage has given you a lot, Ignacio, but it's not going to give you that!"

He raised an eyebrow, and, although his voice was no longer strident, his candor was keen as a blade. "This marriage hasn't given me much, Belén. I do the same work I did before I married you. I eat at your father's table, as I always have. What the marriage gave me was the privilege of sleeping in your bed. There was a time when I thought that was all I'd ever want, to be near you, love you, and have you love me in return. But over the years you pushed me away, went off in your head, retreated into your books with all their more interesting characters. For years now, I see you on the other side of a room, on the other side of a table, dreaming. And what do we have when all is said and done? Zero. We don't make love. We don't touch. We hardly talk. We're dried up, woman. *Secos.* Dry as the dunes."

She snapped the sheet away and swung her legs over the edge of the bed, releasing some candor of her own. "Fool!"

"*Ay, bueno.* I'm the fool, you're the genius."

There was a long pause in which the bed seemed to rock beneath her. Through the walls she could hear her nieces and nephews dart through the corridor, giggling and banging the doors.

"Quiet!" Ignacio thundered, and the children screeched and scattered away like mice. "Look," he said to her, "I don't know how I've been able to stay silent so long. Here is our situation as it really is, Belén: You and I inhabit opposite ends of the earth. Don't tell me you haven't thought so. We share a bed, but we live alone."

"Nacio," she said, suddenly fearful, "are you in love with someone else?"

"Pah!" he scoffed. "Here, in this godforsaken place? How would that be possible?" He left then, grabbing his hat, pulling the door shut behind him. She could hear the clatter of his boots—down the stairs, into the comedor. Dazed, she drew the slippers from her night table drawer, slid them on, and headed for the refuge of her library.

Closing her eyes, she breathed in the familiar smells—leather, paper, mildew. A gecko leapt from the wall onto the low shelf at her right, its pallid body hitting the wood with a dull thwack. She watched it slither over the spine of Sor Juana's *Dream,* then disappear quickly behind.

What he had said was true. Books were her sanctuary. She understood that within her family she was eccentric in this. She was the antithesis of Graciela, who had no appreciation for the contemplative life. Neither was she anything like her mother, who seemed to live only to facilitate other people's dreams and ambitions. Although she loved her father and was awed by him, she knew that she was not remotely like him; she was no doer, no person of action. She was happy to live in her head. She understood, too, that she was not like her great-aunt in Trujillo, for all Ignacio's delusions about their similarities. Although she loved the old woman, although she waited anxiously for her letters, Tía Esther was a character from a larger world. Her totem was a *tsantsa,* the shrunken head of a cougar. It was nothing so tame as a book.

But, as Belén leaned against that library door, she understood that it was her own husband with whom she had the least in common. It seemed only yesterday that her father's foreman had come calling, dark hair slicked back and shining, a spray of orchids in his fist. She had been astounded to realize that he had come looking for her. She had seen him come in and out of the house every day, sit quietly at her father's table, consuming his meals. But as far as Belén remembered, they had never exchanged more than a greeting.

In time, he was courting her avidly and, somehow, with an imagination full of romantic stories to amplify his every visit, she began to encourage him. Ignacio spoke softly, listened intently, whispered sweet compliments about her long neck, gray eyes, small hands. He was a man of few words, but she could see he had a good heart, a rock-solid decency. He would stare at her plainly when he came to call in the Sobrevilla living room, ask politely about whatever book she happened to be holding, watch her worry its pages nervously. She loved the way he answered Don Victor's questions, always direct, unafraid to disagree on the practicality of this or that invention. Her father seemed to rely on him, admire his quiet fortitude. Weeks passed and Ignacio continued to call in the late afternoons, and they would sit together in the sala, always in the company of Doña Mariana, who would plant herself in a distant chair and look up from her needles now and then to smile approvingly. One day, when Doña Mariana was absorbed in her knitting, the foreman dared to touch Belén's hand. The feel of his rough fingers changed everything. She began to dream of them searching her skin. When he took a pencil from the side table, a scrap of factory paper from his pocket, and scribbled *I love you with all my heart,* she turned it over and wrote in a careful hand: *So I confess to the crime of adoring you . . . go ahead, dear one, punish me.* She put the pencil to her chin and then added an inscription. *From a poem by Sor Juana.*

Two months later, Padre Bernardo married them. There had been a year of passion after that, when the blood of every heroine from every novel she had read pulsed through her veins, lending their marriage joy. She would read poems lamenting lost love and run to the gate to greet him, covering his sooty chin with kisses. She would read Zola's *Germinal* and thank God that her legs were wrapped around a factory worker, a man who labored with his hands. Belén's library had served Ignacio then, inspiring her to ardent heights. She had only to close her eyes and her imagination would channel the loves of the Western world. But, in time, her fictional heroines marched off and went back to their books, where they'd always lived more comfortably. The ardor waned, reality surfaced: When she spoke to him of Ruben Darío or Clorinda Matto de Turner, he would answer with a vacant stare. When he spoke to her about the factory, the purification of river water, the digesters, the beaters, the mesh—she would grow anxious to get back to Martín or Don Fernando, and the romantic distractions of her long, red shelves.

Years produced a thick wall of indifference. There was no bitterness, no rancor, nothing like the poison he had spat at her that morning. There was simply a shared neglect. The two of them floated off into far corners of separate realms, until they ceased to talk, ceased to make love, as distant as two wary animals.

No. Ignacio hadn't said a word that wasn't true. That he'd said them aloud was the surprising thing—that, in the course of a few minutes, he had told the truth and destroyed their cathedral of silence. Now, looking at it coldly, seeing the marriage for what it was after he'd pick-axed the walls, she understood why she had hesitated on that first day when she saw him in the doorway. There was nothing connecting them. No bridge. No string. No filament. Nothing at all.

5

Thousands of fireflies had invaded the master's workshop. They were everywhere: on the great table, on the shelves, on the sill of a window. *"Ayañahui,"* the gardener whispered to himself, recalling the word he had used as a child. For an instant, he was running along the banks of the Rio Tapiche, trapping the flickering insects in the caverns of his hands. *Ayañahui.* Devil's eyes. But once Pedro's eyes adjusted to the dim light of dawn, he saw they weren't fireflies at all, more like butterfly wings, translucent, fragile, radiant. But wings a man's eyes could see through? He had never imagined such a thing. As he came closer, he registered their dimensions. Long, flat, set out in neat piles. His father had told him of warriors with capes made from hundreds of bats' wings, stitched together with sharpened bird bones. Could the light of fireflies, somehow, be merged into a seamless whole?

Don Victor was certainly capable of producing marvels. Pedro had been in Floralinda for only four seasons of the rain, but he had seen things here that he'd never imagined he'd see in his life: floors of baked earth that were hard as stone, a bridge of caoba that climbed toward the heavens, balls of light that brightened the darkness, a roaring monster that spun dry, flying sheets from freshly mown hemp. There was good reason his master was called a shapechanger.

The gardener—for that was what the Sobrevillas called him—was a member of a wandering tribe, born on a riverbank between Despreciu and Pobreza. He was a Capanahua, part of a migrant tribe that stayed in one place long enough to harvest some roots, pull down some vines. His father had been a curandero; his mother, a simple tribeswoman, dispatched to the next world by a virulent snakebite. As a child, he had thought he would follow his father's calling and become a healer; he had always sprung to the task of stuffing a pipe with *mapacho* or rattling the jaguar teeth when the *icaro* songs began. But his voice grew deep as a man's, and still there was no signal that the universe was summoning him in that direction. It was then his uncle came from the "land of the blood-drinkers" and took him off to the cashew groves.

His uncle was an overlord in a cashew-gathering army—rain forest people who had been pressed into servitude harvesting nuts in Brazil, where, it was said, men drank the blood of men. Pedro joined their ranks as a picker, working his way quickly to sorter, and, in time, his uncle rewarded him by making him one of the few chieftains of the oil. When the overlords began bringing in men captured in the wild, pushing them into their camp in collars and shackles, Pedro's job was to train them to harvest the precious substance.

La Compañia, as the overlords called that vast empire, was not really interested in the meat of the cashew. The *cashueros* could take as much as they wanted as they cracked the nuts open, separated the poisonous husks, sorted and sifted them. It was the shell that was valuable—and even more, the oil that could be squeezed from that shell. There was war in a faraway land, they were told. Men toted iron to kill one another. Their weapons required grease for which the foreigners were willing to pay handsomely. Pedro's uncle was getting rich.

Pedro spent seven seasons of the rain in those groves, overseeing his little band of pickers and shuckers, crushing the shells in wooden presses until the precious oil ran freely. But one day, his uncle was told that the great war was over. The whites had put away their guns. He was told that all the men he had mobilized up and down the river could take the collars from their necks and go home.

After months of canoeing from town to town, looking for his people, Pedro learned that his father had died in his absence. Wifeless, childless, weighed down with coins that could buy nothing he really wanted, he wandered the river alone. He had lost the ties to his tribe, and for all

the wisdom he had inherited from his father—spiritual and botanical—
the Capanahua were not about to accept him as a curandero. He was
too old now, too tainted by his service to the termite world.

He came upon Don Victor on a chance trip upriver, in Santa Isabel,
where Pedro was hauling large canisters of gasoline in exchange for a
hammock and meals. When Floralinda's paper barge pulled into the
dock for provisions, he looked up and saw an extravagantly dressed
white man walking the perimeter of the village. He was crouching to
grab clumps of dirt, breaking them open with his fingers, contemplating the quality of the soil. Pedro's father had done the same: He had
studied the earth, smelled it, chewed it, in order to know where to plant
his medicines. Pedro hurried to where Don Victor was standing. He
greeted him and was pleased to hear the white man respond in Shipibo.
Eventually, Pedro nodded toward the dirt and asked him what particular aspect of it had drawn his attention.

"No, no, amigo," said Don Victor, smiling. "It's not that I'm the least
bit interested in this lizard shit. It's that I see that nothing grows on
cleared land around here. There is not one tree to block the sun, and
it's obvious someone once tried to cultivate something, but the soil is
bald. That's what interests me."

Pedro took a handful of earth and put it in his mouth. Don Victor's
eyes widened, but Pedro could see that the white man knew exactly
what he was doing. "What do you taste, eh?" Don Victor asked
him. "What poisons are you finding there?"

Pedro shook his head and kept on chewing. "Back in my hacienda,"
Don Victor continued, "I don't have this problem with the barrenness.
The traders in Pucallpa told me long ago that I would never be able to
grow anything along this river. They said that eventually the jungle poisons would seep in. But that hasn't happened. Year after year, my hemp
gets taller, my coca fuller. I worry about the time when the poisons will
come."

The curandero's son spat out the mud, then cleaned his mouth with
his fingers, wringing the black liquid from his tongue. "It's not a poison,
señor. Nothing has seeped in. This dirt has no life in it. No taste at all."

All at once Don Victor realized Pedro had more than a passing familiarity with these matters. He asked him why Floralinda's fields were so

productive when they were only two hundred kilometers upriver from the depleted banks of Santa Isabel. "It's the hemp, señor. If hemp is what you are growing, it explains why your fields are so green. Hemp puts down long roots; it feeds the soil. But you can do more to make your land thrive. Do you strip off the leaves when you harvest the hemp? Do you turn them back into the earth?" Don Victor shook his head. "When you start to do that regularly," Pedro counseled him, "you can be sure your fields will stay green." Don Victor gaped at this bit of information. His men had been stripping the branches before the paper-making process, but they would burn the leaves, or dry them to smoke in their pipes, or dump them into the river. It hadn't occurred to anyone, including Don Victor, to return the leaves to the soil.

"How is it you know so much, hombre?" Don Victor asked.

Pedro smiled and shook his head. "I listened to my father, señor. He was a very wise man, a curandero."

The son of a curandero—that was all Don Victor needed to hear. He asked Pedro to come with him to Floralinda. "As my gardener." He spread his arms wide, palms up, as if he were offering Pedro a viceroyalty.

From that day forward, Pedro was Don Victor's personal agri-culturalist—tasting the soils, determining when one crop had to be alternated with another, deciding where to plant the rice, how to space the yams, when to dig up the yuca, how much coca leaf they would need to pay off the factory workers. But adjusting to Floralinda had not been easy. Working for La Compañia in the cashew-harvesting business had made Pedro a wary man. He did not trust white people, oppor-tunists who came in with promises and left with no warning. He was not one to get drunk with the bar-hangers at Chincho's, pinch a girl on the bottom, go home and take a stick to his wife. To start with: There was no wife. He had resigned himself to it. Except for quick couplings with whores here and there along the river, he had never had a woman he wanted to call his own. He had been taken from them too early, sequestered for years in a barrack, cast out to travel alone.

There were many reasons why coming to Floralinda was a good turn in Pedro's life. He moved into a roomy shack, was given the responsi-bility his own tribe had denied him. His satisfaction became quickly evi-dent: in the factory's fields, which grew taller with every season; in

Floralinda's rich harvests of fruit; in the little garden of orchids that soon sprouted on either side of his doorway. But perhaps most rewarding of all was his friendship with the servant Boruba. She had been raised by Shipibos—a branch of the great tribe of Nahuas—of which his people, the Capanahuas, were a part. She was lovely in her ample girth, with a smile as merry as a girl's, and although the Sobrevilla children referred to her as an old woman, she couldn't have been much older than thirty seasons of the rain. She had come out to the patio when Don Victor led him up the walk on that first day and had somehow instantly understood that he was a drifter—disoriented and shy. Her welcome had startled and pleased him. *"Ea Boruba,"* she had said. I'm Boruba. *"Chipi mina."* Your sister. She told him that she was the grandmother of the wild boy he had seen running through the coca, and a widow. He quickly learned that she could be stern with the villagers, strict with the master's youngsters, but to him, from the beginning, she had been kind. She explained that her father had been a Barbadian black, her mother an Indian rubber-tapper who worked under her father's whip. It was why Boruba's hair stood out in a crown of black curls, unlike any woman's he'd ever seen, whereas her face, much like his, was copper.

He swept the floor of Don Victor's workshop, thinking of Boruba's laughter and the hatful of butterflies that had prompted it. As he pushed at the cellophane tatters, a large piece broke loose, and he picked it up. The paper wafted from his fingers, stuck to his trousers, floated in the air like feathers, before he snatched it back and thrust it in his pocket. He reached down and took more, stuffing both pockets. Walking away, he glanced through the window and saw the mango on the piano. Filled with an idea now, he took out his cellophane and searched for that first scrap. He worked quickly, knowing the fields needed his attention. It was already late morning. Overhead, a condor wheeled under the rising sun.

When he got to his shack, he plucked a striped lily from his garden— pale white, with purple streaks, and a trifurcated tongue. He wrapped it carefully in cellophane so that its delicate crown was encased in a bubble. He secured it with grass, thrust the stem into a clay pot of water, and placed the flower, very gently, under his hammock. Then he took off his shirt and headed for the hemp.

That night, even as the monkeys howled in the trees and the Sobrevillas chattered around the dining-room table, he stole out under the starlight and placed the wrapped lily at the foot of Boruba's door.

Graciela lay on her bed and studied her nakedness: small breasts with dark nipples, one larger than the other; a navel with its tiny knot; two moles just above the groin, beyond the rim of hair. When she was small, she had asked her mother why it was that jungle people went naked, and that if nothing was wrong with it, why couldn't she? "There is *nothing* wrong with it, Graciela, but you are different from those people. You are enlightened," Doña Mariana had answered. "You are descended from Eve, who ate from the tree of knowledge. Like her, you must cover yourself."

The explanation made no sense. Graciela had always suspected that those who went nude were the enlightened ones. What good was all the knowledge if it hampered Eve's soul and left her mortified? Rain forest people seemed free, unafraid—unfazed by their nakedness.

In her youth, she would study herself in the mirror and wonder if a man would ever be drawn to what she saw there. She was thin, compact as a boy. But when her nipples hardened and her sex warmed under her own scrutiny, she understood what eyes could do—"eyes," as crooners moaned in boleros, "those muzzled tongues of love." Now, in this prime of life, her eyes were her only lover.

She longed for more. She yearned for the moment when a body lifts into weightlessness, rises in ecstasy, reaches a vertex where skin has no meaning. She had taken to stretching herself out in the evenings, in the privacy of her room, under heavy mosquito netting, listening to the sounds of night. She felt too anxious to sleep, too dreamy to wake. Not since her husband, Nestor Sotomarino, had slung a bag over his shoulder and headed into the trees had she felt such a promise of change.

She had been glad to see him disappear into the jungle and prayed she would never see him again. That had been five years ago, when Pablito and Silvia were small but perfectly capable of understanding terror. They had heard the screams behind closed doors, seen the bruises on her cheeks, the welts on her arms and legs. One day they peeked through the keyhole and saw the knife. He was waving it at her, babbling demands, and the sight made them cry out in fear. Graciela was grateful when her father burst in, seized her husband by the collar, and showed him unequivocally to the door.

Watching Nestor depart—his body growing smaller in the distance, until he was no larger than an earwig and the green swallowed him in—loosed something in Graciela, a mix of dread and deliverance. As days wore on and he didn't return, as bruises faded along with the memories, she learned what it meant to breathe. She began to hope for a new life. In time she realized that circumstances had not changed, she'd simply entered a different limbo. She was minus a husband, but still the same mother, the same daughter. With the passing of boy and dog, a force field in her life had shifted. It was just a hunch, but she found herself clinging to it, there, in the dark of her room.

Long ago, when the family had lived in Pucallpa and she was a girl of twelve, the gypsy Maruca had predicted the failure of her marriage. The crone had leaned forward in her chair of mirrors and studied the entrails at her feet, muttering and poking them with a bamboo stick. When she was satisfied that she had seen all there was to see, she beckoned the girl forward and grabbed her groin with the powerful vise of one hand. "Feel this, little bird?" she said, frowning. "This is what he will want. When he finds it elsewhere, you will lose him. You'll see."

And so it had been. Nestor's profligacy was well known along the river. He tried working in Don Victor's factory but knew nothing about machines, cared little about the business, and had gone off for months at a time, only to return a little drunker, a little meaner. Rumor had it that he had another woman in Contamana. They said the woman would have nothing to do with other men, that she lived with a baby in a shack by the river, selling baskets. Whether the child was Nestor's, no one could say for sure. Word reached Floralinda that he had fled to Brazil—that he couldn't risk returning because he had raped a skin trader's woman on a mud bank of the Ucayali; there was a price on his head.

The rumors did not square with the man Graciela had known. She had fallen in love the moment she'd seen him, a phenomenon she'd heard of but never understood until it happened to her. He had docked in Floralinda in a barge that was moving tinned goods downriver. She had watched from the distance: his burnished shoulders, the way his hair tumbled into his eyes, the wide smile, perfect teeth, chiseled jaw. His curls were bleached caramel by the sun; his eyes were a radiant amber. He was the most beautiful man she had ever seen. Who, except a hardened diviner like Maruca, could have predicted that such an angel would bring so much misery?

Their courtship had been short. Don Victor had disapproved, but the padre had urged him to give Graciela his blessing. She was clearly in love, racing to the dock every time he came through, her arms flung out like a supplicant's. The priest argued that they were beautiful together: she with her piercing black eyes, he with his winning smile. Eventually, Don Victor relented. They were married in the church, with the Virgin of Copacabana looking down and a hacienda of souls in attendance. Nestor worked at the factory at first and seemed to get along with Jaime and Ignacio, but, as Graciela began to bear him children, he would take longer and longer trips on the river. By the time their son was born, he was too partial to rum. By the time their daughter walked, he had taken to bullying. It always started the same way: He would stagger in stinking of drink, cooing for love. He would paw at Graciela's breasts, grab her between her legs. She began to grow frightened, repelled by the cruelty of his hands.

"Mami," Pablito would say, turning up his face, "why is he always so angry?"

"I can't imagine, darling," she would say with genuine wonder. "But your father and I were married before the Virgin. God will watch over us."

God did watch over them. As did Pablito and Silvia. They peered through the keyholes, pressing their ears to the walls, gauging the pivotal moment when their mother needed a little fist to come rapping. Behind her husband's rum fury, Graciela could hear her children whisper, "Let me see! No! Let me see!" Silvia would beg and Pablo would shush her, make her go back to her room. And then the boy would open the door, walk in. At first, Nestor shooed him away and turned to his wife with even more urgency. But Graciela so feared that Nestor would strike their son that she began shooing the boy off herself. In the end, she relented to Nestor's desires, if only to quiet him. But for all the evidence of her misery, Graciela succeeded in hiding it from her father.

Don Victor moved in a fog, between workshop and factory, oblivious. Her mother was another matter. Doña Mariana kept watch on her son-in-law's comings and goings, and in the mornings after a loud night, she would frown over her knitting, urge her daughter to seek help from the padre. If Nestor burst into the house, eyes narrow with drink, Doña Mariana would put her face in his way and speak plainly: "*Señor machito,* go back outside, sober up. Leave my daughter in peace."

One day, as dawn crept into the hacienda, Nestor stumbled in after a month's binge on the river. He lumbered up the mahogany steps, flung open the bedroom door, and roared for Graciela to take off her clothes. When she protested, he grew so angry that his shouts woke Don Victor, who ran into the corridor, gun in hand, thinking he'd find an intruder. But he found only children, clasping each other's hands, huddled against the door. They cried out when they saw their father fumbling with his knife. It dropped from his hands, pierced the floor. In frustration, he yanked their mother from the bed and punched her squarely in the face.

By the time Don Victor drove the brute from the house, the night had left indelible bruises on Graciela's eyes. The plum-colored rings never faded, and they had the curious effect of rendering her lovelier. The men at Chincho's bar began calling her La Bella Morada—the beautiful purple one.

In the five years since Nestor's departure, Graciela had worked to lose herself in her music. She staged whole zarzuelas in the living room, casting the family in supporting roles, acting extravagantly in cameos, running to and from the piano, as the program required. But she had begun to doubt that life would hold more for her. She had no husband. She had spoiled her children irremediably. In any case, they would grow up and away from her, and she worried that she was becoming a jittery, apprehensive woman.

She had taken to observing the marriages around her. Her older sister seemed the soul of stability. Though Belén and Ignacio had opposite interests, they had reached—like poles of the earth—equilibrium. Ignacio inhabited a realm of machinery and concrete, where hard exigencies ruled. He was a quiet man, hardworking, brooding—dealing in things he could see. Belén, on the other hand, was his antithesis. If their marriage was successful—and certainly it seemed to be—it was because they had had the wisdom to reach across the ravine of difference without surrendering a hair of who they were. When they were with the others, they hardly spoke, hardly touched, but Graciela imagined them grabbing at each other hungrily on their side of the wall. There were no children to distract them. For years, Graciela had pitied her older sister's barrenness, until she considered the fury her own pregnancies had provoked: the way Nestor had sneered at her swollen belly, the quick sex, his look of disgust afterward. What she would have given for her marriage to be more like Belén's, her husband more like Ignacio.

Her brother, Jaime, was another story. He had been loved with all the abandon a family reserves for the baby. He had been spoiled, pampered, adored, and he returned every indulgence with corresponding extravagance. He was vibrant, funny, bighearted. But it was as if the scale of his personality had exacted a perverse calculus, as if it had siphoned a corresponding vitality from his wife. Elsa was a brittle little thing, wavering between indifference and imbalance. When she wasn't making inane conversation, she was squelching her husband's exuberance or raging at the amas, berating them for not teaching her children better manners.

And yet, Graciela marveled, her brother had fathered three cherubs by the woman. Rosita, Marco, and Jorge were as merry and affectionate as their father. For all the ill temper Elsa had imported, her children countered with an equal joy. How could such a disagreeable woman have borne such offspring? As Graciela pondered that paradox, gauging her brother's marriage, she had to admit there was little logic to love.

How to explain, for instance, the marriage of her mother and father? Don Victor and Doña Mariana were constantly bickering, divided on everything, from how to pray to how to raise children to how to braise porcupine in a peanut sauce. But they were deeply in love; anyone could see that. When he emerged from his workshop, bragging that his latest discovery would transform that godforsaken backwater, beggar the Brazilians, bring President Odría's generals scurrying from Lima to cover his chest with brass—his wife's eyes would glow with pride. She loved him with all the enthusiasm of a schoolgirl; the evidence was in her gestures: the way she walked to the other side of the table to spoon sugar into his coffee; the way she tidied her hair when he entered a room; the way she kissed him on the temple as he dreamed in his rat-tan chair after dinner; the way she mounted the stairs briskly to bed.

Graciela had burst into their bedroom once while they were making love. She hadn't known it at the time—she had been a mere girl, and naive—but it came back to her now like the curve of familiar landscape. She had run in, chased by a nightmare, and found them naked, glistening in the dim light of a candle, frozen by the suddenness of her intrusion. Her mother's body was splendid when her father dismounted it: golden, voluptuous, with a shiver of red pubic hair that radiated from the wings of her belly to the inside of her thighs, so that her sex looked, for all the world, like a cleft copper heart. The adults had tugged at the bedclothes frantically, pulled the sheets up to their chins, but she had already registered the shallowness of their breathing, the pungent odor of their skin. She had never erased that moment from her mind's eye. Sitting alone in her room, sliding her fingertips along her belly in the stillness of morning, she felt the down on her neck rise.

Belén drew Tía Esther's letter from the trunk at the foot of the book-case. She had reached for this particular one so often that her hands knew exactly where it was in the rows upon rows of correspondence she had accumulated there from her father's godmother. Now, in the early gray of a Thursday morning, with Ignacio's words still stinging her heart, she wanted to read it again. She pulled it from the worn envelope and unfolded it carefully on her lap.

Dear Belén,

I am sitting here, peering through the carved wood of the balcony to that spot on the avenue where your father's littlest sister saw her last bit of sky. My God, how I loved her. China was my godchild, you know. As are you, dear. As is your father. They tell me she died screaming my name, yelling about a cat. I've never gotten over it. That mangled little body—your father's desperate sobs. Poor boy, he wept for nine days.

I never had a cat. It most definitely was not a cat the poor child ran after. I've told your father my story many, many times since that terrible day, but I cannot rely on him to pass it on with any accuracy. I certainly never thought I would ever be writing it on paper. But fate is strange, dear. I also never thought I would have a correspondent like you, someone I could confide in.

The truth is, now that you are twenty, you are old enough to know this story, and I, at my sixty-five-year-old ripeness, am certainly old enough to tell it. So find that good chair in your rosy red *urucú* library, darling, and make yourself comfortable. Here is the story of a woman and her impossible love.

I met him on a trip to the Huallaga Valley. I was not much older than you, twenty-one. My friend Pelusa, a tour guide in Chiclayo—a vivacious girl who loved the company of foreigners—persuaded me to accompany a group of ten Norwegian photographers who had just come west from the interior. They had spent a number of weeks trying to find the Jivaro—those headshrinkers who live out there in the remote Amazon. For photographs! Imagine! In any case, they came to Chiclayo with their cameras and equipment, but after a few days of recuperation they wanted to go east again. They told Pelusa they didn't want to go over the cordillera and into the Huallaga without a translator. Since my English is not so bad, and since the Norwegians only spoke English, Pelusa persuaded me to go. It might prove interesting for you, Esther, she said. Well, unlike the Sobrevillas, we Paniaguas never had money. The Norwegians were offering what seemed like a queen's ransom: five hundred *soles* in cash.

Remember too, darling, that I was young, foolish, and far too adventurous for my own good, so it should come as no surprise that I fell in love with one of those Norwegians. Lars was his name and, in time, he returned my affections. He was golden-haired, towering, with an appetite for life that was infectious. I cannot remember much about the mountains or our ride through the cordillera. Nor can I tell you much about the Huallaga Valley when we finally came upon it. I'm sure it must have been splendid. My eyes were riveted on Lars. Every day was an opportunity to look at him, every night a chance to sit by his side. We were in love and free to pursue it wherever it led us. It was the most blissful month of my life.

Since I am not writing this from Sarpsborg, Norway, you already know how the story ends. Before he boarded the ship that would take him home to his wife, we stood awhile on the dock in Trujillo. He said he would love me forever. His shirt was wet with my tears. When the ship's whistle sounded, he reached into his bag, pulled out the precious trophy a Jivaro had given him, and handed it to me. It was a *tsantsa,* the shrunken head of a cougar. Lars had told me about it before, always in reverent tones, and indicated it was his greatest treasure. But I was a west-coast girl. I had never seen one, much less held one in my hands, and it shocked me. It was a ghoulish little thing, its face grizzled—two beads where its eyes should have been. It was more hideous than anything we're used to seeing here in Trujillo, though we're used to seeing a lot, living as we do near the ancient burial grounds. Understand, dearest girl, the heartbreak of the moment: I loved the man. So I took the thing, although I was taken aback by it. The head of a brained animal as a token of love! As Lars walked up the ramp into that cavernous boat, I realized that the furry little token was all I had of him. Over the next months, I grew quite attached to it. I couldn't sleep if it wasn't on my night table. I put it in a birdcage for safekeeping. I didn't want anyone to touch it. For me, it became more than a shrunken head or a shriveled symbol of life. Strangely, that ugly little relic came to stand for Lars himself: his boundless laughter, his stillness on a starry evening, the way his eyes mirrored the sky.

Of course, I never saw him again. He never wrote. I didn't expect him to.

The *tsantsa* stole my soul. And then it stole beautiful China, my moon-faced doll. Yet, despite that horrible consequence, despite the thirty years that have passed, despite this decrepit shell I now inhabit, I am still in love with Lars. I want you to know this. I don't know why. Come live with me in Trujillo, child, and I will tell you everything.

Sending you all the affection this old heart can muster,
Your Tía Esther

* * *

Jaime sat on a stool at Chincho's bar, one foot propped on a rickety wood table. He was nursing a tin tumbler of rum. Beside him, the dog lay dozing. In the far corner, under the overhanging palm thatch, laborers from the factory were chewing coca leaf and sipping fermented *chicha*. From time to time, they would break out in laughter, or issue raw curses and swat at the mosquitoes that hummed overhead. The night rains had come late and hard, and steam rose from the mud, shrugging the insects to life.

The barge from Pucallpa had pulled in an hour earlier and increased the hacienda's population by four. A few tables away, the barge captain, an Australian with yellow teeth, was holding forth in an improvised pidgin, regaling three unkempt companions with tales about faraway lands. "I'm telling you, mates, whatever you've seen natives do on the Amazon don't sabe-sabe nada with what I seen those savages do along the Indus River! They whack cabezas with machetes! Flick, flick, thud! Never seen nothin' like it. They make this river look like a bathtub of *maricones,* I'm telling you. I drove barges up and down during the worst of their *chingado* uprisings—the Hindus killin' the Musselman, the Mussels killin' the Hinduman, *no importa.* I seen 'um swim up to the deck with sabers in 'um teeth. *Carajo, hermano! Has visto algo así?* Big time in Pakistan! And that was before Hyderabad went to Hydera-*worse!*" He roared at that, throwing back his head so that the lantern illuminated the chasm of his mouth.

"How about the women, man," said fat Chincho, leaning over the bar, black eyes gleaming. "They say they something else with their veils and their shakey shakey. You seen them dance like they do?" He was shirtless and sweating, and he stepped out from behind the bar with a bottle in his fist, wiggling his belly, making his fleshy breasts tremble. *"Carajo!"* he shouted with glee, and slammed the bottle on the wooden counter. "You seen those turk ladies dance?"

"Shit. I seen it all, Chincho. I seen it all, goddammit. And now I'm seeing the bottom of this devil drink. You poured me short, you greedy little pig! Fill it up!"

Chincho waddled over to the Australian's table, flicking a rag around his bare knees as he went, warding off the mosquitoes. He topped up the Australian's cup with a generous portion of rum and stood with one hand on his hip, waiting.

The Australian slapped three shiny coins on the table and watched the barman swipe them from the rough wood into his apron pocket. "*Oye*, fat man," he said. "You know the doll with the delicious ass in the big house up there?"

Chincho glanced quickly at Jaime, but the young man seemed lost in thought, smoking a cigarette, gazing at the palm thatch above their heads.

"You mean La Bella Morada?" Chincho whispered, leering.

"Is that what they call her?" The Australian looked quizzically at one of his companions—a man with a deeply scarred face.

"No, hombre," the pineapple skin answered. "No. La Bella is the daughter of the old engineer. The woman you're talking about is a servant."

"A servant?" Chincho frowned, running a mental census of the asses in that household, until his mind stopped at the teacher's. "*Ay, pues, gringo*," he said. "You mean the woman in charge of the brats." His hands were thrust into his apron, and he rattled the coins there fitfully.

"That one," the Australian seconded, nodding. "What's her name?"

"Marcela," Chincho sighed. "Sweet Jesus, what a butt." He rapped the table with his knuckles.

"Marcela! That's the name!" the gringo yelled, grinning with childish glee.

Jaime was jolted out of his reverie. "Ay-ay-ay," he heard the barge captain say, as he ran his fingers through his grizzled hair. "The teacher! The one with the perfect ass!"

Jaime rose from his chair, stamped out his cigarette, tossed a few coins on his table, and whistled softly for the dog to follow. He turned and waved at Chincho, who bowed obsequiously, one hand over his heart. Ambling home through the ferns, Jaime contemplated the captain's rapture. It hadn't occurred to him that the children's teacher even had an ass.

He stepped through the mud, feeling a melancholy sweep over him, as it had on and off since his father had summoned him to his workshop that morning and shown him the samples on his table. Don Victor had lifted each sheet of cellophane as if it were a sacred document, explaining his vision for the paper and the factory conversions it would require.

Jaime had nodded to everything he heard. Yes, the samples were beautiful. No, he never imagined ordinary hemp could be rendered transparent. Yes, it might be profitable to spin it in quantities. No, there was no reason to doubt that they could get the acetic acid. Yes, he would look into it. No, as far as he knew, no one else in that area was producing cellophane. But, yes, he would find out. Yes, he would do it all, yes.

But he had not been able to shake the melancholy. Even as his father had held up the tissue triumphantly, there was something not altogether right about the image behind it. A slight distortion came with the transparency. It was that split-second dread that led him to deeper vexations.

He didn't love his wife. He hadn't been able to think of much else all afternoon. He had accepted it for years, but he had found himself sitting at Chincho's that evening with an overwhelming desire to say it to Elsa plainly. Why would he do such a thing now? What would it prove? He had always made an effort to put a bright face on things. Elsa had followed him to this faraway hell, after all—to a life that was inimical to everything she had known in Trujillo. She had given him three perfect children. He couldn't blame her if she was turning into a grotesque version of herself; the jungle had a way of doing that to people. He had seen madmen glide by on the river—eyes wild, cheeks blistered, minds wrung by that devil's maze.

Why, then, did he have a sudden urge to confront her with the realities of his disaffection? Men lived for years in unhappy alliances, fulfilling pledges made before God, taking a little pleasure where they could. Why kick in walls with a truth that served no purpose? Why couldn't he just tamp down this sudden, irrational desire to speak his mind? Why couldn't he force his attention elsewhere? Why couldn't he distract himself with another woman, as sensible males had done throughout history? And why hadn't he ever noticed the teacher with the beautiful ass—a woman who was being worshipped this very minute at Chincho's—who had been under his roof all along?

* * *

Don Victor rose before the sun, removed a butterfly net from a nail by the door, and strode out into the damp of an early morning. He found the insects low on the mahogany trees, clinging to the lichen, or scattered by the roots, like litter. Their wings were folded and veined—camouflaging their brilliance. He lowered his net over them and one fluttered open. He marveled at its iridescence: the whorls of green, sprays of flamboyant yellow.

He scooped them up, dropped them into an empty lard can, which he had perforated with tiny holes, and slid on the lid quickly. Walking back to his workshop, he could hear them throwing their fragile bodies against the tin. He hung his net, placed the can on his massive table, switched on the light, and went about his first business of the day, which was to test the strength of his various batches of cellophane. He stretched sheet after sheet on a wooden frame and pressed a series of weights against them. By the time the cock crowed, he knew which was the most resilient.

Doña Mariana was alone in the dining room when he wandered in, lost in thought. The sight of her there startled him, but he approached her chair, pecked her cheek, and said curtly, "Good morning, dear."

"The first Thursday of the month!" she sang cheerfully, as she poured him a cup of maté. "The barge from Pucallpa is in. I looked out our window at first light and saw it was already in the dock. It must have arrived last night."

"Very good, darling."

"We have letters from your old aunt, Victor. Marcela just brought them. You know how much Belén looks forward to those letters. God knows she worries the old ones until they fall apart."

"Yes, I know." And then, as an afternote, "Has the teacher gone off to return the mailbag?"

His wife stirred her coffee dreamily, her mind still on Belén. "I'm sure she will before the children go up, darling. They're in the kitchen now, having their breakfasts."

He dispatched his bread, cheese, and guava without another word, drank his pungent infusion of maté. By nine o'clock, long before the priest usually came to bestow a blessing on him, he left. Crossing the patio to his workshop, he glanced toward the dock and saw the four bargemen—spindly as bottle flies—unloading the crates.

Before long, he was on his way toward the dock, preened for courtship. He had groomed his mustache to two finely waxed crescents, dressed in a shirt of crisp linen, and donned his Cajamarca hat with its band of black satin. If Yorumbo's brew had failed to sweep the teacher's charms from Don Victor's imagination, there was a reason: Yorumbo had assumed the problem to be in the past, not the future. The memories of old loves were now indeed gone, leaving much room for Don Victor to contemplate a new one.

Marcela was exactly where he suspected she would be: ambling down the road, her hair uncharacteristically loose, the empty mailbag slung over one arm. He placed his hands on the dome of his hat and began to run, eager as a schoolboy, shirttail fluttering behind. When she heard his feet on the dirt, Marcela spun around and her hair swirled like a dancer's skirt.

He caught his breath, struck by that loveliness. Perspiration sprang in beads along his forehead. "Good morning, Señorita Marcela," he said, and when he tipped his hat jauntily, twenty-four yellow winged butter-flies flew from beneath it, fleet as quicksilver, soaring toward the sun.

6

If the people of Floralinda sensed something shift with the passing of the blue boy, they felt the whole machinery change course when they learned about Don Victor and Marcela. Within an hour there was hardly a soul who hadn't heard about it. And if someone managed to sleep late, or be stirring a pot over a fire, or by quirk of fate be off hunting boar in the forest, they heard it by the end of the day. The story of the butterflies reached such exaggerated proportions that those who actually witnessed the event began to doubt their memories. "El cambiador ran from the house like a crazed boy," a fieldworker was heard to say. "When he reached the teacher, she whirled around to look at him and—wahhhh!—his brains flew out of his ears."

They understood something momentous had happened: something uncontrollable, tectonic. If someone had said that the factory would now produce paper an eye could see through, that a plague of truth would coil its way through the mansion, that everyone who passed under that roof would acquire a new appetite for love, they would have shrugged their shoulders and said, *So? We knew something like that would happen. It was only a matter of time.* Seeing the shapechanger there on the road, at the height of his abilities—his very self transformed into a boy—they knew he had graduated to more than irrigation systems made from coconuts. Cooked plants that were rendered transparent, tongues that were made to stop lying, hearts that yearned to be free again: and now a change of a different kind.

So it was that all of Floralinda began to long for a transformation. Men began dreaming of fortune. Women began pining for love. Monkeys hopped through the fields as if hemp could bear fruit at any moment. Pigs began to gaze past their troughs at flowers across the road. Even Marcela, who had come from Iquitos to the third floor of the Sobrevilla mansion sure that she would live out her life as a spinster, began to believe that something in her person—her clever mind, her agile wit, her appreciation for the patient accrual of a good education—had somehow translated into an irresistible magnetism. There was no doubt about it: The old man had ogled her, created a spectacle for the sole purpose of delighting her. She was capable of provoking desire.

She giggled when she saw the butterflies climb the air, covered her mouth with her hands. "Your hat!" she said. "How on earth did you get them in there?"

"Anything is possible, my dear," Don Victor said, wiping his forehead with his sleeve, "if a man only wants it enough."

They had walked toward the dock together even as the rest of the hacienda gossiped about the flying head-matter. They chatted about inanities: the fullness of the mahogany trees, her father's job in the shipping office in Iquitos, little Pablo's cleverness with numbers. At the end of the conversation, as he was about to step onto the concrete platform of the factory, she stopped, shifted the empty mailbag on her shoulder, pushed her glasses up the wide bridge of her nose, and asked, "Will you perform your hat trick, señor, for the children?"

"No, Señorita Marcela," he answered, crossing his arms on his chest. "That trick I will only ever do for you."

* * *

Trujillo, 1952

Dearest Belén,

Here is the news from civilization.

I am sitting behind the carved balcony that overlooks Orbegozo and, through the slats, I can see hundreds of fieldworkers spill down

Avenida Independencia. They are shouting, waving their fists at these houses, angry. If it weren't for an equally belligerent throng of soldiers—hundreds—that rattled into the city yesterday in a noisy procession of trucks, those men might be stomping into our foyers, running upstairs, doing who knows what to the women.

God knows I can't blame them. I am, in turns, heartsick and furious about the events of the last few months. I know I've written to you many times before about Victor Raúl Haya de la Torre, that brilliant man who is trying to make a bid for the presidency. He comes from one of those middle-class families that has little to lose by sullying its hands with politics. My God, what a voice—a silver-tongued orator if ever there was one—talking about justice and the rights of the peon, a shining new future for Peru!

Well, days after General Odría's coup, when Haya de la Torre began to rail against it, a company of army thugs poured into Trujillo and shuffled him off in the cover of night. For months we didn't know where they'd taken him. And then he disappeared completely. Finally, we've learned where he is—safe and sound in the Colombian embassy in Lima. His supporters in the past haven't been so lucky. I still remember the day the army came here, gathered them all up, and marched them off to the dunes of Chan Chan. They were slaughtered, you know. Who knows in what numbers?

Darling girl, I wish I could write to you about the bougainvillea, which is heartbreakingly beautiful this time of year, or the goats your uncle ordered roasted for his garden party last Sunday, but all I can think of is the rank butchery in this godforsaken country. And the people outside waving fists.

Read your books, darling. Life is better when we imagine it. Infinitely better in our heads.

Your loving Tía Esther

* * *

Yorumbo's vine, smoke, and stones had achieved more than ridding Don Victor of the old lust and opening a way for the new: His mind was sharper, nimbler, more focused than ever. The ritual had cleared his head. By the end of the day, when he looked out the window and saw Jaime walking toward the house, Don Victor realized he had never worked so vigorously. In the course of fourteen hours, he had finished mapping the reconfiguration of the factory. Before him on the work-table, illuminated by the flicker of lanterns, was a pile of crumpled paper and a long, narrow white sheet—carefully drawn, painstakingly labeled—with his plan for the redesign. Refitting the machines would be a challenge, but possible. He would need to introduce a string of acid baths, find a way to accelerate the belts so that the cooked pulp could be extruded at a faster rate. Tomorrow he would lay out the whole scheme for Ignacio and together they would finalize the details. Ignacio's knowledge of the existing machines would be essential in implementing the changes.

Yes, it was remarkable how quickly after the ayahuasca it had all come to him. When he had returned to his tidied workshop, cleared of all rustle and refuse, he had the sense that his skull, too, had been purged and dusted, each nettlesome bit of history shooed out so that the machinery could reel again.

There was little that could compare with the order of a well-run factory. That lack of clutter, economy of design was what Don Victor respected about the jungle. There was no unnecessary accumulation here. Drop a handful of raw meat into the black of night and it would be gone within the hour, scarab beetles swarming to devour it to the bone. Leave the bone, and a fungus would soon finish the task, its chemicals decomposing the matter within days, reducing it to a fine dust. This was a lesson quickly learned by a traveler in the Amazon. Perspire, and butterflies will race to the skin. Defecate, and metallic blowflies will plunge in to consume the excrement. Die, and predatory bats will shred a body in a thousand directions, ridding the earth of any evidence of its existence. The jungle, in short, was master among shapechangers, genius at bringing the dead into the realm of the living. All would be broken down, built again, in the jungle's slick wheelwork of resurrection.

Recently, to test its properties of decomposition, Don Victor had carried bits of cellophane out to the forest's edge, buried them at the base of a matapalo tree, where its shallow roots were knit with a pale yellow fungus. When he returned a day later, the cellophane had disappeared and, in its place—a swarm of rice-colored maggots.

"All flesh is grass," as Padre Bernardo would say when called to preside over a funeral in Floralinda, "and all the goodliness thereof is as the flower of the field." Flesh to dust, dust to seed, seed to bloom, bloom to flesh. But on the business about how dust became dust— about how life fed on life in order to fulfill God's harsh miracle—the churchman did not need to elaborate. The Lord's factory was swift and efficient, especially in the tropical forest. Was it any wonder that rain forest people would rather burn their dead and drink their ashes than see creatures gorging on the remains? Here nothing was wasted, nothing missed. No memory. No history. All process.

Don Victor stood and admired his diagram showing the long train of cellophane production. The harvested hemp would be threshed, mashed down with pima cotton. From there the pulp would be transported on a mechanical belt, dumped into a deep vat of filtered river water, and boiled under a wide coal fire. Three chemical baths would follow in churning succession: with acetic acid, with sulfates, with bleach. Beaters would take the mix down to a smooth pudding; sieves would separate the pith. After that the paste would pass through the nozzles, shoot over the racing mesh into the giant dryers, and emerge at the other end—bright bolts of a new generation.

Don Victor's brain had been restored by the witchman's ministrations, but it was the vision that followed—the *encanto* of the stones— that had given him a clear picture of what he needed to do. As he lay in his big brass bed the night after his visit to Yorumbo's tambo, a dream had come to him. It had been precise, detailed, allowing him to see every stage of the modifications. When he had awakened to a coolness on his tongue, as if the stones were still resting there, the diagram was a full-blown image in his mind. He had taken a sharp pencil and sketched it, hardly stopping to consider what he was doing until the process was mapped out in its entirety. After that, it was a matter of figuring the final proportions, redrawing it in detail, and listing the ingredients: the requisite tons of dried hemp, the corresponding percentage of cotton linters, the barrels of acid and chlorine, the coal.

When he appeared in the dining room for dinner that night, his mustache was combed and waxed, his collar bleached and starched, his black bow tied pertly under his chin. He had slicked his hair with pomade, and the unruly mass was uncharacteristically tame. In his vest pocket, in place of a handkerchief, was a tuft of cellophane, thrusting up like a cockscomb.

He entered the room, rubbing his hands. They were all there—Jaime with a bottle in hand; Elsa with her stiff lace collar; Graciela in a flamenco dress; Ignacio fiddling with his tie; Belén smoothing her hair behind her ears; Doña Mariana giving him a little nod from the opposite side of the table. Even Marcela was there, blinking and shifting nervously in her chair.

Before the soup was served, Belén noticed the cellophane. She pointed at it with a little smile; he plucked it out and handed it to her. She held it up to the candlelight and marveled at the image of her father through its vitrescence. "What's this?" she asked with all the wonder of a child. "Paper? Whatever for?"

"You see how we live in the Stone Age!" Don Victor exclaimed, half-appalled at Belén's reaction, half-delighted at the opening it gave him. "The rest of the world is racing ahead, using this paper in hundreds of ways: for sealing cigarettes, displaying candy, wrapping meat, storing dresses, shipping machine guns. We are living in this haven, with the possibilities of cellophane everywhere around us, and this woman doesn't even know what it's for. Take a good look, my child. They need that paper in Paris; they need it in Lima; they need it in New York. Soon, very soon, we'll be giving it to them. From our factory right here, in Floralinda." He swiveled from left to right grandly, like a rare bird displaying its colors, and winked openly at the teacher. "As my old professor Doctor Laroza used to say, 'There's no place on earth that technology—smartly conceived and skillfully delivered—cannot improve!' "

The sheet of cellophane traveled from hand to hand, glistening over the soup plates as each diner considered its promise, marveled at its cunning—a paper that you could see through! A wrapping that did not hide! As they graduated to fish and yuca, they congratulated Don Victor on his foresight, his genius.

Jaime drank to it.

Graciela wrapped the paper around her fist and noted its pliancy, observing how her hands were perfectly visible: the olive skin, the oval fingernails, the fine blue veins.

Ignacio, being the most sensible, asked Don Victor if it was really possible to create something so elegant with machinery that was now producing heavy brown sheeting. It seemed impossible that one mill could produce such radically different products.

"Ignacio, my boy!" shouted Don Victor. "Look no farther than across the table. Behold the woman who has been my wife for almost forty years now. Impossible as it may seem, she produced your brother-in-law—that rum-sucking monkey over there. Eight years before that, she produced your brilliant wife. Who would have guessed one person could produce such vastly different children? Our factory is no different, hombre. We have all the right equipment; I just need to move it around. I need to tinker with the Fourdrinier, make slits out of holes, add a number of acid baths, speed up the belts. I'm telling you—by Jesús, José, and Santa María!—as soon as Jaime pays a visit to Lima and finds us the buyers, we'll start the modifications. The curandero cleared my head of all the nonsense that has cluttered it lately. I drank the stones, and the *encanto* came to me, clear as a road map. You'll see all the drawings tomorrow."

He paused there, as well he might have, since that very point in the evening marked the nexus of a complete shift in the conversation, as if Jesús, San José, and Santa María had reached down from their celestial heights and thrown a lever in the opposite direction, so that the entire engine of logic and deliberation went hurtling off on another track.

"The curandero?" said Doña Mariana, a frown tugging at her brow. "*Ay, hijo,* don't tell me you went off to that quack and had him puff all over you with his smoke and voodoo. All that *pasapasa* and abracadabra! What's wrong with your blessed Virgin of Copacabana? What's wrong with that church you built down the road?"

"My sweet darling," Don Victor said, smiling broadly, "bird of my paradise, *vida de mi vida,* light of our days, Padre Bernardo is a good man and an excellent priest, but if I had gone to a monastery with him for forty days and forty nights he would not have been able to scare the image of that woman from my head. Yorumbo did it in the course of an afternoon."

"That *woman*?" Doña Mariana said, her eyes wide with disbelief. "What woman? You mean Vanessa? The hun who ran the hostel on Pachacuti? The one with hands like Bavarian hams?"

Don Victor was less struck by his wife's words than by the simple fact that the pink-breasted woman was back in his skull, name and all, knocking about his brain in all her flaxen glory.

"Doña Mariana," Elsa piped in, "you cannot be serious. After that priest came here and admitted the fraud that he was? That preposterous confession about the dancer, do you remember? The hips? The park? How could you trust that man to light one more candle in your church much less counsel your husband on spiritual matters? There is nothing—*nothing*—more base and vulgar than a man of God flouting his priestly vows. I say it's disgusting. I say that, given the choice between counsel from that man and counsel from a savage, Don Victor was right to seek help from the savage."

The next comment, hard as it was to fathom, came from Doña Mariana. She raised herself out of her chair, put her knuckles determinedly on the table, and nearly spat the words at her daughter-in-law. "Priestly vows? Pardon me, but what do you know about priestly vows, O sainted princess of the sugar palace? Do you know that your children— God bless them all in their beds—are great-grandchildren of a priest?"

There was a moment when it seemed as if all the air had been sucked out of the room. The diners shrank into their chairs and then leaned forward with equal intensity: "What are you saying?" "Mama!" "She can't possibly mean it." "Is this some kind of joke?"

But Doña Mariana slammed her fist on the table with uncharacteristic fury and said it again. "That's right. That's the truth. My father was a priest. My mother and sister and I suffered the consequences. You've all been sitting there, seething at that poor, suffering padre, and all of you—to the last person—are related to a greater sinner. You are all tainted. Now let's see who has the nerve to cast stones." She scanned the table, glowering.

"Well," Graciela said after a long silence, "at least we can hope that my grandparents, whoever they were, were in love. I'd give anything to love someone so much that the rules didn't matter." The comment hung in the air until Doña Mariana folded her hands and sat down.

"That's more than I can say for my marriage," said Belén, and the entire circle stiffened, looking from her to Ignacio and then back again. "Or mine," Ignacio said simply, putting his fork on his plate with a sharp click.

"Señora," the children's teacher said to Doña Mariana, straightening her napkin, "with all due respect, not *all* the people at this table are related to sinners, as you put it. I am the exception. None of my ancestors is a priest." She cleared her throat primly. "These things do need saying, you know. The truth, as I tell the children, is vital in human affairs." Here she peered at Don Victor to see if his eyes were on her. They were, but not in the way she'd expected. They were wide with alarm.

"Well, well," said Jaime, running his fingers through his hair and loosening his collar. He had had too much to drink. He was grinning and slurring his words. "Tonight was the night I was going to say something I've wanted to say for a long time, but I see that my news pales in comparison to the tidings being shared at this table. Let's see if I have this straight. Number one: Tomorrow we start reconfiguring the factory to make a paper that isn't really paper, yes?" He held up Don Victor's cellophane, flicked it with a finger. "Two: My older sister finally lifts her face from her books to announce—surprise!—she's not happily married. Congratulations, Belén, you're human, like the rest of us. Three: My grandfather was a priest. *Uy-uy-uy,* there will be hell to pay. Four: My father had to call on his curandero to get a certain Vanessa off his mind. Really, Don Victor. At your age! Five: Graciela is starving for love. My condolences! Six: The teacher has a beautiful ass."

Everyone gasped. The teacher reddened.

"Seven?" Jaime said, looking around. "Did I miss something? Is there a seven?" His tongue was thick, but he could be understood perfectly. "Oh, yes, of course! Elsa, this one is for you, so, darling, listen carefully.

"Seven: I don't love you anymore."

Elsa blanched and looked around the table, but she found no one looking back at her: Doña Mariana was glaring at her son, shocked by his uncharacteristic insolence. Elsa's sisters-in-law glanced at each other but then immediately averted their eyes. Dinner was over very quickly after that. Don Victor and Doña Mariana rushed into the sala, whispering furiously. Elsa marched off to her room. Marcela grabbed a cigarette from the alabaster box and scurried out to the patio to contemplate Jaime's comment about her physical attributes. Graciela took Belén's elbow and led her into the library. Ignacio helped Jaime to his feet.

For all that the dinner-table confessions might have interested her that evening, Boruba did not have her ear pressed to the door. She was leaning against the washtub, turning a cellophane-wrapped lily in her hand, listening to the young amas chatter. She recognized the bloom from Pedro's garden: its creamy whiteness, its purple streaks. His tiny plot was the only place she had seen such a flower. Clearly, he had meant it as a show of affection. But what was that radiant skin?

Four miles away, where the river turned a sharp corner north, dawn came with a shrill beginning. *"Iwishin!"* called a high, frantic voice. The witchman turned in his hammock, fearing a displeased spirit. But his wife peered out and saw the girl, stamping her feet so that the beads on her ankles shivered. "Yorumbo!" the girl called again. Her hair was matted, the *urucú* patterns on her skin smeared from many days on the river. A string with ivory-colored capybara fangs rattled around her neck.

Yorumbo's woman immediately recognized the marks of status. She roused her husband, then went out into the dawn to calm the intruder, but the girl seemed inconsolable.

When Yorumbo emerged from the door of his tambo, she threw herself at his feet, pressing the top of her head into his shins. *"Ápa minu, ápa minu,"* she moaned. She had come about her father, whose high rank was evident on her skin. She was a Jivaro, of the tribe of head-shrinkers. He could see that from the tattoos along her collarbone. But she was far from home. He noted the breasts, high and full, imprinted with tiny hatch marks around the nipples, evidence of marriage. He saw the smears of *urucú* along her legs and arms and concluded that they were vestiges of a nuptial celebration, but it was odd that those marks should be so carelessly defiled.

He raised her up, pointed to the *urucú*, and asked when she had been painted for marriage. His voice seemed to calm her. She ceased her sobbing and, once she collected herself, explained her predicament.

Her name was Suraya and her father was Mwambr, great headman of the fearsome tribe of *tsantsa* warriors. They had been at war, as Jivaro often were, with a tribe whose women they had kidnapped. Bloody battles had followed and the jungle had been littered with decapitated bodies. Jivaro warriors had worked through the nights to empty the skulls, flay back the skin, boil down the faces, then sew the hide into tiny pouches, packed with a dense, hot soil. Yorumbo knew about the Jivaro practice of stealing a dead warrior's soul by spilling his brains on the ground, consigning him to spiritual limbo, and dangling his head from a war belt. He nodded for her to continue.

In the last battle, she told him, the bird people had swept into the Jivaro camp to take back their kidnapped women. The Jivaro lost one man, but they fought fiercely. Not one of the women was surrendered. Two men of the attacking tribe had surrounded Mwambr, but the Jivaro's fiercest warrior, Kikuru, plunged two swift spears in their backs. When the bird people finally fell back in retreat, Mwambr honored Kikuru by offering him his daughter's hand in marriage. Suraya could not go against her father's wishes, so allowed herself to be painted with *urucú* and tattooed with the hatch marks of matrimony. But there was much that troubled her about the man. She had watched him swat children away with the butt of his spears. She had seen him force one of the abducted women to her knees and take her from behind, like a rutting monkey. She had seen him whack off a prisoner's ears, though the unfortunate had pleaded for mercy. She didn't want to bear such a man's children.

When her tribeswomen finished painting her, Suraya had run into Mwambr's hut and begged him to offer his warrior another woman, although she knew this was pointless and only served to strengthen her father's resolve. In the end, she had fled, after the ceremony was over. She waited until her husband was asleep, drunk on fermented yuca, and then, in the cover of night, she stole away to the river and took an abandoned canoe. She had paddled all night and all day without stopping. On her third day, she encountered a Cashibo family heading downriver.

She showed them her hands, palms up, in supplication, pleaded with them to guide her to a powerful sumiruna. They told her of Yorumbo and where she might find him. Other travelers helped along the way.

She wanted to be purged of the evil eye, she told Yorumbo—she wanted to be stripped of her past self, made new. She was sure Mwambr had sent tribesmen in pursuit, and she wanted to erase her trail.

Yorumbo searched the young woman's face to see whether she spoke the truth. He knew from past experience that the Jivaro were ruthless. If her story was true, she was fierce indeed. It was something in her eyes that won him—a mix of humility and defiance. She was bold enough to have broken with her father but wise enough to fear the spiritual consequences. She had done the right thing to seek out a sumiruna and put her fate into the hands of the gods.

The girl was a cat, he could see that—a true puma, bounding her way to freedom. It was obvious in the way she moved as she spoke: She was light on her feet, agile. There was a reason one cat had sought another, brought her predicament to his door. He decided to help her.

He gave her a vine of abrasive tamshi and instructed her to go down to the river and scrub away the residual paint on her skin in preparation for a fuller cleansing. He told his woman to freshen the girl's hair with the fruit of the tutumo tree. When they returned, he readied his pipe and ordered Suraya to lie down on a bed of reeds he had prepared for her. He blew *pumasacha* smoke—a powerful drug—over her body. As she began to writhe, he called on the spirit of the cat to enter her and drive away any weakness. He threw dust on her heels to signify that she no longer needed to run. He dragged grass across her back to remove all trace of former allegiance. When he stopped singing the *icaro*, he saw that her trance was over; she was perfectly still. The sun was already in the afternoon sky. The girl slept for many hours. Yorumbo and his woman could see that her flight had exhausted her. When she finally rose and went into their tambo, it was dusk.

They talked for a while quietly, sharing the yams that Yorumbo's woman prepared for them, and then Suraya began to look about inquisitively at the straw walls of the hut. There was a glint of the prowler in her eye, and the shaman registered it and counted his magic successful. Already, she was seeing the world like a lone animal. When she offered him the string of teeth from around her neck and thanked him for his hospitality, he told her she could stay until she felt strong enough to continue upriver. He would help her stain the canoe with cumala dye and urine so that even its maker wouldn't recognize it.

She pressed her forehead into the back of his hand.

It was then that he took out the box to show her the knife with the leaping cat. He told her that he should have known, on the day the shapechanger had brought it to him, that a cat spirit would come calling for it. He hadn't realized it until the *pumasacha* smoke had spoken to him, but now he knew: The knife was for her. "Bring out the shapechanger's flying lion," the smoke had whispered. "It will give her the strength she needs."

Suraya listened, marveling at the way the two box halves separated like a clam to reveal the blade nesting inside, but the sliver of film that shielded the weapon suddenly billowed up and floated lazily to the ground. She watched the cellophane descend gently, floating on air, catching and flinging the light. It landed not far from her toes. She squatted down to take it between her fingers even as the sumiruna continued to talk about the dagger, turning the cat in his palms, telling her how it had guided her to him. She lifted the glossy substance to her nose and sniffed. It rested against her mouth momentarily, cool and slick as the skin of a frog. Yorumbo glanced down and saw her lips through the paper, saw the depth of the girl's fascination. And then he realized, with lightning intuition, that Suraya had not come for the knife—or for the cat that made its handle. She had come for the substance that accompanied it. She had come for the white man's shine.

* * *

My Dear Belén,

Forgive me for allowing more than a week to pass without writing, but not only has the interval had a clear purpose, it has turned out to be positively providential. I write now to announce an important decision.

During the past few days, Trujillo has been locked in a fog so pervasive, so suffocating, I cannot remember another like it in all the

eighty-one years of my life. We cannot breathe. We cannot see. If
our neighbors have sprouted tusks on their jaws or horns on their
heads, we wouldn't know it. When we step out of doors, it's as if we
were swimming into a murky sea. The wetness curls into our eyes
and throats, fouling us with all manner of afflictions. Your cousins
have some form of the grippe. I myself am plagued by a mysterious
catarrh of the bronchials that makes me sound like a man. Your tío
Alejandro has been forcing us all to drink pisco in great quantities,
claiming that alcohol will do us good in this algid season—warm our
veins, put a little fire into our chests. But all it has done so far is
make us drunk as baboons. Isabelita, who is hardly eight, grew so
inebriated with her father's remedies that she ran from the house
giggling and naked except for a thin little petticoat. It took three of
your uncle's manservants groping around in the fog for two hours to
find the skinny little thing and bring her home. A phalanx of soldiers
escorted them.

So, perhaps it is the fog that has forced me to the decision that
this letter announces—you know how superstitious I am. I simply
do not trust a season that prevents me from seeing my feet. Some
diabolical hex is at work out here on the coast. I have forgotten what
the other side of this street looks like. I have forgotten whether the
basilica has one cross or two. This is a devil city, I tell you, and I do
not want to end my life here. I'm tired of the way your uncle's
friends laugh at the way I dress, tired of the way I always seem to
embarrass this household. I may be an old woman, but I still have a
will, a brain, and a pair of strong legs. Which is all to say: I am
leaving this godforsaken city and coming to Floralinda.

I do not know when or how I will do it, but I want you to know,
dear goddaughter, that you can expect me soon. Someday you will
look out and see a boat, and your ancient tía will be on it—a tired
old woman with the heart of a mountain goat. I simply must get out
of here.

Well, fine, if you want to know the truth, the fog isn't the half of
it. Ever since Haya de la Torre's men were taken off and butchered in
Chan Chan, I have hated this place. So you see, it's been quite a
while that I've felt this way about Trujillo. I hate the sugar fields. I

hate the big mansions. I hate the old birds who limp around here claiming to be daughters of viceroyals. (How much royalty can a city have one hundred and thirty years after the revolution?) I hate the way they stare at my Chinese dresses. They have become Hitlers, holding court over tea in the Hotel de Turistas. They've even sprouted nasty little mustaches.

There is more: that phalanx of soldiers marching out of the fog with Isabelita. Now that the steel-fisted orangutan who calls himself our president is trying to lock up anyone who does not agree with him, this place is crawling with troops, studded with guns. The rich are delighted. They invite the generals to lunch. I don't want to stay here anymore, my dear. I'd rather swing from the trees.

An old gypsy once told me that I would die with water coursing beneath me. Well, she couldn't possibly have meant Trujillo, could she? Not unless I fling myself into the sea. You must never dismiss what the dark gifts can teach you. I know you have difficulty with this. When I come, I'll explain.

Now, please, do not send me calculated letters telling me about anacondas and poisonous ants and sharp-fanged piranhas. They will not put me off. Remember, I have climbed mountains with Norwegians. I am a stubborn person. This mind will not change.

Receive much affection, Belén, from your elderly aunt who longs to behold your dear face.

                                        Tía Esther

7

Truth moved through the Sobrevilla house like a rude guest, striding into rooms where it wasn't wanted, interrupting the flow of conversation, trumping the witchman's medicine, upping the amperage of every exchange. Don Victor admitted to Doña Mariana that he had been having a long, ardent, and loveless affair with the Dutch hostelfrau in Quillabamba even as he had proposed to Mariana in her mother's garden, even as he had pledged love on his knees. Doña Mariana wept when she heard this, hiding her face in her hands, but before he had time to pass her his handkerchief, Don Victor was hearing a reciprocal confession. It seemed that she, too, had not been altogether chaste on the day of his proposal. For a year, she had been involved in a brief but highly charged liaison with the owner of the bookshop, La Librería Minerva, which was situated, as it happened, just down the street from the frau's bed-and-breakfast. The young bookseller would call on Mariana's mother, bring an assortment of volumes for her consideration, and while she studied them, he would excuse himself and retire to the walled garden in the back to smoke a cigarette. Mariana would slip out and join him. They would kiss at first, but before long his fingers would be under her blouse, down her skirt, caressing her as if she were a finely bound volume. "I'm telling you all this, *querido,*" she said to her husband, "although I atoned for it long ago in my father's confessional. If you tell me your truths, I must tell you mine."

It was more than he'd cared to hear.

Jaime awoke the morning after his outrageous disclosure only to confirm to his wife that he no longer loved her. For the sake of their children, he wished it weren't so, but he could no longer lie. If Elsa decided to go on taking refuge in endless, undelivered letters to her cousins or in the strange green canvases that crowded their room, he would not try to stop her. But he had to act on his convictions. "From now on," he said, "I will hide nothing. I will act openly. So that anyone who cares to look can see the truth of what goes between us." He added that he was telling her all this with a heavy heart because, in all candor, he seemed to be losing his relish for life altogether and that, if it hadn't been for the dog and its life-affirming laughter, he might have taken a spear, pierced his veins with curare, and lain down in the forest to die.

"I wish you'd go ahead and do it!" Elsa screamed, driven by a corresponding urge to speak the truth. "At least I could go back to Trujillo as a respectable widow!"

Marcela, being anything but immune to the penchant for flagrance that was coursing through the household, caught Jaime coming out of his room after his conversation with Elsa. She asked if he would mind stepping into her schoolroom briefly. Without hesitating, he followed. To his surprise, none of the children was there. She closed the door, took off her glasses, and, with a coy murmur, told him that she found him highly attractive and had been drawn to him long before last night's dinner, the passing of cellophane, and his bracingly piquant compliment. She unbuttoned her blouse, took his hand, and slid it onto her breast, which greeted his fingers with a tight little nipple. "Come here tonight," she told him. "I'll be waiting."

Jaime's reply was polite, but unequivocal. He removed his hand, and said in as gentle a voice as he could manage, "Thank you, señorita. We don't know each other well, but I like you. More to the point, Rosita, Jorge, and Marco like you. You have marvelous gifts. You are a calming influence. God knows this household needs a bit of moderation. Your invitation to me is more than a little tempting—you can't imagine how tempting, really—and my compliment to you last night was no more than a simple statement of fact. Your figure is lovely. But, in all truthfulness, I won't be standing at your door tonight. Had you told me the same thing two days ago, I might have reacted differently. But last night, in my drunkenness, I spoke my mind, and now I can't do anything else."

Belén, overcome with a desire to talk to her husband, marched to the factory and pulled him outside. *"Querido!"* she yelled over the din of the threshers, "I can't think of anything worse than to be buried alive in that room for the rest of my life, no matter how many books are in it! Forgive me, darling. I promise to be a better wife to you!" When he heard it, he put down his tools. He studied her eyes as if he were trying desperately to see what lay behind them; seeing the love, he folded her to his heart.

Graciela went directly to Padre Bernardo, not to his ramshackle confessional. She wanted to see his face. "Padre," she said, "I need to talk about that young woman of yours in Puno."

His lips tightened.

"No, no," she protested immediately, "I've said it all wrong. I don't want to pry into your life. I want to disclose something about myself."

"What is it, child?"

"Ever since your story about those trysts in the park, I've been unable to think about anything else. All day long I imagine it—I put myself there in your shoes."

"In Puno?"

"Not in Puno. In love."

"I see." He scratched the stubble on his chin. She went on to say how much this worried her, that a longing for love seemed impossible in her circumstances, and that she hoped she could learn from him how to put desire behind her—to have the fortitude, even after tasting love's sweetness, to walk away.

"I've had the same dream night after night since you told us that story," she confessed. "I don't know what to make of it. I wake up ashamed and then, by nightfall, I'm longing to dream it again."

"Tell me."

There was a well of infinite serenity in his eyes. She took a deep breath and spoke quickly. "It is night and I am alone. A stranger walks into my bedroom. I don't know him, have never seen him before, but it is as if I have been waiting for him all my life. I allow him to stroke me, kiss my body, trace my belly with his tongue." She stopped there and looked at the padre. He was listening thoughtfully and nodded for her to go on. "That is all, Padre. That's the gist of it. Every night I wait for the dream. And every night it's the same. I thought perhaps you could help rid me of it the way you rid yourself of that girl."

The priest suggested that she pray for forgiveness, that she say a hundred Ave Marías. But he added, with all candor, that she certainly didn't need to model herself after him. He was a priest, after all: He'd had to set himself straight and return to celibacy. On the other hand, if her husband were dead and gone, there was no reason to believe she might not love again. "There is nothing greater that a human can aspire to than true love, Graciela," he said. "God gave you that faculty for a reason." He put his hands on her head, blessed her, and told her to go in peace.

In a dank room in the servants' quarters, Boruba took a well-worn book from the three-legged stool by her hammock. It was a book Belén had given her, although Boruba could not read. The words seemed an endless procession of ants scurrying across paper. But the illustrations were of familiar Bible stories a missionary had once told her—Noah and his ark, Moses in the bulrushes, the sweet-faced Virgin making her way on the donkey. She extracted Pedro's flower from the heart of the book where she had pressed it last night and saw that in its new two-dimensional form it had the look of a prayer card. The lily was still in its cellophane and, when she turned it in her hand, she noted how the wrapper accentuated its beauty. She considered the gift for some time before she tucked it back into the book and went to the kitchen. She took four sweet-potato caramels from under a dome of mosquito netting and wrapped them in a square of cellophane she had retrieved from the floor of the dining room. She tied her little package with red jute and carried it straightaway to Pedro, who was, at that very moment, seeding a fallow field. When he saw her making her way toward him through the coca, he put down his hoe and ran to meet her. She handed him the sweets. And then, to her surprise, she found herself telling him how much her dead husband had loved sweet-potato candies. He nodded, untied the string carefully, peeled back the clear wrapper, and dropped one into his mouth.

Later, Boruba wondered why on earth she had felt the urge to mention her dead husband. But it was true what she had said to Pedro. Chang had loved those candies, licking his fingers and grinning as he devoured them, his bright black eyes pinched into slits. He was an odd little man—rangy and nimble, with skin as yellow as ripe squash. He had been a laborer in Mr. Meiggs's sugar factory, among the first to follow Don Victor to Floralinda.

He loved the roundness of her, the way her flesh jiggled when she walked. It wasn't often a man saw a fat woman in the jungle. He remembered his mother had once told him that across the sea, in the faraway place their people came from, flesh on a wife was a good thing—a happy sign of prosperity.

And it was so: Boruba was a happy person. The first time she saw him, she laughed openly at his bowed legs, slanted eyes, at three long black hairs that sprouted from a mole on his chin. When they made love, he laughed openly at her joy.

In time, she bore him a little girl with golden skin and a petulant mouth. But their happiness would not last. Chang disappeared one night when she and the newborn were sleeping. They found his body ravaged by an animal—most likely a panther—down where the river took a sharp turn to the south. The beast had devoured him, leaving little more than his bones. But it had left his unmistakable chin, with its mole and three hairs intact.

The more Boruba thought about it, the more she knew that she had spoken to Pedro about her husband because she wanted him to know everything. She wanted him to know what lay hidden in her heart.

Truth being unstoppable once a family is itching to tell it, revelations followed upon revelations in that house. On the night before Jaime set off for Pucallpa to find buyers for cellophane, Don Victor called everyone into the sala and said that he had an announcement about a small but crucial point of family history. It seemed a threshold moment, remarkable for two reasons: first, that Don Victor would want to announce anything about family history, it having been taboo for so long in Sobrevilla parlors; second, that he was able to remember any history at all.

He waited until all his progeny were gathered in one room, including the five noisy children, who tumbled in last, pulling the dog behind them. The little ones took their places on the colorful rug, shushed one another, and waited for the news.

What he had to declare, he told them, probably had no compelling importance except that it was God's truth. The evidence for it was gone. The people affected were dead. As far as he could determine, no one in this house had felt history's cold hand reach down the generations to reveal it, but since he was suddenly endowed with a crystal-clear memory about such matters, he was obliged to pass the information along. "Do you see the pretty way Graciela's eyes tilt up?" he asked them. "Have you noticed the subtleties and complexities of Belén's brain? Are you fond, as I am, of that round, sunny face of Jaime's? There's a reason for it, children, although in all my sixty years no Sobrevilla has dared say it. The truth is: We're a little bit Chinese."

There was a gasp of surprise around the room. Elsa threw her hands up at that point, frankness being a force too irresistible. "I don't know what it is with you people," she said. "I think you are thoroughly insane."

8

Jaime rose stiffly. He had spent the night on a hard rattan chair in the library. He slipped on his boots, shouldered his rucksack, and carried the box with the cellophane samples out onto the patio. There was a sweet scent of mashed hemp in the air. It was five o'clock, before the light of day.

By the time he reached the dock, his three men—two Huitoto workers and one Aymara field hand—were rigging the boat, fitting the motor for the journey to Pucallpa. They had brought enough provisions for five days, and they had added machetes, iron pots, knives, for tribesmen who staked out positions on the river, demanding bribes. They packed these into the stern and roped them in, for the trip against the current would be rough.

Jaime reached down to bid Papu good-bye, scratching his neck then nudging him away. Halfway up the bank, the mastiff turned and cackled playfully. Jaime chuckled too. He couldn't help himself. But then he pointed toward the path that led back to the house and the dog ambled away, forlorn.

The men pushed off into the river. Fog hung over the Ucayali, clinging to the water's surface so that it was impossible to see more than forty feet ahead. They paddled silently, the only sound the soft plash of their oars. Half a mile downriver, they switched on the motor, and the sudden roar sent screams of tree life pealing through the dew-hung forest.

The river grew calm after that. There was no traffic except for the rare canoe gliding by in the distance, ferrying a hunter from one bend to another. At one point, the boat churned through a slough of reeds and scared out a flock of snow-white egrets. They fluttered back wildly, then wheeled up majestically over the trees.

By mid-morning, they had rounded the first ninety-degree elbow of their journey and were heading toward Resbaladera when the fog lifted to reveal a teal-blue sky. They looked south and saw a riot of color soar overhead from canopy to canopy—macaws, traveling two by two.

Jaime took a piece of dried *charqui* from a bucket and settled into the stern, ripping off mouthfuls of the leathery pork with his teeth, savoring its salt. He scanned the shore, taking in the river life: A herd of alligators were forging through mud, their snouts iridescent with green flies. A haughty toucan rocked side to side on a low branch. A troop of black monkeys appeared in the distance, swinging noiselessly through the fig trees.

The girl was kneeling on the west bank of the river when he saw her. He could tell from the angle of her body and the circular motion of her hands in the water that she was washing something. She was completely naked. Her breasts were full and round, their mahogany nipples visible even from that distance. He watched her shoulders move as her hands worked. Something glinted in her hair. Behind her on the shore was a black dugout perched on two logs, freshly painted.

Hearing the hum of the boat's motor, the girl rose to her feet slowly. She shook out her palm-thatch brushes, eyeing the boat all the while, tilting her head in the sunlight. Suddenly a thousand lights flickered from her hair.

Jaime shouted to one of the Huitotos to cut the motor. The man pushed the flange and the engine hushed to a purr. "Over there," Jaime told him, pointing to the place where the girl stood. "Take us there."

The man swung the prow of the boat westward, fighting an implacable current. As the motorboat sped toward the riverbank, the girl thrust her brushes beneath the canoe and whirled around to face them. She seemed firm, resolute, unafraid. The four men scanned the trees behind her, wondering how many of her tribesmen lurked there.

Jaime could see that she was even lovelier than he had imagined from the distance. The eyes were wide, slightly tilted; the well-oiled skin as smooth as brown marble. From either side of her lips, dry reeds bristled like whiskers. A string of tattoos ran along her collarbone. Her legs and breasts were slick with fish oil. But the trait that most struck him, apart from her astonishing beauty—the salient feature that had lured him across the Ucayali for a closer look—was the cellophane, wound into her long black hair. There, in the full sun of day, the ribbons sparkled like impossible mirrors.

Jaime called out in Shipibo, the only indigenous language he knew. *"Bari!"* he shouted. Sunshine! *"Mapu!"* he added. From your head! She lifted both hands and fingered the braids on either side of her face. Just that morning, she had opened the box with the cat knife, cut the shine into strips, and twisted them into her hair.

Soon he realized she didn't understand the language entirely—she chattered back in words that were unintelligible. He reached down toward the floor of the boat, unfastened the box with the cellophane samples, and sprang into the hip-deep water. The girl took measure of the white man as he made his way through the current. She had only heard Mwambr speak of the termite people, of their vicious and powerful magic. This one did not seem hostile. His face was open, the expression in his eyes warm.

He pointed to her hair, then to the large wooden box under his arm. She cocked her head curiously. He slid back the clasp, flipped open the top so that it swung back on its hinges, then tilted the box so that the girl could see the glittering paper inside. She gasped and danced back, one hand over her heart.

Jaime tried every indigenous word he could think of to elicit some information: Where had she found the cellophane? He suspected it was a discarded cigarette wrapper, although in the jungle the insects would have devoured it quickly. But how had it gotten there? He'd never seen cigarette packs except in large cities. Smokers here rolled their own. Even in Iquitos, the largest city along that river, vendors sold cigarettes individually, doling them out one by one. Where had she come upon such long, thick strips of a material the likes of which he, who traveled up and down the river regularly, had not seen in the rain forest outside of his father's workshop?

He waved his men ashore and they, too, asked her the same questions—in four different languages—but she only babbled on incomprehensibly. Desperate to communicate with the enigmatic woman, Jaime was ready to shout in frustration, until he heard her say three syllables that explained everything: "Yo-rum-bo."

"Yorumbo?" he said. "*Mapacho?* Sumiruna? Curandero? Ayahuasca? *Pumasacha?*" using every word he could think of that referred to a shaman and his cures.

"Haa!" she responded, with an emphatic shake of her head. "Yorumbo. Haa! Haa!" Then she ran to the black canoe and returned with the slender cardboard container. She opened it to reveal the treasure inside.

Jaime started when he saw his father's knife lying in her palm so neatly. And then the realizations came one after another: The cellophane in her hair was Don Victor's. Yorumbo had given it to her. Many were the ways such a thing might come to pass. But there it was, alluring as it could be, curled into her ink-black hair, summoning him across the water.

For seven years now, Elsa Márquez de Sobrevilla had comforted herself with the knowledge that she had married a good name. Despite her father's sly reference to some hint of family scandal in recent Sobrevilla history, she was sure that the venerable Don Carlos Sobrevilla, whose handsome portrait still hung in the Club de Trujillo, came from a long line of aristocrats, sons of viceroyals, whose pedigrees reached into Spain.

The day she turned fifteen, the scions of Trujillo society began to court her, but, for all their good connections, none seemed particularly attractive. That changed one afternoon at the club's annual garden party when her cousin Matilde introduced her to a group of recent graduates from the university, among them a young man with a dazzling smile. Matilde presented him as the nephew of the distinguished Don Alejandro Sobrevilla, whose spacious *casona* was just down the avenue. Elsa, who had recently celebrated her nineteenth birthday, was surprised that she'd never met the young man before; his family lived so

near. That afternoon, she studied him openly. He was a handsome man
with an appealing manner. She was enchanted by the stories about his
father's hacienda in the interior. When he told her that he would stay
in the city another year as an apprentice in his uncle's law office, she
went to her father, Alberto Márquez y Márquez, and asked him to
extend Jaime an invitation to dine at their table. Within a month, he
was a frequent guest at the house. Before the year was over, his ge-
niality had won over everyone in it. The evening he called on Alberto
Márquez to ask for his daughter's hand in marriage, he expected to be
asked to give an account of the Sobrevilla fortunes, but the old man,
who had six older daughters to give away in marriage, simply slapped
him on the back, handed him a glass of brandy, and said yes.

In all that time, no one had spoken to Elsa of the dead Angélica
Paniagua and her dead Chinese daughter. No one had thought to point
out the eccentric old woman in cheongsams who hobbled around Tío
Alejandro's house.

To learn now that she had been fooled, that the children of her marriage were descendants of clerics and coolies, was sickening. Elsa
searched the features of Jorge, her youngest, and found the damning
evidence: the full-moon face, the round bow lips, the eyes with their
epicanthic folds. As the granddaughter of a sugar baron—as a Márquez
y Márquez—she knew what that bloodline meant.

How had she failed to see the truth—that a family in good standing
would never have left the coast? Don Victor was part Chinese! She
might as well have married one of her father's field laborers.

She yearned to return to her family's stately palace on the main
square of Bolívar's city. She was desperate to depart this wilderness
where Indians swatted at airplanes as if they were flies just beyond their
noses, where travelers welcomed a stew of snake flesh as if it were
ambrosia. She longed for the company of her cousins, with their cosmopolitan banter about film stars and fashion. She longed to confide in
her sisters about the miseries of her predicament: about being a
Márquez who had unknowingly married down; about being the mother
of three slant-eyed children.

The Márquez family had been avid importers of coolie labor. There
was evidence of this in the endless rows of musty albums in the family

mansion. She remembered rifling through them as a child and stopping at one of the photographs: a grimy canecutter standing in a field, his feet chained to an iron pole, his hair in a stringy queue. Was *that* her children's ancestor? Another photograph haunted her: a Chinese slave shoveling gull guano in the islands off Paracas—marooned, ragged, eyelashes white with dried excrement. When she was a schoolgirl, she had giggled at the strange little men who filed through Trujillo in the early morning, sweeping the dung from the streets: the way they shuffled along as if their feet were still shackled, the way they grew long nails on their little fingers so they could dig at their earwax, the way hairs sprang from their moles. *"Chinos cochinos!"* her brothers would shout. Filthy Chinamen!

Although she had never met him, she had always suspected that Boruba's husband had been a *chino*. The grandson was a pronounced yellow before death rendered him blue. Then again, why wouldn't an Indian marry a Chinaman? Animals mated across species—flagrantly, along this river.

No. Being a descendant of coolies would not sit well in her father's house.

But that her children were great-grandchildren of a priest was worse: the depravity of that woman, her mother-in-law, standing and delivering the news so brazenly. The shame. Even if Jaime were to do her the mercy of going into the rain forest and sticking his veins with curare, how could she return to Trujillo with those children?

Elsa knew she needed to keep her distance from these people until she could devise a plan. To board a boat unaccompanied was impossible: She had heard of women raped, left at the mercy of savages, killed, because they had traveled alone. If she wrote to her father for help, she would need to tell the truth about the Sobrevillas. She knew Alberto Márquez might soften at the sight of her tears when she confessed, but she also knew he could be ruthless; if he read the news in a letter, he might banish her from the family entirely. He had done it before with Veronica, his own sister, a shy little spinster who had run off with her music teacher. Alberto Márquez had declared her unworthy, ordered her room emptied of its belongings, and purged her name from the family will.

As days passed, it was as if a sickness had crept into Elsa's body. She began moving through rooms like a disoriented creature, bumping her shoulders into walls. More than once, she put on her boots—the good, high leather ones that had been made for her by her father's shoemaker— and scampered out to the patio, getting as far as the brick barricade. But one sniff of the damp river air, one glimpse of the dark, impenetrable jungle would send her running back into the foyer, clambering up the stairs.

She began taking her meals alone, growing ever more sullen. She told Boruba she wanted breakfast, lunch, and dinner delivered to her room under the silver dome that sat on the dining room sideboard. Three times a day, one of the tiny Huitoto maids struggled under the weight of that tray to feed her. And with every day, Elsa grew more impatient.

The verbal abuse would start when the maid tapped the door with her bare toe. "No shoes?" Elsa might snarl. "What are you, a monkey?" As the wretched servant weaved her way in under the gargantuan silver, Elsa would have other things to say: "Miserable midget!" or "I won't eat your slop!"

But she did eat it—every time, every bite. In the sanctuary of her solitude, she would tuck the white napkin behind her collar, settle into the chair with the red brocade pillow, and apply the old silverware with relish. She averted her eyes from whatever displeased her: the hideous scar in the great dome of silver, the reason why Don Alejandro had tossed it into a crate bound for the Ucayali; the moth-bitten napkins, mended with threads of another color; Don Carlos's old pewter goblet, its every dent another insult; the cup with no handle—only one was intact, and, at Doña Mariana's insistence, reserved for the master of the house.

Already inured to those imperfections, Elsa ate her food and dreamed of escape. She imagined that her father, aware of her homesickness by some miracle of paternal intuition, had dispatched someone to fetch her. The more she gazed out at the river, the more she was convinced that he'd actually done it. She would finish her meal, dab the corners of her mouth, and stand at the window for hours, humming a little tune. One morning, the maids arrived to discover her dressed in a hat, high shoes, and gloves. Every day after that when they brought breakfast, they would find her arrayed in finery. Always, she would shriek at them when they appeared, and always, when they returned to retrieve her tray, there she would be, standing at her window, watching the river. She came downstairs rarely now, and only to slip out to the patio for a better look at the dock. As time passed, the people of Floralinda began to notice her, staring out from that second-floor lookout. "There's Señor Jaime's woman," they'd say, "cracked as an egg under a chicken!" and then they would cluck their tongues.

If the news about Padre Bernardo's long-ago sin had shocked the three hundred and seventeen souls who inhabited Floralinda, it wasn't evident in the pews of his church, where the faithful continued to gather to hear his homilies and gaze on his richly bedecked Virgin. There was, at first, a spirited gossip—like a bad night of crickets—visualizing the carnal details of his vernal union. Had the two frolicked in the park, naked? Had the woman, like Eve, initiated it? But before long, the padre's sin seemed slight: forgivable even. What were transgressions of human desire compared to the savage laws of the jungle, where questions of life and death ruled? Within days his sin was absolved as a human error and the friar as another fugitive from a difficult past.

There were few in Floralinda who weren't chasing redemption, looking to alter their lots. Someone was always headed for the next bend in the river, for the point when one's past molts like a snake's. Lepers, their faces eaten by disease, rowed past, peering from rags, seeking a shaman with a cure. Skin traders, perched on carcasses, slid past in canoes, stalking the one big kill that would buy them prosperity. Veterans of distant wars, eyes red from too much carnage, stopped briefly for provisions, then moved on, daring the river to show them its worst. Travelers were not rare in Floralinda. They would stumble in wearily, make their way up the road, then glance up at the house as if they had crossed into the afterlife.

So it was that when Doña Mariana emerged from a visit with Padre Bernardo, she hardly noticed the gringo with the long leather bag who was tramping up the dirt path. Most likely he was a weary traveler, washed ashore for a morning, wanting a little boiled water for his canteen, a bit of yuca for the journey. She had more important things on her mind. She had gone to see the padre about her husband's alarming inclination to bring up every detail of his past indiscretions.

Father Bernardo had braced himself when he saw her walk into his church, assuming she had come to further discuss his sin. But when he heard her out, he gave her the full benefit of his pastorate. He told her that it was not unusual for a mind so stimulated with work to find respite in memories of another time. His expression changed when Doña Mariana explained that Don Victor's new memories were not particularly comforting. They were largely of dalliances with women, of past family humiliations, and the solace seemed to be in the confession, not in the memory itself. The padre responded that it would have been far more appropriate for Don Victor to have aired such revelations in his confessional.

The padre rolled his eyes when she told him about her husband's visit to the witchman. "Señora," he said, "I've warned him a thousand times about his visits to pagan healers. If I could have my way, every last one of those charlatans would be packed off to monasteries, where they might learn a thing or two about healing." But he patted Doña Mariana's hand anyway and promised to counsel Don Victor on these matters.

Such were the preoccupations that engaged Doña Mariana as she marched homeward, past the workers' shacks, past Chincho's bar, past Filomena's pig corral. At first, when the gringo with the long leather bag addressed her, she didn't hear him.

"Pardon me, señora," he said for the third time. "I'm looking for a place to stay. Is there a *posada* in this village? Anyone who will loan me a hammock?" Gradually the man's face came into focus.

The Spanish was perfectly grammatical, although the accent was broad. He was grimy and unshaven, as if he had been riding the current for days. When she asked him how he had come, he pointed behind to the river, which was visible over the rise. There, at some distance from the dock, she saw a motorized canoe.

He was not tall, but his shoulders were square. The face was hard—chiseled and narrow—but the hair was pale yellow and the eyes as blue as a parrot's tail feathers. Judging from his features he was young, perhaps the age of her son. She had heard of blond, blue-eyed children abducted by tribes and raised as their own: Rain forest Indians believed them to be gods; they were smitten by the blue, by the hair the color of sun, so rarely did they see sky. But this was no "white Indian," as those lost souls were known. Too much signaled a recent foreignness: the plaid shirt, the leather boots, the watch, which gleamed from his wrist like a beacon.

She explained that Floralinda was not an ordinary village but a hacienda with a paper factory. There was no *posada* here. But then she nodded toward the long, flat structure on stilts in the distance. "That's where the unmarried men live—the bachelors," she told him. "I'm sure someone can find you a place to sleep there."

He thanked her and, as he shifted his leather bag from one shoulder to the other, he told her his name was Louis Miller. It suddenly occurred to her to wonder why the gringo's bag was so heavy. Gun traders, revolutionaries, and *pistoleros* often trolled the river—the Peruvian Amazon was thick with them—but they tended to travel in pairs and stick to well-populated towns. Perhaps he was a lone marauder, importing trouble. "Are you carrying guns?" she asked outright.

"Oh no, señora," he answered. "This satchel is packed with metal stands and mapping instruments. That's why I'm here. I'm mapping the Ucayali's tributaries for the New York Geographical Society. There are a number of deviations between Contamana and Nauta that have never been drawn accurately."

"*Ay, bueno,*" she said, softening. "Then I'm sure my husband will not object to your staying over there." Perhaps Don Victor might even be interested in the fellow. She put out her hand. "I am Mariana Francisco de Sobrevilla, wife of the chief engineer. Why don't you join us for dinner? Our house is up this path. Our cook always serves at eight o'clock. If you come at sunset, I can promise you a little sherry."

Don Victor sat by the tambo and watched the girl with the beautiful breasts pull long tubers of yuca from the earth. Squatting behind her, Yorumbo's woman peeled and chopped the day's harvest. Don Victor had been explaining to the witchman that his medicine needed to be stronger. Not only had the image of the Teutonic woman entered his head again, he was daydreaming about the young teacher who lived upstairs. "But that's not all," he told the curandero. "My house is a nest of bees, and all they do is buzz. They say words that should never be spoken about things they should keep to themselves."

Yorumbo emerged from his marmoreal stillness when he heard this. He opened his eyes, took his hands from his knees, and put his fists squarely on earth. "They are telling their truths?"

"They are telling their secrets, sumiruna. Truths nobody cares to hear." He twisted one end of his mustache and added, "They're not the only ones who do it, mind you. I do it too."

The witchman looked into the shapechanger's eyes and saw how troubled he was. "There is a difference between the truth of the world and the world as a person sees it. We cannot know the truth. But if you are telling me that the people of your tribe are experiencing a plague of the tongue, then there is nothing my medicine can do to stop it. That is a force greater than any I can conjure."

"You mean I must live with this?" Don Victor asked. "It will never change?"

"No. It will change. But maybe not in the way you want it to. I will tell you a story, shapechanger. Listen. Long ago, a plague of tongues came over a tribe called the Idainapi. It was when I was a boy; my father told me about their troubles. The Idainapi began to speak their minds openly, against all tribal law. The young told the old what they thought of them, insulted them to their faces. Women spoke words to men that only women should hear. It got so that nothing was sacred. Nothing secret. The people tried taking potions of piri-piri, thinking that, because it cured snakebites, it would stop tongues from wagging. They made plasters of capinuri bark and went to sleep with them over their mouths, thinking that, because trees are silent, they would wake up the next morning mute. But none of those medicines worked. The plague of tongues continued, bringing a wake of other plagues behind it." Here the old sumiruna stopped and sighed.

"And so?"

"And so, after the plague of the tongue, there was a plague of the eye. And after the eye, ears. Then fingers. So it went, until one of the

Idainapi, wiser than the rest, spoke up and said he would listen no more to his people. He would listen to the river, heed the advice of his spirit creature, leave that encampment, and follow the line of the forest."

"Did he?"

"They all did. They dispersed like a pod of seeds. I've searched all my life for an Idainapi. I've asked every wanderer whether he is one. I wanted to know if the story my father told me was so. But then I understood that my search was pointless. You see, if the tribe has survived all its troubles, I will never meet one of its members. At least I will never know whether I do. A true Idainapi will not reveal himself to me. It is the one secret he must keep."

Don Victor drank the ayahuasca then, puzzling over that lesson. He was convinced that if he could just see through the eyes of his spirit creature—as the wise Idainapi tribesman had known to do—the way forward would unfold clearly. He lay on Yorumbo's straw mat, fell into a dream state, and, in a vision as vivid as his last, he soared over the river, between the high banks of the emerald forest. He saw his own house in the distance, and then, as he mounted the wind over the hacienda, he saw all the movement below as if he were a fly over Señor Urrutia's perpetual-motion machine and the human heads floating beneath were perfect little spheres of steel. There was Elsa, in her hat, standing at the window. There was Graciela, shooing her children into the kitchen. There was Doña Mariana, trundling her way to church. There was a stranger, stepping from his canoe, heaving a leather bag over his shoulder. There was Ignacio, shouting instructions over the thresher. There was the priest, watering a plant in a tiny clay pot. There was Marcela, yawning and stretching her warm little arms from the sill of her third-floor schoolroom. And there was Pedro, kneeling before Boruba's door with his hand on the great, scarred dome that had served generations of Sobrevillas, from Andalucia to the Amazon. Boruba opened her door and stepped into daylight; Pedro looked up and smiled. He lifted the silver service and a parrot flew out from under, pounding its bright green feathers, soaring toward the sun.

* * *

Louis Miller strolled down the road toward the bachelor house. A little sherry? The promise of it seemed impossible after the last three days he had spent on the Ucayali. The day before had been especially hard. He had pulled his way along the shore, clutching at grass from Libertad to a nameless node on the river—a diastole containing two islands. He had stood on the western shore, measuring the landforms through the loupe of his quadrant. Then he had walked the scant mile due north through clouds of stinging pium and boroshuda flies to the coordinates where he expected a lake to be. Eventually he had found it, but not before he hacked through to a teeming nest of Isula ants, whose fierce mandibles had chewed through his trousers, leaving welts along his calves. Sherry. The very thought seemed ludicrous. In this wilderness of mud?

The sight of Floralinda had been a deliverance, although he had had no idea such a place existed. He heard the thrum of the factory before he saw it. Skimming downriver northwest toward Punto Alegre, he rounded a bend and there it was: a concrete foundation that dominated the shoreline; a long white building that seemed to run half the length of it, and thrusting up—a fat chimney, spewing a column of black smoke into the sky. He had passed the dock where a team of bare-chested men rolled great spools down wooden planks onto a loading platform. He could hear the squeal of conveyor belts and the plangent roar of an engine. Rowing ashore north of the dock, he had seen a man in overalls walk from one machine to another, stopping to adjust the instrumentation.

Exhausted, he had moored his canoe to a fallen tree. The last good sleep he'd had was five days ago when a petroleum worker in Contamana had offered him an extra hammock for the night. All he had wanted from Floralinda was a little water, a few hours on his back.

Sherry.

He had seen the mansion over the rise, beside a hemp field, down a path that was thick with ferns. He thought he was hallucinating. He'd been told that apparitions were not uncommon in the Amazon rain forest—especially if a traveler was nearing exhaustion. But after he'd rubbed his eyes, the mansion was still there.

That was when he saw the woman. She was tall, commanding, in a dress of black cotton that was belted, with a full skirt and high collar.

Around her shoulders was a mantilla of fine lace. Her hair, shot through with silver, was gathered in a knot at the base of her neck. In the heat of the late afternoon, she seemed yet another apparition. She was so utterly exotic, so out of place. He stood transfixed, watching her advance, reminded of museum paintings he'd seen long ago as a boy in Chicago. Dutch school, perhaps. But Peru? In the jungle? Midway through the twentieth century?

Floralinda had not appeared on any map he'd ever seen, but it was here, all right, with its pigs, its ramshackle bar, and its otherworldly resident: a specter from the past, inviting him to an aperitif.

Doña Mariana heard a sharp rapping on the great front door and hurried out to the balcony. She looked down at the slick blond hair, the clean shirt, the hands thrust casually into his pockets, and hardly recognized Louis Miller. The cartographer was the very picture of well-being; it was remarkable what a razor and a little sleep could do. She called down merrily in English, "Hello, mister!"

Don Victor, who was at that moment tucking his cravat into his shirt, knew very well that an American would be sitting at his table that evening. When Miller had presented himself at the bachelor house, one of the workers had gone directly to the factory to report it.

"The cartographer descends!" Don Victor sang out as he adjusted his collar. "The coordinates align!"

Belén answered the door and escorted the young American into the vast room with its ebony piano and gargantuan armoires. She studied the man as she poured him a glass of oloroso from a squat decanter of cut crystal. He seemed perfectly at ease in Spanish, and, if it weren't for his hair and his marked accent, she might have thought he was a traveler from elsewhere in South America. After the initial formalities, they sat there primly in silence—she on the couch, he on a chair. Miller gaped at the elaborate room around him: the rattan and leather furniture, the massive mahogany sideboards, the grand family portraits, the immense, colorful carpet with its geometric Inca design.

"Welcome!" Don Victor said as he strode into the room, arms flung wide in greeting. "All manner of men have found sanctuary under this roof—soldiers, priests, medicine men, and governors, not to mention every stripe of riverine flotsam—but a cartographer? Never. You are our first. Welcome, sir. We are honored. My hacienda is at your disposal."

The American was quick to say that he was no explorer, no Colonel Fawcett on the verge of momentous discovery. He was merely an employee in the service of a New York firm, contracted to refine maps of the Amazon tributaries.

"My dear man," Don Victor answered him, settling into his favorite chair. "I didn't say you were an explorer, I called you what you are: a cartographer. We are not ignoramuses here: We know the difference. Cartography is a science—a very precise science, to be perfectly precise! Explorers? Pah, they're nothing special. The river is crawling with fools looking for El Dorado." He leaned back into the rattan. "You see, Mr. Miller, we appreciate science in Floralinda. You might even say that we Sobrevillas are the Venetians of modern science along this river. You have strayed into friendly waters, señor!"

"But tell me, Don Victor," Louis Miller said, "why is Floralinda not on the maps—not in America or Peru? I've seen military boats trolling up and down the river one hundred miles north of here doing their coca surveys. You'd think they'd want to know about this town."

"It's just as well they don't," Don Victor answered. "It's a working hacienda, not a town. You can't call it a community in any civic sense."

"With all due respect, señor, many working haciendas along the Peruvian coast are recorded by Peruvian army maps: Cartavio, Chiclín, Paramonga, Salamanca, Santa Ana."

"Perhaps you are right, Mr. Miller, but I can only rejoice that Floralinda is invisible. Put us on a map and the next thing you know census takers, missionaries, politicians will be riding up and down this little stretch of river trying to make us a part of their world. We live freely here. We work hard, do what we can, but we don't answer to anyone but God. Someone puts you on a map, and then the petty potentates come with their itchy fingers. We don't want it! We want to be left alone to do our work."

"How long *have* you been here, may I ask?"

"Twenty-two years to the month. Belén had just turned fourteen years old. I was thirty-eight."

"And this glorious house? How did you manage to build it?"

"Mr. Miller, I am an engineer. What's more, I am a native of Trujillo and a graduate of the Escuela de Ingenieros in Lima. If, with all that cultivation and learning, I couldn't build this house, you could count me an idiot."

"But the materials, the tools!"

"All from the jungle. The staircase and walls you see here are caoba, what you Americans call mahogany. The tools we used to build them are all from Lima, via the rolling river. The tiles were made by an *azulejero* from Iquitos. It may take us longer to build something, but we do it as well as anyone. And with less. The staircase you saw in the front hallway doesn't have a screw or a nail in it. It's all in the cutting, the fitting, the grooves. There are challenges here in the Amazon—floods, termites, the impenetrable jungle—but the coast has its challenges too. Engineers there learn to factor the earthquakes. If you count the challenges, you need to count the gifts, and they are legion here: The varieties of wood—there is nothing like it on earth. The natural stains. The rubber. The botanical riches. A good engineer learns to adapt."

The American listened raptly. The rest of the family had trickled in, and while he nodded politely to each, he was entirely focused on the remarkable figure before him. He had forgotten his sherry completely, and it sat, full to the rim, on a side table. Elbows propped on his knees, he listened to the story of how paper had come to Floralinda, and how the factory on the bank of the river had grown to supply the entire region. There was no bag, no box, no paper in any of the major towns on the Ucayali that did not originate in Don Victor's pulp vats. "All of it delivered in barges up and down the river," the papermaker told him. "Being a cartographer, you know very well: It's impossible to move anything overland in this jungle. The river is the only way."

"Now perhaps would be the time, Papa, to tell our guest about your cellophane."

Graciela was leaning on the wall, just inside the doorway. Her head was back, resting on the mahogany and, to Louis Miller's mind, against the dark of the wood, her skin seemed incandescent. Circling her eyes were two lilac rings, like the fine colorations of a bird. The sight of her drew him with the force of a lodestone. He rose almost involuntarily, held out his hand. She came forward to take it. She was wearing some sort of costume: cinched at the waist, flared at the ankle, celadon green. Her figure was small, but perfect in all particulars. Her hair was a long tumble of russet. A warm perfume rose from her breasts.

Being a man who searched out terrain for a living, Louis Miller had learned to live with the unexpected. But this place seemed to have no end to surprises. First Doña Mariana in her old-world dress. Then Belén, opening the door with a prim welcome. The old man's cravat and sherry seemed like crackpot affectations. But nothing had prepared him for Graciela, whose fragile beauty bore a quick hole in his heart.

"So, Graciela!" Don Victor spoke finally. "You want me to talk about my cellophane? For months I've been working on this new process secretly in my workshop, and you want me to spill it all out to this illustrious gentleman—from New York, no less, and whom I've only just met?"

There it was. The truth, leaping from Don Victor's mouth—blunt and unvarnished. It was unclear whether or not the others knew that a plague had invaded their household, but if they didn't know it then, they would understand it completely before the evening was over. A sickness had taken hold: an irresistible urge to unburden their minds, hold nothing back, empty their heads of the most trivial thought.

"Please," the American said, sensing the phantom of something passing, "I don't need to hear secrets. I am neither illustrious nor am I from New York. I'm from Chicago, actually. Rockford, Illinois, to be precise. I'm simply grateful to be in this room."

"Here it is, if you must know then," said Don Victor, ignoring the apologies entirely. He drew a length of cellophane from his breast pocket; he always seemed to carry a bit of it now. Opening the paper carefully, he pressed it onto his knees and then held it up, between the thumb and forefinger of one hand. "My cellophane. *Our* cellophane, I should say. When my son returns from Pucallpa with orders, we'll start the machines running. It's part hemp, part cotton. In other words: part leaf of cannabis, part wool of the field. It has sky in it; it has dirt. It has

Huaman, lord of the heavens. It has Pachamama, goddess of the earth. It is bird. It is cat. Condor and puma."

The cartographer stepped forward and took it in his hands. "Marvelous. Just marvelous," he said, turning it over and over. "You make this here in the jungle? In your factory down by the dock?"

He lifted it up and turned toward Graciela so that her face was caught in it, like a fine portrait behind glass.

"At the moment, I make only limited quantities," Don Victor answered. "But before long, it will be all I make."

"You can't be serious," Ignacio blurted, unable to contain himself. "Only cellophane? What about the demand for brown paper we've built over the years?"

"I am perfectly serious," said Don Victor, glowering. "In time, Ignacio, I promise, you will forget we ever made anything else. This is what we engineers call a true leap of progress."

"You like what you see through there, don't you, Mr. Miller?" said Graciela, incapable of curbing the immodesty. She was smiling at the cartographer, whose gaze remained fixed on her.

"Nonsense," said Doña Mariana, being equally candid. "He's admiring your father's paper. Now, children, let's go into the comedor. Boruba's about to call us. I can hear her feet on the tile."

Louis Miller folded the cellophane to its original size and handed it back to his host. "Hemp and cotton. That's just extraordinary, *Doctor Ingeniero*. From two dense substances—a paper that is clear as glass."

Don Victor smiled broadly and raised his shoulders as if they were wings.

The night would be a turning point for the Sobrevillas. For if they believed indiscretions had been aberrations, they would now understand indiscretions had become the rule: What was in their hearts would soon be on their tongues. The first course had hardly been served when Marcela began trumpeting her thoughts. "I don't know what goes on at Señor Chincho's bar," she said, "but whenever that barge captain comes around, funny things happen. I think they're pulling pranks. Last night, he sent someone up here with another note for me. I can't make out a thing it says."

"Another note?" said Doña Mariana, looking up from her *sopa de tortuga*. "I didn't know there was a first."

"Neither did I," said Belén. "Although Jaime told me about that pirate. He's a mercenary. He fought in the wars in Africa and India. For money."

"Really?" said Marcela. "Well, I don't know anything about that." She patted her lips with her napkin. "But if a man were going to write a woman a note, you would think he would write it in a language she could understand. The handwriting is atrocious. I think it must be in English."

"I could read the notes for you, if you like," Miller said, looking up brightly.

"Could you?" she said, and from the neckline of her starched white blouse she drew a scrap of brown paper that looked, for all the world, like a remnant from the factory floor. "This is the latest." She handed it across the table to Miller.

He opened the scrap and read its contents with mounting alarm. When he was through, he set it on the table with a tense hand. His cheeks were flushed.

"Well?" said the teacher. "What does it say?" She leaned forward eagerly.

It was a terrible message, obscene and unspeakable, but the coccus of truth had yet to infect the American, so he cleared his throat, smiled wanly, and lied. "Oh, it's a perfectly innocuous little message," he said. "The fellow wonders if you'll loan him a book."

"Ah!" the teacher said, cocking her head in surprise.

"A book!" said Belén. "The pirate *reads*! From Jaime's accounts, he's a drunk and a lout. He'll probably use it to wipe his ass!"

"Belén!" Doña Mariana exclaimed, rising from her chair, but she lowered herself quickly, seeing that her daughter was as surprised by the vulgarity as she was. Ignacio threw back his head and roared.

"*Oy*, Belén just can't imagine living without one of her books," Graciela piped in, sensing the atmosphere lightening. "Can you imagine her loaning her books to anyone, least of all that Australian?"

"No, you're wrong, Graciela," Belén countered, quick as a Naca-Naca snake. "I'd give up that whole library—and every book in it—in exchange for a baby of my own. A lusty, bouncing boy." Ignacio, who had been relishing his wife's wicked coarseness, suddenly stopped laughing. Tears glistened in Belén's eyes.

"To have babies you must make love!" Doña Mariana's voice rang out. A loud charivari of clattering plates came from the kitchen as Boruba scrambled to put her ear to the door. Boruba knew, of course, that to make babies one had to make love. But, as she had been advancing with two fully served plates on her palms, thinking of Pedro, the butterflies, the parrot—her mistress's voice filled her with a fizz she could barely contain. She stumbled toward the conversation like a zealot toward the Word.

"Why is everyone staring?" Doña Mariana looked around the table, her eyebrows raised in surprise. "Am I telling you anything you don't know? You want a baby, Belén? You must make love. Put your energies into it. Be resourceful. Seduce your husband. Thank God your priorities are finally straight!"

Everyone's eyes searched their plates desperately. But silence being an irresistible vacuum, the matriarch's voice soon sprang to fill it, embellishing her theme about a woman's duties to a man. "Young wives so often forget!" she said, tapping the table with her forefinger. "There is no housework, señoras, no obligation more important than making love to a husband. Plan! Be inventive. Think of it as taming a large animal. First you lure him with play. Then you immobilize him with attention. Finally, you fill him with pleasure. Do this rigorously, and I promise: He will never stray from your side."

Miller looked about in awe. Had he stepped into a sanctuary for free spirits?

"I am not in the least ashamed, children," Doña Mariana continued, "that the golden moments of my life have been in the arms of my husband. When he took me for the first time, on the night that my father married us, every pore of me, every hair, came alive. I was electrified. But I've told you that so many times, querido."

The kitchen door flew open and the wide frame of Boruba tumbled forth like a rock in a mud slide, in a fall that reverberated through the house.

"Enough!" Don Victor shouted. "What devil has possessed us?

Yesterday we were sensible people; today we are raving maniacs! I don't recognize any of you anymore. I don't recognize me. My dear wife, I love you beyond reason, but I have heard you say more about us in this dining room, frankly, than I want the world to know. And if I feel disoriented, what must this poor, lost cartographer—who just happened to wander into this asylum—think of the Sobrevillas now?"

9

If Don Victor could have seen into the heart of another man's heart, he would have understood that the poor, lost cartographer was anything but disapproving of his family. Louis Miller left the house elated, as if a brisk wind had blown through his chest.

It was a feeling Don Victor would have recognized.

Curious, that feeling of froth in a man who is falling in love—the ferment that fizzes his brain and lifts him like a toy into the fly gallery. He does not *fall*. "Your feet are on earth, but in truth you are floating," Yorumbo said when the shapechanger visited him with those symptoms. Don Victor told the witchman about the hat, the butterflies, and the teacher; and the witchman nodded, lifting his hands, so that they canted up into the air. "Yes, pacu—a man rises to desire."

But Don Victor's mind was so filled with the teacher that he hardly listened; he nodded reflexively and told the witchman another story.

Don Victor had been on his way to his workshop, deep in thought, when the parrot in the front hall had cried out and startled him. He'd had a powerful urge to take it from its cage and thrust it under a large shining dome in the other room. Instead, he went straight out the door, bought a macaw from a villager, placed it on a tray under an inverted basket, and set out to find the teacher. He found her with the children, on the top floor of his own house.

The woman stood, smoothing her hair while the children rushed toward their grandfather, reaching out with fat little hands. He raised the covered tray high in the air. "No. Not for you."

He extended the gift in her direction. "For you."

The shapechanger lifted the basket and the bird rose in the air as if it were shucking the jute with its wings. It came to rest on the teacher's shoulder, looked about at the gaping faces, then flapped a mad, scarlet course out the window, toward the sky. The children shouted and clapped their hands as it flew off toward the sun.

"You are sick with this woman," Yorumbo said, clucking his tongue.

"Yes," Don Victor replied.

Yorumbo shook his head. "You come speaking riddles, pacu. You say you are speaking the truth. But it is not so. There is no truth on this earth. Truth comes when we enter our spirit creatures, or when we die. All those truths you think you are telling one another are only secrets about lust."

"I'm tired of it, sumiruna. I don't recognize my own family. I can't imagine how we got where we are."

"Something happens when a person speaks his heart, pacu. Others measure themselves against it. They want what that person has—they long to feel what he feels, or love as he loves, or speak as freely as he has spoken. Soon they all speak their secrets. That is the plague of tongues. And then, when all the secrets are out, when the past is cracked open, people want more. That is what you are doing with the teacher, pacu. Chasing the want. It is not truth. It is not love. It is a plague of hearts."

There was a long silence before they spoke again. The shapechanger did not ask to take the vine, or drink the stones, or fly like his spirit creature. He was there to talk, and the two of them passed a pipeful of *mapacho* and carried on, until the conversation came full circle.

"You surprise me, pacu," said the witchman. "I would never have guessed a man of your age and wisdom to chase after butterflies and parrots." Then he went on to deliver the lesson Don Victor would mull over for days: "You talk about nothing but that teacher. So much talk. You must remember: She is a passing thing, like a feather on a burst of wind. Your head is full of confusion, pacu. You speak about truth as if it were light—bright as the eye of that shine you are making. But truth is a stone, heavier than love. Only the spirits can carry it.

"One thing more," Yorumbo said, putting a hand on Don Victor's shoulder. "You say you can see through your paper. But that kind of seeing means nothing. A man sees through water and air, doesn't he? Just as a man sees through water to find a fish, just as he sees through air to find a bird, you must see past your shine to find what your heart really hungers for. The burden of your paper, pacu, is that it will force you to look elsewhere."

Once he arrived in Pucallpa, Jaime made his way to a tumbledown warehouse owned by Maximo Huamán, a bagmaker who was one of Floralinda's best customers. Maximo told him about Alfonso Suárez, a businessman in Lima who represented small factories and haciendas along the coast. Although Maximo added that Suárez skimmed hefty percentages from every paper deal he facilitated, he was the only agent Maximo could think of who represented independent businesses. Jaime took down all the information carefully. Accepting a lift from a young engineer returning to Lima, he rode the asphalt highway from jungle to capital, his head filled with cellophane dreams.

The trip did not disappoint him. Alfonso Suárez was a little bullet of a man—bald, with a face like a rodent's and a formidable prow of teeth—but he turned out to be amicable, open to new opportunities, and surprisingly effective from the start. Suárez confirmed that no papermaker in Peru was producing cellophane. A number of companies—Country Club cigarettes, Farinelli candies, Donofrio ice cream—were paying a premium to buy it from foreign sources. As far as Suárez could determine, one outfit—Du Pont—held the monopoly and was charging exorbitant fees. That company was headquartered in Wilmington, Delaware, on the shores of the gringo sea. Within twenty-four hours Jaime had Suárez's assurances that he would represent the Sobrevillas, and, judging by the pliability and strength of the samples—he projected that Floralinda would undercut Delaware's prices and become Peru's primary supplier. After that, there were opportunities in Brazil,

Colombia, Ecuador. If the factory could expand, there was no limit to the future.

But two days later, Suárez outdid his promises. By then, he had contacted six manufacturers. If the Sobrevillas could maintain the quality of the samples, he told Jaime, if they could charge sixty percent of the American selling prices, if they could diversify with an array of colors and produce quantities in a timely fashion—they could expect to be given the business. According to his reckoning, a one-hundred-kilogram roll of cellophane could fetch twelve times the price of a similarly heavy roll of brown paper. Jaime imagined how pleased his father would be.

The rigors and prospects of commerce were not the only things on Jaime's mind as he made his way home from Pucallpa, traveling with his cohorts, scudding along in the swift current. Mingling with the weighty issues of factory output, rate of harvest, competitive pricing, was an unforgettable image: the naked girl with the cellophane braids. Gentle as a petal, the memory of those eyes, lips, skin lit on his mind's eye. He longed to see her again.

As his boat approached the tiny town of Resbaladera, he scoured the western bank for the girl and her black canoe. But the town came and went with no sign of her: only a cluster of small children sitting on a pier, staring back, motionless; behind them, a string of huts, perched on stilts. After that came an endless tangle of matapalo, a swoop of snowy heron, a cloud of pierid butterflies adrift in the sunlit woods. He had almost given up hope of seeing her when, about five miles north of Resbaladera, he saw a canoe jut from the shore like the spine of an alligator. She was squatting beside it, scraping the scales from a long silvery paiche, and the tiny, transparent disks flew from the fish like a fountain of airborne jewels.

His three men saw her too. One turned to the other, nodded toward the figure, and then, instinctively—as if they knew all along what he was hoping for—they shifted their oars and headed in her direction.

Jaime wondered whether she would recognize him; whether she would remember the box, the cellophane, their laughter. Suddenly, he was gripped with fear that she would plunge into the forest and disappear forever. "Ha-a-a!" he called, waving his arms like wings—up and down, up and down, as if he were marooned and she his only hope on the horizon.

She lowered her hand slowly, dropped the knife, and then her arms flew out from her sides, pumping the air vigorously. She leapt again and again, her sinewy legs springing under her so that her knees bounced high to her belly. As the boat drew toward her, she laughed and yelled words he could not understand. *"Iyat-su!"* she called out to him. *"Iyatsu! Iyatsu!"* Brother. Clansman. Boy.

Don Victor was not in a happy state of mind. If the thought of the teacher was making him dizzy, luring him into the ether, his thirty-seven-year marriage was pulling him back, exerting a force in the opposite direction. He loved Doña Mariana as one loves one's hands—the very thought of life without her was impossible. He stole glances at her as she sat knitting. Her firm mouth, large brown eyes, energetic fingers were so familiar: comforts to him, really. She was to life as furnace to factory—the active core, the source of heat without which little else would function. Watching her over the rim of his dog-eared journals, he marveled at her strength, her love of family, her loyalty, and he wished he could throttle the imp of desire, come down to earth again.

He took to laboring over mathematical equations, shouldering new problems, reckoning the magnitudes. Being an engineer, trained in the laws of physics, he knew something about pitting weight against weightlessness. He sat after dinner in the presence of his wife, and then, long into the night, he willed himself to think of Marcela as a fleeting force field—electric, magnetic. As a feather on a burst of wind. She was, he told himself, no more than a temporal infatuation: an unwanted, discomfiting vertigo. He would remedy the foolishness by pondering, a pastime with a decidedly downward motion, a verb that wears gravity on its back.

So it was that Don Victor became suddenly, alarmingly proficient at pulling sad images from memory, heaving them forward, worrying them until wee hours of day. He took out the old monkey fortune he kept in a child's wallet, safe in the far corner of a drawer, and contemplated its warning that someday he would face something dire. Was there anything

more dire, he reflected, than living in this wilderness, subject to raven-
ing beasts, to flood, to the random will of the river? Was there anything
more dire than the miseries he had suffered in Trujillo: the loss of a
father, the family's cruel snub of his mother, the heartbreaking death of
his beloved sister? Was there anything more odious, for that matter,
than his own abandonment of his responsibilities?

He recalled his mother's face the day he sailed from Trujillo to Lima
to begin his studies at the School of Engineers. Doña Angélica had
accompanied him to the port and walked with him to his ship, trying
to impress upon him that he had an obligation to his family. "If I'm
sending you off, Victor, it is for an education. I want you to come back
and put all that knowledge to good use. I expect you to excel at your
studies, abide by the rules, and, four years from now, I want you home.
I want you to find a good wife, settle down in your father's house, and
make your future in Trujillo."

"Don't worry, Mamá. I'll be back. You can be sure of it." But, after
that morning on the dock, he had never seen her again.

Twenty years later, his brother Alejandro had sent a terse letter to
Floralinda, written on the magnificent desk he had appropriated from
Victor. Their mother was dead. She had been the casualty of a military
maneuver. By Alejandro's account, the army had marched into Trujillo
to suppress a rebellion. The generals claimed that the workers had been
training at night with rifles, when they weren't out laboring in the cane
fields. Soldiers were ordered to round them up, tear open their shirts,
and arrest anyone with bruised shoulders or callused trigger fingers. *The
army was just doing its duty,* Alejandro wrote. *We can't have laborers running around with guns, for Christ's sake.* The Army of the Republic proceeded to march the unruly peons to the dunes, whipping their backs
with pistols. When Doña Angélica heard of it, she ran out of the house
to protest, but by then the city was swarming with workers, shouting
and brandishing machetes. She had just reached the boulevard when
six army trucks released soldiers into the foray, waving their rifles in the
air. In the chaos, Alejandro was told afterward, the butt of a rifle struck
her head. She died instantly. Alejandro closed the letter saying that she
was now buried in the vault next to Don Carlos. Over the body of their
little sister.

Don Victor had reeled with grief. For weeks, his mother's tiny face had loomed before him, and for weeks, he could hear her voice, imploring him to come home. He was pondering again the weight of that filial betrayal when he heard a gentle rap at the door. The clock told him it was near midnight. Surely everyone in the house was asleep. Perhaps it was an errant bat, lost in the dark. He raised his chin from his hands. *"Pase, si es humano!"* Enter, if you be human.

Father Bernardo was suddenly there, in the shadow of the doorway. "Victor!" he said warmly. "I was taking the night air, reveling in God's creation, when I saw the candle in your window. May I sit with you awhile?" The padre had come to lighten the ballast, as Doña Mariana had begged him to do.

That night, they spoke of many things Don Victor had never discussed with anyone but his own wife: about the gypsy caravan with the whirling knives and the terrible death of Chína; about Don Carlos's ignominious end on the threshold of his lover; about Doña Angélica's death at the hands of the Peruvian military.

"Blessed Jesus!" Padre Bernardo said, when he learned about Don Victor's mother. "That's horrible!"

"It is. I never saw her again. The army killed her without so much as a wasted bullet. Had I been in Trujillo as I promised I would be, perhaps it never would have happened. Had I been there and it *had* happened, I certainly would have known better than to bury her alongside my father. It was the last thing that poor woman wanted."

"You can't blame yourself for *that*, friend."

But Don Victor just sat there, staring into the dark of the window. "To tell you the truth, Padre," he said finally, "I had put the whole sad business out of mind until tonight."

"Why do you think that is?"

"Because I have a powerful urge to stray, Father Bernardo. The only way I can fight it is to weigh myself down with such memories."

The priest frowned, but Don Victor sailed ahead, unable to contain the truth now. "I've been to my shaman, you know."

"Yes. Your wife makes a point of telling me," the padre said, sighing. "You know how I disapprove of that, Victor. Mumbo jumbo will only cloud your mind."

"No, Bernardo. Yorumbo's medicine actually helps me to think more clearly. Just the other day, he told me that there are three things that weigh most heavily on a heart: truth, which is impossible for us to carry; love, because it is far greater than desire; and clarity, for it forces us to see the world."

"He has a point."

"But there is something that weighs even more, Padre."

"What is that?"

"Sin. Although I wouldn't have known how to tell Yorumbo what sin means in the context of his culture. Simple, ordinary sin."

Sunday, in the early afternoon, Graciela and Louis Miller strolled along the path that divided the hemp from the cotton. It was a gray ribbon of dirt, rutted by the traffic of handcarts that shuttled between field and factory. Macaques scampered back and forth across it, their leathery fingers picking at seeds.

The two ambled slowly, surveying the open field, talking about inanities, feeling the buoyancy in their hearts. Earlier, when they had set out on their walk toward the wild orchids by the river, Louis Miller had asked where her husband was and she had responded with surprising candor: About Nestor's abuses. About his banishment from the hacienda. About the scene with the knife, years before. Her heartbreaking admission had hung there like a yoke, binding Miller to her solitude. Registering the effect of her words, Graciela turned the conversation to superficialities. Now that the mood had lightened, so had the freight on his heart.

"I seldom walk here," Graciela said, "but it's lovely, isn't it? You see how the monkeys come when the men aren't here? It's so much more peaceful on Sundays. So much prettier a place." She pointed out to where the butterflies lingered over the hemp in a shivering cloud of yellow. "Look at how many there are! It's the female flower that attracts them."

There were thousands of butterflies, dipping and soaring in concert, a furling carpet of life. The plants were waist-high and full—two days from harvest. "Even hemp has its genders," he said. "And—wouldn't you know?—the female is sweeter. Nature is sensible that way."

She laughed so merrily that he turned to look, taking in her loveliness. She was beaming, her eyes lit with a girlish joy. "Do you ever leave this place, Graciela?" he said. "Do you ever get away?"

"I go north to Iquitos once in a while, but the trip back is always hard, and I don't like leaving the children for long."

"But they have their cousins and their aunts to mind them."

"I know. But I am not a restless person, Luis. I don't mind staying in one place. As long as I have my music. As long as I have my family."

He thrust his hands into the pockets of his white linen jacket and searched for something to say. A flock of papagayos swooped low over the cotton, then banked swiftly toward the far wall of forest.

"The teacher," he said finally. "Did you say she is from Iquitos?" He drew out the slip of brown paper the woman had handed him across the table.

"Marcela? Yes," Graciela responded. "She's a very good teacher. Iquitos is known for its schools."

"She may be excellent, but she obviously doesn't know English. Actually, I'm relieved she couldn't read this filth."

"What do you mean?"

He flicked the paper in the air between them. "The note from the Australian. Thank God she didn't understand a word of it."

"But he was only asking to borrow a book!"

"That isn't what it says."

"Oh!" Graciela shook her skirt, dispatching a winged flurry of insects. "Why did you lie?"

"It was a polite lie. The note was crude."

"Read it to me!" She stood with her hands on her hips.

"I couldn't possibly." He thrust the paper into his pocket, took her hand, and kissed it.

It was brief, but she could feel his breath on her fingers. She took his arm and they walked down to where the yellow casuarinas grew. She pointed out places where she had played as a child. She told him about how she had loved to dance for as long as she could remember: the flamenco, the bolero, the waltz. She confided in him about her love for her mother and father, her worry about her brother's marriage, her admiration for her sister's mind. He, in turn, spoke about his family in Chicago. His father had been a banker, well-to-do until he lost everything in the Great Depression. One night, when Louis was twelve, his father kissed him on the head, went to bed, and never woke up again. They said it was a heart attack, but as they carried him away the boy saw the vial of pills on the bedside table. It wasn't discussed, but he always suspected suicide. In time, his mother remarried and had three more children, but they were much younger—he hardly knew them. Now they were scattered across the United States of America, with houses and children of their own.

"Why aren't *you* married, Luis?" Graciela asked him.

"I suppose because it never occurred to me. I've been infatuated with women, but never enough to marry. I like my freedom," he said.

Ambling under the stately trees her father had planted twenty years before, she showed him the spot where Basadre was buried and told him about the coughing dog, the blue boy, and her sense that those deaths had signaled a shift in her world's alignment. So many strange things had followed: the padre's confession, Belén's yearning for a baby, Doña Mariana's behavior at the dinner table. And then, of course, there was the arrival of Louis Miller himself, like the opening of a new day. They stepped into the shade and continued their conversation, less now for words than for what went unspoken. He reached a hand from his pocket to pluck a bright red begonia from the edge of a sea of ferns, and when he did so, the note flew into the air. Neither of them noticed. They were too busy looking at each other. When he handed her the flower, her face shone like a lambent sun.

The expression on Graciela's face did not escape the men at Chincho's.

The bar was filled with customers. The morning had been hot. The women had returned to the shacks from Padre Bernardo's ten o'clock Mass, sending their husbands in the other direction, looking for male company and a long, stiff drink. The fat bartender scurried back and forth to the tables, wielding trays of corn liquor and sweeping men's salaries into his apron pocket. Perspiration trickled from his neck. He might not have noticed had the men not commented so loudly: the gringo kissing Graciela's hand. The Australian barge captain slapped the table when he saw it, and they all turned to watch La Bella Morada and her suitor walk down the path arm in arm like two boulevardiers. The captain snorted, the men snickered, but they couldn't take their eyes off that spectacle of the heart. They downed their *chicha,* measuring themselves against the love, wanting what another man has, feeling their giddiness rise.

10

Perhaps it was the weight of so many decorations, perhaps it was the responsibility of being an officer in President Odría's army, but on the morning General José Antonio López turned onto the path that led to the Sobrevilla house, his range of vision was down. He was a little barrel of a man, his modest height belying a hearty appetite for power. He moved quickly, lips twitching with intent, eyes fixed on the ground, marking his own advance. His small hands were clasped behind, and as he made a mental count of Victor Sobrevilla's violations, he marked each by stretching a finger—until all ten were taut as talons on a bird of prey.

He had heard of Floralinda as far away as Iquitos. Traders had told him about it: a real hacienda with a factory, fields of crops, and a full-fledged business up and down the river. The man who owned it was known as the shapechanger. Not only did he have all the magic of a shaman, he was as rich as God.

General López made discreet inquiries about the Sobrevilla business, and as he and his men pushed upriver from Iquitos to Pucallpa, he jotted the information down in a spiral notebook stamped with the flag of Peru. He was contemplating the fact that he had filled no less than sixty-eight pages with incriminating evidence when a slip of brown paper trapped between two fronds of a fern, tight to the soil, caught his attention. He bent down and picked it up. There were words on it, scrawled in an uneven hand—black and angular, like a row of ill-tempered vultures. *Dear Marm,* it read, *I'd like to snug my mug in your rug.* But since the sentence was unintelligible, written in a language he did not understand, he did not know what to make of it. He shrugged his shoulders and stuffed it into his pocket. It wasn't often one came across epistolary matter in the jungle.

There would be more that was unfamiliar: the mansion, for instance, which loomed like a wood behemoth over its thick, black stilts. And then there was the lovely young woman pacing the patio, peering over the low brick wall in the general direction of his ship. She was delicate, nervous as a sparrow. Lace ruffles circled her wrists and throat. Her dress was silk—a pale shade of yellow, long to her ankles—the type ladies wore in the city. Her high-heeled shoes were brown leather, with straps and an open toe. She was so absorbed that she didn't notice him until his boots were heavy behind her.

"Ay!" she said, whirling, her hands flying to her face. Her eyes were the color of amber, skin as translucent as china, lips like an open berry.

"Buenos dias, señorita," he said, and doffed his hat in greeting. She raised briefly to her toes.

"Buenos dias," she answered. It was a small voice—high and reedy, and he was reminded of his cousin in Lima, a refined woman with the face of a porcelain doll. She had been educated in a Swiss finishing school. Never married.

"Permit me to introduce myself, señorita," he said. "My name is José Antonio López. I am a general in the Army of the Republic. In charge of the Fifth Military Region. I have come to speak with the engineer Victor Sobrevilla Paniagua. This is, I presume, his domicile?"

"Yes, General. This is Don Victor's house and I am his daughter-in-law, Elsa Márquez de Sobrevilla—"

"Ah!" he interrupted. "You are a señora. Forgive me, you look so young."

She was struck by the formality of his language, the manliness of his shoulders, the impeccable creases in his trousers, the dark green jacket hung with medals and red and gold braid. For a fleeting moment she thought he was the one she had been waiting for—her father's agent, come to rescue her at long last. It would not have been the first time the Márquez dynasty had sought help from the military. But no. Slowly, she brought the palms of her hands together. "I'm pleased to make your acquaintance, señor, but I'm afraid I will disappoint you. Don Victor is not here. He left in his canoe early this morning. His wife, Doña Mariana, has gone off to church, as she does every day."

Elsa had garnered this information when the maid came up less than half an hour before, bringing breakfast. She had been relieved to wake up and find her husband's side of the bed undisturbed. Since Jaime's return from Pucallpa, he had been outwardly civil, especially in front of the children, but every night, he had retired to another room in the house. He had come home a different man. Now they were operating with a new understanding—as if the truth about them were so transparent that no explanations were necessary.

The general tapped his sides in frustration. Politely, Elsa led him to the table under the potted cherimoya, and once he was comfortably in a chair, he told her why he had come.

He was making a sweep of the lower Ucayali, he explained—a cadastral survey. President Odría, head of state and chief general of the army, had begun a new program to monitor the cultivation and harvest of all coca leaf in Peru. Henceforward, every grower, every hacienda, and even the occasional farmer would have to register his crops with the military junta and turn over control to designated army officers. The army would return a fair market price, but the generals—not the growers—would be in charge of subsequent use and sales. All this had been determined carefully by the president's Centro de Altos Estudios Militares in Lima, and a Coca Monopoly had been duly recorded and blessed "by that apotheosis of international fairness, the newly formed United Nations." He looked at Elsa to reassure himself that she understood. "Dear lady, forgive me for pressing a point that may be entirely obvious to the cosmopolitan woman you seem to be, but when I say the United Nations I'm not talking about a cabal of a few heads. Do you know that that august body is attended by the highest ranks of more than one hundred independent countries?"

But he didn't wait for an answer. The general went on to say that he had been making a routine survey of the army's many thousands of hectares of coca cultivation along the Ucayali when, by chance, he had learned that the owner of Floralinda was also a grower. He wondered why no one had bothered to inform the army operatives in Iquitos or Tingo María. The announcements of the new policy had been made on January 1, 1950—more than two years before.

"I don't know the answer to that," Elsa said, still standing. She was impressed with General López's elegant turns of phrase. It wasn't often the river tossed up men with such command of the language. She told him that the hacienda grew coca and cannabis, but they did not sell either crop. The cannabis—or hemp—provided fiber for Don Victor's paper. The coca, on the other hand, was traded, sometimes for provisions, sometimes in exchange for work. Many of the laborers in Floralinda were from tribes upriver in the jungle highland—*coqueos*, accustomed to chewing the leaf.

"Of course, señora," the general said grandly. "I know very well that people in the interior have chewed coca since the days of the Inca. They need it to lighten the hunger, lighten the burden, lighten the agony of a racing heart. It's as integral a part of the Andean tradition as *vin du pays* to Burgundy!"

He could see he was making an impression. He put an elbow on the table and leaned in for full effect. He told her then that the Coca Monopoly had ancient antecedents. When Jesuit priests ruled the Amazon, they claimed a percentage of every farmer's harvest, dividing all arable land into two parts: the fields of God, whose harvests belonged to the Church, and the fields of man, which a farmer could plant for his own profit. The arrangement had assured the Church a lucrative income. President Odría's new law was an elegant variation of the same concept: Under the Coca Monopoly, all coca would grow in the fields of God, except that God was now the government. "The installation of the government's Coca Monopoly, dear madam, is simply a new precaution being taken by an enlightened man. Our president is a brilliant general. A man of energy. Finally, we are setting things straight in this country."

The fields of God! Elsa was convinced she was in the presence of the sort of splendidly uniformed man her father so often invited to his table. "President Odría, yes!" she offered pertly. "I believe I've heard the name!"

He studied her, absorbing the possibility that a civilized woman in a fancy dress might actually not know the name of her president. "You are from along this river, señora?"

"Oh, no!" She laughed. "My family is in Trujillo. My father is Alberto Márquez y Márquez."

Márquez . . . Márquez. He tapped the table, trying to place the name. "Sugar?" he said finally, his eyes widening.

"Sugar," she confirmed, and then folded her hands and smiled.

The general looked at the woman with new appreciation. What on earth was the daughter of a sugar magnate doing in a remote swamp? But then he registered a slight strabismus, a lack of focus in the eyes. There was something odd about her demeanor. Beautiful, but odd. Who knew what circumstances had brought her here?

He explained that his boat, the *Augusto Leguía,* would be traveling downriver to Requena, Nauta, and points north, but eventually it would return. "It goes without saying, señora," he added, thinking how long it had been since he had seen such an enchanting face, "that it would be a pleasure to see you again." The last time he had had a woman was when his soldiers dragged one out of a rancid brothel, the back of her hair in knots. But this Elsa Márquez de Sobrevilla, in her yellow silk and lace ruches, was the very picture of freshness.

He stood abruptly and asked when the master of the house was expected, but she only shrugged and said she didn't know. Maybe tonight. Maybe tomorrow. The general clicked his boots, in European fashion, and bowed solemnly from the waist. He donned his hat and thrust his hands in his pockets. "Oh," he said, "one more thing. Could this be yours?" He handed her the missive he had rescued from the dirt. Then he put a forefinger jauntily to the rim of his hat, smiled broadly, and departed.

The general's parting words drove Elsa into the house, trying to parse their meaning. Having absented herself from dinner the night the Australian barge driver's note had been passed across the table to Louis Miller, she didn't know the history of the paper in her hand. When she tried to read it, she understood nothing, except perhaps the capital *I*, which she had learned somewhere along the way as the first-person pronoun in English.

"Could this be yours?" he had said. Was the courtly general *presenting* the note to her, as in: Might these thoughts be your thoughts too? Or did he believe that it already *belonged* to her, as in: Here is your property; I recognize the mark. The first interpretation was certainly possible, but the second was not. He couldn't have been *returning* it to her (or to them, if you happened to read it in the plural—*you* meaning the entire household), since the note was certainly not hers nor was anyone in the house capable of writing an English sentence.

She knocked on the library door and asked Belén for the English dictionary. "English?" Belén said, frowning. "What on earth for?" But she handed it to her anyway. Elsa carried the massive tome upstairs to her little desk by the window. She took a pen and a sheet of paper from the drawer and smoothed the note so that it lay flat before her.

Dear was easy enough: It meant *querida*, as in *mi querida señora*, the greeting used in any civilized letter. *Marm* was harder. There was no entry in the dictionary remotely like it, save *marmalade*. Why would anyone be called such a thing? *I'd* was problematic for the odd diacritic that followed the pronoun, but the next word, *like*, was easily translated: *parecido*, meaning similar or the same. She made a note to herself of the secondary meaning, the verb: to be fond of. *Snug* meant to be happily sheltered—an informal, dialectal usage. *My mug* was the same as *my cup*, but without a saucer. *In* was *adentro*, inside. *Your rug* was *tu alfombra*, your carpet.

She paused to consider her translation: *Dear Jam, I am similar to shelter my cup inside your carpet.* It hardly made sense. Could it be: *Dear Jam-like person* (meaning sweet), *I am like a cup, resting upon your carpet?* She wrote that out on a fresh page, held it up, studied it. Yes, perhaps that was it. However, when she recalled the general's behavior on the patio—his formal comportment, his verbal embellishments—she concluded that she was being too literal. She was sure he was a complicated, subtle man. He knew about *vin du pays*, after all. Perhaps, like her childhood tutor, a charming Burgundian with an imagination, the general was employing a playful mode of communication. ("Open that hard head of yours, *chérie!*" the Frenchman would say. "Think large! *Plus grand!*") Perhaps the general hadn't meant for the words to be read closely; perhaps he had meant her to read the imagery. She scratched out the sentence, put the pencil to her chin. She needed to raise the level of her analysis. Forming each letter meticulously, she wrote down another translation: *Dear Sweetness, I am a chalice trembling on your threshold.* Yes, better. She lifted her face to the window, and her eyes fell on the place where the path veered left then made a straight line toward the dock. Quivering with elation, she penned her final version: *Sweet madam, my boat awaits you.*

The pieces fell into place after that. His inelegant stationery was easily understood: The dock was littered with brown scraps of paper, flung here and there as the heavy rolls were wheeled out to the barges. The nervous hand was obvious: He had composed his correspondence as he walked up the pathway. The motive was not difficult to fathom: He may have stepped on these shores to carry out a cadastral survey, but seeing her from afar, he had added something to the agenda. Her Paris clothes, her studied grace—her west-coast elegance—had won his fastidious heart.

Fueled by her mad discovery, she began to fashion a plan.

Between the last bolt of brown paper and the first bolt of cellophane, Floralinda hung in a kind of limbo, lingering between old and new. Don Victor, Jaime, and Ignacio busied themselves with changes in the production process. The pulp had to be finer, the cooking time longer. More caustic soda was needed for the digesters. A curing stage became essential: A giant tub was constructed so that the cellulose could soak in carbon disulfide and reach the necessary thickness. The headbox had to be refitted with flattened nozzles; Don Victor fashioned them himself from old valves salvaged from Mr. Meiggs's machinery. The Fourdrinier needed additional sprinklers and trays to bathe the viscose as it sped over the suction roll into the presses and dryers. Each change needed trial and preparation, and the strong spirit of patience.

There was more marking a kind of limbo. Don Victor saw the object of his fantasies everywhere: trotting up and down the stairs with his grandchildren, grading penmanship notebooks on the patio, strolling the fields in late afternoons with the laughing dog. One day, as he was tinkering with the controls on the factory's cookers, he watched her walk briskly down the road toward the barges. Approaching tentatively from behind the huge ball digester, he heard her summon one of his dockworkers. "Señor!" she called out. "I have a question."

"*Sí, señorita,*" the worker said, removing his hat.

"The tall Australian captain," she said, "does he drive his barge through here every week? Or every other week?" The man scratched his head and confessed he didn't know. "*Ay, ya,*" she said, clearly disappointed. Squatting there, by the belly of his iron vat, Don Victor watched her pout all the way back to his house, twitching her siren's tail. And so, between hard days at the factory, forced memories of old family tragedies, and regular visits to Yorumbo, Don Victor hovered at the frontier of longing, weighing the burden of sin.

Marcela was flattered by her master's ogling, but she didn't take it seriously. She was grateful, however, for the greater epiphany it had given her: that under her glasses, her careful guise, lurked a beauty of epochal proportions. She spent her off-hours recalling Jaime's words about her buttocks, turning this way and that in front of a mirror, wondering about the conversations that took place at Chincho's tables. In this, she found herself dwelling especially on the unmistakable attentions of the gruff man who called himself John Gibbs.

It had started with his notes. The bits of paper had begun to appear on her weekly trips to the dock when she went to fetch mail from the barges. She had hardly noticed him until the day he thrust the first one in her direction. Crumpled, hastily scribbled and folded, it told her that at least he was a literate man. There were few who could read and write on that river. And although, when he spoke, he only managed a pidgin— complete with droll winks and exaggerated gestures—he tried to communicate as best he could. When his barge docked in Floralinda, he brought letters and small packages up to the house to save her the effort of coming down in the early mornings. Shy and unkempt, he would wait by the casuarinas, shuffling his big boots. When she saw him there, she would amble toward him, summoning every phrase of English she had ever heard along the dock of her native city: "Welcome!" "Heave ho!" "Cigarette?" "Chiclet?" Marcela was biding her time about the Australian, wondering when he would make his next move.

Doña Mariana, too, was in a kind of limbo. She headed for church earlier every morning, eager to look on the padre's face and contemplate his life drama. Here was a man who had wrestled demons—who had tasted temptation, fallen in sin, but managed to put Satan behind him. He hadn't succumbed to his appetites entirely, as her father had, but walked a hard road to redemption. Sometimes she would lose track of her rosary and simply stare at his pink face in the distance, his lips moving in prayer. "You know, *querido,*" she said one night as she poured a glass of oloroso for her husband, "ever since the padre unburdened himself about that woman, I feel drawn to him like a sister. I can't say that I understand it—never having had a brother—but it's true."

Louis Miller stayed on in Floralinda, using the excuse that he needed to recalibrate his instruments. He laid his metal stands and measuring devices out on a tarp and checked each methodically. He borrowed oil from Don Victor's workshop and reconditioned his motor. Every evening, after dinner, he would sit on the patio with Graciela and tell her about life in America, about his travels around the globe. Graciela, for her part, would enter the house tense after these conversations, and end the day at the piano, improvising chord progressions. So monotonous, so relentless was her playing that Don Victor would rise from his bed, stomp to the edge of the second-floor landing, and command her—for the sake of Jesús, José, and Santa María—to stop all that racket at once.

In those days of suspense and transition, Ignacio did not dare reach out to the other side of his hermetically made bed, but he would linger in Belén's library, study her shelves, choose books by her favorite authors, and bring them upstairs so that she could read aloud to him. She would sit beside him in bed and read the tales of Ricardo Palma, the poetry of Sor Juana, until his eyelids drooped. When she saw that he was asleep, she would close her book and stroke his hair into the night.

Elsa wrote letters to her cousins, saying that she would soon see them in Trujillo. It was a matter of arranging a military escort, she explained, but she had made contact with a simpatico general in the

Army of the Republic, and it was only a matter of time before he bore her to safety on the *Augusto Leguía*. She made no mention of her husband or children.

Jaime found reasons to set out on the river. Twice he traveled to Contamana to buy barrels of caustic soda from a soapmaker, although he might have asked any worker in the hacienda to make the trip in his place. He insisted on going to Orellana alone to harvest long rashers of the dense wood paxiuba, which were needed to construct the acid vats. Once, in the dark hour of a morning, as he pulled his boat onto the shore where the girl waited, he thought he saw his father on a nearby bank, pushing off in the opposite direction. Realizing that Don Victor had just made a visit to Yorumbo, Jaime wondered whether the girl, too, had seen him. There was no way to ask her the question.

Boruba dreamed of having a child by Pedro but was too shy to do anything but pace the frontier between hope and initiative. She would see him hard at work, planting a new row of cotton. She would wave at him from the distance, wondering when he would stand in her doorway again, and with what new surprise. Pedro, for his part, waved back over a sea of hemp, knowing there was more he could do to make her laugh again. Much, much more, if only he could get all the planting done. What wouldn't he do to see her smile, watch her lovely, round body tremble with pleasure, make her forget the dead?

So it was that the residents of Floralinda lingered between the known world and paradise, longing to close out one life, breathe in another. Padre Bernardo called it prayer. Yorumbo called it purification. To Don Victor it was merely good science: A cellophane maker needs time to adapt the valves, adjust the solutions, refit the machinery. Once he is ready, the rest follows naturally. He mixes the hemp with the cotton and acid. He adds the water and heat. He cooks down the nature, flattens it out, renders the whole thing transparent. And then he steps through to the other side.

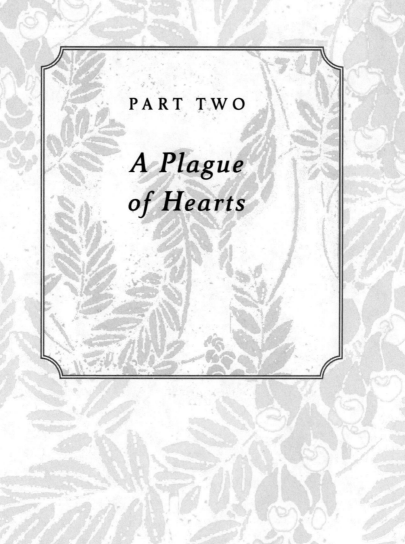

PART TWO

*A Plague
of Hearts*

11

The Virgin of Copacabana was covered with feathers and beads. Long black hair streamed from her head. A cape of dried yellow casuarina flowers was draped around her shoulders and a brightly woven Jesus sprang from her breast. Flickering in the dim light of the candles were bits of cellophane, twisted into her straw skirt. With a brass sun above and a tin moon beneath, she was resplendent, glorious. Don Victor felt a sudden sense of well-being—that feeling of comfort that would come when his mother made her way through the dark, kissed him good night, and said the Virgin was hovering above, watching him. Here she was, with her palms reaching out, as if he were a long-lost prodigal.

Padre Bernardo looked up from his desk, which was little more than a wood plank to one side of the altar. When he saw the papermaker, he rose slowly, like hope through a weary heart. "Good afternoon," Don Victor whispered, and bowed slightly from the waist, as was his habit. He took a seat in the front pew and leaned in with his fists on his knees. "We never did build you a proper presbytery, did we? Here you are with your desk still in the church."

"No, Victor. I count myself fortunate. You built me a fine church with a floor eight feet from the ground—the floods and the termites have a long way to travel before they reach my sandals." He smiled.

"Your Madonna has blossomed," Don Victor said, nodding toward the Virgin. "I almost didn't recognize her."

"Yes! The people dress her. The women are always making her things, weaving her clothes. The hair is from Filomena, the seamstress; she cut off her own two braids to make it. Those baubles you see, some are real silver. Travelers on the river come to ask her blessing and, before they go, they festoon her with offerings. She's well loved, our Virgin."

"She is magnificent, my friend. It makes my heart glad to see her. Especially, as you can imagine, adorned with my paper."

"Ah. That is the work of Boruba and your gardener. I came in one afternoon and saw them threading those bits into the *chuchería*. Very pretty, don't you think?"

The image of Boruba and Pedro spending afternoons together flitted past like a bothersome gnat. The cook had grieved the death of her grandson for months, but lately Don Victor had seen her coming from the crop fields, flushed and animated. Something was going on. Experience had taught him that managing a hacienda was like steward-ing a large family. Life got in the way. He was reminded of Pepe, one of his best workers—a man he could always count on to mash pulp to the right consistency. His wife had caught him in flagrante with another woman and chased him from Floralinda, a knife swinging over her head. Don Victor never found another pulp masher to match him.

"May I ask," the priest said, "to what I owe the pleasure of your visit? It's been years since you last set foot in this church."

With the startled look of a man who has wandered into a room and suddenly forgotten his purpose, Don Victor turned back to the padre. "Yes, yes," he said. "I'm here for two reasons, Bernardo. The first is to ask you to bless the new cellophane production when the factory starts up next week. It will mean a great deal to the laborers, and, naturally, it will mean a great deal to me."

"Of course, Victor."

"The second reason is that I want to have a more personal conver-sation with you, if you will allow it."

"Ah!" said the Franciscan, leaning in. "You have come to talk about sin."

"No, Padre. I have managed quite well with that, thank you. It takes effort, but I have a strong will. This is a different, more pressing matter."

Don Victor reached under his vest and drew something from his pocket. It was a tattered antique wallet, from which he plucked a tiny scrap of pink paper, creased and worn thin by time. It looked, to the padre, like a child's prayer card.

"I have carried this document for forty-eight years. This is what led me to the Virgin of Copacabana, and it was she, as you very well know, who led me to you. So, as I see it, this little relic is the reason you and I are sitting together today. Now that we are on the verge of a new venture in this hacienda, I want to start fresh, make a clean breast of things. I bring it to you in full view of our Virgin."

"Are you here to make confession, Victor?"

Don Victor hesitated. "Well, no. I've come to tell you the truth, that's all."

"Ah. I see. The truth."

"Yes, Padre."

"*Ya, bueno.* I won't stop you. But I'll tell you that I'm a bit alarmed by this new compulsion to speak one's mind. Not least my own. It's as if Satan himself had got his hands on our commandment not to lie and is wagging it in our faces, making a mockery of it. A man who divulges a long-held secret is not necessarily a man who tells the truth—he never has been and never will be."

"I agree with you, Padre. I've said as much to my family. And, if it makes any difference, my curandero has said the same. I'm not here to tell you of scandals or secrets. I simply want you to know what brought us together."

"Hmm," the padre said, folding his arms and sitting back in his chair.

"I didn't learn of the Virgin of Copacabana from the nuns at the Convent of Santa Clara."

"No? Well, you certainly didn't learn about her from your curandero. That's a prayer card you're holding, isn't it?"

"No. It's a gypsy fortune, handed to me by a monkey—a macaque, to be precise."

The priest raised his eyebrows. Don Victor proceeded to tell him about Negrita, the toy cathedral, and the dwarf who held court in Trujillo's main square every Sunday.

"And you've come now, after all these years, to tell me that you built this church and supported my work here only because a monkey—a macaque, to be precise—told you to do it?"

"I do not doubt the power of the Virgin," Don Victor said quietly. "I never have."

"But what you are holding is devil's work. That gypsy hocus-pocus is nothing more than idolatry."

"Please, Padre. You have been, for better or worse, my family's spiritual adviser for twenty-two years now."

The priest raised his hand. "I have been the padre of your hacienda, Don Victor. I have blessed your paper. I have married your children. I have baptized your grandchildren. This is the first you've ever asked my advice. I am your spiritual adviser? Fine. You know I will not refuse you my guidance. But if you have come with a gypsy fortune expecting me to tell you what I think, you must be prepared to hear me."

"Good. I accept your conditions." Don Victor quickly handed the priest the paper.

Padre Bernardo sighed, took the fragile pink scrap, and began to read. Don Victor watched him intently. The priest's eyes widened when he came to the part that said the gentleman would prevail if he prayed to the Virgin of Copacabana, but it wasn't with approval. He wanted to smack the prediction down on the wood and take this opportunity to counsel Don Victor on the wickedness of sorcery, the affront of seeing the Virgin's good name on a gypsy talisman, the dangers of visiting the curandero. Instead, he decided to open his heart to the poor, deluded man—listen. He did as he was told and read all the way through until the final warning: *There will come a day when you face something dire, for which you cannot prepare. When that hour comes, you have two choices: Fight with all your will; resist any failure. Or fly above it, see its God-given value, surrender to a greater force.*

He folded the paper and set it down on the table between them. "Smart monkey," he said. "Good advice."

"My question to you, Padre, is this: Have I reached that fateful day? I've carried this fortune for most of my life and I've never encountered anything—not even an arrow at my throat—that made me fear for my future. But suddenly I feel I am standing at the edge of a new world. Maybe it's the cellophane. On the one hand, it's a miracle. On the other hand, as I don't have to tell you, I will forfeit a great deal if this business doesn't thrive. That's why I'm asking: Do you think I stand, as this fortune suggests, at the verge of a terrible failure?"

The padre studied Don Victor's face. "You realize you are asking me to comment on a piece of paper that has nothing to do with God's plan."

"If God is great, this paper is part of His plan," said Don Victor sharply, tucking the fortune into the wallet.

"Yes, of course. But put your fate in the hands of God. Not in a heathen prediction."

"As I see it, I can be in both hands. God brought me the monkey, and the monkey brought me the Virgin. It's all one and the same, isn't it? The god of my curandero is your God is mine. As my aunt Esther used to say to me often during my childhood: In the face of magnificent creation, our symbols are paltry things."

"Victor," the padre said with impatience. "I don't have a crystal ball. What precisely do you want from me?"

"Your prayers, Bernardo. I don't know what will become of this venture—it's a big gamble. I am entrusting this entire hacienda and everyone in it to a vision I hold in my head. More than anything I've ever wanted in life for my family, for me, for this patch of God's earth, I want it to succeed. I want it to prosper."

It was suddenly clear to the priest that Don Victor believed in the power of the monkey prediction every bit as much as he did in the Virgin. He had brought it here, into the heart of his church, to ask the Almighty's protection against it. The audacity was breathtaking. Didn't he know that he couldn't have it both ways? On the one hand, his voodoo. On the other, his God? "I can pray for you, Victor," the priest said sternly, "but I cannot promise your cellophane will prosper. God does not bend to the desires of man."

Don Victor was craving success, anticipating the glory of producing cellophane in the Amazon, envisioning his factory on a poster in Señor Urrutia's workshop, complete with a boy's face pressed to the window. The curandero had been right. The plague of secrets had become a plague of want. It was not enough to have built the only paper factory in the rain forest, not enough to be known up and down the river as a shapechanger. Don Victor wanted the kind of fame written about in books, taught in schoolrooms, dreamed about by young men. He imagined himself as Eiffel incarnate, engineer of the impossible, builder against the void.

He tramped through his hacienda, surveying the land, barking orders to the laborers. He took to the fields to measure the height of the hemp. He hung Yorumbo's feathered ropes and magic gourds from poles around the newly planted cotton. At dusk, he could be seen inspecting the day's accomplishments, his wide-brimmed eucalyptus hat unmistakable in the distance, his boots digging into the mud. There was no doubt about what he wanted. The desire was so naked, so manifest and unremitting, that all Floralinda began wanting it too.

There was something more. His will in matters of sin was weakening. He had not foreseen the second plague, the virulence Yorumbo had predicted. So strong were Don Victor's desires that he began to forgo his heavy disciplines. He let his fantasies rise to whatever heights they would go. Within two days of his visit to the church, he was climbing the steps to the third floor of his house, with a bundle tucked under his arm. He found Marcela in the middle of a mathematics lesson. There, with her little breasts just discernible under her cotton blouse, she was perched on a high stool, holding up cards with numerals on them. Don Victor scooted the children out the door with the news that Boruba was making sweets in the kitchen. Then he turned to the teacher and commanded her, "Open this now. Put it on."

She blinked quickly behind her thick glasses. Running her tongue along the rim of her upper lip, she took the package from his hands. She pulled one end of the jute string, and the brown paper fell open to reveal something like a clump of dried grass. "Take it out! Take it out!" he said impatiently. "Put it on."

"But what is it, señor?" she asked, genuinely puzzled. She lifted it out with two fingers, as if it were the tail of a dead animal. In one rustling motion, it tumbled out and hung from her hand to the floor. It was a skirt of straw remarkably like the one that was tied around Padre Bernardo's Virgin, with bits of cellophane twisted into it. Her mouth agape, she turned to look at her master.

He was smiling down at her. If she had thought that his pranks with butterflies and parrots were passing fancies, harmless antics, she saw now that she had been wrong. There was hunger in his face. Slowly, she dropped the paper to the floor and drew the skirt toward her.

"That's right, that's right," he said. "Put it on."

She did as she was told and tied the brittle thing around her.

"Now take off those clothes you have under it."

She reached behind her back, undid the hooks, and pushed her cotton skirt down so that it fell to a heap around her ankles.

"Come, Marcelita," he said, but it was he who stepped forward. He slid his hand through the straw, between her legs. She drew a sharp breath as she felt his fingers, surprisingly gentle, skimming the bare skin, touching the pink heart of her cut. "I've been wanting this for a long time," he said.

It wasn't that this sort of thing hadn't happened before. Marcela's cousin—the one with the tobacco stains on his teeth—had done it when she was eleven. Her squat, porcine uncle with the stubby fingers had done it when she was fourteen. The government bureaucrat in Iquitos whose children she had tutored when she was just fresh out of teachers' school had done it whenever they were in a room alone together—put his hands on a number of her forbidden places. But in all of her two years in Floralinda, it had never occurred to her that Don Victor might do the same. He had always seemed so dignified, so aloof, so content in his person and marriage.

Still, it was intoxicating to have such a powerful man yearning for her—so hungry that he would climb the stairs in the middle of the day. And yet, even as he fondled the flower of her vagina, even as she grew wet with his resolve, Marcela had not wanted this. How would she ever look Doña Mariana in the eye? It had been Doña Mariana who had traveled to Iquitos, asked the nuns at her old school to recommend a young teacher, knocked at the door of her former employer and saved her from his unwanted attentions. And now here she was again, trapped between a man's fingers and her job. What could she do? Guilt mounted with pleasure. Don Victor's eyes were shut, his breathing heavy. When the children began clattering up the stairs again, she gasped with fear. He opened his eyes, withdrew his hand, and left, leaving her to scramble back into her clothes, bewildered.

For as long as she could remember, Marcela had liked the idea of sex—she loved exploring her most secret places. She loved to stroke herself, discover the precise touch that most delighted her. But whereas in Iquitos she had never thought of herself as particularly attractive, in Floralinda she began to feel the pleasures of a man's regard. Not the leers of the laborers with their snorts and grunts, but the open stare of a foreigner who longed for books. John Gibbs came to occupy that place in a young schoolteacher's heart that imagines what she might do for a man. He was awkward, even a little pathetic, and clearly in awe of her. He had taken to shaving, putting on clean shirts whenever he delivered the mail. Just that morning he had come with a stack of letters—several from the paper agent in Lima, two from Doña Mariana's sister, and one small package addressed to Belén in an elderly aunt's elaborate hand. What would John Gibbs think, Marcela wondered, if he knew that she was the object of Don Victor's peculiar fantasies, standing in her schoolroom with his fingers on her sex?

Belén hastily opened the little package from Tía Esther. With each passing week, she feared the octogenarian would make good on her promise and brave the long, perilous journey into the jungle. Every letter was happy confirmation that she was still sitting in the old *casona*. But this time the package contained more than a letter. There, with the familiar onionskin paper, was a red satin artifact, folded neatly in the shape of a triangle.

Trujillo, 1952

Dear Belén,

With this letter I send you a Chinese hat. Isn't it clever? So shiny and red, with its bright yellow tassel. It belonged to your great-great-grandfather Wong. He was my mother's father—the father of your

grandmother Angélica. Your father never heard about him from his
mother, because all Paniaguas were forbidden to mention his name.
Wong Hsing Tao. There. I have written it down. We cannot deny it
now. Perhaps Wong's hat will bring you a bit of magic.

When I get to Floralinda (God willing!) I will tell you more
about Old Wong, but here are a few things on paper to insure that I
don't lose my nerve. What you hold in your hands is Wong's
wedding hat. He wore it in Huarmey—a tiny village by the sea,
south of Trujillo, where he owned a dry-goods store. He married a
widow, a dour little woman, whose triumph of missionary work came
the day she saved him from Buddha. She was María Nazaret Botero,
shunned by society for marrying the coolie, although she came from
a fairly decent family in Cajamarca. In any case, as the story goes,
Wong loved the little missionary beyond reason, following her
everywhere, showering her with presents from Canton, which was
where he was from before a gang of Portuguese thugs hoodwinked
him into boarding a ship bound for this world. They sold Wong and
a boatful of two hundred Chinamen like him to a Peruvian hacienda.
Four months later they were disgorged onto the godforsaken guano
islands off the coast of Peru to mine birdshit so that the world could
have more soap, more fertilizer, more bombs. Your great-great-
grandfather was resourceful, however, and when he won his freedom
after ten years of indentured labor, he gathered enough money to
start a street stand in Huarmey, where he sold freshly slaughtered
chickens and smoked ducks. Eventually, it became a store, and then a
formidable street-corner emporium, the Palace of Wong, with pretty
trinkets shipped from his family in Canton.

Who knows what the appeal of the right-godly María Nazaret
was! Perhaps, as they say, those who rail against sin make for ardent
bed partners. In any case, there was copious evidence of their mutual
attraction: She gave him seven sons and one daughter. The baby girl
was at once a great blessing and their final undoing: A blessing,
because of her beauty, which was truly astonishing. But the undoing
is what this letter is about.

Her name was Catalina Wong, and she grew up to be my mother,
your father's grandmother. She was raised, according to Chinese

custom, in a sheltered environment, hardly seen, behind the high walls of Wong's corner compound, which by then he had transformed into a magnificent building with a red lacquer sign that arched over the door in the shape of a dragon.

My old aunt Carmen told me that my father, Homero Paniagua, fell in love with Catalina Wong by chance, when he saw her through a window. He was spending the night in Huarmey—a little rest stop on the long trip from Chiclayo to Lima. The first time he laid eyes on her face, Aunt Carmen said, he was sitting in his modest inn, looking out, with a cup of café con leche in his hand and a leather bag at his feet. A beautiful woman appeared at the door of the Palace of Wong, under the dragon. She crossed the street and walked one long block, directly in front of him, to church. She was lithe, graceful, with tiny hands, heartbreaking bow lips, and blue-black hair that trailed down the back of her immaculate white dress. For six more mornings, Homero Paniagua sat at that window and watched Catalina emerge from the store, go to church, and, an hour later, make the trip in reverse. It occurred to him that he should go to the Palace of Wong, look around, and see why the young woman always launched her daily ritual from those portals. But he was too shy to follow that impulse. On the seventh day, when he thought a decent enough interval of time had passed, he asked the innkeeper who the lovely girl was, only to learn that her father was Wong himself. The woman was Chinese! No more information was necessary. Homero Paniagua packed up his horse and set out for Lima. But the memory of Catalina's face haunted him, and four months later, on his way back to his family hacienda in Chiclayo, he conquered his shyness and approached Old Wong to ask for her hand in marriage. Wong didn't hesitate: He wanted a better life for his daughter, although he well understood the diabolical bargain under way. The rest of the story I assume you can deduce. Homero Paniagua confided in my aunt Carmen, his older sister, all the details of Catalina's ancestry, but he swore her to a lifetime of secrecy. He said nothing about Old Wong to his parents. He forbade his children any information about Catalina's family. There was a rule in the house that there were to be no questions.

Wong's wife, the missionary, died of sorrow, because she was not allowed to see her beautiful daughter again, and Wong, who loved his wife more than reason, ran out into the sea on the day she expired, claiming that he was swimming his way home to China. Naturally, he drowned. This hat, darling, is all that is left of him.

You live with such stories of your own out there in the jungle, I doubt that any of this will seem very strange. But hearing my mother tell me these things on her deathbed was as otherworldly an experience for me as any I had with Lars, under our great canopy of stars. Chinese? She might as well have told me we were descended from headshrinking cannibals. If my old aunt Carmen hadn't confirmed it all long after my mother and father were dead, I might never have believed it. Of course, as you well know, I have come to love the yellow blood that courses in our veins. I am smarter for it. Stronger. And so are you. To hell with the tea ladies in the Hotel de Turistas.

Faithfully, and with great affection,
Your very own Esther

Yorumbo knew that when the headshrinker's daughter went off in the early hours of morning, she was meeting the shapechanger's son. He had seen them from a distance, on the bank of the river, gazing silently out at the water. Once, as he slipped down to the river to catch fish for his woman, he had sensed something above him, and when he glanced up, the two young people were perched in a tree, murmuring to each other.

He had recognized the man from long-ago visits with his father—the pleasant, open face, the gentle black eyes, the sudden, irresistible smile. Yorumbo wondered at what point on the terrified girl's trip upriver she had met him. He wondered, too, at the magic that had come to pass. He himself had been its intermediary: He had given the Jivaro girl the puma knife, the box, the skin of diaphanous shine. Days later, she had appeared beside the son of the very person who had made them—as if the young man had been conjured by a spell. This was no coincidence.

Yorumbo knew that his spirit creature had revealed this to him as a gift. It was not something to be spoken of—sent ear to ear. He did not tell the Jivaro girl that he knew of her white visitor. And she, too, being a lone wanderer in a far artery of the universe, kept her new friendship to herself.

The Jivaro headman was weary. His hair was matted under his yellow cock-of-the-rock feathers, his face smudged with bird blood and black paint. Two long braids hung to his shoulders, plaited with a thick red string. Four *tsantsas* hung from his neck: three males, one female. He was known to his tribe as Mwambr, the Great Man, an *unt*. At his side was his fiercest warrior. Forty more warriors were dispersed behind, concealed by the trees, each with a blowgun and a full quiver of darts. They had been moving swiftly for countless sunsets, searching for the girl.

They stood at the lip of the forest, studying the termite people in the distance. An endless sprawl of bewildering humanity tumbled from the verge of the forest to the river. There were rows upon rows of dwellings on sticks, separated by winding paths. Through the maze they could see the water and the floating structures. The banks were stripped of all vegetation—lined with long, flat constructions, unlike any they had ever seen.

Mwambr put one hand over his eyes to shield them from the sun. He felt disoriented by the light. His eyes were no longer what they used to be—they were weak under the best circumstances—but this hunt for his daughter, which drew him from shade to sun, had begun to tax his energy, his *arutam*. He would need to eat the flesh of the water snake to get back his strength.

Had she been abducted? Had she taken off over water? She had dared to question him when he insisted she marry the warrior beside him, but he could not imagine that she would defy her father, humiliate a new husband, break with her tribe. The bird people must have taken her. There had been provocations: His warriors had stolen four bird women on their last raid.

Wives were in short supply in his part of the jungle, and his daughter was a *tsunki* woman—the type men wanted. He had always feared it. Her mother had said that someday her beauty would bring a bad wind. Now here he was, with his *arutam* dwindling, his eyes aching, and an urge to give the girl up for dead.

Suddenly he noticed one of the floating monstrosities at the river's edge. From it, a row of termite people was descending a plank into the mud. They were covered from chin to toe in cloth, the color of a young alligator before its skin hardens to black. The one in the front had many decorations hanging from his chest—red, white, yellow—glinting in the morning sun. The others seemed indistinguishable one from the next, like a long line of leaf-cutter ants. They marched out to a flat place and stood before their highly ornamented leader. Was he a great warrior? For the Jivaro people, rank was written on the body. Was it true in the termite world?

Mwambr watched the men lift their iron rods and make their way up the bank. He had bartered shrunken heads for those rods in the past. Traders had come to their encampment, stinking of drink, offering a rod for each of the *tsantsas*. He saw now that the armed men were passing into an area where fruits and roots were laid out on the ground, being traded. They swarmed around them like hungry insects.

Surely his daughter was nowhere near here. But where had she gone? He was risking the safety of his tribe to answer the question. This search party was made up of forty of his most agile, ruthless fighters, and the women and children had been left to the protection of lesser men—not one warrior among them. If the enemy decided to raid them, the losses would be severe.

There was no question that the warrior at his side had been dishonored. The morning after the marriage ceremony, when the *kakaram* realized that his bride had vanished, he had become enraged. He had screamed and cursed the spirits—and readied himself for revenge. His sisters had brought him bowls of bird blood and black dye. He had painted his skin for war before Mwambr declared it. That's how badly things had begun.

Running through the forest to the bird people's camp, the Jivaro had prayed to *Ayumpum,* the spirit of life and death. But *Ayumpum* had tricked them. The bird people had moved on. Now, stumbling from one clearing to the next, Mwambr's men were following the river, moving farther and farther from their tribe. What he really wanted—more even than to see his daughter's face—was to creep home, tend his sore shanks with medicines, feel his old woman's warmth.

"*Jinta, ápu,*" the *kakaram* told him. Press on, lord. She's not there. I do not smell her. The warrior's expression troubled him. There was *aru-tam* in it, and the fierce eyes of desire.

Mwambr turned away. How could he be less of a man than this boy, who hadn't seen eighteen seasons of rain? How could he force a weaker will on his warriors? The spirits would never forgive it. Mwambr signaled to the others and they fell in behind, following the rim of trees.

Louis Miller took the front steps in one leap and sprang onto the patio just as one of the amas was carrying out the day's laundry, a sturdy jute basket on her head. When he asked her to let Graciela know he was there, she set down the dirty clothes and scampered inside, propelled by the blue of his eyes.

He felt nervous, uncharacteristically ill at ease. All his life he had been a decisive man, able to push off when his work was finished. He had come to Floralinda by chance, needing to repair his instruments, and now that his work was done it made no sense to linger. But here he was, standing on the threshold of this imposing house, eager to see the woman whose face he couldn't put out of mind.

Within minutes she was there, stepping from the intricately carved portal with one hand outstretched in greeting. He raised it to his lips. He could feel her warmth as she led him inside. They passed the parrot's cage, which was draped with a heavy green scarf. The sala was cool and quiet, its windows shuttered against the sun. It was the hour of the siesta.

She was wearing a loose ivory dress, which allowed him to see the motion of the body beneath it. An ocher shawl was draped around her shoulders. When she flung out her hand, indicating that he should sit on one end of the long leather sofa, the shawl opened wide and he could see the outline of her small, perfect breasts under the cotton.

"I hope I didn't wake you."

"No, no! Not at all!" She sat next to him.

"I've finished my work here. I'll be pushing off this afternoon, toward Dos de Mayo. I must go while it's still light."

"*Sí, sí.* Of course." His eyes, which had always looked at her with tenderness, were hard, his face pale. She wondered if he weren't afflicted with a jungle ague.

"I didn't want to go without telling you," he began, his spine rigid against the arm of the sofa. But his voice trailed off to silence.

"I'm happy you came," she responded brightly, filling the air between them. "You're going back to your country?"

"Yes, of course, eventually."

"*Mm, ya.* So we are saying good-bye." He could see the sadness in her face, but she smiled all the same.

"That will depend on you. I'm traveling north now for three hundred kilometers, and then I'll turn around and go south to Pucallpa. I can stop here in a few weeks on my way back, if you'd like me to. But I don't want to deceive you in any way. I must confess something before I go."

There it was. She had tried to prepare herself for it: the moment when he would tell her how sorry he was about her heartbreaking marriage, that he had enjoyed their warm conversation, that he would think of her often and fondly. But someone was waiting for him in Pucallpa, or Chicago, or New York. He would say it at the end, as if her hunger had been too evident: *I thought it fair to tell you.*

"Confess? We are friends, Luis. You don't need to give me explanations."

He tried to read the topography of her face again but saw only a lovely stillness. He let his eyes travel the portraits on the living-room walls—generations of stillness—as they stared back from richly carved frames.

"No, Graciela. I must tell you the truth."

So, the coccus had curled its way into him now. He could tell no lies, not even polite ones. "*Muy bien,* Luis."

His eyes fell on her hands, folded peacefully in her lap. He imagined them running up her husband's back, or fending off the brute's advances. He imagined them clenched into fists as she pushed two children into the light. He imagined them opening toward him—such small hands, the only parts of her he had ever touched.

"Graciela," he said, "I am almost forty. I'm not young anymore. But I'm fairly content. I have a good career. I have a pleasant apartment in New York, in a quiet part of the city. I have friends waiting for me in distant corners of the world. I have the respect of my peers. I have the good fortune to be someone who loves solitude. In short, I've been a lucky man."

She nodded.

"But I have come to realize that what I desire more than anything in this world is the one thing I cannot have."

"What is that?" she said. Here, she thought. Now: He would tell her about his heartbreak elsewhere.

"You, Graciela. I want you."

She was stunned. She had not expected it, had not imagined that he would pledge love, surrender his independence when she had no independence to return. The weight on her heart was unbearable.

"You don't need to answer," he reassured her. "I know you are married. I know the customs of your country."

"*Te quiero,* Luis," she said simply. I love you. "More than those words can say."

Miller reached out and touched an auburn tendril that hung from behind her ear. "You must go now," she told him.

"Yes," he murmured. "But I'll come back, darling." He took her face in his hands, drew it toward him, and placed his lips on hers. Then he was gone—across the room, over the porch, onto the winding path.

Graciela flew upstairs, her sandals hardly touching wood. She headed directly for her mother's room and opened the door gently. Doña Mariana lay alone on the big brass bed, her dress unfastened and her feet—still in boots—delicately crossed over a small straw mat.

"Mamá," she said, stepping into the room tentatively.

"Yes, *mi amor.*" Doña Mariana opened her eyes.

"Where is my father?"

"In the factory, I suppose. Or in his workshop. You know how he is these days. Full of nerves. No time for siestas." She propped herself up on one elbow and frowned into the light. "Why?" the mother said, worried now. "What is that look on your face?"

"Mamá," Graciela said. She ran in now, unable to contain herself.

"What is it, child? What have you done?"

"I'm in love."

"In love!" Doña Mariana sat up.

"Yes," Graciela said, sitting down on her mother's bed. "God help me, yes. With Luis Miller. I can't hide it any longer. He is the one I want."

The words sent her mother to her feet. Even as she fastened the hooks that ran down the side of her black muslin dress, Doña Mariana began lecturing her daughter. A woman has an obligation to her children, she said, a sacred duty to her family. Only a hussy is ruled by wants. "Don't hold yourself cheap, Graciela!" she told her. "Don't go breaking your heart!"

For thirty-six years, Doña Mariana had struggled to create a proper home in that jungle: The Sobrevillas were *gente decente,* the kind of respectable household she had never had. Here, in an unruly land where men took multiple wives, where women ran naked, and offspring were spawned like so many mosquitoes, she and Don Victor had run a civil establishment. They expected their children to comport themselves with a minimum of manners, help build a wall of decorum against the godless flotsam the river threatened to spew into the hacienda. But things had begun to change. When she had exhorted her children to make love, to revel in life's embraces, she hadn't meant to encourage wantonness. Now Graciela was talking about adultery, admitting she wanted to give herself to a total stranger. A foreigner! It was too much to bear.

"Desire!" Padre Bernardo nearly shouted when Doña Mariana told the priest that someone in her house was contemplating infidelity. "There is no calamity greater than desire, my dear woman. As someone much smarter than I once said, we desire nothing so much as the very thing we should not have!"

"Padre," Doña Mariana said, eager to get to her point, "if a señora is seeking love . . ."

"A señora? Outside the bonds of her marriage? Why, that is a mortal sin." He began a mental scan of the house's residents, wondering who this señora might be.

"Yes, but . . ."

"Ah!" he said, stumbling suddenly on the image of the cook twisting cellophane into the Virgin's skirt. "I take it you mean Boruba!"

"Boruba?" Doña Mariana's eyebrows lifted with surprise.

"Yes!" he said, seeing the image in full now, with the genial gardener alongside. "Boruba is a widow. In her case, seeking love would not be sinful. Her bond of marriage was severed with her husband's awful death. God would not mind if she were to love again."

"Boruba? In love?"

"Who else?"

"It's not Boruba!" Doña Mariana cried. "It's m-my . . ." She stuttered, unable to say Graciela's name.

"Dear friend, good woman, say no more," the friar said, raising a hand. "If anyone understands the diabolical nature of desire, it is I. You recall all too well, I'm sure, my own sad brush with a woman in Puno." Indeed Doña Mariana remembered. "Well, I needed to be taught an important lesson: A priest does not want. A man reaching for perfection learns to ignore his appetite. If one seeks a life of the spirit, one must forfeit the earthly life. And if a married woman seeks the gate to heaven, she will stay true to her man." Father Bernardo saw Doña Mariana's distress. But he saw it not as it was—as a mother fearing for her daughter—so much as a woman fearing for herself. Doña Mariana was on the verge of perdition. His first reaction was alarm; his second was enterprise. With a new rush of energy, an overwhelming urge to save her, he made his way to the far wall, where he kept his teaching materials in three wooden crates propped high on bricks. He reached in and pulled out a gray, dog-eared print.

"Look here, Mariana," he said, hurrying back, dusting it off. "Do you recognize this?"

"Of course. Everyone knows what that is. The Last Supper."

"Correct. There are thirteen people sitting at this table: twelve disciples, one Lord. Now you tell me. Where do you see desire, eh? Where do you see the hunger? Certainly not in Jesus's face. Look at Jesus,

Mariana! His whole presence hovers over the table. Now, look at His disciples. They, too, are above the table! All of them. Save one. Only one has a body below the table. Only one has the sorry organs we all shuffle around with us—the stomach, the bowel, the intestines. Do you see which face I mean, Mariana? The rat face? The snout of the betrayer? And do you see those loaves, the cups of wine? Those things are symbols, of course. As food, they are pointless. As food, they have no place to go. The disciples, like Jesus, live in a higher sphere: eyes pure, minds clean, hearts true!

"Now listen carefully: A woman who has taken a vow of marriage must work to be true to that vow. Otherwise she is a Judas Iscariot. Look at that face there." He jabbed at the lean, whiskered face of Judas, so that the paper crimped under his forefinger. "The wanting too much, the naked craving, the hungry animal! You can smell his intestine! His bile! There it is, Mariana, for us to contemplate: the human burden, our task on earth. The spirit must conquer the lower half. To be a Christian is to struggle constantly against gravity—that terrible pull from below."

Doña Mariana sat in the front pew, startled, but listening raptly. The priest's cheeks had reddened and his eyes were as dark as a moonless sea. He seemed utterly transformed, electrified by the challenge of the straying señora—no longer the serene pastor of the calming word.

"Have you ever stopped to think, Mariana, why Satan is so often pictured as an animal? Why he has long fangs and a tail? It's because he lives below the table. He claws in the dark. He is ruled by his lower half. We have no problem imagining Satan with all the body parts, no? He is a fornicator, mounting indiscriminately, rutting in a fury! A Canis Vulgaris, locked in carnal union! Staggering down the road on six legs! That is what we must fight, Mariana! That is where that woman is headed. You go back and tell her that she, like Judas, is slipping below the table, headed for the fires of hell!"

Doña Mariana left the priest, determined to save her daughter. She marched into the house—face grim, but flushed with purpose. She yelled Graciela's name and waited for her at the foot of the stair. When her daughter appeared, she told her in no uncertain terms that she would not stand by and watch her put her immortal soul in danger. "Listen closely, my dear," Doña Mariana said. "You made a vow of marriage, blessed by God, all the saints, and the Virgin. You have no choice but to accept your circumstances. You must not want the very thing you should not have! When that gringo comes back, remind him that you are a married woman. Tell him you are no Judas Iscariot! And then keep away, do you hear? I absolutely forbid you to see him again."

"But that's ridiculous," Belén said, stroking Graciela's hands. "Nestor is probably dead! *Por Dios,* she knows how that man was hated. He was a leech, a shark. He had so many enemies up and down the river! All that coca he was smuggling. All those guns! Who knows what he was up to before Papa sent him away. Don't worry, Graciela," Belén told her. "I'll help you. When Luis comes back, you can count on me."

Late that afternoon, even as Belén sat in her library thinking of ways Graciela might petition the church for an annulment, another señora went looking for love. Boruba trudged along the perimeter of the razed hemp, carrying a small package wrapped in cellophane.

She had not seen Pedro for days, except from a distance. He and the laborers had been out with their machetes, hacking the hemp back to stumps, piling their harvest onto the handcarts. It had been grueling work, especially in the merciless sun, as boroshuda flies swooped from the undergrowth, angrily drawing blood. Now that the fields had been mown and the hemp transported to the factory, Boruba knew Pedro would be exhausted and hungry. Her brick of dulce de leche layered with guava would be a welcome sight.

She strolled through the shorn fields, holding her sweet gift aloft, swatting away the insects. Beads of perspiration sprang from her neck and trickled between her breasts. When she finally found him, he was sprawled, fast asleep, at the rim of the coca field, where a path verged into the trees. The sun cast an oblique shadow across his legs. She could see his chest rise and fall peacefully. She found a cool place under the shade of the canopy, took off her sarong, wrapped it around the candy, and set it on a rock. Then she settled her naked body onto a soft bed of leaves so that he would see her when he opened his eyes.

* * *

Elsa Márquez de Sobrevilla had hidden her trunk and four suitcases behind the wide bamboo screen in her bedroom. She had been packed for a week, making the business of dressing a challenge. Every day, she opened the locks, rummaged through clothes, pulled out a dress, then repacked the suitcases again.

She had not breathed a word about the general of the Fifth Region of the Army of the Republic. She had decided that, in order to make her escape without notice, she needed to keep him, his boat, and his cadastral survey a secret. It seemed essential, therefore, to avoid family gatherings. She spent days and nights dressing, disrobing, packing, unpacking, or gazing for hours out the window, through which she had a clear view of the dock. *"Elsa, la loca,"* the workers would whisper as they hurried past and saw her there, staring at the river—Elsa, the mad. And they would cross themselves.

On one of those long and airless evenings, Rosita and Marco tumbled into her room and found their mother in her petticoat, on her knees, digging wildly through a suitcase. "Mami?" eight-year-old Rosita said, taken aback at the sight of her impeccable mother clawing in the dark like a hungry animal. Her younger brother, less inclined to see ironies, dove to all fours and pawed alongside.

The *loca* raised her head and looked from one child to the other as if she needed time to remember who they were. She sat back and studied their faces. "Listen," she said, her eyes growing hard, "you are not to tell anyone in this house about these suitcases, do you hear me?"

But, of course, it would be impossible for them to lie.

Marcela had managed to elude Don Victor for days now, racing down the stairs whenever she heard his boots start in the other direction. She felt nimble and clever—like a rabbit that has foiled the fox. Clutching a book Belén had given her, she trotted across the patio. "Papu!" she cried, when she saw the dog crawl out from under the house. "Come!"

Papu dove in and out of the begonias along the route to Chincho's, emerging with mouthfuls of coral blossoms. When they reached the road, Marcela peered across, looking for John Gibbs.

The bartender noticed her first. "Look over there!" he cried out. "It's Little Miss Sweet Butt!"

"Shh!" John Gibbs said, gesturing wildly. His companions fell silent. Seeing the men properly subdued, Marcela continued toward them. She raised the book in the air and waved it at the Australian.

"Shrink my balls!" Chincho whispered. "She's brought you something!" And the Australian stood, scratching his chin in wonder.

"Go on!" urged one of his cronies. The barge driver straightened his shirt, hitched his trousers, and hurried toward her.

"Take it!" she said, when he reached her. "Here." She thrust the book into his hands, brushing his hard palms with her fingers.

John Gibbs's face seemed frozen, eyes wide with astonishment. But he had the presence of mind to reach into his pocket and draw out his bandanna, which he had washed and hung out to dry the day before. The teacher pushed back her glasses, nodded, and, with a little smile that acknowledged the spirit of the exchange, took it from him. Then she and the dog went the way they had come. He watched them until they were well up the road, then looked at the thing in his hand. It was a slender volume—old, brown, cloth-covered—and the words on the spine were stamped in English: *Salt-Water Poems, by J. Masefield.*

The sight of John Gibbs with a book dangling from his fingers was so ludicrous, so absurd, that a roar of laughter burst from the bar. Papu whirled like a weathercock when he heard it. The workers swung cups in the air, laughed in chorus. Sensing the merriment, Papu threw back his great dog's head and laughed back. *Ha!,* followed by a gale of cackles. He dove through the ferns—toward the trees and back again—like a dolphin on a tranquil sea.

Don Victor was carefully avoiding Padre Bernardo, slipping away from the house before the priest could make his appearance. Four times he mounted the stairs to the third floor, eager to continue what he had started with the teacher, and four times she thwarted him by running in the opposite direction, his grandchildren in giddy pursuit. Had he stopped to think about what he was doing, had he taken the monkey's counsel—which the padre had clearly seconded—he might have let go, surrendered to the greater force. Whatever gods reigned in that perverse backwater, they didn't want his hand on Marcela's sweet flower again. But in the face of her evasions, his will became only stronger. As he labored to finalize the cellophane process, as he persuaded the Wycliffe Bible people to deliver chemicals on their missionary transports, as he and Ignacio adjusted the valves and cleaned the spigots, his appetite for the teacher grew hot and hard, like a devil's fork.

Yorumbo recognized that obsession the day before the cellophane machines started. He saw it from the moment the white man parted the elephant grass and walked briskly toward his tambo. Don Victor seemed rash, high-strung. There was little of the easy confidence the shaman had come to know. A strange heat emanated from his skin; he carried the nervous look of a voluptuary, and his chest seemed sunken and thin. "Sick," Yorumbo said when he saw him. He walked up to Don Victor and pinched the loose skin of his neck between two fingers. "You're lusting. I see it in your color. You itch. You want. You're letting your testicles rule you. You need to drink the stones."

"Pah!" Don Victor said, and swatted his hand away. "I haven't come here for you to tell me that, sumiruna. I want to fly. I want to ride the condor. I'm about to start the factory again, and I want to know all will go well."

Yorumbo clucked his tongue, but he went, nevertheless, to fetch the ayahuasca. He had never been able to say no to the shapechanger.

Soon the condor rushed through Don Victor's gut, rose up his chest, and burst like a shot from his forehead. Riding the damp air, he saw his factory through the fog of a dim morning. The workers were dumping the last cartful of hemp into the thresher; the fields were mown, the leaves turned back into the soil. The vision was quick, efficient, and the purgative left him light and clean.

When he rowed back to Floralinda in the late afternoon, he saw Marcela in the distance, walking along the dock with the black dog at her side. Don Victor leapt from the canoe, tidied his mustache, and made his way toward her. She was moving slowly, her back to him, but he sensed she was studying something in her hands. By the time he reached her, he made out what it was: an ordinary piece of blue cloth, folded neatly into a square. "Marcela," he said, and she turned to face him, slipping the kerchief behind her.

"Don Victor!" she said, surprised. If the workers watching had expected Don Victor to doff his hat now and release another cloud of butterflies, they would have been disappointed. He seemed anxious, a gray tinge limned his features, and the muscles in his neck were taut.

"What is that? What are you hiding?"

"Nothing, señor, a piece of cloth, a gift from a friend." She brought it in front of her, and indeed it seemed harmless enough—a cotton scarf in a checkerboard pattern, the kind a river man might wear on his head.

"Marcela, you are driving me insane. I have tried to visit you several times now, and every time I do you avoid me. At night you lock your door. I won't have it. No one has ever locked a door against me in my own house."

The silence sat between them like a stone.

"Come, Marcelita," he said, his face softening, "Tomorrow, everything will change. Tomorrow we start up the factory again. Tomorrow is the first day of a miracle. Let's have our own little celebration, shall we? Leave your door open for me, mamita. I'll come to you tomorrow, after the festivities, when all the lights are out."

Belén could see from the expression on Marcela's face that she hadn't come to the library to gather the mail or chat about some fine point of grammar. One hand worked the other nervously. Something was clearly wrong.

"Thank you for the handsome book, Señora Belén," the teacher said. She hesitated, then blurted the truth. "I passed it on to the Australian."

Belén laid aside the letter she had been writing. "You actually took that note of his seriously?"

"He doesn't strike me as the sort who would make an idle request."

Belén's mouth gaped in disbelief. "That's the point! There's nothing idle about it!"

Marcela looked at her feet.

"Could it be you know less about men than I think you do?" Belén asked her.

The teacher shrugged, clutching her skirt with both hands. It was the gesture of a girl, not of a woman of twenty-five years. Suddenly Belén was filled with pity.

"Marcela. Sit down."

Marcela went to her quickly. She took a seat and leaned in. "What is it like, Señora Belén, to be settled? To be in a house with your man?" Her little face looked earnest and serious.

"What do you mean?"

"I mean . . . how did you fall in love with Señor Ignacio? How did you know he was the one?"

"I suppose I was lucky, Marcela. He came to my door. He said he loved me. I had never had a man pay attention to me before. And suddenly there he was."

"Men pay me a lot of attention," the teacher said glumly.

"I'm not surprised."

"It must be nice to be safe from all of that."

Belén thought about her marriage and its stubbornly sexless years. She longed to take the young woman into her confidence—she seemed a knot of nerves. "Marriage is a comfort, Marcela. But don't fool yourself. No woman is ever safe."

Marcela could not contain herself any longer: "What would you do, señora," she cried out, "if a man was making unwanted advances?"

Belén was sure now that the Australian was the lout she had predicted him to be. "Unwanted advances!" she said. But when she saw the teacher's eyes, pleading for counsel and sympathy, she reached out and took her hands. "You don't have to accept that behavior from anyone, Marcelita. You are an intelligent woman, most attractive, with every reason to expect a man's esteem. If he doesn't show you the respect you deserve, ignore the barbarian. You don't need him. You don't need any man, for that matter. Look after your own desires, Marcela, put yourself first. A woman can get by perfectly well. On her own."

* * *

The next morning, when the call of the piracuru signaled the start of a new day, Padre Bernardo emerged from his church in the new cassock Filomena had sewn for the occasion. Behind, on a bare wood plank and shouldered by four girls in clean yellow shifts, stood the resplendent Virgin of Copacabana. The priest saw that all was as it should be: Children with scrubbed faces lined the road to the factory; beside them, their stolid mothers, clutching the household pots. He nodded a warm approval. The procession could now begin.

The men had been at the factory since dawn, preparing it for his blessing. They had filled the steam vats, oiled the machinery, checked the digesters for the volume of fiber, the flow of purified water. Don Victor was adjusting the apertures on the ball digester when one of the workers scaled the roof and shouted that he could see the padre on his way. Don Victor dusted the dirt from his blue linen suit. His hair was damp with the morning's exertions, but he was in high spirits. He slapped his workers' backs as they gathered, asking about their families, shaking their grimy hands.

More than one hundred men of every size and color—Shipibos, Huitotos, Boras, mestizos—spilled into the open area. The pulp shovelers wore borrowed shoes—unmatched, ill-fitting—fetched that morning from crates by the main door. The field hands went barefoot, bare-chested, in trousers that hung in shreds. But all were dressed in cellophane illusions. Great sheets of it had been displayed on the inside wall of the factory. Don Victor had produced so many samples that they passed from hand to hand, shack to shack, dimmed by a thousand fingers. If Don Victor had worried about infecting them with his lofty illusions, it was too late to stop it now. The clear paper had invaded their dreams, inflated their appetites.

Doña Mariana stood under the casuarinas, surveying the priest's procession. Her face was lit with pride, alive with her husband's achievements. The padre gave her a spirited wave, and her face beamed back, clear as the morning sky.

Doña Mariana led her household forward and they fell into formation after the Virgin. The noisy procession rattled on, down the road— Graciela and Belén were there, whispering intently about Louis Miller;

the teacher was tying a kerchief around her head. Boruba, short of breath, herded the young along in their Trujillo hand-me-downs; the hacienda's children tripped after like a flock of wild goats. Last, like stony panjandrums wielding their relics, came the straight-backed mothers, with makeshift instruments. Banging their pots, they filed past the lush fields where the yuca, coffee, and towering papayas flourished. Months later they would remember it: *Everything was in bloom in those early days of the shining paper, all ripe for the picking, ready to grab, as if God, the ápus, and Pachamama herself were offering us their blessings.*

When the parade reached the factory, the men came forward and lifted Father Bernardo onto the concrete platform. The Virgin—her ornaments wobbling and clattering—was set down beside him. The priest threw his hands into the air, the crowd hushed, and all three hundred and sixteen souls knelt on the hard earth before him. "Benevolent Father!" Padre Bernardo shouted, and a flock of macaws lifted from the dock and swooped overhead like a heavenly answer. "Sweet Jesus! Gentle Son! Look upon my beloved brothers and sisters! Help them to walk in the light, not in darkness! Teach them to know the difference between angels and devils! Help me to free them from sin. But see them, above all, Lord, as creatures made by Your hand, destined for salvation. Give them the strength to labor for their bread. Accept their work as a celebration of Your glory. Raise up their hearts—toward love!"

It was then that a most remarkable thing happened. The strips of cellophane that Boruba and Pedro had twisted into the Virgin's straw skirt—dozens of bits of gossamer—were caught by a breeze and loosed from their purchase. They twirled, floated on air, then billowed up and out toward the sea of people, before wafting down into open hands.

Soon after that, the machines rumbled to life. The valves opened, steam rushed from the boilers, and the factory at long last began its cellophane production. The prediction that the monkey had handed Don Victor forty-eight years before came to pass: The papermaker prevailed. The cooked pulp, smooth as pudding, came shooting from the headbox into the first acid bath. The felt bands caught the opaque viscose and plunged it into three more trays, until a clear film cohered and sped into the dryers. The rollers squeezed out every bubble, every imperfection, and pressed cellophane flew, crisp and shining, onto the waiting reels. So it was that the factory began to produce a new kind of paper and the secluded little world of Floralinda set out on an irreversible course toward the modern day. Somewhere within them, the people felt it: They, too, had been altered, regenerated. They, too, were transparent and resplendent. A demon of want was among them now, flicking a shimmery tail.

12

Even as Doña Mariana twisted in her big brass bed—even as she dreamed of hell's flames dancing up the road, looking for Graciela—Don Victor lifted the sheet, swung his legs to the floor, and tiptoed toward the door. Not since his afternoon dalliances with the pink-breasted Vanessa or his hot couplings with the whores Refinata, Nora, and Porfiria had he anticipated sex with that singular ingredient, that galvanic enhancement: sin. But if he had worried about remembering the pleasures of his youth too clearly, he needn't have. He was not thinking about the past at all. He was imagining the future, throwing his whole mind forward, anticipating his profligate fortunes upstairs in the teacher's bed.

He slid his hands up the mahogany banister he had built more than twenty years before and felt his way along the walls until he reached the teacher's bedroom. He pushed open the door, and there on the narrow iron bed, in a thin, cotton nightgown that glowed in the sputtering candlelight, was Marcela. She had been reading, but when she saw him, the book fell from her hands. She gasped and drew up her knees.

He took the book and set it on the night table. Then he pushed her shoulders gently onto the pillow. She didn't resist. "If he doesn't show you the respect you deserve," Belén's words reechoed in her brain, "ignore the barbarian." She understood what she was meant to do.

Marcela clutched her hands high on her chest like a grim patient and fixed her gaze on the flickering shadows on the ceiling.

Silently, he drew up her nightgown and began stroking the fine down on her thin little thighs. He ran his fingers up over her hips and onto her stomach, where he could feel the umbilicus protrude like a small stone. He felt her breasts with their small and defiant nipples, then drew his hand down between her legs. She sighed, as if all the will were rushing from her body, fleeing for life to the back wall. She began to moan, softly at first, but then as he found her wetness, her voice grew more resonant, louder. "Shh, Marcelita," he whispered, and quickly began to fumble with the string that tied his pajama bottoms. But she didn't stop moaning. Never could he have imagined such sounds from so diminutive a body. In the half-light he could see her fingers now vigorously working her own sex; and her voice was rising steadily, like the noon whistle at Mr. Meiggs's sugar refinery. Her body was so rigidly arched against her own ministrations that it looked as if she might break.

Don Victor was momentarily paralyzed, his throat tight with panic. He pulled his trousers closed and backed away. Against all conceivable reality, her wail grew even louder. Terrified, he rushed from the room just as the teacher exploded in high, shrill cries. He stopped on the staircase, unable to believe his ears, reminded—in a most untimely impingement upon consciousness—of the shrieking of seagulls on the seashores of Trujillo, a sound he hadn't heard for forty-two years. But just as he made the connection, Doña Mariana emerged from their room, pulling her robe around her. "*Querido!*" she said, spotting him there like a large beetle, impaled on the newel of his own staircase. "Who is that? What on earth is that bellowing?"

"Sick," he said. "She is sick." His voice was thin, almost frail. Outside, the frogs had ceased calling.

"Who?" The word boomed like a foghorn.

"The teacher. She had me quite alarmed, darling." After all, it was not a lie.

Doña Mariana swept up the stairs, as if Marcela's life hung in the balance. Stunned by the turn of circumstances, Don Victor retreated toward their bedroom only to collide with Graciela, who was suddenly in the hallway full of questions. He opened his mouth to answer, the impulse to tell the truth strong now, but before he could, his wife was rushing downstairs, her gray hair aloft like wings on an avenging angel.

"What is it?" Graciela asked, recognizing her mother's expression too well.

"*La profesora!*" Doña Mariana spat in disgust. "In her own bed! Pleasuring herself!"

How could anyone hold it against the woman—in the privacy of her room, getting by perfectly well on her own? It was true that Padre Bernardo had taken it upon himself to teach his young students what he knew they would learn if they were in a school run by nuns: You do not touch your private places. You do not surrender to your lower half. To fornicate with your fingers is to fornicate with the devil. But the woman was far from home, far from her own people, with nothing to occupy her save the progress of five tiny minds; at least she was keeping her moral disintegration to herself. As Doña Mariana contemplated these things, she added the teacher to her list of worries: the increasing nervousness of Don Victor, the barrenness of Belén, the madness of Elsa, the dangerous appetites of Graciela, and now the ear-splitting debaucheries upstairs.

"I must admit I was aroused by that little escapade," Don Victor said, releasing the simple truth in all its blazing purity as his wife climbed back into the wide brass bed.

"Of course you were, *mi amor.* It's only natural—an animal instinct. When a person hears someone in the throes of pleasure, he can't help wanting it for himself."

"Funny. Someone else said that to me recently." He tried to think who, but he was too distracted by the growing rigidity of his manhood. He reached out and took his wife into his arms.

Flushed with pleasure, Don Victor rolled over and surrendered himself to the darkness. As he drifted into the margins of sleep, the image of Yorumbo appeared in his mind's eye. The shaman seemed real. His earrings—tiny cowrie shells, strung together by the dozens—shivered in the late-night air. The sweet scent of verbena, which Don Victor remembered from his childhood garden in Trujillo, permeated the air. "Everything on earth has its roots and sprouts," Yorumbo said cryptically. "One thing leads to another, every seed has its children, and if you follow the sprouting vines, you will understand the great web that is this universe."

This was a concept Don Victor could understand, having been taught well at the School of Engineers in Lima. His professors had said it a thousand times, drumming their fingers on thick, moldering textbooks: Every action has a reaction. Every force has its counterforce, every invention its ramifications. It was simple physics. He nodded his consent.

"You may not see it, you may not feel it, but the next thing you say, the next way you move, the next thought that enters your head, pacu, will go like a ripple into a great river. We are all bound together in that way. You breathe in, you talk, your words ride the air toward me. I take in that same air, breathe it out, send it on. We feed on a single thing— it is the life force that connects us. If you understand this one thing, you will know all I can possibly teach you."

As Yorumbo spoke about motion and connection, Don Victor recalled Señor Urrutia's ball bearings: He pictured the way one bounced off another at the point of impact. He remembered the old engineer's contraptions in the window on Garcilaso de la Vega—their endless circuits and conduits, the little balls rolling up and down chutes with what seemed like infinite energy. "Yes, sumiruna," he said, "the wise ones in my world teach the same lessons. They call them the laws of the real universe."

"The real universe?"

"Yes, real. As in what you can see. The physical world." He said it in Spanish—*el mundo físico*.

"And what is not real, then, according to your wise men?"

"What you cannot see."

"How do your wise men see anger, then? Or love? Hunger? Satisfaction?"

"Those are what we call imponderables, sumiruna. They belong in a different category than the things you can feel and touch."

"But they, too, have their roots and sprouts, pacu. They, too, send ripples into a great river."

"I don't doubt it. But you cannot measure them."

"Yes, you can. If you look, you can. That is what I am telling you."

"What do you look for, if there's nothing to see?" Don Victor asked, recalling the hidden fan behind Señor Urrutia's perpetual-motion machine.

"Why do you need to see it?" the shaman continued. "It is there. Do you see the evil eye? No. But it is there and we need to purge it. Do you see those tiny lights in the night sky above us, shapechanger? Those eyes of the spirit god? They are made of what we are made. Do not doubt it. Every insect, every bird, every animal, every human is tied, pacu. We are one. We live, we feed, we die, we are eaten, we live again. We go forward binding the universe to us, and we are bound to it in return. When you see that life is connected, you will understand that it has no end."

The next morning, Elsa awoke with a start. In her dream she had seen her trunk and four suitcases bobbing up the Ucayali, somewhere between Floralinda and Paca. She sat up and rubbed her eyes. It was mid-morning and the house appeared to be in that tranquil state of female rule in which the only evidence of men was the whir of the distant factory. The image of all her possessions traveling jubilantly toward Pucallpa without her was troubling; she determined to put it out of her mind. She threw back the sheet, pushed open the mosquito netting, and went to her writing table by the window where she could see every corner of her room. One glance told her the luggage was behind the bamboo screen, just as she'd left it. Surveying the river, she realized how absurd it had been to worry—the image of all her pretty satins and laces drifting away on that fetid water was no more than the random detritus of an overactive imagination, feeling its way to daylight. She couldn't help but laugh at herself—before she spotted the tiny figure of her husband, standing alone on the shore.

Jaime was in a jipijapa hat, looking out at the river with his fists planted firmly on his hips. His boots were sunk into the mud of the northern bank, at the farthest point from the factory. A yellow cloth dangled from his left hand. Elsa followed his line of sight to where a black dugout floated out on the water. Inside it was a native from the interior. A wild woman. She wore no garment, no head cover, no paint. She was standing, in all the comfort of her God-given nakedness, waving one hand, shouting something to Jaime. Her other hand gripped a pole, which held her canoe against the current.

It was, on the face of it, not an unusual sight. Travelers on the river often shouted to those on shore, trying to barter provisions, warn about approaching perils, scrounge a necessary tool. But when Jaime raised his hand with the yellow cloth and shook it like a flag, Elsa realized she was witnessing more than a passing encounter. The girl turned her head and stared upriver as if she were thinking something over; then she pulled up her pole, sat down, and took up an oar. She paddled her way toward him. Visibly pleased, he stuffed a corner of the yellow cloth under his belt and waded into the water. When her canoe was close enough, he drew its prow toward him. Then, nimble as a feline, she hopped out and helped him drag the boat to the riverbank, where they secured it to a tall clump of grass.

Jaime pulled the cloth from his belt and shook it out between them now. Elsa could see that it was a frock, the simple yellow shift that Padre Bernardo insisted the schoolgirls of Floralinda wear at the point of puberty, when their breasts grew swollen and their hips began to flare. The Indian shook her head stubbornly, her long black hair slapping against her shoulders; then she crouched in the mud and hugged her knees like a child. Jaime took off his hat, put his hand on her arm, and said something. She rose and let him slip the garment over her head. Once her arms were through the armholes, he pulled the dress over her breasts, and it cascaded down to her knees. She looked down at herself with the startled look of an animal that has just encountered its own reflection, but Jaime clapped, and that gesture amused the girl. She laughed, and pulled at the dress playfully. After that, he led her through the undergrowth toward the factory: he, with his hands clasped behind his back; she, babbling into the air, or stopping to pick up the cellophane scraps that littered the length of the riverbank.

When they reached the main road, the mastiff scrambled from his place under the house and bounded toward them. Jaime saw him and called out, his voice inaudible through the roar of machines. The girl screamed when she saw the huge black dog galloping toward her. She put her hands to her mouth and staggered back, terrified. Elsa couldn't help but laugh at the silliness of it—jungle savages so rarely saw dogs.

Elsa took out her hairpins, shook loose her hair, and ran her fingers through its waves pensively. Perhaps the girl was related to someone who lived in the hacienda. Jaime was always helping a random passerby, offering favors to complete strangers. It was annoying, really, to see him pay so much attention to a brute Indian when he had given so little of it to her. She kicked a stray slipper across the carpet. It skipped onto the floorboards and slid to where her massive trunk stood waiting. She focused on its familiar black leather, trying to calm the fever in her mind. She studied her family's insignia with its two lions in sharp relief—*Márquez y Márquez,* it said and, under it, *El azucar de los reyes.* The sugar of kings.

How preposterous, she thought on further reflection, to dream that her trunk could float.

"She is a Jivaro, Father. I found her upriver, near Pampa Hermosa. Your curandero had taken her in."

The papermaker had followed his son to the far side of the concrete, and there, sitting on a ledge, hunched against the din of the machinery, worrying a handful of cellophane scraps, was the girl from Yorumbo's tambo. In the yellow school shift, she seemed young and innocuous. "Yes," Don Victor replied. "I saw her with Yorumbo. She's a Jivaro? You don't say." He turned to the girl and spoke to her in Shipibo. She stepped forward, her chin raised defiantly. He smiled when he saw that, but it was clear she hadn't understood a word.

"What is her name?" Don Victor asked his son.

"Suraya."

"Suraya," the older man said, and held up his long fingers in greeting. Her hand shot up like a banner.

"*Ápa,*" she said in return.

Don Victor studied the girl. "A Jivaro, eh? She's probably lost," he conjectured, crossing his arms gravely. "If she is, it's only a matter of time before her tribe comes looking for her. Believe me, we don't want her here when the headshrinkers come. Unless, that is, you fancy having your conk bounce from a chuncho's belt."

"We could hide her. She could be useful. She's strong. Very strong."

"I don't doubt it, my boy. But what's the point? We don't need this girl."

"I want to help her."

"That's nonsense. The Jivaros don't need your help."

"I don't think you understand," Jaime said, and his voice suddenly deepened, prompting Suraya to turn and study him. "I care what happens to her. Since the day I went to Pucallpa to find buyers for our cellophane, I've cared what happens to 'this girl,' as you call her. I brought her here out of respect for you, because I wanted your permission to give her a home here in the hacienda. She is far from her people and I'd like to see that she's safe. She has nobody else."

She has Yorumbo, Don Victor thought, but he didn't say it. He rocked back on his heels and considered the situation. There was more than charity between his son and the Jivaro—that much was clear. He looked from Jaime's wide-open features to the pierced, wary countenance of the girl. Reading the old man's eyes with perfect accuracy, Suraya gripped the hem of the yellow dress with two hands and with one deft motion pulled it over her head and off. She flung it down on the hard floor between them. Without so much as a glance back, she turned and walked briskly over the concrete, headed for her canoe.

When his children told him about the trunk and four suitcases hidden behind Elsa's screen, Jaime had felt something like deliverance. The reaction was instantaneous, unequivocal, and the coldness of his own heart surprised him. But that same afternoon, when Graciela took him aside and whispered, "I'm in love!" he felt something new enter his bloodstream. "Real love!" she said. "Don't tell me it's wrong. Don't tell me I shouldn't feel it. I can't deny myself something this sweet, Jaime. I'm wildly, irremediably in love! He's brought me such happiness at last."

Graciela in love with the American! The thought of it seemed so unlikely. But if Graciela's shriveled heart had sprouted a new love, why not his? If she could put a broken marriage behind her, why couldn't he?

Wildly. Irremediably. The words ran a mad course in his brain. Until Graciela's confession, the state of his own feelings had been inchoate. He had grieved over his wife's madness, been buoyed by the sad, sweet love he felt for his children; he had felt his heart lift with Suraya, known the quick stab of fear that he might never have her and that his youth was slipping irretrievably away. But on the night Graciela told him about Louis Miller, he drifted into uneasy sleep in Belén's library, and a dream he had had many days before came to him yet again.

In the dream, he went to Yorumbo's tambo and called to Suraya. She flew out of the straw hut to greet him, flinging her arms around his neck, grazing his arms with her cinnamon breasts. The feel of her skin lingered like a rash—warm and tingling. The strips of cellophane that once shone from her hair were braided together now, coiled at the base of her throat. He took her hand and led her to his boat. They sped to Floralinda at sunset, scudding downriver so swiftly that her hair flew out behind.

Squinting against the wind, her eyes became shining jewels, the color of topaz. The moon was high in the sky when he led her through the ferns to his house. She seemed strangely tall, weightless as ribbon. When he looked down, he saw that her legs were crossed at the ankles, her feet floating above the earth.

They arrived at the house as his family gathered in the sala, taking their nightly *copitas* of port. "The wooden girl did not come on foot! She was suddenly there!" Don Victor cried, throwing his big arms wide, quoting the great poet Neruda—and Jaime immediately understood him to mean that she was as magnificent as a ship's figurehead—a sleek, brown caoba goddess. They all raised their glasses and praised the beauty of her skin, her slick cellophane collar. When he took her upstairs, he saw Elsa's luggage sitting out in the front hall, packed and ready to go, just as his children had described them. There was a hole on one side of the trunk, just above the two lions of her family crest, and through it he could see the eye of the madwoman, watching as they passed by.

The dream ended with that jolting image, but as he lay on Belén's couch, it struck him with the force of an omen. When morning came, he went to Filomena's pig corral and asked the seamstress for a shift like the ones she sewed for the schoolgirls.

The next day, he had rowed upriver to Yorumbo's hut. He found Suraya sleeping in a hammock in a corner. She woke with a little smile but refused to go with him when he tried to lead her to his boat, even growing sullen and belligerent—clearly, she was a person of her own mind, beholden to no one—but she watched studiously as he took a stick and scratched the river's contours into the dirt. He put a mark where Floralinda lay. Yorumbo looked on from his door and understood it.

In the end, she came to him.

The dream had little to do with reality in every detail but one. He was in love with her. Wildly, irremediably—the virus had taken hold.

So when she pulled the dress off and walked away, he did not hesitate. He apologized to his father, for filial piety was deeply ingrained in his nature, then he picked up the dress, ran to Suraya, and drew her toward the house.

Boruba was slumped on a stool in the corner of the kitchen, her forehead against the wall, but she sprang to her feet when she heard the squeak of the back door opening. In her hand was a long steel knife.

"Calm down, calm down!" Jaime said, laughing, but one look at her tired eyes and clammy skin told him that she was ill. He left Suraya to gawk through the doorway—she had never seen a house, much less a table, a stove, a row of pots, and so many sharp implements in such splendid profusion—and fetched Boruba a cup of cool water. Her face was as green as a newly hatched turtle, but she drank quickly, collected herself, retied her sarong, and insisted she had nothing more than a touch of river cholera. Narrowing her eyes now, she watched the girl inch into the room, shoulders hunched, as if entering a cave. Suraya trailed her hands along the unnaturally smooth surfaces—the wood counter, steel sink, tile wall—and studied the strange, nappy-haired woman warily.

Jaime explained to Boruba that he had brought Suraya to Floralinda because he felt responsible for her welfare. He had found her on the banks of the river, wearing nothing but his father's cellophane. Fate had meant him to bring her here. He hoped that Boruba would give her a hammock in one of the back rooms and see that she ate. In return, he said, the girl might be persuaded to help with the cooking. Boruba's face, which until that moment had been as stern as a granite monument, softened. She wiped her face with a rag and looked around at the work she had yet to do. There was fish to skin and bone, yuca to chop and fry, plantains to poach in milk. She promised him the girl would be looked after.

Jaime patted Suraya on the hand and returned to his work at the factory. The day might have proceeded uneventfully but for the fact that Elsa had seen the entire drama from her perch by the window. Piqued by curiosity, she came down to the kitchen to take closer measure of the girl. The sight of Elsa's extravagance in the doorway—the peach chiffon, the elaborate hat, the sequined purse—so frightened Suraya that she leapt under the table. Elsa giggled, relishing her effect on the barbarian.

"What are those sticks in your face, you misery of an animal?" Elsa asked her. "Whiskers?" And then the madwoman hissed like a cat until the sound so dismayed Boruba that she moved to put out a soothing hand. But Elsa spun around, her eyes wild and fierce. "Don't touch me!" she shouted. At the door, she issued her instructions. "Set a place for me, cook. Tonight, I eat with the others. But remember: Serve me the whitest part of the fish. Boned! I will not put up with those sharp little needles. Do you hear me? Not one!"

Alfonso Suárez entered the sala rubbing his hands, sniffing the air—the sleeves of his white shirt rolled to his elbows. It was clear the heat had overwhelmed him, for he had removed the jacket of his charcoal-gray suit and it hung, limp and damp, over one shoulder. Ignacio made a matter-of-fact introduction, without pomp or exaggeration, although everyone knew very well who their guest was. He was the paper agent from Lima, their conduit to the wider world: the one who had made all the connections, flooded Floralinda with orders for cellophane, trumpeted their little factory in every corner of commercial Peru.

Being a hostess of considerable experience, Doña Mariana invited the little man to inspect the guest room and take a brief siesta. She knew that upon arrival in the jungle, a city person wants nothing so much as to see the clean bed he will sleep in and know that it is a good distance from ground. She took him upstairs to the vast room overlooking the hemp fields.

"Señora," he said, wriggling his nose as she led him up the stairs, "I cannot tell you what miseries I endured on that purgatorial boat! Five days!"

He surveyed the appurtenances in his quarters with unabashed wonder: the large carved bed with its snow-white mosquito netting; the smoking chair with its delicately crocheted antimacassars; the Portuguese tile table with its ceramic bowl and pitcher for fresh water; the towels and sheets sprinkled with bay rum. Doña Mariana showed him the wire apparatus Don Victor had fashioned and affixed to a back post of the bed. One tug and a bell would sound in the kitchen and another in the maids' quarters. If he needed something—anything at all—an ama would come running to attend to it.

"Servants! Bells! What welcome words, señora!" he cried. He thanked her fervently as he rummaged through his leather bag, removed a prettily wrapped gift, and pressed it into her hands. It was a finely wrought silver pot for chili sauce, with an ornately carved lid and spoon. Pleased, she set it on the aparador in the dining room and headed for the kitchen.

Boruba was sprawled on her stool, with her back to the wall, snoring. One of Padre Bernardo's schoolgirls was squatting on the floor, peeling and chopping the yuca. Doña Mariana noted the girl's industry and made a mental note to thank the padre for having the foresight to send her. Then she shook Boruba by the shoulders and gave her the evening's instructions: "Listen closely, my dear. I absolutely do not want Señorita Marcela at the dinner table tonight," she told her firmly. Doña Mariana didn't say so, but the thought of looking at the teacher's face when the last she had seen it was glasses-askew, panting in ecstasy, was too much to bear. "I don't care how you do it, but make sure she knows: She will have her dinner upstairs. In any case, there will be someone sitting in her place. A very important guest, Boruba! I expect everything to be superb!"

As it happened, Boruba outdid herself—her fresh paiche stew flavored with cumin and pumpkin was colorful, elegant. The yuca was fried to perfection, served with slices of lime and sprinkled with chopped cilantro. The plantains, poached in milk and flavored with brown sugar, were crowned with fresh guava and accompanied by coffee and sweet-potato candies. Even Elsa, in her chiffon finery, poking the fish with a fork, couldn't find a bone to complain about. It was the attendant conversation that was so unpalatable.

Suárez had strutted in, refreshed by an afternoon spent between rum-scented sheets. From the start, he quickened the air with his city sophistication. "Oh, what a New Year's gala you all missed this year in President Odría's palace! If only you could have been there, my dears! The boom of the cannon! The endless limousines! The spiffy generals with their shiny, tall boots and brass decorations!" He described the waiters with their red bow ties and white gloves at Lima's Club Nacional and how everything in the country seemed to hum with corresponding order. He regaled Don Victor with stories about paper being made along the west coast by W. R. Grace, a famous American company. He reported that Grace was using waste from Peruvian sugar mills—crushed cane left behind in the extraction process. The result was pure profit for the Americans and a way for the haciendas to dispose of useless detritus.

"I know something about sugar paper!" Don Victor said triumphantly. "I've made it myself in my workshop!" His wife signaled a happy assent. But the mention of west-coast commerce did not have a happy effect on Elsa. "Sugar?" she sniffed at Suárez. "If you're talking about sugar, I take it you mean Márquez y Márquez."

"Oh yes, I do mean them," Suárez said. "Those *sinverguenzas*! Bandits! You know about them? You know about Alberto Márquez y Márquez? He makes out like a thief on all sides. He even peddles his garbage!"

Elsa stiffened, her wrists arching like scorpions. "The man you are calling a bandit, señor, is my father!"

For the first time that evening Señor Suárez was at a loss for words.

"Well, my dear girl," Don Victor interjected brightly. "You can hardly blame our visitor for taking that position. He is a champion of small businesses and, after all, your family owns every stalk of sugar cane in Trujillo. Señor Suárez has come all the way from Lima to support our little factory, so he can be forgiven for his opinions. Let's just thank God that here in our jungle backwater no one is counting the cane. No one is keeping track of who owns what. We're all upstarts in the Amazon. I say bravo to that!" He raised his glass in the air.

"Is that what you think, Don Victor?" Elsa snapped. "You think no one is keeping track of you?" And then she did exactly what she had been working for weeks to avoid. "For your information, señor, there is a general I know who is keeping track of who owns what! In fact, he is quite interested in your coca! It seems you've been delinquent. You should have surrendered your coca to the army long ago. It's the law in this country—don't you know?"

Things went bad quickly after that. Jaime turned to their guest. "Señor Suárez," he said gently. "My wife cannot be held accountable for what she says. She is more than a little unbalanced. She cannot help herself. The jungle has had a very deleterious effect on her mind."

"Oh?" Elsa said, striking back now. "Shall we talk about unbalanced minds, dear husband? Shall we talk about the *loco* I saw this morning, chasing through ferns after a naked girl? Shall we talk about how he brought that little Neanderthal, *pim-pam-púm,* into the family kitchen?"

"No, no, darling." Doña Mariana was certain now that her daughter-in-law was so far gone that it would be inhumane to judge her by her behavior. "You have it all wrong, dear. The girl in the kitchen is a child from Padre Bernardo's school, and I can assure you she's not naked at all. Perfectly clothed, in fact. In her yellow tunic." She reached across the table to pat her daughter-in-law's hand.

"What you all should know about the young woman in the kitchen," said Jaime, his face flushed with emotion, "is that I love her. That's why she's here. That's what you all should know."

Elsa laughed out loud, then covered her mouth with gloved fingers.

Don Victor's eyes widened with comprehension as he looked across the table at his son. "You brought the Jivaro into this *house?*"

"I did," said Jaime. The entire family looked at one another in confusion. The conversation appeared to be about someone they were supposed to know—someone in their own house, possibly in the next room—but no one was sure who she was exactly. "Yes, she is here, Father. Under your roof. And I'm telling you and everyone else at this table that I love her," Jaime added. "Wildly. Irremediably."

Graciela blanched.

"A Jivaro?" the man from Lima said in a parched little voice. "A headshrinker?"

In Alfonso Suárez's defense, it would have been difficult for any visitor, however acute in his powers of observation, to understand what was happening at the Sobrevilla dinner table. How could he know that no secret could shock this family? Secrets had batted about their house promiscuously for weeks now. People in the room were resigned to hearing the most intimate news about one another. To those who have learned that one grandfather is a priest and another is a coolie, what is a headshrinker in the kitchen? The truth was the truth and that was the end of that. It no longer made anyone angry. It no longer made Doña Mariana shoot to her feet and pound the table with her fists. It no longer made Belén sneer and Graciela gasp and Jaime throw another drink down his gullet. So, to Alfonso Suárez's great surprise, the Sobrevillas adjusted their napkins, sipped their coffee, passed the sweet-potato confections, and the conversation rolled on, like the mighty river.

"The Jivaro, yes!" said Don Victor, sighing. "Ah, well. Perhaps I am fated to be fed by Jivaros. They once almost fed on me!"

Alfonso Suárez dabbed his lips with his napkin and looked around anxiously.

"The last I saw a Jivaro," Don Victor continued, pouring his guest a full glass of pisco, "was many years ago, but I remember it as if it were yesterday. It was the dry season and I was traveling along the Marañon River, which, as I'm sure you know, my dear Suárez, is the great tributary north of here. I was trying to decide where to establish this hacienda. I suppose that would make it almost twenty-five years ago, when that big, handsome son of mine was only a little boy." Suárez nodded and gulped down his drink. "There were five of us shipping out from Iquitos in a trawler. Lord! What a pile of sticks it was. All rotten and green with slime! I was in the company of four Shipibos, brave men. Two are still with me and, to this day, labor in this hacienda—God bless them!"

"That must be Flavio and Antonito," Ignacio added. He turned to his father-in-law with interest. He hadn't heard this story before.

"Yes, precisely," Don Victor confirmed. "Flavio and Antonito. One night we secured the boat in what seemed a safe enough cove and hung our hammocks in the trees. We roasted some deer we had hunted upriver, then went to sleep sated and comfortable, with our netting pulled over us. But suddenly, in the middle of the night, I felt a sharp prickle in my neck. When I opened my eyes, there was a Jivaro, a dart at my throat, with eight of his tribesmen about us. My Shipibo friends were tied to four separate trees. The Jivaros were preparing to decapitate them. You know how they do! Whick, whick! Before they flay your skin and shrink your head."

"Tía Esther wrote to me that she has a Jivaro *tsantsa*," Belén said simply. "It's of a cougar, I think. Given to her by a Norwegian."

"Yes. I remember it well," Don Victor said, and nodded at her. "It used to sit on the night table in her bedroom." Belén glanced across the table at Ignacio, who was listening intently. "Anyway," Don Victor went on, "the Jivaro dart went into the mark! It pierced my throat right here, and the poison began to flow. I felt it travel my veins, descending like a hot snake into my chest. That's what curare does, Suárez! It makes a sharp course toward the heart! I felt an unbearable pressure against my lungs, as if one more breath would be impossible, but then a miracle happened: A canoe full of Machiguenga floated by. No noise. No warning. Just like that—*zzzzz*—by they went, skimming along the water, and suddenly twelve eyes were staring at us through the black of night! They were painted for war, with their spears pointing straight up. It so unsettled our captors that they went running into the trees. One of the Machiguenga warriors must have seen the dart in my throat, because he gave me a quick jolt of *ojé*—up my nose, right into the bloodstream. If it hadn't been for him, I would have been a *tsantsa* on somebody's belt now, with stones where my eyes should be."

"Oy, querido!" Doña Mariana exclaimed, clutching her hands to her bosom, her eyes lit with affection for the manliness he had exhibited, not only with the Jivaro on the river but in bed on the night before. "That is fascinating! And you tell it so vividly, with so much color, Victor! What a memory! And what's more—have you realized it, *mi amor?*—there's no Vanessa, not one hussy in the story!"

Suraya knew that what ailed Boruba was no disease. She had seen the woman sick in the morning, pointed to her wide belly, and made little rocking motions with her arms. Boruba smiled. She had suspected the same thing herself. She was pregnant with Pedro's child.

But the universe, as Yorumbo had said, is tied fast by roots and sprouts. One little shoot leads to another. Boruba was understood so well by Suraya that Boruba proceeded to understand someone else. She took one look at Graciela's gaunt face over the breakfast table and saw that her heart was devouring her body. In those eyes, with the plum-colored rings around them, Boruba could see the image of the gringo—there was no mistaking it.

Louis Miller, in turn, glanced up from his tripod on the western shore of the river and saw the *Augusto Leguía* steaming its way south toward Floralinda. Standing on the deck was a general of the Army of the Republic, cutting a formidable figure with his binoculars, the medals on his uniform glinting in the afternoon sun. Behind, like a string of ants, was a row of soldiers, leaning forward and shouting to one another in the wind. The cartographer took off his hat and wiped the perspiration from his brow. He understood that, in some fundamental way, the forces had shifted along the Ucayali, but he didn't know how. He longed to be on the fast boat with the army man, speeding south, to where he had left his heart.

General José Antonio López, in turn, twirled the dial on his binoculars and brought an image into closer focus. It was a man, staring back at him from between two trees on the eastern bank of the river. His cheekbones were painted black. His long braids were plaited with red string. A cap of brightly colored feathers clung to his head. His mouth was set in a grim line, as if he had good reason to monitor the army's property, but the general saw an indisputable weariness in the eyes. He studied the face. The face studied the general. And yet, when General López handed the binoculars to the soldier behind him, the soldier saw nothing but trees.

The barge sped like a gray ghost past the village of Bretaña. Through the dark, John Gibbs could see the dock and the proliferation of shacks along the shoreline—pricks of light against the great curtain of forest. It was night; he was alone. In one hand, he held the volume of poetry. With the other, he felt its ragged leather, swollen pages. He ran his fingers over the raised letters on the spine: *Salt-Water Poems, by J. Masefield*.

He had been hesitant to take it out in the daylight. He had worried that his mates, in fun, would grab it from him, toss it to one another, and throw it—irretrievably—into the rushing river. He brought it to his lips and remembered how the teacher had held it out to him: those outstretched fingers, those small, cinnamon hands. When he closed his eyes and slipped into his dreams, he could almost smell the sweetness.

Alfonso Suárez stayed in the Sobrevilla house only long enough to see how ingeniously Don Victor had rigged the machines and how well Ignacio managed the paper process. He had far more orders than the small operation could deliver, but as limited as its capacity was, the factory seemed a model of efficiency. With clever pricing and a close oversight of the accounts, Floralinda's cellophane could make inroads, establish a customer base, grow.

The family was eccentric—perhaps even a little mad—but, as the days passed, their ways ceased to trouble or surprise him. What sane human being would choose to live in this hell, at the brink of oblivion? He could tolerate the aberrant conversation, the outlandish behavior and questionable manners, as long as Don Victor continued to fill his cellophane orders. Suárez inspected Mr. Meiggs's reconfigured machinery, took a tour of Pedro's well-tended fields, but in the end he wasn't much interested in how the hacienda was getting things done. He was a practical man: What interested him were the ways Floralinda's production might be expanded—the potential acreage it would take to double or triple its output. After three days and three nights in the sweltering humidity, tugging on Don Victor's wire for the amas to come pick lizards off his screens, or swat away spiders, or remove horned beetles that shuffled under his bed as if they were oxen bearing heavy loads, the agent was exhausted. He swore to himself he would never return. He packed his clothes and, deciding it would be a terrible waste to leave a perfectly good silver chili pot in this backwater, tiptoed downstairs to retrieve his elegant gift. He stuffed it into his bag, instructed the crew of his chartered boat to start the engines, and made his rounds of farewell. At the factory, he proclaimed Don Victor's decision to make cellophane in the heart of the Amazon pure genius. The ambition was formidable, he said; the execution breathtaking. How bold! How brash! Paper, in the Shangri-la of botanical possibility! He unfolded a wad of cash, paid the Sobrevillas in advance for the first five shipments of paper, and secured their promise that the factory would soon operate around the clock.

Alfonso Suárez departed, leaving a curious vacuum in the air, forcing the family to think about their future. The brown paper Floralinda had produced before had been durable, but it wasn't unique—other mills in Peru were making it. The bagmakers and printers up and down the Ucayali had complained when they learned that Floralinda had ceased to produce the sturdy paper, but Don Victor's competitors in Pucallpa readily took the business. Cellophane was different. The Sobrevilla factory was the only one of its kind in the country. Don Victor had achieved his miracle. His children had been so caught up in their loves and confessions that they hadn't stopped to consider what that might mean.

After a silent and ruminative supper on the night of Señor Suárez's departure, the Sobrevillas dispersed, wandering off into various corners of the house to contemplate life's changes. Graciela went into the kitchen to see about the ailing Boruba, who had shuffled in and out of the dining room balefully with every plateful of carapulcra, kneading her back with one fist. Jaime stepped onto the patio and leaned over the wall to watch Suraya, who was hanging out rags to dry. Don Victor went into his workshop and spread out diagrams of his crop fields to see how he might fulfill Suárez's expectations. Doña Mariana brought him a strong cup of chocolate, kissed his head, and retired to the restorative clicks of her crochet needles; but she couldn't quite put out of mind the picture of the teacher in her autoerotic fever and the pervading guilt that she had not told the priest about it. Elsa, who hadn't shown her face since the night of Señor Suárez's arrival, took out her palette and oils and resumed painting her furious canvases. Above, at her third-floor window, Marcela imagined a barge making its way to Iquitos, and John Gibbs on it, holding a book to his heart.

Belén slipped into her library, prepared to light the gas lamps, but she saw that they were already burning, although no one was there. Apart from the blaze of light, everything was just as she'd left it. The illustrated *Mitología Romana* was still on the sofa, a garnet ribbon trailing from its pages. To its side, exactly where she had put it, was the folded, red satin cap of Old Wong. But she sensed someone had been there, rummaging through her books. Her gaze swept over the furniture until it fell on the table next to her reading chair. Two volumes lay there, glittering like lacquer boxes. One was her collection of stories by Ricardo Palma, the other *The Book of Good Love*—both sheathed in cellophane. She picked them up and turned them in her hands, marveling at the ingenuity of the idea. She could see through to the spines, the ridges, the stamping; even the worn edges were visible.

"Do you approve?"

She whirled around to find her husband standing at the far corner of a bookcase, arms folded across his chest.

"*You* did this," Belén said softly.

"Yes."

"Why?"

"Because I know that you love those books, and because I thought the cellophane might protect them."

Ignacio stepped into the light, and she took in the hard line of his jaw, the onyx glint of his hair. He laid a copy of Sor Juana's *Dream* carefully on the table, its new cellophane cloak gleaming.

"*Dream,*" he said. "Impossible for me to understand that woman's poetry, but I enjoyed wrapping it all the same. Speaking of dreams, shall I tell you what I dreamed last night?"

She sat on the edge of her reading chair and smiled up at him. "Tell me."

"I was back in Huánuco," he began, pacing back and forth. "My father was alive and his electrical shop was open. He was showing me a miniature model of the new lamps around the Plaza de Armas. He had duplicated it perfectly: Every street, every building—every tree!—had a replica. Where each lamppost should be, he had put a tiny bulb. All the complicated wiring was hidden between two sheets of plywood, so that with just one throw of the switch—*pum!*—Huánuco was alive with electricity, a shining city against the night. I was a boy when he first showed it to me, and in the dream I had last night I was still a boy. No more than seven or eight."

Belén smiled at the thought of him as a small boy in short pants. "The dream didn't end there," he continued. "He and I are in his shop. It's nighttime and his city on the table is glowing. There is a knock on the door and he goes to answer it. I hear him say, 'No, señora, you have come to the wrong address. Your husband is not here. Why don't you go ask over there, across the street, where the owner is just locking up.' He closes the door and comes back shaking his head. 'Poor woman,' he says. 'She doesn't know where her own husband is.' I look through the window and see the woman go past. *Such a tiny woman,* I think to myself, *no taller than a girl my size.* She turns as if she'd heard me think it. When she's facing me, I see that the woman is you."

Ignacio stopped and looked up at Belén. She seemed stunned, as if he had lifted a corner of his soul and revealed a whole universe. "What a strange and beautiful dream," she said finally.

He nodded. "It moved me somehow. I felt it was trying to tell me something about you—something about us. I wish I understood it."

"The simplest flower is hard to understand," Belén said, quoting Sor Juana. "What happened," she asked then, "to your father's model of Huánuco?"

"I never saw it after he died," he answered. "It was shuffled into another room, then to the back of the house. Later, when I tried to find it, I was told that it fell apart." Ignacio turned the newly wrapped *Dream* in his hands. "Pity, isn't it?" he said after a while. "Such a perfect thing, that miniature city of Huánuco. I thought it was indestructible."

Belén took the cellophane-wrapped copy of *The Book of Good Love,* put Old Wong's wedding hat on top of it, and mounted the stairs to their bedroom. Behind her, the sound of Ignacio's boots echoed on the mahogany, causing Doña Mariana to look up from her tatting and make the almost certain connection that the two were retiring together. They had not done so for years.

While Ignacio lit the gaslight, Belén told him the story of her Chinese great-great-grandfather, Old Wong, and how Tía Esther had sent Belén his hat in hopes it would bring her a bit of love's magic. Ignacio took the red satin triangle, stroked the yellow tassel thoughtfully, then opened it and set it on his wife's head. Delighted, she drew him toward her and kissed his mouth.

They fell onto the bed, looking into each other's eyes, searching each other's faces as if they'd been caught by surprise. And then they disrobed and made love, slowly, so that Wong's hat stayed on Belén's head until the very end, when it tipped back and tumbled to the floor. They made love again and again, and *The Book of Good Love*—scribbled six hundred years earlier by a priest in a Spanish dungeon, wrapped that very night in the clarified cellulose of Floralinda's hemp fields— rocked back and forth, winking its lights on their walls.

13

Padre Bernardo had not read the Archpriest of Hita's naughty *Book of Good Love,* as Belén had, but he knew the book's essence: Good love is divine. Bad love is wicked. And, if priests have a task on this earth, it is to teach the difference.

It did not escape the people of Floralinda—with truth following on truth in that remote bend in the river—that the padre had been first to openly confess his wickedness. Perhaps that was why, as the plague of want spread its germ through the hacienda, they did not hesitate to sit at his confessional and divulge their secret longings. They knew that their priest would be the very model of compassion. He had been in bad love himself.

The day after Alfonso Suárez departed, Doña Mariana awoke feeling she could no longer delay telling the padre about the teacher. She sat in the front pew of his church, put her hands on his ramshackle desk, and whispered, "Padre Bernardo, there is someone in my house so sick with desire that she pleasures herself in full earshot of everyone!" Padre Bernardo listened thoughtfully, nodded soberly, and concluded that, once again in that time-honored way of well-mannered ladies, Doña Mariana was referring to herself. Could it be that Don Victor was so consumed with his cellophane, so distracted by commerce and witchery, that he was neglecting his husbandly duties? The priest responded with delicacy, maintaining the sham carefully. "Pleasuring oneself is not a good thing, of course," he told her. "I always try to teach young people not to do it. But it is a venial sin, and forgivable. Much worse would be to act on that vile impulse and consummate a carnal alliance that violates the Commandments. Be patient with this woman," he counseled. "Her intentions are admirable, ultimately godly." He sent her off, making the sign of the cross over her and marveling at her struggle to preserve her purity. His prayers were doing their work.

But as his confessional began to ring with similar admissions from others, he began to grow alarmed by the rank concupiscence that was overtaking his congregation. He found himself listening to a remarkable litany of wickedness that forced him to think like a sinner before responding as a man of God. "Father, at night, when my woman is asleep, I go into the fields and *niki-niki* with my neighbor's wife." Or "Father, is it wrong? Is it bad? My husband sticks his thing in my bum!" Or "Father, how many Ave Marías for fornication with my tongue?"

His worries were made worse by Graciela, who slipped into the booth at the hour of the confession and whispered that she wanted to commit adultery. She said that she had wanted to sin for more than ten days now, and that the desire had become unbearable—an ache that intruded on her every thought, affected every nerve end of her body.

He was taken aback by the coarseness of her words, wondering what poison had oozed through the walls, traveled the house, sickened both mother and daughter. He knew immediately that it was Graciela he was listening to, as he knew every female voice in that hacienda, even when women took pains to mask them by pinching their noses with fingers. It could well be that Graciela was trying to disguise herself, he thought, but the guttural voice that was addressing him from behind the confessional curtain made him wonder—if only fleetingly—whether a demon had invaded her body.

"How many years, child, has it been since your husband left you?"

Padre Bernardo was shocked by his own question. In his eagerness to help Graciela, he had revealed that he knew exactly who she was; he had committed an infraction a father confessor should avoid at all costs.

Graciela, too, was shocked, but only that she had been so transparent.

She paused, realizing the awkwardness of her situation. "Five years, Padre."

"I see," he said. "And the object of your desire is here in Floralinda?"

"Not now. But he will return." At which point the priest understood everything. Graciela went on to say that she knew it was an *amor loco* and impossible, for the man would only go away again—next time to an impossibly distant place. Was she wrong, bad, hateful, she asked, for wanting to love and be loved?

"No one is hateful in the eyes of God," the padre answered. "God's love for us is boundless. But you, my dear, have made a marriage covenant with Nestor, and that covenant was blessed by God, in this very church, under the eyes of the Virgin of Copacabana."

"But Nestor tried to kill me!" Graciela wailed. She was arguing with the priest, breaking every covenant of the confessional.

"Graciela, think of your children!" the padre snapped from the other side of the grid.

If the padre had planned it meticulously, he could not have found better words to pit Graciela against her demons, for if she was in bad love with Louis Miller, she also adored Pablito and Silvia with as good a love as any mortal could muster. Her children were, for her, the essence of sacredness.

She left Padre Bernardo's confessional with a clear, unmistakable directive to weigh her children against the force field of her desire—to think about Silvia and Pablito's welfare. Padre Bernardo had been far less clear about what to do with Louis Miller. She pulled her scarf around her shoulders as she marched down the dirt road past the workers' shacks, wondering why the priest hadn't demanded that she cast the gringo from her heart and be done with it. It was what she had expected him to do.

Boruba was next in line for the padre's ear, and she lowered her aching body with great effort, sinking into the chair with a moan. The padre recognized the heavy breathing that followed, as well as the unmistakable voice with which she apologized for her slowness, but he restrained himself from welcoming her by name. "I am listening, my child," he said.

"*Oy*, sainted Padre," she said. "I've come to tell you about a great miracle, which is at once a great sin, and so I require your blessing as well as your pardon."

The priest sighed. By that time all of Floralinda knew of her condition. The engine of truth had sped through the hacienda far faster than the cook could waddle her way to church.

"I am with child, Father," she blurted, "and I am not married."

"Is the father of the child married?" the priest said, forcing himself to pose the question.

"No, he is not."

"Then, Boruba, why don't you marry him and make it right in the eyes of the Lord?" he cried. "A child is a kiss from heaven!"

"Oh, thank you, Padre Bernardo!" Boruba's relief was so great that she shouted it for everyone in the church to hear. "Will you marry me to Pedro?"

"Of course I will!" he shouted back, and then instructed her to recite one hundred penitential Ave Marías. She left as breathlessly as she had come, mumbling her prayers as she pulled back the curtain.

There was a long line of workers' wives after that, seeking forgiveness for the awful truths they had told their men, and the even more awful truths they had heard in return. Knowing their identities full well, the padre made mental notes to call on the husbands and offer his prayers. But when the padre suddenly heard a male voice on the other side of the curtain, he had to work hard to place it—so rarely did men attend the confessional. The voice was young, vibrant—definitely familiar. But at the point when the man said, "Is it a sin, Father, to love a woman who is not baptized?" the guessing was over. The priest knew that Jaime Sobrevilla was speaking and that the woman in question was the Jivaro in Boruba's kitchen. It hadn't been hard to spot the young woman with the reed holes on either side of her face. Even with all the hubbub of Alfonso Suárez's visit, the padre had seen her there in her yellow tunic. He had walked through the house as he did every day—flinging the sign of the cross over Don Victor—and puzzled over who she might be. There were eighty-one children in Floralinda, forty-seven of whom were girls, but few of them were of the age to wear the lemon-colored shifts. He knew exactly who they were. When he asked Filomena for whom she had last sewn a yellow dress, she had shrugged and replied, "Jaime."

"My dear man," the priest said, squaring his shoulders, "if the fear of sin has brought you to this confessional, that is a good thing. If you and the unbaptized Indian conceive, that is bad."

Jaime hesitated. "So, Padre, what you are saying is that the unbaptized Indian should be baptized, and once she is baptized all will be well?"

"Jaime, for God's sake!" the priest blurted, in all exasperation. "What I am saying is that the Jivaro girl should be baptized, yes! That hardly needs saying! Everyone is saved who is baptized in the name of the Lord. But why are you sitting there asking theoretical questions as if we were discussing politics over a cup at Chincho's? This is a confessional booth. Have you forgotten that? Have you forgotten what we do here? And why aren't you acknowledging the real transgression—the part about cheating on your wife?"

Doña Mariana found her grandchildren swarming in anarchic confusion. They were chasing one another around the schoolroom, pulling on one another's hair. The teacher sat at her desk, cradling her head in her hands. On the floor lay a dry flask of ink. "Silence!" Doña Mariana screeched into the uproar. The children scrambled to their places, faces flushed with mischief.

But the teacher remained as she was—a monument to human suffering. "Marcela, my dear," Doña Mariana said, touching her tenderly on the arm. "Forgive me for being so hard on you, sending your meals upstairs as if you were a leper. I did not realize until today how difficult your life must be. How brave you are in your circumstances. A lone woman struggling to be good!"

The miserable teacher looked up, hardly believing her ears. She could see the children glance from her bewildered face to their grandmother's, and back again. She saw the compassion in Doña Mariana's eyes.

"I understand your predicament, dear girl. Living such a solitary, sacrificial life in this faraway hacienda. Your fortitude is admirable. Godly, in fact."

Marcela began to cry. Whimpering, at first, and then with such sobs that her shoulders began to shake.

"There, there, *mijita*. Don't cry."

"It's been so hard!" Marcela erupted, realizing now that her plight was so apparent, so pathetic that even the culprit's wife was feeling sorry for her. Tears gushed from her eyes.

"Yes, of course it has been hard."

"You can't imagine!" the teacher bawled on. "First the butterflies, then the parrots, then the fingers! I'm only human! Understand? Only human!"

She was right that Doña Mariana couldn't imagine it. Butterflies? Parrots? The older woman crossed herself against the sudden suspicion that the teacher had been applying those creatures to her nether regions—but she understood, perfectly well, the part about the fingers. "Yes, of course, you're only human, darling." She lifted the tiny woman up by her shoulders and embraced her. "All is forgiven, Marcelita. Hush, hush, please. All is forgiven now."

Graciela drew the magnificent dress from her armoire; it rustled out like an eager creature. Gathered at the waist, ruched at the neck, voluminous in the skirt, it was the garment she had dreamed into being—the dress that, for what seemed like countless days now, she had imagined wearing on the night she and Louis Miller would finally make love. There was so little to be done: a small adjustment to the sleeves, an easy trim at the hem.

Would she have the strength to turn him away? Would she be forced to uphold a bond that no longer existed? She had tried to make her marriage to Nestor a good love. She had borne him two beautiful children. When Don Victor had sent him off, Silvia was a baby, still suckling at her breast; Pablo was only five. If Nestor were to walk back into their lives, right now, tonight, would her children even recognize their father?

She took the dress to the mirror and held it before her. "Look at your eyes, Graciela," she murmured, studying her purple rings. "That's what your husband gave you. Two little angels and those eyes." She turned the dress right and left, listening to the way it whispered to her, feeling the way it moved. She brought one leg forward, hooked it around the wide skirt, and kicked, making its four layers snap up like wings. She cocked her chin. "Look proud, *jelenedra*!" the gypsy Maruca had commanded. Look fierce! Graciela frowned into the glass and stamped her feet in a rapid staccato, remembering Maruca's exhortations: "Make me a face that shows the strong heart behind it! Make me a woman who stands on her feet!"

If Don Victor now knew that the teacher enjoyed having fingers on her little mount of Venus, it was becoming clearer and clearer that those fingers might never again be his. Doña Mariana commandeered all her free time. She was taking the teacher everywhere—off to Mass in the early mornings, out to a walk before siesta time, down to the sala in the evenings. One day, during the children's school hours, Don Victor charged from factory to house, hot with hope, intending to interrupt Marcela's lessons, only to see his wife huff and puff up the stairs toward the third floor, bearing a pot of steaming maté for the teacher. One night, Doña Mariana even brought her into the bedroom! As he dragged wearily in, there was Marcela, in her robe, with her thin little cotton nightdress visible under it, sitting on Doña Mariana's dressing stool, having her hair brushed. He had to admit that seeing her there in such intimate circumstances, with his wife's fingers stroking her hair and those big eyes peering up under her thick glasses, made him want her so much he could hardly contain himself. He strutted around the room, blustering on about one thing or other, and then when Doña Mariana finally kissed the woman and sent her off, he couldn't wait to clamber into bed and take his wife's breasts in his hands.

Doña Mariana, for her part, wondered what herb the witchman had given her husband to make him so suddenly virile. On the other hand, she worried about his general state of health. If the witchman's potions were giving him an appetite in bed, they were taking it away at the dinner table. Don Victor seemed more and more gaunt by the day. She resolved to be more attentive to his diet.

In truth, Doña Mariana was attending to everyone's troubles, spending her hours bustling from one want to another. There was so much to do on behalf of so many: She frowned at Elsa's ghoulish paintings, reminding her daughter-in-law that no good would come of them. She took the Jivaro girl down to Filomena's to order another dress. She put poultices of chamomile on the cook's fevered brow. She sat on Graciela's bed and talked about the shame of Mary Magdalene. She counseled Belén to eat tubers and roots. But mainly, she trotted up- and downstairs, championing the fine spirit of her grandchildren's teacher. There was no moment of the day that Doña Mariana might not burst into a room, trailing Marcela behind her, babbling on about what a good wife she'd make if only she had the patience to wait for the right husband. To Don Victor's distress, his mamita had become a remote dream.

In this mood of melancholy frustration, Don Victor sat alone one night, in the gloom of the darkened sala. Swirling his prune-black port in his father's old pewter goblet, he listened to the chirr of nocturnal life and thought about Don Carlos's famed oyster-bed mistress. How much easier on a man to cross town at an appointed hour and find a warm woman waiting—even if you have to run the gauntlet of her husband's gun—than to sit in the same house with the object of your lust and a well-meaning but meddlesome wife. Doña Mariana had extinguished the lamps and retired upstairs with Graciela and Marcela; he could hear their happy chatter above him. Outside, the winged beetles continued to fling their hard bodies against the window screens, drawn to a brightness now gone. From the forest he heard the caterwaul of monkeys and the reechoing of bats as they whirred east toward the river.

Although it was late, Don Victor longed for company. He rose in the dark, felt his way through the house, and stepped into the moonlight. Down the patio, across the road, he could see the men at Chincho's, their spirited gestures silent against the buzz of the jungle. No, he would not seek them out tonight. His needs were far deeper than liquor. Seeing a bright gleam in the distant church window, he was drawn to visit his friend.

He walked down the path, under the lambent moon, marveling at the fullness of his hemp fields. Farther on, he could see the coca, shivering in the breeze. Here and there, jutting up like great mantises, were the tall bamboo totems Yorumbo had created to protect his crops. For as far as his eye could see, the fields were flourishing. The seed had gone into the land, the earth had nourished the seed. The jungle had brought dreams to life and been good to him. He breathed in the thick night air, savoring its perfumes—mango, lily, cannabis. And then, riding the same air, came the sound of men's voices, from the direction of Chincho's bar.

"Son of a whore!" one worker said.

In the light of Chincho's torches, Don Victor could see Pedro hunched over a table with the other men, listening intently. "Yes!" someone else yelled. "But that son of a whore is no fool. He swept up from Arequipa, marched into the presidential palace, and stole the country!" "That wasn't all he did!" a third shouted. "He outlawed the people's party and stuck its leader in jail!" "Not in jail, asshole," the first worker said, pounding the table. "The man is in a foreign embassy in downtown Lima. It's worse than jail. A jail, you can break into. Or you can bribe the warden. An embassy is like being marooned at sea." So. They were talking about politics.

Alfonso Suárez had given Don Victor a lively report on President Odría's coup, but he had made the new regime sound like a good thing—the country was running again. The army was back in power. The communist upstart Haya de la Torre, whose incendiary speeches had fomented a rebellion in the docks of Callao, had been smart to sequester himself in a foreign embassy. The generals would just as soon put a bullet in his neck.

Don Victor had never cared much for politics. His father's campaigns for this and that general were dim history now, a rich man's attempts to bend the law in his favor. Since the time of the Inca, the military had served the ruling classes. And so, Don Victor supposed, it was natural for the poor to worry about a general in the presidential palace. But it all seemed so pointless here. This was the jungle, where power was decided by nature and a man's will to use it. Not by ridiculous little men in epaulets and gold braid. He wondered if he shouldn't give every worker in his hacienda a little gift to mollify him: a pig. Or perhaps a goat.

"Compadres!" Antonito, one of the pulp shovelers, shouted as he sprang onto a chair. "The army has banned workers' strikes. Now is the time!" Don Victor drew closer. "We need to take matters into our own hands!" Antonito continued. "Before you know it—" But he stopped there, and Don Victor realized that the man had seen him in the shadows.

Best to face the men squarely, Don Victor decided. He crossed the road briskly, one hand raised in greeting. His workers fell silent. Antonito slid back into his chair. The others stared down at the tables as he passed. Only Chincho called out, "Hey, boss!" He was grinning like an idiot, drying a tin cup with his apron. Don Victor continued on, hands clasped behind his back. Dirt crunched under his boots. The men's conversation resumed. Only now, he noted, they spoke in whispers.

A pig *and* a goat, he decided. Over the years, he had learned that generosity was an easy counterweight to a worker's yearnings. An unexpected gift never failed to quell the want. What was it about his cellophane that was causing such foolery among his workers? They had never seemed so petulant before.

He reached the church and mounted the steps, gazing up at the sky. It was lit with a galvanic circuit of stars.

The priest was still awake, reading at his desk, by the light of a spitting candle. "Twice in two months now!" he called out when he saw the haciendado. "After two decades of neglect!" Don Victor crossed himself as he approached the Virgin and moved quickly to take the padre's hand.

"Sit, sit!" the priest said.

"Have you ever stopped to think, Bernardo," Don Victor said as he lowered himself onto the front pew, "that the stars above on a night like this are made of the same thing we are? And that what we do down here is tied to what floats up there?"

The priest pinched his lower lip—it wasn't like the engineer to expound on the philosophy of life. "I hadn't thought of it that way, Victor, but, yes, I do see what you mean." He looked at his friend closely, searching his face for a sign. "What's on your mind?" he said finally.

"I mean, things do connect, don't they? I was thinking about this as I walked over here. Men's bones feed the dirt. The dirt feeds the seeds.

The seeds grow to plants. The plants make the paper. One ball hits another in the complex, intricate circuit that is our universe."

"But it's not without purpose."

"No, no. I didn't mean to say that it had no purpose."

"In the great, unknowable world God has made, Victor, I do believe there is one plan, with one heart and one circulatory system, if that's what you're trying to say," the priest said.

"And do you believe that we all feed on a single thing—and that that thing is the life force that connects us?"

"Yes. And that force is God's love."

"That's what I wondered. That's what I came to ask. I am thinking about the great connectedness of things, and whether if—as Christ teaches us—all men are brothers, can it be that man's gods are brothers too?"

"Well, Victor. I suspect you are asking the wrong question. There is only one God. You are His son, nothing more, nothing less. As am I. As is every soul in this hacienda, whether they have found Him or not. We are as related as children in a big family. That is the great connectedness of things. If you understand that one principle, you will know all I can possibly teach you."

Don Victor thought about that for a while, but the mention of children in a big family scooted his mind upstairs, so that, before long, he was three floors up, back at the teacher's threshold, thinking like a child himself. "Do those who sin, Padre, have a place in the kingdom of heaven?"

"Yes. We are all flawed. All sinners."

"So, if I have a place in heaven, why should I worry about sins?"

"Because the sins we mortals send forth into the world ultimately come around to strike us—they race up behind when we least expect it. Sin is a giant carousel, Victor, in which God turns the wheel full circle. It all catches up eventually. The last shall be the first, you know, and the first shall be the last."

"Like a circle of dominos?"

The priest laughed. "Like a circle of dominos."

"Like Señor Urrutia's ball bearings," Don Victor murmured.

"Hmm?"

"Nothing, nothing. I was just thinking of someone I once knew."

Padre Bernardo nodded, and put a comforting hand on his back.

Doña Mariana was beginning to think that her life had always been ruled by other people's wishes. She had come into the world because a priest had lusted after her mother. She had left home to chase after her husband's dreams. She had raised three fine children and was now raising *their* children. Here she was, at the promontory of life, with fifty-seven years of service behind her, and she was still tending the rumbles of other stomachs, worrying about someone else's desires: As she lay in her gigantic brass bed, staring at the little brass balls that seemed to orbit the predawn around her, she listened to the faraway hum of the factory and thought how little she asked of life.

If she hadn't begun her day in this frame of mind, she might simply have bustled along, the engine of efficiency that woke the servants with a sharp rap on their doors, the spirited matron who planned all the meals of the day, the caring mother who looked after her family's every necessity, doted on grandchildren, spun her own cotton, and crocheted their clothes. But, as it was, she sat alone in the early-morning light of the dining room. When had she demanded anything that wasn't for someone else's benefit? When had she drawn attention to herself?

As a child, she had always imagined that she would grow up to have a large family, a white stucco house, a retinue of servants dressed in crisp, blue uniforms. Warm bread would be delivered to the gate every morning—fresh tamales in the afternoon. The neighborhood ladies on walks to the plaza would peer through her windows and see her impeccably behaved children, sitting at the table, smiling blissfully; her handsome husband would be there too, snapping the morning edition of *El Noticiero;* and the ladies would envy her good fortune. Just as Doña Mariana was conjuring that happy vision, she heard a man's voice in the kitchen.

"Of course I'll marry you, *chukri,* if that's what you want." The voice was speaking Shipibo. "Of course we will make our child whole. But have you forgotten that you and I are from the great tribe of the Capanahua? We don't need the white man to tell us what is right. I've been realizing this, Boruba, as I listen to the workers down at Chincho's. We are living our whole lives as pawns to someone else's dreams. Ever since my uncle took me off to work in the cashew groves, I've been a servant, answering other men's orders. That's fine. That's the life I have been allotted. It doesn't mean I have to take on their ways. Don't forget I was a curandero's son. I don't need that padre to tell me what to do."

Doña Mariana recognized Pedro's voice—the steady tone of control, the unmistakable pitch of authority she would hear when he was in the field, talking to his men. But this morning the words were subversive. She felt a deep ripple of dread.

As Doña Mariana listened—half in wonder, for she hadn't imagined such conversations went on in her house—she learned that a wave of petulance was surging through the hacienda. "Listen to me, Boruba," Pedro said, "these aren't just my thoughts. There are many who share this feeling. All over this country. The revolution started far away, the workers tell me, along the seashore. Canecutters rose up. Then factory laborers. They were being treated like animals, paid nothing, and a man named Haya de la Torre told them they deserved more. We Indians were a mighty people before the conquista, he said. United, we could be mighty again. But," Pedro exploded, "the president decided that kind of talk was treason! A big fist came down on Haya de la Torre, crushed him just as people were beginning to listen. Peru has been stolen, Boruba. Now the generals are bullying their way through the highlands, putting the fear of God in the Indian, selling the country to foreigners, keeping the white men rich. That's why the rebellion is here now, pushed inland to this river."

As Pedro told it, racial fury was now fizzing steadily along the Amazon like a lit wick headed for dynamite. The president's military machine was arresting troublemakers everywhere. "Boruba, please listen to me," he said. "They say the army is pushing electric prods into men's asses, dropping boys off cliffs. You think I want the white man's church, Boruba? I do not. You can do what you want, *chukri*. You can worship at the foot of that wooden Virgin if it makes you happy. But ever since we went together to twist cellophane into her skirt, I've been thinking very hard about this. What has that church given us? All it makes are demands. What have any of these white people *really* given us?"

Surely not everyone in this hacienda was such an ingrate, Doña Mariana thought. Indignation pierced her like a needle and traveled the length of her veins. Surely the roofs over their heads, the food in their bellies, the clothes on their backs, the Christian education of their children meant something to that throng of jungle humanity.

When Don Victor arrived at the breakfast table, she wasted no time in telling him. She pulled her chair close and whispered the whole thing in his ear. When she was finished, Don Victor raised his napkin and daubed his mustache. "*Querida,*" he said, "the workers on Peru's coast are always looking for trouble! And the dumb-ass generals there have nothing better to do than run around after them. But they're far away! This is the Amazon! Those things don't happen here! It's why we came in the first place. These people don't care that my father died in a scandal, that your mother slept with a priest, that our children's ancestor was a coolie. It's enough here to put a little food in your belly, have a bag of coca to chew on, dream to your heart's content. Why would these people mount an insurrection against a system that keeps them alive? I heard the men talking about these things down at Chincho's. It's just politics, *querida*—something to gab about over a cup of *chicha*. Don't worry your pretty brain. I have it all under control."

Doña Mariana took heart in those words, so confidently spoken. Boruba did too, listening behind the door. The two glanced toward heaven, made the sign of the cross—and then went about their busy day.

Suraya arched her back, threw her arms over her head, and stretched her fingers toward the ceiling. She was tired, after a long night of love.

Slipping into her yellow tunic, she tied the string belt around her waist and went to the iron snake on the far side of the room. She opened the flow of its rusty spigot, as Boruba had taught her to do, and splashed her face with river water. She had seen so many marvels here that they no longer astounded her. The cavernous house, the constant roar from the factory, the odd family rituals, the people from so many different tribes gathered to produce that shining substance: At first, these things had startled her, but every day brought a new level of familiarity. She wandered the hacienda in a pleasant state of enchantment, marveling at Don Victor's tools and the ways they transformed the world around him; she was in awe of Doña Mariana's ability to spin thread, weave clothes for the young; she was amused by the plates on the tables, the sheets on the beds, the little bell in her room that rang when somebody needed help; she was touched by the friendly man in the brown robe who brought her small pages, like leaves, with images of a lovely woman—eyes looking skyward, hair covered by cloth.

Suraya liked Floralinda. There were daily reminders that her spirit creature had been wise to make her ride the river. She was meant to be in this place.

At first, the people of the house had been as curious about her as she about them. The children came and put their fingers in her whisker holes and begged her to wear her reeds. When she did insert them, thrusting the ends into the dirt first so that they would not slip their hold, the little ones would clap their hands and laugh. The young woman who lived at the very top of the house wore a much more elaborate decoration on her face—highly polished shells, through which her eyes were visible—but even after Suraya had let that woman feel her reeds, the woman had not returned the courtesy: She had not allowed Suraya to finger her shells. Perhaps, Suraya thought, the woman was a fish person, ruled by the spirit of water. She had heard that fish people were difficult creatures to touch. It had something to do with their skin, which was slippery, and far more sensitive than fur or feathers.

In her idle time, when she wasn't chopping vegetables or scrubbing a floor or plucking and dismembering a chicken, Suraya would puzzle over the people who lived under that roof. Who were their spirit creatures? Were they ruled by land, air, or water? Here, in this place where everyone seemed to be a traveler, tossed together by fate, it wasn't easy to know.

The shapechanger was a condor. Yorumbo had told her so. But his wife might be anything; she had no animal mannerisms, nor did she wear any tattoos or ornamentation that would reveal her spirit. The

woman with the blue rings around her eyes was definitely a cat; Suraya
had seen her holding a shiny dress, springing about on her feet. But the
woman who never left her room, who screeched like a hawk and
perched incessantly at the window, was clearly a bird, and dangerous.
She would need to be watched. Suraya couldn't make out the spirit
creatures of the others, or of the hairless little man who had come to sit
at the big table on the day she arrived. But Boruba, whose skin was
always glistening with perspiration, was most definitely a fish. Kai-me,
whom she loved beyond reason, had the wide, full face of a puma, with
eyes that tipped up at the corners. Lying in his arms, looking up at the
gold in his irises, she was sure that her spirit creature was looking down
at her and that, in a universe with so many new rules, she had found
something akin to home.

Every night, after the Sobrevillas had climbed the stairs to bed, Jaime
retired to the empty library, put his lips to the screened window, and
whistled softly: three times—two short, one long. Within minutes,
Suraya would slip through the door, her shift clinging to her body, her
nipples hard under the cloth. He would never forget the night she
appeared naked, just as he had first seen her, with cellophane in her
hair. Except that the paper was woven with casuarina blossoms, purple
vine, and turquoise feathers—and the whole towered above her head
like plumage. In her hands she carried a stone, as smooth and yellow
as a serpent's egg. She knelt in the center of the room and tugged on
his pant leg. When he had flung all his clothes, one by one, into a chair,
she pulled him to his knees, pressed the stone to her forehead, and
placed it between them on the carpet. He did the same. Next, she
pressed the stone to each of her eyes and laid it down again. He did the
same, his desire for her mounting. From nose to lips to chin to neck to
chest, each of them pressed the stone into various parts of their
anatomies, until she reached her belly. At which point he was so filled
with want that he pushed it aside and took her in his arms. They made
love with her headdress splayed on the carpet, its perfume invading his
soul.

They didn't need to talk. They didn't need to trade opinions about this or that or comment on the weather. There was meaning in their tones of voice, narrative in their gestures. He understood when she was angry. He understood when she wanted tenderness. He understood when something delighted her. And she understood these things about him in return. Often he would marvel at the redundancy of language. For her to utter a comprehensible sentence to him was as unnecessary as an infant asking to be kissed. He remembered holding his children when they were first born, staring into their faces for hours, reading every nuance of comfort or discomfort. Gazing into Suraya's eyes as she looked up from the tangled splendor of her hair, Jaime felt it wouldn't matter if he never spoke another word in his life.

14

M ore champagne!' No, no. Too abrupt. Slow it down. Stretch it
out—he's not one for short sentences! 'My king, my very own
sweet *generál*, don't be so lazy, you bad, bad boy! Don't just sit there
looking handsome! Pour me a little champagne, won't you, darling?
Give me a drop more!' Ha! Yes! That's perfect!"

For weeks now, Elsa had chatted with her reflection in the mirror,
practicing her repartee, pursing her lips prettily. She imagined the general opposite her at dinner, turning an eloquent phrase, savoring her
rejoinders. Night after night, she took his hastily scribbled note from
her pearl-studded purse and set it out on her writing table. *Snug, mug,
rug:* She had memorized the shapes of those words by now. It was
difficult to imagine the potentate with the tidy mustache producing
that anxious black scrawl, but how cosmopolitan of him to write it in
English; how clever to pen it as he walked; how cunning to disguise his
plan!

She visualized them strolling arm in arm across Lima's Plaza de
Armas. They would walk under the blaze of the lamplight, anticipating
a ball in the president's palace. Perhaps they would dine at the nearby
Hotel Crillon, at a table providentially graced with lilacs. She would
breathe in their fragrance and listen to the purr of his voice. Lifting a
flute of pilsner (or pisco, or pernod, or pinot), he would launch into

witty accounts of ancient campaigns (of Saladin, or Hannibal, or Napoleon), replete with marching slaves and intermezzos of local color.

Pacing her room during a particularly vivid flight of fancy in which she envisioned herself on a brisk promenade on the Jirón de la Unión, she tripped on a corner of her carpet, exposing an irregularly cut panel in the floor. She thought nothing of it until she kicked the rug into place and noticed that something beneath rattled slightly, as if the wood were loose. Folding the rug back again, she took a closer look. It was a small slat of wood, an improvised lid, no longer than four or five inches. She put one fingernail on either side and lifted it with care. Underneath, she could make out the space between the floor and the first-floor ceiling. She leaned in to study the cavity, quickly surmising that she was looking down at Belén's library, but a pale little lizard leapt out and startled her so that she fell back on her haunches with a cry. It scampered toward the wall. Perhaps the gap was nothing more than that—a hiding place for vermin—but she peered once again into the murky grayness. As her eyes adjusted, she realized she was looking down on a man and a woman, naked and making love. Quickly, for her shock was greater than her curiosity, she dropped the slat into its groove. All she had seen was the suggestion of a face, two legs, and a man's naked back, but it was enough. She straightened the carpet and sat there, covering her mouth with her hands.

All night, she dreamed of the shadowy lovers, rolling and thrusting in the dark. The dreams were vivid, lifelike. Her mind turned again and again to the image of the man's arching spine, his driving buttocks, and each time, she would spiral to consciousness, wet with desire.

When morning finally came, she rummaged through her suitcases, pulled on a simple dress, and ran downstairs to the library. Agitated, she paced back and forth, studying the ceiling. She was backing toward the door when Belén came in the room and saw her. "You can hurt yourself walking backward," Belén said, as if speaking to a child. "You could fall and crack your head open like an egg."

"Oh!" Elsa spun around. "It's you."

"What are you looking for up there?"

"I'm looking for you, Belén! Did you sleep well?"

"Why...yes."

"And Ignacio?" Elsa felt a mean smirk come over her face and tried mightily to suppress it.

"He's up and off to the factory. Why?"

"Oh, I don't know. Just curious. Don't mind me!" Elsa giggled to herself. "I'll go now." She moved toward the door and Belén stepped aside, bewildered, but just as Elsa reached for the doorknob, she stopped. "There's a hole in my bedroom floor," she added simply, almost in passing. "I wonder if you knew it was there?"

"Oh, that," said Belén. "I put it there years ago, before you came to the hacienda."

"You?"

"Yes, me. Your room was mine when I was a child, you see, and I was convinced that the characters in my books came to life at night, when everyone was asleep. Of course, much as I tried to spy on them, I couldn't." She smiled. "Have you been looking through my little hole?"

"Yes." Elsa narrowed her eyes.

"Well then!" Belén said, laughing. "I hardly think you're seeing much come to life either!"

Stunned, Elsa fled the room.

Later that night, when the house was dark, she lifted the slat and again saw the lovers. It seemed they were playing a game. Each stretched a hand forward to a place between them, then pulled it back again. The scene was as formal as a ballet—the motions swift and graceful—until the figure on the right reached for the one on the left and drew it hungrily to the floor. Beyond that, all Elsa could see was a woman with an iridescent fan splayed around her face. Moving over her silently was the shadowy form of the man.

She was sure the woman was Belén, but she couldn't believe the man was Ignacio. The figure was tall and rangy, whereas the foreman was short and square. The shape of the shoulders seemed familiar, but she couldn't quite place it. More frustrating, she was distracted by the enormous tussock on Belén's head. What was that monstrosity? Clearly the woman had read too much—the headdress looked like something out of an Egyptian storybook. But most puzzling of all: Why would Belén talk about the peephole so nonchalantly? Did she mean Elsa to witness her infidelity? It was so flagrant a taunt, so vulgar. Horrified, Elsa slid the wood over the hole and went to sit in the dark at her table. She folded and unfolded General López's invitation. Now that the most civilized Sobrevilla had sunk to a new level of debauchery, she had to extract herself from their house as soon as possible. If only López would arrive.

But for three more nights, Elsa watched Belén and her mysterious lover ravish each other, plunging into a depravity she hadn't imagined possible. Fueled by prurience, goaded by desire, she shooed off the lizards and put her eye to the floor. Night after night, she saw Belén take the stranger into every orifice and rut him like a demon beast. The face in that frenzied hell was only partly visible, but as far as Elsa was concerned, ecstasy altered reality. Belén was Belén, but she looked different somehow in the sex act—her shadowy breasts seemed inflated, her ghostly buttocks muscular.

Elsa felt weak and used, as if she, too, had been coupling for three nights on the floor. She staggered to bed in the wee hours of morning, her head reeling with sexual exhaustion. She needed to get out. Now. The man in the uniform would be her angel of deliverance.

The last thing General López imagined was that he was the answer to anyone's prayers. But on the fourth morning, as Elsa sat down to the table by the window, there he was, standing on the dock, looking like the very model of a savior. She leapt to her feet and waved a lace handkerchief. He seemed to give a little nod in return. Clutching a hand to her heart, she wept tears of joy.

She took a clean piece of paper from her stationery box and wrote with as steady a hand as she could manage:

My dear General López,

How lovely to see that you are back in Floralinda, just as you promised you would be. To answer your kind invitation—yes. Of course, I will come with you on your boat. My bags are ready. I am so grateful for your exquisite delicacy of feeling. There is much I long to tell you about this sad and wayward place, the least of whose offenses are its coca violations.

Ever yours, Elsa Márquez y Márquez

With a sharp tug on Don Victor's wire bell pull, she summoned Boruba's new girl, pressed the note into her hand, pointed out the window, and instructed her to deliver it to the man on the dock—the one with all the ornaments on his chest.

Suraya ran through the undergrowth. She disliked man-made roads, preferring the feel of foliage between her hard, bare toes. She clasped Elsa's envelope to the belly of her yellow shift. She hadn't understood a word of the woman's babble, but she felt sorry for her: the urgent way Elsa thrust the paper into Suraya's hands, the hungry look as she pointed toward the dock.

Suraya could see through the mist that the man was still there, although his tribesmen had gathered around him. He was clearly an *unt;* his floating palace was the most elaborate she'd ever seen. Lit by a night of love and captivated by the figure of that chieftain, she danced her way through the ferns.

The soldiers of the Fifth Military Region fell into formation. Squinting into the afternoon fog, they surveyed the hacienda: On one side were workers, shoveling the steamy pulp from the concrete floor into wheelbarrows; on the other, the girl in yellow, running like a nimble animal, back to the magnificent house. "The Republic of Peru summons Victor Sobrevilla Paniagua!" an adjutant shouted, and one of the factory's laborers darted into the factory, trembling with unholy dread. It wasn't often the river brought agents of the iron fist. The worker scooted into the long building, hissing to his cohorts as he passed, "Shut your mouths. The green jackets are here."

Emerging from the factory, Don Victor was momentarily startled by the sight of so many uniforms. There were at least two dozen soldiers lined up along the river, shouldering heavy rifles. The pulp shovelers gawked, wondering whether their halfhearted conversation down at Chincho's had prompted something so dire as a military intervention. But the capitalists were forever summoning generals. Wasn't that how it always was?

Don Victor's appearance so stunned the general that he had to force himself not to laugh out loud. What was that ridiculous contraption on his head? Two tin cups were clamped against his ears. A metal brace vaulted his head. A tuft of grizzled hair shot up from the apparatus, the rest lay shackled against his skull. His mustache, long enough to groom into a magnificent set of wings, drooped from the sides of his mouth. There were stains on the shirt. His trouser legs were so wide they whipped like two torn sails behind him, slapping his calves as he walked. The general couldn't entirely suppress the impulse to laugh: His face broke into a smile. The workers traded looks, sure now that their employer had made a calculated alliance with the visitor—the army was there at Don Victor's invitation. And Don Victor, seeing warmth in the general's greeting, decided to be genial in return.

"Welcome to Floralinda, sir," he said, offering his hand, but as soon as he spoke, his face was filled with confusion. He couldn't hear his own voice. He pulled off the metal device and his hair sprang up like a doll's. The general could no longer restrain himself. He exploded in high, jolly laughter and extended a friendly hand.

"Señor Sobrevilla, how do you do," he shouted over the din of the factory. "I am General José Antonio López, head of the army out of Iquitos. This is quite an operation you have here."

"I understand it's not the first you've seen it," Don Victor shouted back.

"Quite right. I had the distinct pleasure of chatting with your daughter."

"Daughter-in-law."

"Ah, yes, of course." The general rubbed his chin. "Is there somewhere we might sit and talk, señor?" He turned quickly, and his gun came into view.

All at once, Don Victor recalled the rifle that had dispatched his mother from this earth. The memory darted through like a pesky insect. But he pushed away the thought—dismissed that old, instinctive anger—and shouted for his workers to bring something to sit on. A giant straw parasol was plunged into the dirt, for the sky above was darkening, and two stools were arranged underneath. The general's company stood watch, their backs to the great bronze river.

"I gather you make cellophane in that factory," López said, swatting a fly from his neck.

"Correct," Don Victor answered.

"It strikes me as incredible that anyone could produce something so elegant in this jungle inferno."

"One might think so, but it is perfectly sensible to make it in a place where plants thrive."

"What plants, specifically?"

"Hemp, cotton, mainly. Sometimes we use cetico, but only rarely."

"Anything else?"

"Not really. Cellophane can be temperamental."

"How about coca? You grow coca leaf here?"

"Yes, we do. But only for local consumption."

"Local consumption! How many people live in this hacienda?"

"Three hundred and twenty, give or take a few."

"All of them chew coca?"

"It's not unusual for the haciendas along this river to provide coca to the workers. That's just how it is. They chew it the way you and I drink coffee."

"I don't need a lecture on *coqueos,* señor. I know very well how the leaf is used." The general's spine stiffened. "How many hectares do you dedicate to coca?"

"Oh, I couldn't say, really. Look here, General, what is your point?"

"Your fields are illegal, señor. You must register them with the army and turn over all sales to our offices. That is my point."

"Sales? With all due respect, that is ridiculous. There are no sales. As I told you, it is for local consumption. What they don't chew, we dump into the cookers and use for fiber to make paper."

"That is not what I've been told."

"Told by whom?"

"By an informant whose name I will not divulge. He is quite knowledgeable about your fields and factory. I have a map here of your crop allocations." The officer reached into his breast pocket and took out a white envelope with his name written on it in a delicate, cursive hand. "Oh, pardon me, not this one." He seemed momentarily flustered as he put the letter back and reached into the other side of his jacket. "Here it is. Here." He drew out a parchment folded many times over. When he opened it, Don Victor could see that it was an accurate rendering of his hacienda.

"That's quite impressive," he said, "but old. Several months ago, we reapportioned the fields to grow fiber for cellophane."

"But the coca remains the same, does it not?"

"The coca, ah, yes. That is true."

"Well, señor. My men need to look around your hacienda. When you disburse coca to your workers, you must either instruct them to pay an army representative, or you will pay that army representative on their behalf. That is the law, and if I need to leave a soldier here to enforce it, I will not hesitate to install one."

Don Victor rose to his feet. "That, sir, is preposterous. Sell coca to my own people? Absurd! I thought that kind of exploitation ended a century and a half ago when Peru chased the Spaniards home. The army can't just come in here and take over. What I grow on my land with my own labor belongs to me."

"Not according to President Odría, it doesn't." López stood and thrust out his chest. "Today we start the survey of this hacienda, and we'll stay as long as we need to. You have a choice. Cooperate with me or answer to the minister of defense. He has ways to bring culprits in line."

"What you say is tantamount to extortion, General. You will get no cooperation from me." Trussing his head with his metal device, Don Victor stormed back to the factory.

General López straightened his jacket and calmly made his way up the road, toward the big house. A number of workers who had gathered in front of the great ball digester watched him walk up the hill.

"See that?" Flavio said. "The army's not going anywhere. The old man has just made a deal with the general."

"You fool," Antonito said. "Can't you see Don Victor is in a rage? They were arguing! He didn't summon that green jacket here."

"How do you know?" Pedro shouted. "Maybe Don Victor's upset because the general just told him the river is crawling with rebels!"

"Look," said Flavio. "Over there." He nodded toward the soldiers.

They were at ease, smoking cigarettes. "Now look there." He pointed to the general, who was halfway up the path to the house. "Does anyone look nervous to you? That green jacket looks as comfortable as a cousin on a Sunday visit!"

The next thing they saw would corroborate Flavio's summation completely. There on the patio stood the *loca,* smiling and rubbing her lace-gloved hands as if salvation itself had arrived in the form of the Army of the Republic. When the general marched up the steps like Pizarro toward his queen, she smiled down with open gratitude. The two sat together under the potted tree, but not before he bowed like a lowly vassal.

But truth is truth. Illusion, illusion.

"My dear General, how happy I am to see you." Elsa was radiant in pink organza.

"Not as glad as I am to see you, dear lady." She seemed lovelier than he remembered. A hint of anxiety lit her features.

"You received my letter, I trust?" she asked.

"I did. Are you in danger?"

"Oh yes, señor. Terrible danger. Terrible."

"You are a vision, señora—more beautiful than on the morning I first met you. Allow me to kiss your hands." She obliged him. "Now tell me, what could possibly be so wrong?"

"I will tell you as much as I can, although there are things, you understand, that a refined woman cannot mention. You must know how grateful I am that you have come to deliver me from this purgatory."

López was surprised by her words, but pleased to have his suspicions confirmed. Something smelled wrong in this hacienda. He was sure of it: To start with, there was that haughty jungle lord, dressed like a clown, dismissing a division general—an emissary of the president!— as if he were a bothersome gnat. And then there were those men by the factory, gathered like a row of magpies, yakking conspiratorially. He turned back to the pretty woman. "I want to know more. Tell me what you mean by 'purgatory,' *princesa,*" he said.

"*Princesa!* What a wonderful word you use! But shhh! We must whisper. Tiny, tiny voices. You can't imagine how people in this house can pry. All the peepholes!"

It was worse than he thought. The poor woman seemed slightly unhinged. "Calm yourself, dear. *Calmate bien!*" He leaned in, took her hands. "Tell me."

She took a deep breath. "Priests having children."

"Really?" It was not the answer he had expected.

"Yes. Awful."

"And...?" He determined to be patient, coax her gently.

"And Chinese coolies! Forced to procreate with their masters!"

"You don't say. Here? On this river?" He could see now that he would have to humor her.

"A coolie's bastard is here in this house! And his children and grand-children!"

"Hmm. I see." He sat back, wondering how to talk to the woman—so beautiful, so fragile, and under such obvious strain. "So, Señora Sobrevilla, how exactly do those things, awful as they are, put you in danger?"

"Please, General. Don't call me Señora Sobrevilla. That name is offensive to me. My marriage is, in effect, annulled. I am quite sure that Rome will approve it. The name is very simply Elsa Márquez y Márquez, but please call me Elsa. You needn't be formal."

"Do you fear for your physical safety, Elsa?"

"No. Not now that you're here, José Antonio."

He smiled. He could certainly use this woman.

"You would not believe what is allowed to happen in this house, José Antonio. We might as well be living in the trees, picking the fleas from our fur."

Suddenly a voice rang from above. "Elsa? *Elsa!* Are you talking to yourself again?" They looked up to see Doña Mariana's face at the balcony. "Oh! Good morning! I apologize. I didn't know anyone else was here. I'll be right down."

"Oh my God!" Elsa whispered in alarm.

"Is that the haciendado's wife?"

"Yes."

"Just don't mention what you've told me."

"But you don't understand, José Antonio! I can't help myself! If it's true, I say it. So does everyone else around here, believe me."

"What on earth do you mean?"

"The truth! The truth! I can't help it."

"Here, give me your hand again, Elsa. I am here to assist you. I make you that pledge. Just quiet down."

"There you are!" Doña Mariana said, hurrying out to the patio.

The general introduced himself and explained his presence. "I've already informed your husband, madam. The army has assumed control of all coca cultivation in the country. We are here to carry out a survey of our fields."

"Yes. I do think I remember something like that being mentioned at the dinner table. We didn't really believe—"

"I told you!" Elsa said, reddening. "I told all of you! The general came here the morning Don Victor went off to the curandero! You remember—to rid his memories of Vanessa." Her hand flew to her mouth, but she couldn't stop. "You weren't here either, Doña Mariana. You were off with that reprobate priest."

"Elsa! General López, you must excuse our Elsa. She's a little . . . you know. Harmless, but . . . Perhaps you'd like to meet my other children? Please do come into the house. We'll be more comfortable there. I'll try to find Belén—"

"Belén! Oh, General! She's the worst of them!" Elsa wailed. "If you only knew the depravities to which that woman has sunk! Fornicating on the floor with a stranger!" López stepped back, amazed by what he was hearing. Was she mad, as the matron seemed to imply, or simply telling the truth? His informant had told him that Don Victor was arrogant, insufferable, maybe even a little cracked by a long tenure in the jungle, but he had not said Floralinda was Gomorrah.

"That's enough!" Doña Mariana erupted. "If you weren't slapping that hand over your mouth, I'd do it myself! It's one thing to be insane. It's another to insult my children."

"It's all right, señora. Quite all right," López said, suddenly exasperated by the quarrelsome women. "I must go. My troops are waiting for me. Much as I would be pleased to meet your daughter, of course." He paused and then added for Elsa's benefit, "In any case, my boat will be docked in Floralinda for another day or two. But do tell me, Señora

Sobrevilla, where might I find a sample of that famous cellophane? I neglected to ask your husband to show it to me."

"You haven't seen it?" Doña Mariana said, genuinely surprised. "Well, of course I'll fetch some."

"Thank you," he said, bowing as she disappeared into the workshop. Then he turned to Elsa. "Stay in the house for another few days," he commanded her. "You'll be more useful to me here."

"You'll take me away?"

"If that's what you want. Be quiet now. Here she comes."

Doña Mariana rushed toward them, holding the shining paper. "Here you are, General." She put a hand to her heart.

"Thank you, señora. That's very kind. Ah yes, this is cellophane, all right. Very fine, very pretty." He folded it into a small square and tucked it inside his coat.

"Will you look at that!" Flavio shouted at Pedro. "The old lady just gave that general *money*! You *see* it? You see her give it to him with a hand over her heart?"

And so, there it was. The workers had seen it all clearly: There it was, as it always had been, ever would be. The general was in the employ of the Sobrevillas. He would do their bidding. The bribe in his pocket had been his price.

* * *

Dear Belén,

Thank you for all your efforts to dissuade this old heart and keep me "safely" in Trujillo, but my mind is made up. I do not want to die in this city. The monster in the presidential palace is too much in evidence here, as far as we are from Lima. His soldiers are everywhere. The strikes have been quelled and the organizers have fled inland. The rich will get richer now, and Odría and his generals will see to it. All the poor wanted was a bit of warm food in their bellies, a bit of God's light in their lives. Now what they have is cold steel at their backs.

What you say about Floralinda, with its harmless insanities, strikes me as far, far better than this tomb of the walking dead. There's no point in your writing to me again, *hijita*. Alejandro has promised to take me to Pucallpa once the fogs subside. From there, I'll come on the river. Of course.

Tía Esther

* * *

Mwambr gazed through the mist at the floating bunker in the distance. He and his men had been following it as it churned its way upriver. The loathing he felt for the termite warrior had been instinctive, consuming. He detested the arrogant stance, the ornaments on the chest, the stomping on shore, as if he were lord of the river. And yet every day seemed to bind their fates closer together. It was not until Mwambr saw the roaring forge by the riverbank—its stinking spew, its green rolls glinting like the eyes of a reptile—that he realized his fate was spooling more quickly now. The sight of his own daughter, approaching the warrior, confirmed it. Mwambr felt his blood leap like a nimble panther. He was filled with wonder for his spirit creature, the force that had propelled him against all weariness. It had led him to Suraya. His men did not know her right away—not from the back, with her hair pulled up, and the yellow cloth draped over her body. The *kakaram* did not smell her blood. But Mwambr knew his daughter immediately. Her gait was unmistakable—that surefooted step with its cleanness of motion. That smooth, easy lope of a cat. The moment he recognized it, he felt his *arutam* rising—the fire in the chest that makes warriors forget fear. She came to a stop before the evil headman, her bearing prouder than any Jivaro warrior's, and he was reminded how much he loved the girl. Issuing a soft whistle from the side of his teeth, he ordered his men to retreat soundlessly, into the shelter of green.

Forty miles to the south of Floralinda, where the river begins its relentless east–west zigzag, the barge lurched in the rain. The Australian looked up from his book. He had read the same poem so many times that its words were burned into memory.

I must go down to the seas again, for the call of the running tide
Is a wild call and a clear call that may not be denied.

He would read the other sixty-seven poems at leisure, then flip to the same page and feel the hair on his forearms rise. It had physical force, that verse. How had she known it would move him? How had his raunchy proposition—scrawled on a drunken dare—produced such a generous response? He wanted to thank her, tell her that she and her book had come to mean more than all the coromandel in China, but she had come for the mail with the old señora at her side, and the words had flown from his head. Oh, yes, that hatchet-faced biddy hanging on to her elbow was right to worry: He was a mean dog, loose dog, tied to nothing so much as freedom. Spawned in a brothel in Darwin, flung out to sea at ten, he had learned all he knew about reading from old sailors. He had learned all about love from old whores. Now here he was, a foolish man on a fetid river, with a teacher breaking his heart.

Sixty miles to the north, pushing his way upriver, Louis Miller nursed a bad arm. It had been almost a month since he had seen Graciela, and, struggling against time and the vicissitudes of the river, reason told him he wouldn't see her for another two days. Somewhere south of Dos de Mayo, the rain and the mud had forced him to pull ashore, lug his waterlogged motor into a skin trader's reeking hovel, and hang his equipment in three hammocks to dry.

In exchange for a place to stay, Miller had offered the skin trader help with six alligator corpses, but when he tried to grasp one by the tail, the creature drew on its last bit of strength to strike him with it. He fell hard on the riverbank, breaking the long bone of his arm. After that, he could only sit at the door of the shack, watch the river swell, and listen to his host butcher carcasses. The hacking of flesh lasted for days.

Once the motor had dried, he started upriver again, but a flatboat of hysterical Indians ferrying bananas in the opposite direction warned him that a troop of armed rebels was moving downriver with a dory of soldiers in pursuit. For twenty-four more hours, Miller stayed with the skin trader, and on that second night—as promised—two boats drifted by and he counted the shadows of twenty-one heads. The rebels skimmed past, with nothing to illuminate them but the glow of cigarettes. The next morning, a company of stone-faced soldiers slipped silently in the same direction, hunched against the driving rain. One called out, "*Oye,* gringo! You seen any shiteaters with guns?"

"None," he called back, and thrust his canoe resolutely into the current.

15

Belén's cellophane-wrapped books glistened from her bookshelves, bathing the library in light. Omar Khayyám's poems nestled against *Don Quixote,* which in turn rubbed shoulders with Guy de Maupassant's short stories, and so on, causing a voluptuous friction from El Inca Garcilaso down the ages to Karl Marx.

Watching Ignacio's hands move over the cellophane in the very room where his wife conducted her nightly orgies filled Elsa with agitation. She squinted through the peephole at shelves that glittered by day, phantoms that coupled by night, and longed for the general to give her a sign, send for her. It wasn't easy playing the spy.

The rain had ruined everything. Although the factory was churning cellophane beyond Alfonso Suárez's wildest expectations, the general's coca survey had come to a sudden halt. Elsa remained in limbo, waiting for deliverance. At first, the soldiers had braved the downpour, venturing into the fields to determine what grew where. Elsa saw them race through the torrents with sheets of gray oilcloth flapping behind them. But by the next afternoon they had stopped entirely. They seemed more interested in monitoring Chincho's, where laborers huddled under the palm thatch, dreaming of insurrection. The green jackets took their positions on the deck, under their hastily rigged awning, training their binoculars on the bar's motley population day after day, until they were as fixed to Floralinda as ticks to a hapless goat.

"We're under occupation!" Don Victor roared, roaming the moldering house, knocking his wax-paper umbrella against the floors until the parrot complained and the dog slinked along the walls. At the factory, the laborers threw themselves into their work. The very thought of President Odría's electric prods up their asses was all the inspiration they needed—they were determined to prove, beyond any soldier's doubt, their patriotic credentials. The rain worked in their favor. Water flooded the vats and cleaned the pulp. Rolls of red and green cellophane spun efficiently from the reelers and they began to accumulate, until there were endless stacks lining the long wall of the factory. The army was making Don Victor rich, but he didn't factor it. All he could think of was the butt of the rifle that had struck his mother dead on a long-ago, faraway morning. Come nights, he stood on the patio, drenched in rain, shouting, "*Viva la revolución, hombres!* If Peru got rid of the Spaniards, we'll get rid of those pigs on our dock!" At Chincho's, the workers scratched their heads in confusion.

Day after day the soldiers did little more than sit there, occasionally slipping out to buy a pig from Filomena, butcher it on the muddy banks, roast it under a tin shield, and collect rainwater in great, metal drums. The torrents became so violent that the barges ceased to appear and the river seemed free of human traffic. The jungle groaned with the weight of water until trees fell like tired colossuses, bringing down webs of vines. Eventually, the river was so swollen that water creatures flung themselves onto the flooded banks, abandoning the great rolling waterway. Frogs surged up the mud, coughing and chirping, confusing the night with day. Eels slithered through ferns, leaping in giddy arcs. A twenty-foot anaconda surfaced on the deck of the *Augusto Leguía* and sent the general into his first round of combat. He called to his soldiers to bring out their bayonets. The giant serpent slid languidly over the bobbing vessel, barely registering its attackers as they lunged back and forth, taunting it with their weapons. Finally, it raised its head, bared its teeth, and pushed itself to the edge, where it plunged into the river, leaving a whirlpool behind.

The work in the fields came to a standstill. There was little for a worker to do but stare at his wife across his table or out a window at the pouring rain. Even as days passed and Pedro and Boruba were married (in spite of his misgivings, in the white padre's church with the Virgin of Copacabana smiling down on him), even as Boruba waddled happily back and forth from her husband's shack to her master's kitchen, the fields lay sodden and unattended, and the seeds were not tamped into the soil.

From time to time the rain abated, waning to a drizzle before it resumed with force. At just such a moment Elsa—always standing vigil—caught sight of a vision that terrified her. For seven years she had painted apocalyptic scenes of a barbarian invasion, and suddenly the barbarians were there, rows and rows of them, creeping along the jungle, staring out at the hacienda's imposing structures. She squinted, trying to get a better look at the fierce faces. The dense forest canopy protected them from the deluge, but even so, paint streaked down their skin. In their hands were long lengths of bamboo and, dangling from their waists, bundles of tiny spheres.

In a state of acute panic, Elsa ran down to the sala to warn the family. But as soon as she finished describing the jungle savages, she couldn't help saying a word or two about Belén's savage fornications, and clutched by the additional fear that she wouldn't be able to keep the rest of her secrets, she went scurrying back upstairs. Doña Mariana shook her head, clucked over her crochet needles, and said to the rest of them, "Didn't I tell you that those wretched canvases would come to no good?"

Savage fornications. For the rest of her days Belén would wonder how it was that Elsa knew so much about her secrets. Belén would not have called it "fornication," but there were many words like it that might have been used to describe her recent obsession: carnality, fleshliness, copulation, sex. How was it that a recluse who confined herself to her room could guess Belén's new joy with such accuracy?

Making love for Belén had become a nightly ritual. Ignacio would open the door of their bedroom to find her standing there, wearing nothing but Old Wong's hat. The sight of her under the symbol of the Chinaman's passion would stir equal passion in him. That red satin cap with its dangling tassel spoke of love, marriage, sacrifice. There was something at once erotic and wistful in the sight of his wife's beautiful body—slender, childlike, golden—waiting for him under it.

"Come here, my sweet Shanghai princess."

They would make love in a heat. And then afterward they would linger long in their conjugal embraces.

Locked in Ignacio's arms, Belén murmured that Elsa had discovered the peephole she had made as a child. Ignacio chuckled at the image of Belén as a young girl, drilling a hole in the floor, her face in a purposeful frown. He drew her close and kissed her on the forehead. But the following night, as he continued to swaddle his wife's books in the library, he looked up and saw an opening with a dancing light through it, as if someone above were watching.

Belén, too, sensed Elsa's eyes on her as she sat in her library and tried to read, her mind tugged by the memory of Ignacio's hands. What instrument of witchery, what idiot gift of perception, had made Elsa able to spy her there in the daylight and know about her nights elsewhere?

For eight years, Belén had scrupulously tended her frigidity. Her bed was made according to long-standing instructions: two sheets folded vertically and anchored at the foot, so that she and Ignacio would crawl into bags of their own—an ingenious device to prevent skin from touching. But on the night she discovered him wrapping her books, everything had changed. It was as if the barrenness of those long years had given them resources they didn't know they had. Kneeling, standing, on the bed, in a chair, wherever they could within the confines of their room, Belén and Ignacio sought each other's pleasures. Elsa had called it savage. An observer might well have: the fevered reaching, the constant hunger, the unabashed demands. Fornication with a stranger? The accusation was not entirely inaccurate: Belén and Ignacio had been estranged for a hundred moons. For all her confusion, Elsa was onto something. A new wildness peered out from her sister-in-law—a rawness no one had imagined was there.

Asked to give a layman's explanation, Don Victor's professors at the School of Engineers might have explained the events in Floralinda this way: Just when you think you've perceived a subject clearly—just when the glass, or the light, or the peephole has allowed you to observe it with certitude—nature fools you. Blame it on perspective, on distortions in the medium, on the demons of simulacra: You can't always believe what you see. In optics it's called an aberration—when light is imperfect, when rays fail to converge to a sharply defined focus. It can be due to a flaw, to the distance, or perhaps even to a failure in the optic nerve. Astronomers know this as the aberration of heavenly bodies: You think you see a star to the left, but in fact it is to the right, because, though every hair on your head is in place, you are reeling through the universe at considerable velocity. This is very like the moment when you gaze out the window of a moving car and the rain looks as if it is falling sideways. It is not. Its trajectory is a plumb line toward the center of the earth, following the brute pull of gravity. But if you are planted serenely in your seat, it is hard to factor that you are rushing along the earth's surface, and so what you think you see happening isn't happening at all.

Don Victor was certain his workers saw him as simpatico. Yorumbo was fooled into thinking that Don Victor's problems were sexual. Padre Bernardo would have sworn that Doña Mariana was battling temptation.

And Elsa: She was persuaded that Belén was making love to a stranger. Until the night Elsa looked down the peephole and heard the man say with perfect clarity, "My darling!" For all the hours she had spent watching him, this was the first she had heard him speak. In one terrible, mind-illumining moment, Elsa realized that the dark of night, or the distance from floor to floor, or the wretched business of trying to see through a hole had tricked her. It wasn't that a light had switched on and Elsa was suddenly able to bring more skill to the task of spying. It was the voice. Once she heard it, she saw with absolute certainty the outline of Jaime's body. She recognized the span of his shoulders, the muscled back, the solid trunks of his legs. It had been so long since she had seen him naked. But now Elsa understood what she was looking at: her own husband in heated coupling with Belén. How could she have missed it?

Like an astronomer computing the aberration of starlight, she dropped Jaime into the equation, figuring how that velocity might alter the picture. The fact that her husband was rutting downstairs meant little. As far as she was concerned, he was an animal, the spawn of a priest and a coolie. In her mind, she had divorced him the moment she'd learned of his tainted bloodline, or perhaps the instant she'd laid eyes on the general. She had put the man so out of mind that she hadn't seen the obvious sooner.

Jaime and Belén.

It was at that exact juncture in her qualitative analysis that Elsa let out a scream that reverberated through the hacienda like a cathedral bell at the Inquisition. Then came the invective—"Perverts!" "Incest!" "Criminals!"—at such a pitch that even the rush of rain couldn't distort them.

The instant Doña Mariana heard screams, she reached for her robe and rushed to the next-door bedroom. Don Victor crossed his arms under his head and sighed. He no longer suspected that his cellophane was causing this madness. He was sure of it. Some *duende* in the headbox, some demon in the digester, some evil eye in the rollers had brought the hacienda to this vale. The evil eye: He should have asked Yorumbo to visit the factory, gathered the sumirunas from up and down the river, insisted that they all carry out a ceremony to purge it.

His wife's fearful whispers about insurgency seemed preposterous. The workers weren't going to rise up against the army, no matter how much he hectored them. They were trooping like ants past that damn boat every day. They were working long hours, doubling the factory's volume. A haciendado couldn't ask for more. The factory had just sent off its third shipment of cellophane, and it made his heart swell to see giant spindles of the stuff, wrapped in strong cardboard, roll down the ramps of the dock onto the southbound barges. When he and Ignacio organized two shifts so that the mill could run day and night, the workers had grumbled, complaining that they had little time to eat or sleep, much less make love to their women. But Don Victor moved quickly to appease them. He sent word via the barges to have a hundred goats delivered to Floralinda: one for each worker's family. Then he announced very clearly, so that all in the vicinity could hear it, that the goats would be followed by an equal number of pigs.

Watching that ragtag refuse of a capricious jungle file to work in the mornings, he often wondered how desperate their lives must have been to spur them to board a barge and come to a hacienda just because he asked them to. What misery had they known before? Year after year they slept in those shacks, rose before the sun, shuffled out shoeless to make something they couldn't eat, couldn't use, whose utility they could hardly fathom. All of it for a modicum of pay, a roof over their heads, a little food, a handful of coca. And why were they suddenly working so hard? What spell did that army boat have over them?

As he lay in bed staring at the ceiling, it seemed he, too, had always been under a spell one way or another. He had risen one morning forty-eight years ago, walked across the square with his tía Esther, been handed a prophesy by a monkey, and the rest had played out just as the fortune dictated. All of it had been written, every turn in the road pre-recorded, right up to the moment at hand.

Doña Mariana returned, her spine stiff with alarm. "Ay, Victor!" she said. "I've reached my limit! That viper is now smearing *all* of our children. You won't believe the slanderous poison she just spat at me! She told me that she saw, with her own two eyes, our youngest and our eldest, rutting like dogs downstairs."

"Jaime and Belén?" Don Victor sat up, incredulous. "Not possible!" he concluded with a laugh.

"Of course not! But it's not in the least amusing, *querido*. You should see her." Doña Mariana recounted how she had found Elsa on her knees in the middle of the room, the carpet thrown back to reveal a hole in the floor. Her face had been red with rage, the veins of her neck bulging. Her long hair was tangled, coated with dust. "Look for yourself!" she had shrieked. "See the foul descendants of the priest, your father!" and then she had cackled in a most repellent way. Doña Mariana had peered into the aperture as directed, but she could perceive nothing in the haze save the occasional gleam from the books in their cellophane. Doña Mariana had to explain—and it was the first her husband heard of it—about Belén's hole in the floor.

"Belén bored a hole all the way through the subfloor?" Don Victor remarked. "I had no idea the child was so resourceful!"

"Listen to me, Victor. I tried to calm Elsa. I tried to make her get back in bed, but the woman would not be consoled. I know Jaime hasn't been a good husband to her lately, but really, can you blame him? Can you imagine watching your wife deteriorate like that?"

"It would be hard."

"What could I do?" Doña Mariana sighed. "I told her that men were men, impossible to predict, and that I hoped my son would be a better husband to her in the future. But she stood there and shouted that she didn't care about my son anymore. All she wanted was for the world to know the truth. And then, quite suddenly, in the middle of all that, she said the most inexplicable thing: She said she wanted me to summon General López. She said she wants to make an official report, detailing the exact nature of Jaime's crime."

"What?" Don Victor shouted. "I will never admit that dog into this house, no matter how many medals he slaps on his shoulders! He's just a uniform! I know his kind! My father was always paying off generals for this or that. They're cocky sons of bitches, but they'll do anything for a price."

Doña Mariana waved him off. "That's not all, *querido*. Elsa insists I bring him to her room, so that he can hear her report in complete privacy."

"No!" Don Victor snapped. "Never!"

It was agreed then, because Doña Mariana was convinced that good, Christian prayer could help anyone in extremis, that she would summon the priest instead.

They tried to sleep after that, but their daughter-in-law's screams had left them shaken. Don Victor wondered out loud if they wouldn't be better off tying her to a bed and gagging her with a cotton towel. As a boy, he had heard that his teachers, the nuns of Santa Clara, kept madwomen under control in exactly that way. Indeed, he'd heard proof of it behind his schoolroom walls—a mournful and muffled moaning. Don Victor told his wife that if muzzling was good enough for the nuns, it was good enough for him. Doña Mariana, on the other hand, wondered out loud whether, when the rainy season was over, they shouldn't send the wretched woman back to her father's mansion in Trujillo, where she couldn't infect the children. They talked of these things into the night, feeling that life's gears had shifted and fate was drawing them in another direction.

When morning came, one of the amas was dispatched with an umbrella to fetch Padre Bernardo. The good-natured father splashed up the walkway, holding a wad of cellophane litter he had found floating, like shimmering fish, in the puddles. He handed it to the ama, listened to Doña Mariana as he removed his waterlogged sandals, then padded briskly upstairs.

"You!" Elsa bellowed when she saw the priest standing in her doorway. Higher up, on the third floor, Rosita, Marco, and Jorge paused over their coloring books and wondered whether their mother would now rise up and float away, as the maids had said she would do. Another eruption followed—so fierce and sepulchral that no one missed a word of it: "I ask for the army and I get a fallen priest!" And then, the biting postscript: "Without shoes!" After that, they heard only the rain, the rumble of the factory, and frantic voices behind the door.

Padre Bernardo emerged several hours later, gaunt and bedraggled, his face as waxy as a resurrection candle. He gripped the banister like a feeble old man. Doña Mariana stood at the doorway of the sala and beckoned him inside.

"Ay-ay-ay, señora," he said. "A thorny case. A spiny, thorny case." He sat on the edge of the leather sofa, looking at his hands as if they were a stranger's. When he finally raised his eyes, Doña Mariana saw they were brimming with tears.

"She told you about the hole in the floor?" she asked him.

"Yes."

"And what she saw through it?"

"Yes."

"Well, surely you don't believe it, Padre. It's ridiculous! A terrible, heinous lie."

"No, no. I don't believe it, but you must not call it a lie, señora. She's not lying, and she's not to blame if her words appear malicious."

"Padre, please. Do not talk to me in riddles. I'm a reasonably bright woman, but I don't understand a word you're saying. You don't believe her, but she's not lying? And those lies that aren't really lies may appear malicious but they're not? Where is the sense in that?"

"It makes perfect sense if you understand what is involved here. That poor child is possessed."

"Possessed?"

"By Satan."

"Oy, por Dios." Doña Mariana's mind whirled back to her childhood fears of Satan—a terror that any minute, through no fault of her own, the horned monster might appear and drag her down through a cleft in the earth, into hellfire everlasting. "How can you be sure?"

"I've never been so sure of anything in my life. I have not encountered a case of possession myself, but I read a great deal about it when I was at the monastery in Puno. There was a very famous incident in Loudun, France, in which perfectly sane Ursuline nuns began raving like your Elsa—"

"Don't call her *my* Elsa! She is accusing my children of abominations. She is the furthest thing from *mine*."

"All right, as you wish . . . raving *like* Elsa. There." He shook his head. "Señora, please listen. It's important for you to understand what's at stake here: Those French nuns—they had all been perfectly normal, but one morning they woke up writhing in their beds like snakes. On the same day, the Mother Superior reported that a huge black ball appeared in the convent out of nowhere. It rolled through the refectory and pushed those same poor, unsuspecting nuns to the ground. They never saw the ball coming, but suddenly it was there, on top of them, and just as quickly it was gone. Later, they swore they heard skeletons clanking through the corridors. They saw visions of ghouls through their windows. They began to bellow like animals, leer like lunatics, issue obscene accusations. It was Satan, you see, señora. It was Satan inside those women. They were just vessels. It was *his* voice, *his* wickedness—not theirs."

Doña Mariana looked at the priest impatiently. "So. What do you suggest we do, Padre? If you ask me, I say we should put that vessel on a barge when the rains let up and send her upriver to her family, where she can't contaminate the children."

"She needs to be exorcised, señora. You don't deal with the devil by sending him off in a boat. If you ignore him, his black force will rip through your house just as it ripped through that Ursuline convent."

"Oh, God!" Doña Mariana cried. She could face almost anything—floods, panthers, a plague of termites—but the thought of the devil in her house was terrifying. "What happened to the nuns, Padre?"

"When they identified the devil among them, they killed it and the possessions stopped."

"We have to *kill* her?"

"Not her. *It.* We need to kill the devil."

Doña Mariana imagined the beast in all its terrible corporality, with powers far beyond those of the gentle man who stood before her. How could Padre Bernardo possibly be God's weapon against the dark prince? Even worse, how could the priest possibly expect *her* to play a part in the battle? "Kill the devil!" she whispered. "How in the world did we come to this?"

The priest straightened, digging one elbow into the sofa's soft arm. "Surely you know, Mariana, that this household has been in the thrall of the devil—flirting with pagan practices—for a very long time now."

"We most certainly have not! What on earth do you mean?"

"Don Victor's shamans. His monkey fortunes. It's one thing for the natives to practice that black magic, but for a baptized Christian it's the door to perdition. I've told him this many times, but he doesn't listen. And it's not just Don Victor. There's Graciela and her gypsy dancing— *gypsy dancing,* for the love of God. The gypsies even *say* their feet are possessed! No wonder she's lost her head over that American. And that isn't all: I have to assume that you know how Jaime has been carrying on with the Jivaro who works in your kitchen. He is so inflamed by that girl that he hasn't stopped to ask the Virgin for forgiveness."

Doña Mariana had heard Jaime say that he loved the girl, so the priest's words came as no surprise. But she rushed to defend him anyway. "How do you know he hasn't asked the Virgin to forgive him? How do you know that?"

"Because he told me so in the confessional."

The padre reeled back when he heard that breach from his own mouth, but he quickly regained his composure. Even after months of experience, blurting the truth made him dizzy.

"*Jesús, José, y Santa María,*" Doña Mariana said, crossing herself and drawing her shawl tightly around her shoulders. "What can we do?"

The priest rubbed his chin and thought for a moment. "Señora, you should give Elsa what she wants. Indulge her. Keep her calm. I will consult my books, pray for God's help, and try to prepare myself for the task. An exorcism is a serious business."

Doña Mariana sat very still after the padre left, turning his words over in her mind. She couldn't fault anyone for falling in love—the forces of love had been too powerful in her own life. If Jaime was infatuated with the Jivaro, she couldn't hold it against him. Men were men, after all. And Graciela's fascination for gypsies was only in dance, limited to flamenco. On the other hand, Don Victor's forays into the occult—his purgative sessions with Yorumbo, his hallucinogenic journeys on ayahuasca, his belief that a condor spirit guided his soul—were more dangerous. She had never approved of his shamans, or his heretical view that one faith was as good as another, or his claim that the more gods he had at his disposal, the likelier he would be to succeed on this earth. Surely these sacrileges had roused the devil. She would wait for word from the priest, but in the meantime, she steeled herself to go against her husband's wishes. If she had to betray him in the short run to save him in the long, so be it. She would instruct Elsa to dress for a visit with the general immediately. She would obey the priest's directive to keep her calm.

She knocked on Elsa's door three times—once for the Father, once for the Son, and once for the Holy Ghost—then flung wide the door. But what she found there was not a wild woman raving about a hole in the floor. It was a model of fashion, a vision of perfection such as she had seen only in the magazines sent from time to time by her husband's brother. Elsa's hair was pulled into a low chignon and garnished with three saffron orchids. Delicate gold twigs swung from her earlobes. Her dress was of maize-colored satin, bare-shouldered, with a minimal bodice, cinched waist, and a skirt that tumbled to the floor in thick folds. Peeking from the hem was a fine ivory crinoline, stitched with flowers the color of pale corn. She was as sleek as a gazelle, as elegant as a queen, but her eyes exuded a glow that was unnatural—as if they contained molten steel.

"You have summoned the general, as I asked you to?" Elsa asked, her voice calm and, to her mother-in-law's surprise, almost sane.

"I . . . I was about to," Doña Mariana answered. Now she was sure Satan lurked inside the woman—how else could she have anticipated a decision made seconds ago? She backed out of the room slowly, trying to compose herself. "I see you're ready to receive him." She pulled the door after her with a soft click.

The general sat behind a spare wooden desk in his quarters, conferring with Nestor Sotomarino. The coca runner was curled in a chair, cleaning his fingernails with a knife. The boat rocked vigorously from side to side, tossed by the torrent, and a lamp swung from the ceiling in a wide arc, but neither man seemed to register it, so locked were they in conversation. "Elsa wants a ride on the *Augusto Leguía*, eh? Little Miss High Life wants to leave?"

"That's what she says."

Nestor chuckled. "I knew Floralinda would get to her sooner or later." He gave López his sunniest smile. "Well, well! Go ahead! Bring her onboard. I'd like to rub my nuts against her."

López laughed. "You keep your hands off," he told him. "She's mine."

The general found Sotomarino repulsive, but soon after his soldiers had arrested him, he'd realized the man would be useful. He had been ferrying coca over the Colombian border for years. He was a small-time criminal, buying leaves up and down the Amazon, selling them to foreigners who transformed them into something more potent. Sotomarino had boasted of his powers with a knife, and the general believed him: He had seen him disembowel a boar with one quick turn of the wrist. "Make yourself scarce just a day or two more, Nestor. I'll

let you know when you can visit your son-of-a-bitch father-in-law." He
slapped a hand on the table. "That high-handed prick! Thinking he
runs the world with his cellophane! We'll soon bring the bastard down
to size." There was a sharp rap on the door and a guard shouted that
one of Doña Mariana's maids was out in the rain, calling for the general.
General López stood, leaned over his guest, and hissed, "Do as I say,
Nestor. Sit back. There will be plenty of time to square with the old
man. Trust me."

The general followed the maid with his black cloak furling about him,
negotiating the rain cautiously, like a crow on two feet. When he
arrived, Graciela was in the foyer beside her mother. "Ah," he said, kissing her hand, "you are as pretty as described. You must be Señora
Sotomarino."

She pulled her hand away sharply. "You know my husband?"

"Dear lady!" he said. "The maid who ushered me here referred to
you by the name Sotomarino. . . . Have things changed? Are you going
by another?" He smiled grandly.

"N-no," she answered tentatively, "of course not." And then she
added quickly, more than anything to reassure her mother, "Yes. I am
Graciela Sotomarino."

"General López," Doña Mariana said soberly, "I'm warning you now
that you will hear things from Elsa no sane person would utter. You
must not believe a word of it. She is deranged. I am allowing this meeting only to keep her calm."

"Deranged?" He had to stifle a laugh. Elsa Márquez y Márquez was
a little eccentric, perhaps even a bit unhinged, but "deranged" seemed
altogether excessive. "I see," he added quickly, "de-*ranged*," and he said
it with as earnest a voice as he could manage. "I understand you completely, señora."

Admitted to Elsa's room, the general slipped in silently, turning the
lock behind him. Doña Mariana put her ear to the door, but five minutes went by and the only thing she heard was the high whistle at the
factory, marking the middle of the morning. She resigned herself to the

probability that Elsa was scribbling a denunciation. There was nothing to do now but have faith in Padre Bernardo's wisdom.

In truth, there had been nothing to hear between Elsa and her visitor. No greeting. No conversation at all.

At the sight of the magnificent female before him, the general was rendered speechless. She was a golden goddess, a bird of paradise. For a fleeting instant he thought he was dreaming. She was, in every sense, his fata morgana—the reason a man works his way up the army, stripe by stripe, medal by medal, hoping to reach his final pantheon with an unobtainable woman, a pale-skinned beauty of the upper class. He reached out and took her hand. She gazed at him evenly, the fiery light in her eyes traveling from his chiseled chin to his black mustache to the coruscating medals on his chest. He drank in that haughty beauty, the naked shoulders, her musky perfume, and then bent to kiss the silky white skin of her knuckles. She threw back her head, issuing a sigh of pleasure. He glanced up, but all he could see was the ribbon of arm, the curve of a shoulder, the long arc of her neck. He turned her hand, kissed her wrist, felt the pulse of her heart. And then his lips moved to her forearm, to the inside of her elbow, up her arm, along the rim of the satin neckline until at last he reached the taut skin of her throat.

She was as smooth as fine porcelain, fragrant as a garden, and when she lowered her amber eyes to meet his, he felt a sudden warmth travel his groin. She took his hands and placed them high on her bodice, so that he could feel the curve of her breasts. Eagerly, he cupped those worlds with his fingers. They were firm, high, luscious as ripe melons. He pulled down the satin decisively and suddenly they were there—two ruby aureoles.

They rushed to make love, wrestling with their clothes, edging toward the bed, which lay like a pedestal behind her. As he flung his trousers to one side, the slip of cellophane given to him by Doña Mariana flew out of his pocket and landed beneath her writing table. Frantically unhooking her bodice, Elsa slid wholly naked from her dress and clambered onto the bed, where he took her silently, like a dog.

When they were finished, they lay on their backs, listening to the torrential rains. Finally, she spoke his name.

"José Antonio."

"Darling?"

"The house has become an inferno."

"I know," he laughed. "Flames are licking your bed."

"I'm serious." She rolled over, put her head in the crook of his shoulder, and began her denunciation. With no trace of outrage, no tears or recriminations, she related what she had seen night after night for twelve days: a man making love to his sister—inexhaustibly, insatiably, in three orifices.

"You are a brave girl," he told her, genuinely admiring her mettle—the soldierly way she gave her report. "I like your courage. You and I are made of the same stuff."

In truth, he was not particularly alarmed. People too long in the jungle became savages—he had seen it happen before: the multiple wives, the snot-smeared bastards, even the occasional cannibalism. Incest was the least of it. It quickly became clear why the family was trying to portray Elsa as a lunatic. She had kept a critical distance.

As he dressed, he instructed her to be patient for a few days longer, until the rains subsided and he had devised a plan. For the moment, he reassured her, she couldn't be safer. The peephole had been, in a way, a godsend. She had the Sobrevillas so worried about what she had spied there that they were willing to cooperate.

He slipped out the way he had come, encountering nothing but the savory aroma of Boruba's cooking, which made him long, fleetingly, for the pleasures of his wife's table. Marching through the front hall, he headed for the rack by the parrot's cage, where the maid had hung his cape. The bird issued a piercing squawk when the general twirled the black canvas around his shoulders. Papu, slumped in the opposite corner, opened a languid eye and flipped a halfhearted tail but drifted back into sleep. Only the kitchen girl noticed his exit. She glanced through the door as he ran into the deluge, her face like a tempest moon.

"Tell your señora that everything's under control," he shouted to her. "I'll be back tomorrow."

16

The day after the general's visit, the house so surged with evil, so rippled with apprehension that the amas swore they could see spirits with black capes and long teeth streaming in through the windows, shaking the rain from their wings. They herded the children upstairs and sprinkled salt on the windowsills. Doña Mariana saw shadows perched on the silver, faces frowning from the rafters, the endless wink of cellophane from the bookshelves. She began to carry a long bamboo stick at all times, whacking it against the walls.

Suraya, too, felt the malevolence. Two nights had passed since she'd seen the evil eye. High over the bookshelves, a light had flickered and traveled its way down the glossy membranes. She had tried to see where it had come from, but it was quickly dark again. There was only the night, the floor, and the feel of her lover's skin. Moments later, the eye opened with unmistakable clarity. The *ayañahui* met her gaze directly. Then came the voice, the shrieks, and the sounds struck her soul like keen little hooves, so sharp that she covered her ears to protect them.

There was no doubt in her mind that it was the evil spirit. She had run from the cavernous house, back to her hammock, her brain in a fever. Surely her father had sent it—only a headman would have that power. And the sign could mean only one thing: He and his warriors were looking for her. Had they smelled her? Had they seen her? If the eye had shown itself, they were close.

Jaime, too, had been awed by Elsa's screams. How could his wife know what he was doing, in another room, on another floor of the house?

He hadn't told Suraya that he had a wife. There was no way she could comprehend this. The evening she had arrived, he told his children she was a friend, and, like friends, they had stroked her face, covered her with kisses. Whether or not she understood that the children were his, he couldn't know. Jaime considered these things as he worked that day at the factory. Everything had changed—he didn't need anyone to tell him that. By the time dusk came, he had made a decision. He would take his things and leave the house. He would stay in the bachelors' quarters if he had to, or find himself a shack out where the workers lived.

In every sense, it seemed all the variables in that house had shifted. Elsa lay in bed, filing her nails, pondering her mother-in-law's unexpected complicity. Under her table, the general's cellophane refracted patterns of light that danced, like happy goblins, across the wall. On the third floor, Marcela set the children's terrarium out on the windowsill and saw, against all probability, the Australian's barge fighting the swollen river toward the dock. She wondered what strange force was powering it when the army, with all its manpower and equipment, hadn't been able to budge for twelve days. Even Graciela was seized by a sudden restlessness: She finished the dress, hung it carefully in her armoire, then took a large pumice to her skin and scrubbed every centimeter of her body. Belén folded her lucky talisman carefully into a little bell of red satin, tucked it into a book, and brought it to the breakfast table. She found her father there, grim as a scarecrow, pushing papaya around on his plate. "What's wrong?" she said. "Why are you looking as if you'd just lost your dearest friend?"

"It's Jaime," he answered wearily. "I went into the library to wake him, but he's not there. And not a trace of his things."

"Jaime?" Belén said. "He's probably in the back, with the Jivaro."

Don Victor struck the table with a fist, making the porcelain shiver. "What's gotten into him? Is he crazy too? We have more lunatics in this family than a whole ward in the Lima asylum. Doesn't my son have better things to do than lounge out back with that girl?"

"It's more than lounging. He took all his things there. He lives there now."

Don Victor never finished his papaya. He strode out into the rain and pounded on the first servant's door he came to. When Jaime opened it, he saw the thin figure of his father, dripping like a river rat.

The doorway was so small, Don Victor had to stoop to pass through it. He swabbed his face with one sleeve and glanced around, trying to get his bearings. He had never been in the servants' quarters. The room was no larger than an animal pen. Two hammocks hung from the rafters. There was a three-legged table made from a ring of tree and, under it, two stools of straw. On the far wall, suspended from nails, hung Jaime's clothes. In the corner, carved into the cement floor, was a grimy hole and, jutting from it, a water pipe with a crank. Black flies hovered nearby, droning over a metal pot. Don Victor's eyes turned back to his son, his features twisted in disgust. "What are you doing here, Jaime? Are you mad?"

"Quite the reverse. I'm leaving the mad behind. I'm moving out."

"That's preposterous!" his father irrupted, eyes blazing.

"Why?"

"Because you're my son. Look, I don't care who you sleep with, boy. I know something about that. I've slept with my share of Indian women. You don't have to move into this filthy place. There are plenty of rooms in the house."

"I'm not staying here, Father. I'm going to find a shack out with the workers." Don Victor's eyes widened as he contemplated the possibility that the vaunted rebellion, in all its entirety, stood before him, in the person of his own son.

"You don't belong here with the servants, Jaime."

"Neither does she."

"Then why did you put her to work in the kitchen?"

"Because of Boruba. I thought she would feel safe with her. And she did. Do you think I could have brought her into the house?"

"Of course not!" Don Victor exploded.

"Because she's a Jivaro? An Indian? A chuncha?"

"No! Because a decent man doesn't bring a mistress under his roof." Don Victor stopped, caught short by his own logic.

"I must not be a decent man, then. I have the sick idea that I should be with the woman I love."

Don Victor took another tack. "You cannot do this, Jaime. Have you thought what it will do to your mother?"

"My mother knows I'm in love with Suraya and she hasn't tried to stop me. I'd like to think she understands my feelings. What you really mean to say, Father, is: You cannot accept Suraya. You don't approve of her skin."

Don Victor sighed and shook his head. He pulled a stool from under the table and sat down. "Suraya's skin," he muttered, and looked up in exasperation. "You marry the whitest woman you can find in Trujillo, import her to this jungle, and you think you can lecture me about skin. I have no objection to the Jivaro girl's skin, son. Humans are not coded by flesh. I had a sister once who was as yellow as a bowl of butter."

"What happened to her?"

"She was killed by the wheels of a gypsy caravan. But not before she lived a short, unhappy life, despised by my family. My mother was made to carry that burden the way Jesus carried His cross. My sister was proof, you see, that we were as mixed, as fucked, as any mongrel in this misery of a country. Only my tía Esther accepted our heritage for what it was. Our lily-white family had been so careful to protect itself. 'You are white as white can be!' my father would say to us proudly before La China was born, 'as white as the conquistadors who set foot in Cajamarca.'" But skin, Don Victor went on to explain, was like paper, and, like paper, it could fool you.

"Cellophane is as strong as vellum, but it looks as fragile as glass," he said. "And cardboard isn't all it's trumped up to be. It can crumble like rotten bark."

Jaime watched Don Victor drum his long fingers against the wood of the table. He was touched that his father had sought him out, but he was impatient too. Why was the man rambling on so? "Why do you object to Suraya then, Father," he asked, "if not for the color of her skin?"

"I told you: because she is your mistress. Take her across the road. Build her a shack. You want her to go on being your mistress? Fine. You want her to bear your children? Fine. Just don't lose sight of who you are. You have a wife and, no matter how far gone, that wife is yours in the eyes of God. The children you have now are the only ones the world will ever recognize. Those you have by the Indian will be nature's issue, offered by chance to fortune. I built this house for you to inherit. I don't want my son to become a drooling idiot out in the servants' quarters. Stand up and be a man."

Jaime's eyes bored into his father's. "You amaze me, señor. You call on God when you want to defend the Holy Order. And then you look to Yorumbo to cure your every ache and pain. You bring in your priest. You bring on your shamans. And when all is done, you walk away, believing you're a progressive man. You are not. You're as trapped in the past as a fly in amber. Do you think that when you die, I am going to continue your charade? You are on the Ucayali, Father. You have been here for forty years, more than my lifetime. I have stood by you for a long time, but you can't expect me to hold on to the old ways. If you want the woman I love to live across the road and your son to go back and forth the way your father commuted between his house and his whore, you should never have left Trujillo. I throw your words back at you, Don Victor: You want me to be a man? Fine. That is what I am trying to be."

Marcela sprinted through the empty dining room with Papu in giggly pursuit. When she flung back the kitchen door, she saw Pedro there, slapping the rain from his clothes. Before he could look up, she was grabbing him by the elbows. "Pedro!" Marcela said excitedly. "It's here!"

"What?"

"The barge to Pucallpa!"

"Well!" he said, pushing his wet hair from his forehead. "At least your boss will be happy. At long last, he'll be able to send off his cellophane." But he hardly had the words out before she was pressing something into his hand: a neatly folded piece of paper, sealed with candlewax. "What's this?" he asked.

"A letter for the barge driver, Pedrito. For the Australian man named John Gibbs. Please, take it down to the dock. Give it to him."

But just as she squeezed his fingers over the paper, Don Victor appeared out of nowhere. He stood in the back doorway, by the servants' quarters, staring at the object of his desire in her flustered, rosy condition. Her hair was parted down the middle, tied back hastily with string. Her eyeglasses had slid down her nose. There was something girlish about her pulling on the gardener's sleeve. When he stepped into the kitchen, he saw her lovely little rump quivering under the thin cotton of her skirt and felt a fleeting tug in the pit of his groin. But the sensation disappeared quickly. In the wake of his troubling conversation with Jaime, in the chaos of the last two days, desire seemed an ancient relic now, dead and buried in a sepulcher of preoccupations. In a mood of rising ill humor, he spat out the question, "What's that in your hand, Pedro?"

The gardener looked up, struck by the ice in his master's voice. He couldn't remember when the shapechanger had spoken to him that way. Instantly, Pedro opened his fist and Don Victor snatched away the paper. Marcela gave a little cry, but before she could stop him, the master was out the door.

As Don Victor splashed his way to the factory, he broke the wax seal and tore open the letter. Inside, in tidy script, was a message that was clear for all its brevity: *Dear John, You cannot know how I worried that I would never see you again. Please do not leave Floralinda without trying to talk to me somehow.* He crumpled the paper into a ball, strode across the road to Filomena's pig corral, reached over the fence, and shoved it into a trough.

Doña Mariana had taken to standing in the front hall, as if she were a guard and the stick in her hand a spear. She imagined the house sprouting invisible demons, issuing noxious poisons, with every breath of the she-devil upstairs. She was looking out at the road anxiously when the priest came hurrying up the walk.

"Have faith, señora!" he said, as she led him to the sala. "It will take a good deal of incense and prayer, but I'm feeling confident." He leaned toward her and whispered, "I need to put a crucifix in her room without her knowledge. My prayers must be directed toward an object that is dear to my heart, placed as close to her person as it can be. I've brought the cross that has hung above my hammock since I was a boy. If the devil within her sees it, he will try to destroy it, so it is essential that I hide it well." He drew the heavy iron relic from under the flap of his cassock, kissed it, and tucked it away again. Doña Mariana had seen it many times before, and the sight of it now was comforting.

"You can help me a great deal, Mariana, just by continuing to keep her calm. Give her whatever physical comforts she asks for."

She patted his hand. "Yes, of course. I will do my part."

The padre found Elsa in bed, hypnotized, as far as he could tell, by a flickering pattern of light on the wall. He greeted her warmly, but to no avail.

"Would you mind if I knelt by your bed and prayed a little?" he asked. As she made no effort to stop him, he got down on his knees, took the crucifix from his pocket, and slid it between her mattress and the bed frame. He slipped out shortly thereafter, heading back to his church as swiftly as he had come.

Within an hour the general was there. Doña Mariana greeted him and pointed her bamboo rod toward the stairs. When he entered her room, Elsa was standing by her armoire, wearing nothing but a mischievous smile. His sample of cellophane was clenched playfully between her teeth and her hair tumbled to her shoulders in a cascade of dark waves. One hip was thrust out coyly, so that the tidy brown V of her pubis pointed to one side, like a devil's arrow. The invitation was too delicious. He unbuckled his belt, dropped his trousers, and pulled her toward the bed. But as she leaned back to accept him, the cellophane fell from her mouth, making an impossibly loud whoosh as it floated toward the mattress. The lovers froze, bewildered. The general looked down and saw that his ardor had dwindled. She tried to revive him but, to his chagrin, her efforts were fruitless. "Ay, what a shame," she said finally, and patted the bed beside her. He got in, pulled the sheet to his bemedaled chest, and announced that he was thinking of far more consequential matters.

By the time she had fetched his cigarettes from his trousers, he was talking animatedly. He lit a cigarette and said, "I have a plan, *mi amor*." She sat daintily on the edge of the bed, directly over the priest's crucifix, and listened. "I'm putting someone in charge of this hacienda—as overseer of coca production. And, believe me, the man I have in mind is perfect for the job." The general snickered. "I'll tell him to run this hole any way that he likes! Roast the old bastard, for all I care. Once he's in place, there will be no reason for us to stay, *querida*. I'll bring you on board and before you know it we'll be in Lima, drinking champagne."

She clapped with delight and, as she did, it was as if a thousand ghosts had swept through the room, whispering.

"What do you suppose that is, *querido*?" she asked him.

"Water. The infernal rain." He dressed quickly, pecked her on the cheek, and promised to return. As he raced through the front hall, he saw Doña Mariana in the living room, rapping the floor with a stick—trying to get his attention. He tipped his hat but made no effort to satisfy her curiosity. He lunged through the door without saying a word. Only the parrot bid him good-bye.

Belén wondered how to tell her sister about her secret new life with Ignacio, but she was hesitant to share the happy news, knowing that Graciela had suffered at the hands of Nestor and now stood to suffer even more with Louis Miller.

Graciela had just emerged from her bath and, wrapped in a thin cotton towel with her hair bound in ribbons, she looked small and sad and vulnerable.

"Why are you staring at me that way?" she asked.

Belén couldn't help but answer truthfully. "I worry about Louis Miller."

"So do I." Graciela reached for a bottle of cashew oil and began rubbing it into her legs.

"You worry about his safety. I worry that he won't come back. I worry that he'll break your heart. I also worry that he *will* come back and then leave you again, and so, whether he comes or goes, it will be a disaster."

"Oh, stop, Belén. He'll come back. I know it. And when he does, I hope I'll have the courage to show him how I feel. The padre thinks it's an *amor loco;* he told me that what I'm contemplating is a sin and I should keep my mind on my children. But I *am* thinking about my children, Belén. They deserve to have a living mother, not the shell of the woman their father made me. They deserve to see me alive and in love. And with a good man too."

Belén looked at her sister's fragile body, ringed eyes, nervous hands. "I'll do everything I can to help you."

Graciela was moved by Belén's concern, especially since she seemed to have marital preoccupations of her own. For as long as she could remember, Graciela had puzzled over her sister's marriage—the icy expanse between two polar opposites, their mutually inflicted freeze of the heart. She hoped that behind closed doors Belén and Ignacio were warmer to each other. Perhaps they reserved their passions for bed. In recent days, she thought she saw a new glimmer of vitality between them, but it was probably a projection of her own happy state of infatuation.

"To tell you the truth, Belén," she said finally, "I don't worry about my children. They are healthy, happy, and surrounded by love. It's everyone else who has me worried. Elsa. Jaime. Mother. Father. Boruba. The priest."

"And me?"

Graciela corked the amber bottle of oil and set it back on the table. "And *you.*"

"I know this sounds crazy," Belén said. "So much in this house is crazy. But whatever worries you have about me—please put them away. I'm happier now than I've ever been. And, yes. With Ignacio." She paused there, registered Graciela's raised eyebrow, then added, "I won't lie to you. It hasn't always been so."

"What changed?"

Belén took the book from under her arm and drew the tiny red hat from its pages. "This."

She told Graciela about Old Wong's hat. "I can't really explain why," she said, "but the day it arrived, Ignacio became a different husband. He confided a dream. I told him a story. One small intimacy led to another, and I became a different wife."

Graciela folded her sister into her arms.

"Do you think I've gone mad?" Belén murmured.

Graciela drew back and looked into her sister's gray eyes. "I think you are saner than I've ever known you."

Belén laughed. "Maybe our mother is right. Maybe this house is possessed."

"Poor woman."

"Sometimes I wish we could go back, don't you? Back to the old days when the factory made brown paper—when noise stopped at six, and no one told secrets we didn't want to know. Everything was so normal, so peaceful. Remember?"

"I wouldn't go back for the world! To Nestor?"

"Of course not," Belén conceded. And then, remembering the long, sterile years of her marriage, she added, "No, and neither would I."

"Oh, I'm not so selfish that I don't see the problems in our family," Graciela said. "And all of it topped by that odious general!" She wrapped the towel around her closely and went to the window to see what new activity might be occurring on his boat, for its long gray flank was clearly visible from her window. She peered through the rain, searching for soldiers, but what she saw instead was Louis Miller, up to his knees in river water, pulling his canoe to shore. She took in a sharp breath.

Belén flew to her side. "Your gringo!" she whispered.

Graciela squeezed both her sister's hands. Within minutes she had put on a dress, pulled on her boots, and was racing down the stairs.

Belén stood at the window and watched her sister run from the house. By the time Graciela reached the front path, she was soaked through. By the time she was halfway to the road, her boots were full of water. She pulled them off and flung them away. Rain poured from her face in rivulets, fanned down her arms in wild arteries. By the time she reached the road, her hair was as drenched as river moss, splayed in dark garlands against her shoulders. She splashed barefoot through the giant ruts in the road, her dress wet against her buttocks. Louis Miller looked up, dropped his tools. And then she was in his arms. The rain was pouring down heavily now; a soft, gray haze rose from the febrile earth. But the two didn't notice. Clinging to each other, covering each other's faces with kisses, they didn't mind the rain at all.

* * *

Father Bernardo had directed twelve cycles of prayers to the crucifix beneath Elsa's mattress, and now he was exhausted. His nerves were blunt from sleeplessness. His legs ached from kneeling. There was much yet to do, but much already accomplished: He had prayed fervently three times a day through each of the twelve cycles. He had prepared his instruments: one Bible; two iron crosses; a plaster tablet engraved with the Lord's Prayer; a flask of holy water; a packet of salt; a bottle of blessed wine; a wood box with an extra rosary and another with incense. He had consulted the Rituale Romanum, a document given to him by the bishop when he had taken his Holy Orders in Puno. He peeked inside one of his psalm books, and there it was—yellow with age, carefully folded. When he had tucked it in as a young man, he hadn't imagined that thirty years later he would be pulling it out with such urgency.

The padre knew he was at a disadvantage: He was not trained as an exorcist, whose purity and skills required lifelong preparation. He was not free of blemish; he had sinned, and the devil would use it against him. He had no holy relic—no saint's bones, no shroud of a martyr— to make him invulnerable. He had no ordained assistants to beat back the demon if it tried to possess him. The monks in Puno had warned him that work in the jungle would be fraught with complications and shortages. A priest in the Amazon would need to pray for resources, do the best he could with what little he had, improvise if need be, and trust to Christ and the Virgin.

There were points in his favor: He had done the work of the Lord in this backwater for almost three decades. He was a man of reasonably good health, in middle age, and had brought many souls to Jesus. But his real strength was the Virgin of Copacabana; she had seen him through every crucible of his long self-exile and, in these last few days of preparation, had given him proof of her favor. Her voice had come to him in a rush of whispers and murmurs, as if a roomful of women were praying. Whenever he directed a prayer to the crucifix tucked into Elsa's mattress, he would hear the voice and be reassured.

He went to the main doors of the church and peered outside. He could see that the bottom two stairs were mired in mud. Wanting to keep the way clean for any lost soul in need, he reached for his broom, pulled his hood over his head, and stepped out into the downpour. It was then that he saw the Indian—swabbed with red grease, naked, wandering through the rain. A length of green cellophane was curled into his hand. A cluster of tiny orbs dangled from his waist. The falling water was flooding his eyes, running along his lips, matting the feathers on his head. *"Huni!"* the padre called in Shipibo, but in the gushing squall the man didn't hear him. He shambled ahead, lost in contemplation. The padre shouted again, smiled, and waved his broom. This time the Indian's head snapped around and registered the hooded vision on the landing, the bared teeth, the weapon. He hopped on one foot, checked right and left, then shot like a puma into the trees.

That night the rain ceased. The cellophane machines rumbled to a halt even as the showers subsided—first to a drizzle, then to a fine mist— and then the clouds lifted altogether, leaving the mud of Floralinda to dry in the pitiless sun. The hemp fields were bare. The digester was empty. The workers made their way home to their shacks, eyeing the *Augusto Leguía,* wondering what would befall them now. An eerie silence descended on the hacienda. Don Victor sat in his rattan chair, pondering the fate of his land, his business, his son. There had to be a link in the long litany of his worries. Hadn't both a priest and a curandero told him that everything in the universe was threaded together, that deeds, like ripples, went out into the great, wide world?

At least his workers had been able to load most of the cellophane— one hundred spools of it—onto the Australian's barge. The captain had come staggering up the mud, his legs weak from too many days on the river, clutching a thin burlap bag with letters. Don Victor had seen him making his way toward the house and intercepted him at the spot where the papaya trees flanked the road. He put out his hand for the mail. When the boatman drew the bag to his chest and said, "But Señorita Marcela—" Don Victor had been unequivocal. He had no patience left for the sniveling teacher, for the goddamn army general, for the long rains, the stalled cellophane, this impudent barge captain.

"She wrote you a note, señor," he said, speaking the truth, his temper aflame now. "I decided to spare you its contents." The captain grew quiet and his blue gaze darkened to stormy green. But he accepted the words for what they suggested. He turned, went back to his barge, and pulled anchor as soon as the men rolled on the last bolt of paper.

When Louis Miller arrived at the house that evening, he noted a remarkable change in the papermaker. Gone was the hearty welcome, the expansive gesture, the spirited repartee. As the American recounted his adventures with the skin trader, Don Victor stared past him, only half listening. He noticed, too, that Doña Mariana was uncharacteristically silent, her eyes on her clacking needles, a bamboo scourge at her side. When Graciela offered her mother some oloroso, Doña Mariana seemed momentarily disoriented. "Oh!" she said, eyes moistening with gratitude.

Louis Miller tried to provoke conversation by commenting on the many spindles of cellophane he had watched being loaded onto the southbound barge that afternoon, but Don Victor contemplated the cartographer as if he were a stone. "If you noticed the barge," he said after some time, "then you noticed the pigs alongside it."

"Aha," he said brightly, "the army! Yes, I meant to ask about that."

Slowly, Don Victor emerged from his torpor. His color rose as he told about the general and his pronunciamentos. He sputtered on that he would never surrender a square millimeter of his land; that they would have to carry him away in shackles before he would sell coca to his own workers. He barked that if it were up to him he would blast the boat out of sight with a well-placed explosive. He lamented that the deluge that year had been so unremitting that the hacienda had lost precious time.

Don Victor spoke on, lurching from apathy to indignation, and the cartographer noted the inconsistencies.

"You know, Mr. Miller," the old man said finally, sighing, "there was a time when nothing struck me as an obstacle. Everything seemed possible. All I had to do was want it enough and I would get it done." He stopped there, put one hand to his forehead, and then waved it wistfully away.

"I'll tell you a story: When I was a young engineer in Pucallpa thirty

years ago—long before there was a road from the coast or any possibility of airplanes—I was given the task of fetching Mr. Meiggs's machines
from a port on the far eastern coast of Brazil. Can you imagine it, Miller?
Do you know what that means? I had to move that massive cargo on
the river. The Amazon was barely navigated in those days, and the
equipment was heavier than any boat I could secure—twenty thousand
tons! I had to travel fifteen days through a barrage of arrows to a port
where I could lease a ship sturdy enough. I found it in Manaus. It was
a broken-down naval freighter, and it tipped like a beggar's cart when
we pulled out into the river, but I rode that tub all the way to Macapá—
three thousand miles!—to get those machines. And then I rode it all the
way back, with the great, black Amazon washing up over the deck,
threatening to drown us—those damn iron gins were so heavy. They all
but rusted, and there was many a time I had to hire whole villages to
strap them with ropes and drag them along the banks so that the boat
could make it through shallow water. But I did it, by God. I did it. And
every time I passed a military boat, the whole damn lot of them saluted—
for the sheer magnitude of the task I had undertaken. But look at me
now: Here I am, nothing but an old man, badgered by a tin-badge
upstart with a pole up his ass. For a few leaves of coca, for Christ's
sake!"

Louis Miller was taken aback by the old man's state. But he was
pleased, at least, to have prompted some response. He wondered out
loud why the army was devoting so much time to Floralinda's fields,
especially since there seemed to be far more pressing matters on the
river. He told Don Victor about the sights he had seen—the hard-eyed
rebels in makeshift canoes; the military men with their motorboats and
machine guns. But his information only urged his host to a higher
anger. "Why don't my workers rise up," Don Victor yelled, "instead of
filing past that curse of a boat day after day? You may have seen rebels
out there on the river, my dear Mr. Miller, but there is not one brave
heart here in this hacienda. These people are like everyone else in this
fucked country—all beggars, sleeping on a bench of gold. They say, you
know, that when the Spaniards killed off the Inca, they were careful to
leave the peons. That is what we have now: a nation of killers and
sheep."

For all Don Victor's apparent rage, Louis Miller felt sorry for him. There was no strength in the anger—only frustration.

When Ignacio joined them mid-dinner, Miller observed that even he seemed changed. He was no longer dour-faced and surly. The foreman put out his hand and smiled.

At one point, Doña Mariana seemed to sense Louis Miller's bewilderment. She leaned her haggard face toward him and confided, "If you think we are not ourselves, señor, you are right. Much has happened since you were last here. Back then we were fighting off flies. Now we are fighting off demons."

Being attuned to the observable world, the cartographer marveled at how a few short months could alter a family so completely. Even the cook, who had once been alert and engaged, now seemed listless, shuffling the plates back and forth as if in excruciating pain. One thing, however, had remained a constant: the look in Graciela's eyes. Whenever her eyes met his, he could feel that her love had grown—that if Floralinda had gone fallow in the rain, her heart had countered with an abundant garden.

Still, he instinctively understood the complex etiquette of the household. As he felt Doña Mariana's eyes fix on him, he was careful to be discreet. He did not return Graciela's glances, nor speak to her directly. As they retired from the table, Belén guided him out to the foyer, then whispered quickly in his ear. Louis Miller checked his wristwatch. Ten o'clock. He thanked his hosts warmly and walked out into the night, awed by the eerie silence. There was no rush of water, no rumble of distant machinery. Only the skirling of frogs.

The family did not tarry after dinner. They kissed one another and headed upstairs to bed. Doña Mariana was first to climb the staircase, her husband behind her. They found the teacher on the uppermost step, hugging her knees, tears streaming down her face. "What is it, Marcelita?" Doña Mariana said, hurrying to attend to her, but Marcela swept past and planted herself above Don Victor.

"What did you do with my letter?" she asked, two fists firmly on her hips.

"What letter?"

"My letter to John!" she snapped, blinking away her tears. "And why did he leave so soon?"

"*Oy, por Dios, mujer!* What do you think I am, your pink-assed, feathered little Cupid?" Don Victor sprayed the air with spit, his mustache quivering. "Are servants now issuing directives? Get out of my way! Go to your room! Cross your knees, woman! And keep that itch to yourself."

Louis Miller stepped into the quiet night. Above him were the moon and stars, brilliant sentinels, and a scattering of clouds scudding toward the east. The river was higher than he'd ever seen it, pulsing against the bank—black glistening on black. The factory's ball digester was dismantled, its mouth yawning up like a giant mandible, and the concrete floor lay fouled by the remains of river creatures. In the distance, he saw the army boat. Under a dim torch, sitting out on the deck, was the figure of a solitary guard.

Miller struck out on the road, confident that the dark and the distance would lend him cover against the army's eyes. He passed the Sobrevilla house, which loomed to his right like a weary leviathan. To his left were the fruit groves and shacks, coal black and silent. The road was rutted with puddles, littered with cellophane, and the shreds— blue and green—winked up in mockery. Miller stepped through them, making his way toward the trees. Once he reached the edge of the first stripped field, he switched on his flashlight and pointed it down at the path. He proceeded without haste, monitoring his feet, attuned to the breath of the night around him.

At the crossroad, he looked up and saw her. It was a fleeting vision, far enough away to have the feel of a conjuring trick. She was there, down the path, illuminated by moonlight, and then, just as suddenly, she was gone. In the dark, he couldn't tell whether the high crop that separated them was corn or sugar. The tops had been hacked off, although the plants were as tall as a man. Across was the coca, offering its new foliage up into the sultry night.

He found the clearing behind the coca easily. It was just as Belén had described: an open tract that separated the fields from the trees and pointed the way into the jungle. He noted how the rain glimmered on the forest wall, answering the light of the moon, then turned to take in the panorama, which flared like a wide skirt before him. Over the coca bushes, he could see the house flanked by the barren hemp fields, the broad dirt road, the shacks tumbling away into the night, the fruit trees that partly blocked the bachelor house, and the factory and dock straight ahead. It was rare to see a rise in the terrain of the Amazon, especially so near the river, but he saw, in one sweep of his cartographer eye, the reason why Don Victor had chosen that precise turn on the Ucayali. The land banked up toward the jungle. It was not prone to flood. Each part of his hacienda was perfectly visible from any other part. The factory, whose process depended on water, had been built to cling to the shore, where water could feed its vats and water could transport the paper. It was a brilliant plan.

He heard a rustle and spun around to see a figure walking along the rim of the forest: Graciela, exactly where she should be. She was impossibly lovely, in a long dress that seemed to glow in the moonlight. Around her she clutched a shawl—coral, bound by an ivory fringe. As she approached, he saw her long, perfect legs through the luminous fabric. Across her clavicle, just over the rim of her shawl, was a ruche of the same material, which cast a supernal glow on her face. She seemed to be moving in a dream, fulfilling a hundred fantasies he had had about her out in the rain, along the river. She dropped her shawl, allowing it to hang behind her, suspended on the crooks of her wrists. The dress was transparent. The cellophane pressed taut against her nipples, cradled her breasts, skimmed along her belly, and raked into a yoke just under her navel, where it fanned into layer upon layer of clear paper. The skin of her groin, under the film, seemed to take on another life. It was tense, smooth, as highly colored as a mango. Where her hips flared around her sex, the gossamer gathered in profusion, so that the light dancing on her pubis burst into a kaleidoscope of refraction, making diamonds from shadow and flesh.

PART THREE

*A Plague
of Revolution*

17

The rains had swept to the east and the mist had risen, giving Nestor Sotomarino a clear, moonlit view of Floralinda. He hadn't seen the place for five years. Rolling another cigarette from the hemp in his leather pouch, he leaned into the boat's rail and allowed the drug to coil up his nostrils and permeate his skull with its sweetness. Helping the general gain control of the coca along the Ucayali had proved to be good business, more lucrative than selling the leaf downriver. The money had multiplied many times. But nothing had been so rewarding as the prospect of undoing Victor Sobrevilla. The old coot had gotten it all wrong: Nestor hadn't meant to kill Graciela; he'd only wanted to graze her cheek with the knife, scare her a little. Didn't she understand how much he wanted her? After their first child, she had grown cold— pushed him away night after night until his nerves frayed and his balls ached. It would have been easy to kill her. Easy, too, to slit her father's throat.

He puffed on the cigarette and watched with mild interest as the man strolled past Chincho's tables. Blowing smoke into the warm night air, he wondered where he was headed at so late an hour. The Sobrevilla mansion was perfectly still, dark except for its moonlit walls. He smiled at the thought of the family boxed tidily behind them: the old man asleep, with no clue of what was in store for him; the meddling wife, mute now; the earnest young men with their dry-as-dust women; the frostbound Graciela, in that big bed, alone. Soon they all would be answering to him.

But as his mind floated away under the pleasant influence of the cannabis, something on the far right of the house began to want his attention. It was on the east wall, by the kitchen, and it burst into consciousness as an explosion of minuscule lights. He didn't imagine that it might be a person, until all at once he saw her: a woman, making her way toward the man. Nestor smiled to himself: a maid with a hot little cunt. Perhaps even a teacher. He felt his cock tighten. He flicked his cigarette into the river, grabbed the metal railing, and vaulted onto the dock.

The mud along the banks sucked at the boots he'd been issued that morning, and soon he found he was better off moving across the ferns. He caught up to his quarry swiftly, amazed at his memory of the landscape. Finally, he came to a stop between the fields and the jungle. Nestor crawled into the coca, careful to keep his head down. He took his knife from his belt, put it between his teeth, and shimmied his way forward. Soon he could see the stranger against the wall of trees, standing alone, training a flashlight to the north expectantly.

Nestor heard her before he saw her. There was a rustling, as if a brisk wind were moving through leaves, and then his wife was there, standing before him, naked in a way he had never seen her—smiling, unabashed, offering herself to the man through a crystalline window.

The headman looked down from the crook of a tree and tried to focus. It had taken him a while to fall asleep—the silence had seemed borne on evil. With no rumbling beast by the river, no falling water, his mind had buzzed like a fly over fruit before it fell into sweet oblivion. Now the *kakaram* was nudging him awake, pointing into the clearing.

He saw a male with hair the color of sunlight, a female in adornment such as he'd never seen. Her body was visible through it, in the way that some river creatures are visible in their eggs. She appeared to be young and well-proportioned. Her hair fell in long curls, coiling down like the tendrils of tree ferns. Suddenly it occurred to him she was there to mate with the golden man. So. It was the same for them as for his own people: Lovers left their hammocks to couple among the trees.

Mwambr studied the *tsunki* woman, admiring her fine physical attributes, when all at once a man's head appeared from under the coca leaves behind her. The motion was swift, silent, and the face hung over the scene like the beak of a predator. A knife was clenched in its teeth.

The lovers did not see him. They moved toward each other like mythical creatures—shining, resolute, immortal. Surely, they were two spirit gods, and the armed man behind them a menace. Soundlessly, Mwambr drew a poison arrow from his quiver, fit it into the barrel of his shooter, and drove it into the intruder's throat.

General López gazed up at the wide, blue sky. Should he order his men to take their machetes to Victor Sobrevilla's coca fields and destroy them altogether? Or should he order them to strip the current crop immediately and keep the plants alive for a future season? If they wasted the coca now, it would take two months for new leaves to ripen. By then, surely, the old bastard could be made to surrender the profits to the Fifth Region of the Republic. He dispatched a soldier to find Nestor to help him consider the question, but Nestor was nowhere to be found. When one of the soldiers came to report that Victor Sobrevilla, too, was missing—he had pushed off into the river at dawn—the decision became simple. He would take advantage of the old man's absence. He would harvest the coca today, waste the crop, dump the leaves into the river.

Forty soldiers, stripped to their waists, descended on the fields, burlap bags slung over their shoulders. They spread out quickly, dividing the territory into neat grids, and then they set up barrels for general collection at the far end of the fields. Meticulously, for they had been taught how, they picked off the coca leaves and thrust them into their bags. The general had instructed them to get rid of it all: a clear case of provocation. In the adjoining field, they could see the laborers, swarming over the mud, planting hemp. One was setting out ripe fruit and cashew nuts on the east and west perimeters of that field—gifts to the earth goddess, Pachamama. He seemed more concerned with his incantations than with the soldiers' activities. Where was the revolution? Even the monkeys were listless, forgoing their usual belligerence, looking on blandly from the trees. Relaxed, the soldiers began calling to one another as they worked.

"I'd like a good cup of *chicha* from that fat man's barrel," a soldier from Tacna shouted.

"Me too! Why doesn't López just let us take over that dump?" another from Piura shouted back.

"Who knows? I don't understand it. I don't understand much of anything, come to think of it. The general said it would take three days to harvest this coca, but we'll have no problem doing it in a day. What's his problem?"

"Nestor. He's got the general all wound up. He's been waiting for the day we pulled into this place. You seen his wife? She's one fine-looking piece of ass."

While the soldiers were bantering about the logic of what they were doing, a young private stumbled over something that would change the whole course of Don Victor's future. It was the bloody corpse of a male, naked from the waist up, headless. The neck had been slashed through the cervical vertebra. It was a clean cut, done in a single, forceful motion. In the throat, to one side of the Adam's apple, was a small arrow. Its shaft was a hard reed, clipped back to a two-inch stub.

Don Victor squinted through the mist that clung to the river. A cluster of logs floated by on the water. Not far from the nose of his canoe, a panel of woven palm bobbed up and down—a piece of roof, perhaps, or a wall—and the skeleton of a boar, its bones carved clean by piranha. The river was high, the evidence of its damage everywhere: Dead fish with bloated bellies lined the shore; tangles of vines floated by, swarming with spiders. When he had set out in the dark, he had sensed a distinct caution in the air—the kind of stillness that descends when the jungle perceives danger. He had been careful to wait until he was well upriver before switching on his motor, but the noise, when it roared to life, seemed to make no difference: The monkeys were silent, the birds stayed in the trees. The deluge had washed away the jungle's vigor, leaving a palpable fear in its wake.

He found the witchman out on the bank, as if worry had summoned him there. He was on his haunches, surveying the river; his woman was cleaning a fish. They looked old and small and tired.

Even so, Yorumbo helped him pull his boat ashore. The woman gathered the fish glumly and carried it away in a sling. Don Victor slapped the mud from his hands, studying the wise man's face, which glittered incongruously with fish scales. His instinct was to brush them away, but he realized that he had never put out a hand to touch the witchman. It would have been impossible for him to do so now.

"What brings you, pacu?"

"I was worried about your safety," Don Victor replied. Yorumbo smacked his lips and shifted his wad of coca from one cheek to the other, but he said nothing.

"The evil eye is with me, wise one," Don Victor said finally. "It has sat out the rains and grown. Now it has joined forces with the termite army."

When they were seated in Yorumbo's tambo, Don Victor took a deep breath and started from the beginning. "Last time, sumiruna, you told me that all is connected."

"Yes, pacu. It is certain."

"If that is so, then the bad is connected to the good."

"Yes."

"And there is no such thing as total good or total evil."

"You are beginning to understand the universe, pacu."

"Why is it then, sumiruna, that there is so much bad now in my hacienda? First came the plague of tongues, then the plague of hearts, and then the army, the floods, and now an infuriating chaos."

Yorumbo looked at him tranquilly.

"There just seems to be no end to it. The evil eye is upon me, Yorumbo. I want to know why."

"Sometimes a power is so strong, pacu, that you have to ride it like a fierce animal. And sometimes a power is so strong that you have to stand back and let it pass."

"Will you come back with me, sumiruna? Will you come ride that fierce animal and rid my factory of the evil spirit? Will you purge it and free me from its hold?"

The witchman looked up at him. "Free you from its hold? Pacu, have you lost your ability to see? Do you think the evil spirit has invaded only your shine, your people, your village? Look around. Look at the river. Look at this forest. Look at the bodies floating by on high water. Have you seen anything? Where have you been?"

"I've seen dead animals . . ."

"Not only dead animals, pacu. Dead men."

"Men?"

"Men. Of many tribes. Some from deep jungle. Some of them white, with long beards, toting iron. The spirits are angry, very angry. Yesterday there was a canoe of dead children. My woman and I were standing on the shore, and it went by, riding high water like a curse. They were faceup, pacu, their little eyes plucked out by birds. They had eaten rotten flesh—I could see it in their skin. A great poison is traveling the river now. The floodwaters are carrying a great pestilence. The evil is everywhere, not only in your shine."

The engineer sat a long while. "The river is cursed?" he asked finally.

"It is so," Yorumbo answered.

Don Victor leaned in toward the curandero, his hands out, palms up. "Forgive me, sumiruna. I do not expect you to beat back the poison from this great forest or even from this neck of the river. I only ask that you come with me, bring your magic, help me with one small part of it. If you are right, if all is connected, the circuits will do the rest."

Yorumbo's eyes grew kind. He could not say no to this man. He had never understood why. The spirits had linked them together—it was that simple. He thought about all the terrible misfortunes that had befallen the river and all the purging rituals he would have to undertake. But perhaps the shapechanger was right. A man could only address troubles one by one. "I will come with you, pacu, if you will work to understand something. It is important that you hear what I have to say."

"Tell me, sumiruna."

"You and I are small creatures in a large universe. We are not masters of all we see. For all the *mapacho* I blow on you, for all the ayahuasca you drink, you are no more than a man. A tiny stone in a great river. As you ride this life, you will see bad, you will see good. You will be pulled into whirlpools—you will be warmed by the sun. It is how you see good and bad that makes all the difference. Not everything good is meant to be easy; not everything bad should be met with a struggle. You will not survive a whirlpool by fighting it, pacu. Sometimes, a man gains by giving in."

There was no belt on the headless corpse. No shirt, no identifying trinket—only boots. But for General López none of these things—not even the head—was necessary. "Murderers!" he bellowed, standing before the Sobrevilla mansion and jabbing a forefinger toward heaven.

"Butchers!" he yelled again, more ferociously. "Where is the head of Sotomarino?"

Doña Mariana, who was at that very moment discussing the day's meals with Boruba, took a moment to think what he could possibly mean and what Nestor Sotomarino had to do with it, but by the time she hurried to the front door and saw the men clustered around a body, she knew.

Before she could find Graciela, the general was in her foyer with four soldiers flanking his sides. His eyes were hard, fists clenched, no longer the lighthearted caller. "Where exactly did your husband go this morning, Señora Sobrevilla?"

"When he goes off like this, General, it can only be to his curandero."

"Curandero! A likely story! An agent of the Army of the Republic is dead," he growled, "and I have every reason to believe your husband is responsible." She opened her mouth to speak. *A ridiculous assumption!* she wanted to say, but the man went on, jabbing the air. "No one is to move from this house! I am imposing an immediate lock on this hacienda. I will assign guards to monitor all of you at all times. And I am ordering an investigation. With a full inquest! Whoever murdered your son-in-law, madam, will answer not only to me. He will be delivered to the Ministry of Defense in Lima."

Doña Mariana leaned toward him on her bamboo stick, one hand on her weary heart. "If I may ask—and with all due respect, General—how do you know that the body out there is Nestor's?"

"I recognize him."

She was momentarily flummoxed. How could the general possibly know Nestor?

"I'll be summoning your daughter to identify the body."

Don Victor and his curandero returned at dusk. Standing on the dock, the shapechanger gawked at the headless body on the deck of the *Augusto Leguía* and barked to the general, "You cannot be serious. You will never persuade me that that is the corpse of Nestor Sotomarino. The fool hasn't been here for five years!"

"He came with me on this boat!" shouted the general.

"Is that so?" Don Victor shouted back. "The last I heard, he was running contraband with a gang of thugs somewhere north of Nauta. The only way he'd be on an army boat is in shackles. You are mistaken, General López. That sad wretch is *not* Sotomarino, however much I would wish him dead."

Yorumbo, on the other hand, calmly walked onto the deck and plucked the arrow from the stump of the bloody neck. He held it up for the shapechanger to see.

"What?" Don Victor asked in Shipibo.

"No feather," Yorumbo answered.

Don Victor knew instantly what he meant. A feather signified the tribe that had done the killing. A feather declared war. That it was absent didn't matter in the least to Don Victor. As far as he was concerned, the hacked body, the arrow, the boots were all part of the general's ruse.

At the factory, Don Victor asked if anyone in the hacienda had gone missing, and Ignacio responded that he had already made a point to see that every male in every shack was accounted for. All three hundred and seventeen Floralindans were alive and well, with heads firmly anchored to their shoulders. Don Victor then escorted Yorumbo to Filomena's pig corral and asked the seamstress to give him a hammock for the night and a hearty breakfast in the morning. The curandero would need a good rest and a big meal before his miracles in the sun.

Graciela was frightened, confused. Even when Nestor would stumble in with a bottle in one hand and a knife in the other, she had not felt the panic that consumed her now. She remembered his handsome face, rugged and cruel, with its piercing gold eyes. She remembered his hands: fierce, strong, with their raised scars and hard, muscled fingers. Awakened by the shouts that his body had been found, all she could think of somehow was that she had killed him. She was the one to blame.

She sat up in bed, her palms tense against the mattress: Was she dreaming? And if the shouts, the slams, the hurried footsteps on the stairs had been a dream, had her night of love, too, played out entirely in her head? She looked down at the cellophane dress crumpled in a heap on the floor beside her. Dried mud caked its hem. So. It was real. She had made love to Louis Miller. What higher power had made her a widow on the very same morning?

Surely she had wanted her husband gone, but she had not expected some terrible arm to descend in the night to do her heart's bidding. The news that she was now free of Nestor brought little consolation. All the nervousness in the air—all the weirdness that had twisted through her father's hacienda since the little terrier had staggered down the stair— now seemed as if it had always been pointed toward this moment. She had been right to worry. But if there had been much bad, there had also been good: the unexpected appearance of the American, whom she now loved more than her own life. Perhaps the headless corpse was God's answer to her unfaithfulness. But, if so, it was a strange kind of censure— an ambiguous rejoinder she didn't understand.

It didn't take long for Don Victor to realize that much had changed since the sun came up that day. As he turned into the path that led to his house, two men in uniform stepped from behind the trees, their Mannlicher rifles at the ready. Don Victor felt his fury rise. "This is my property!" he railed. "My family house, for Christ's sake! You have no right to march in here with guns!"

One of the soldiers plucked a long reed of gramalote from his teeth. "That's enough, pops. Go along now. Up to the house."

Don Victor peered to the left and saw a band of workers hunched over a table at Chincho's. To the right, far off in the fields, he could see his son, walking with the American. "Jaime!" he called out, but his voice was too hoarse now; it trailed out into the damp afternoon air.

"Your son is allowed on your grounds," the second soldier said, then added, "and so is your nephew."

"My nephew?" But all at once he understood it. Ignoring the hesitation, the soldier continued, "There is a lockdown on this hacienda, señor. Only servants and priests can come and go from your house, and the people who live with you. Those are our instructions."

"Don't tell me who comes and goes on my property!" Don Victor roared, but when the soldier pointed the barrel of his rifle three inches from his heart, he understood that his protests would be futile. He moved along, up the path, to his house.

Papu was on the patio, chained to the pot that held the cherimoya tree, on the very tiles where the white terrier Basadre had claimed his last breath nine months before. The great black dog looked up balefully, blinking two tear-filled eyes. The sight of that miserable creature bound against nature further enraged Don Victor. He stormed into his workshop and rummaged under the table for his rifles, but the crates were empty. Every gun had been confiscated, every carton of ammunition. He stood up, alarmed, but everything else seemed to be in place: the miniature Fourdrinier, the goosenecked lamp, the copper tub. From the far wall, the stuffed condor stared back in permanent astonishment. A good warrior doesn't need guns, he told himself. The jungle is a haven of spears.

He found the women in the sala with the priest. Doña Mariana was fingering her rosary. Graciela was daubing her eyes with a handkerchief; Belén was sitting beside her, whispering consolations. The teacher was perched nearby, haggard and wan.

"Saints! Look who's here!" the padre said. "Thank God you're safe. We were worried."

"Where have you been, *mi amor?*" cried Doña Mariana, flying toward him.

"Out on the river," he answered. "One lousy day and the army takes over. The pigs are all brandishing guns. What's more, they've taken all mine."

"That's not all, darling," his wife said, her eyes filled with fear. "They harvested the coca this morning."

He looked at her in disbelief. "The coca?" he asked. "But it's barely had time to leaf out!" Don Victor felt a great rage stir in his belly, but almost immediately his anger was displaced by great lassitude: His legs felt feeble and rubbery. He was spent, every cell of his body a burden. He slumped into his chair.

Doña Mariana put a hand on his shoulder. "You've heard about Nestor Sotomarino, *querido?*" she said.

He grunted.

"The general has announced an inquest tomorrow morning. Everyone in the hacienda will be called to testify. Even Graciela."

Don Victor cast a forlorn eye on his daughter. She was staring off dreamily, as if she were in a trance. The thought of her being cross-examined by those louts, marched to that rotting corpse to be interrogated . . . He willed his mind elsewhere. Tomorrow Yorumbo would apply his magic. Tomorrow the eye would close. He looked about at the somber faces and felt his heart lighten. "Have courage, my dears," he ventured. "Morning will bring us new life."

Padre Bernardo exchanged a quick glance with Doña Mariana. "The day will be busy, then," he said. "In the morning, our exorcism begins."

That evening in the bedroom, Doña Mariana stood over her husband, brushing her glossy gray hair, lecturing him about the devil. Don Victor tried hard not to listen. He sat on a stool, removing his boots and socks. On the other side of the big brass bed, the teacher was tucked into a little cot. Don Victor had seen her immediately, but he had said nothing, so numb had he grown to the caprices of destiny. Now, in the heart of his sanctuary, he glanced at the woman again and saw that she had pulled the sheet high under her chin: She was gripping it fast with two fingers, fixing her fevered eyes on his face.

"Does this woman have to be here with us?" he hissed, thinking Marcela's insolence had reached a ridiculous extreme now.

"Of course she does," his wife hissed back. "She is fighting a terrible affliction. Can't you see it there, deep in her eyes?"

"Pssssh," Don Victor responded. He circled a finger in the air as if they had arrived at some acme of the inexpressible.

All night long, Don Victor thought about what his wife had told him: that the devil was in the house, that his curandero was to blame, that his paper was littering the ground, covering Floralinda like carnival confetti. As the hours wore on, he began to feel time grow infinitely longer. The day had begun with the swollen, cursed river. And it had ended here, in his own bedroom, with a chattering wife and the impudent woman he had once lusted after. He felt as if his life had rolled into another dimension and then floated away, out of reach. He felt like a tiny stone in a great river.

Suraya could smell her father. His ambition gorged the air, invaded her throat. She was sure he was there, beyond the green. In time, he would find her. Would he kill her? Would he drag her away by force? The prospects in either case terrified her. There was no way to explain any of it to Kai-me. She looked at him in his hammock with his head thrown back in slumber, the chest rising and falling. How long would tranquillity last?

Before the first light of day, as the chirr of the night crickets waned, she left their shack and walked up the path to the kitchen. She would try to bury her worries in work today. But as she crossed onto Don Victor's land, she saw more evidence of impending danger. Soldiers were perched in the trees, their legs hanging from branches like heavy fruit—guns by their sides, hats on their chests, keeping vigil. Brusquely they waved her by.

Inside, Boruba had set out two tidy rows of mangos and guavas on the worktable. Suraya gathered them in her arms and lowered them to the floor, then took the knife from her belt. Squatting over a board, gripping the wood with her toes, she calmed herself with the daily business of chopping.

She loved this part of her mornings: the feel of the fruit, the first prick of skin, the quick blade, the nimble shuck, so that flesh emerged—lustrous and fragrant. Her mother had skinned fruit with sharp stones. Among her people, only men carried weapons. Here, in this room where men seldom ventured, it seemed all she and Boruba ever did was wield knives: cleaving, cutting, carving, reducing nature to tiny portions. She had never seen so many tools for the task. Suspended on nails, they circled the whole perimeter of the room. At first, she had cut into her own hands, the blades biting her fingers. The smallest and lightest had turned out to be the most lethal. But, with time, Suraya learned how to control each of them. She learned to sever a chicken's neck with a machete, hack through a pig's bone with an ax, snip out a goat's bladder with a scissor. But the instrument she favored most was the knife Yorumbo had given her, and the object to which she most enjoyed applying it was the fruit waiting for her at dawn.

She peeled and sliced the mangos and guavas and laid them out tidily so that Boruba would only need to carry them to the breakfast table. She covered them with a shield of Don Victor's invention—a dome of bamboo and mosquito netting. When she was done, she slipped the knife with the leaping cat into her belt and went outside to harvest the cilantro.

But a lone figure emerged by Filomena's house, and his sudden appearance made her heart jump. It took a moment to realize that the man was not her father. He was stringy and wizened, his hair covered with paint, his body naked except for his decorations. None but the smallest children went without clothes in Floralinda, and so, within the short time she had been there, the sight of bare skin had become striking. The old man was as naked as a Jivaro—his manhood clearly visible. He seemed to be doing a ritual dance: He jumped from foot to foot, threw back his head, but it wasn't until the light danced on his face that she recognized him. Yorumbo. *Iwishin*. How she had missed him! She flew down the path, past the soldiers, to greet him.

When she reached Filomena's corral, she saw that the spirit man was deep into a chant, and so she leapt over the fence, found a shady spot in a far corner, and waited. Yorumbo was as curled as a shrimp, eyes shut, lost in meditation. But his voice was high and strong. Thick reeds of grass—fresh and green—bristled from his face. Instinctively, Suraya's fingers flew to the holes around her mouth. She remained there, still and silent, as the hacienda came to life.

* * *

When dawn illuminated the window, Don Victor awoke to see a slender leg, like a child's, tossed over his sleeping wife. Doña Mariana was cradling the teacher in her arms, her ample breasts serving as a pillow. The little face with its pointed chin looked back from its comfortable purchase like the head of an evil doll. *"Maldita!"* he whispered. Devil woman! He got out of bed, repaired to the corner of the room, where the screen shielded him, and dressed quickly.

Walking briskly to Filomena's, he was furious. Everything now seemed evidence of how far his fortunes had fallen. His factory was silent. His fields were shorn. Elsa was at her window, humming like a frenzied mosquito. Behind him, the dog whimpered. Ahead, Boruba advanced, holding her belly, singing a lullaby. All this before the crow of the cock.

Where was the old sense of order in Floralinda? Where had things gone so wrong? He nodded at Boruba as she passed, and she nodded back, but she didn't have the courtesy to stop her damn singing. Where were her manners?

Even the army was lax and indifferent. The two sentries had their backs to him. They seemed more interested in Chincho's coffee, chatting with the barman as he bumbled over his pot. The only thing that gave Don Victor comfort was the sight of the old witchman in his ceremonial trappings. He saw the door to Filomena's shack flick open, and suddenly Filomena was there, with a tray of food. It was such a welcome vision, so reassuring in light of everything else around him, that he forgot the rain forest rule about disturbing a shaman as he prepares for ceremony. He called out Yorumbo's name.

Yorumbo started when he heard the shapechanger. His eyes were glassy, face slack, as if he had just returned from a great distance. By the time Don Victor reached him, the shaman was his old self. Don Victor put his palms into the air and bowed.

Don Victor looked down at the mud-caked feet of his curandero and felt tears spring to his eyes, suddenly aware of how much the diminutive man meant to him. The realization swept him with such force that he was caught off guard by the depth of his emotion. He had lost track of how many years it had been since his first visit to Yorumbo, but seeing those feet now, knobbed and disfigured by time, it seemed that he had known them all his life, that, very possibly, he held the man in higher regard than his own father. How old had he been—forty, perhaps—when they first had met? He remembered seeing Yorumbo at the door of his tambo, eyeing the tall visitor with calm, pressing a sure forefinger on an arrow as he drew back a bamboo bow. The witchman had never seen a white man and said so. When Don Victor had answered in the language of the river, Yorumbo had put down his weapon and inspected him curiously. Now here they were, decades later, two embattled old men in a decaying corner of the forest. With a heart as gnarled as the toes of his witchman—with his paper ambitions cankered by rain, family woe, and the Army of the Republic—Don Victor gazed at the leathery face and knew that if he ever had loved a man, it was the one standing before him now.

"Tie this luck-bringer around my arm, pacu," the shaman said, handing him a long red string. "It will keep the evil eye from biting." Don Victor obliged, frowning in concentration. Yorumbo thanked him, took the boiled tubers that Filomena had set out for him, squatted, and began to eat. When he was finished, he touched a finger to his chin, then to his forehead. Don Victor understood that he was ready. "These are your tools, Father?" he asked, moving to take up the rod, the pot, and the pipe stacked neatly on the dirt nearby.

"Yes," said Yorumbo, and then he pointed to Suraya crouching in the shadows. "I summoned that girl from your house. She is my spirit partner, ruled by the puma. She will know what to do."

Doña Mariana seemed bolder than the priest remembered, more highstrung in every way. She clutched a stick in one hand, Marcela's elbow in the other. "Good!" she trumpeted when he stepped into the foyer. "The army of God is here!"

"How about the children?" he said, glaring at the teacher, whose lack of attendance in his church had always worried him.

"Upstairs with Graciela. Come in! Come in!"

Padre Bernardo feared he would lose all sense of momentum if he lingered too long in the sala. He had prayed all the way down the road, past Chincho's, past the sullen soldiers, past the poor dog, who was moaning like a lost soul on the patio. With only a glass of Don Victor's sherry for fortification, the priest shouldered his weighty bag and mounted the stairs. Once he reached the second-floor landing, he turned and spoke to the women firmly. "Wait here. I must enter the room alone." In truth, he feared for the women's safety: Doña Mariana was the child of a priest, and he wasn't sure whether the teacher had ever been baptized—they would hardly serve as assistants in an exorcism. The devil, pushed to desperation, would spring on those flaws like a rabid animal. He might tear off their heads, as surely as he had torn the head from the sad wretch in the coca field.

The priest drew his crucifix from his bag and stepped into Elsa's room without knocking. He crossed himself before he closed the door. The women heard the key turn, the lock slip. Then they looked at each other with lightning comprehension. The priest had unblocked the keyhole. They would be able to watch.

Padre Bernardo cleared his throat, but Elsa ignored him. She was lying on the bed, eyes closed, the back of one hand resting on her forehead.

"Beast, identify yourself!" he cried.

Elsa opened her eyes wide. "Fool!" she replied. "You are as stupid as you are depraved. You know very well I'm Elsa Márquez y Márquez."

The padre thrust his crucifix into the air as if it were the sword of Pizarro. "Not you, Elsa," he muttered through his teeth. "I'm talking to the demon inside you." He took another step forward and shouted, "Devil! Snake! Tell me your name!"

Elsa leapt from the bed, her mouth agape, arms outstretched like an eagle poised to fly. The burgundy lace at her neckline hung away from her, like feathers. "Snake?" she sneered. But her adversary stood his ground. "You're the only serpent in here, you fornicating little Spaniard."

Padre Bernardo seemed livened by that response. "Ha!" he shouted. "I see you now, fiend! Demon foe! Begetter of death! Do not dismiss my command because you know me to be a sinner. You can spew all you want about my transgressions, but you must answer to the One who saved me."

"And who would that be, priest—your patron? Has Don Victor sent you here?"

"No, snake! The Lord, Our Father! God Himself commands you. The majestic Christ commands you. The Holy Spirit commands you. You will bend to the Holy Trinity! You will tell me your name!"

On the other side of the door, Doña Mariana and the teacher jockeyed for position, straining to see through the tiny fistula.

"Miserable cur!" Elsa shrieked. "You say you're a man of God, but you're a fraud. You don't deserve to wear the robe. Leave me alone, do you hear me? The general is getting to the bottom of a nefarious murder. What have you done to solve *that* for this dung heap of a hacienda? What have you done to address the bestialities that go on in this house? Scum! Worthless rot!"

She rushed to the window and waved a mad hand at the boat in the distance, but the priest carried on. He lit his incense, fell to his knees. He recited the fifty-third psalm and prayed every bead on his rosary. Then he rose and made the sign of the cross three times in the direction of her head. Fumbling through his bag quickly, he produced his vial of holy water. Later, in the sanctuary of his church, the padre wouldn't be able to remember precisely how it happened: He had been sprinkling the water around Elsa when she twirled and a drop landed in her eyes. Her hands flew up with the sting of it. As she gasped, the room was filled with a rushing noise—as if a hundred throats were rising in answer. "Stop!" she screamed, and, remarkably, the voices obeyed. She slumped into her chair and rubbed her eyes with her knuckles. "What is he doing? What exactly does this monster want?" Her use of the third person excited the padre, having read in the Rituale Romanum that it was a sure sign that the devil was addressing him now. He planted himself firmly in his sandals.

"Serpent of old!" he thundered. "By the Judge of all living and dead! By the Creator of the world, by Him who has the power to consign you to purgatory—retreat to your burning hell!"

"What?" the woman shrieked.

"I command you to depart this place! You and your poisonous minions!"

"That is exactly what I intend to do, silly ass!" she hissed.

"Tremble and flee, Beelzebub. He who commands you is He who commands the winds, waters, and storm."

"I'm leaving on those stinking waters. Wind or no wind. Storm or no storm. On that boat right there, if you want to know."

"Will you bow to the will of the kingdom?"

"What kingdom?" she growled. "Lecher! Debaucher! Goat!"

"The kingdom I speak of is the kingdom of Him who rules over you, of Him who hurled you from heaven and flung you into the bowels of the earth."

"Bowels of the earth! Yes! That's the perfect description for this cesspool. And heaven is where I'm going. To Lima! To Trujillo!"

"Listen to me, Satan, and fear my words. The longer your delay, the heavier your burden. Be gone from this woman! The Father bids you—in the name of His Son, Jesus Christ—go from this house now, go!"

"Oh, go to hell."

"To hell, cacodemon! Back to the everlasting fire."

"You've lost your mind—"

"In the name of the great Almighty, in the name of His sharp sword, I command you!"

"This jungle has turned you into a dithering idiot."

"Get out!"

"Haven't I told you? I'm packed! I'm going!"

"World without end!"

"*Oy, por Dios!*"

"*Dios!*"

"For God's sake . . ."

"Amen!"

Señorita Marcela and Doña Mariana marveled at the drama. The exchange between the priest and the demon was all the more potent for its smallness, a tiny war between mythic beings—spooling, dreamlike—through an aperture the size of a magical amulet, barely the size of a thumbnail.

The two women had tugged at each other's hands, eager to take turns at that elfin opening. Appalled by the demon's words, amazed at the priest's skill at anticipating them, they pressed their flushed foreheads against the brass plate, maneuvering their heads about the doorknob. So astounded were they by the spectacle that they didn't hear footsteps behind them.

"Señora?" Boruba said.

They spun around to see her there, the color of pale *chicha,* clearly aghast. It was remarkable, really, that they were able to register something so mild as astonishment when they had just witnessed the whole spectrum of rage—from divine to diabolical—playing out on the other side of the wall.

"What is it?" Doña Mariana asked.

Boruba had to gather her wits and steady herself on the banister before she could answer. Her own mistress in the act of eavesdropping! The woman had told her many times, and in no uncertain terms, that it was a vulgar thing to do. "There's a soldier downstairs at the door, señora. He wants Graciela to go with him now to identify the body."

They found Graciela minding the children, leaning over their little shoulders as they practiced their penmanship. Whispering the news in her ear quickly, Doña Mariana insisted on accompanying her to the dock. The teacher seconded the old matron. Graciela's face was pinched, but she took the orders calmly. She kissed Silvia and Pablito, tied a light shawl around her, and walked out into the mist, clutching the two women's hands.

The boat was rocking in water made rough by the endless rain. The soldiers paced about in equal turbulence, waiting for Graciela to approach. The general stood at the aft, arms folded, having given precise orders: Watch the eyes, be dispassionate, a female is a capricious creature.

The soldier yanked back the tarp. It was a male body, dressed only in trousers and boots. Its chest was black with dried blood, the stump of its neck rippling with maggots. The hair on its arms had been nibbled to stubs by the larvae of long-horned beetles. Graciela stood firm, holding her breath against the odor. It wasn't the first time she had seen a body ravaged by the jungle.

"Shall I remove the trousers, señora?" the captain asked, leering.

She glanced up. "You don't need to." The rings around her eyes, normally a pale lavender, had deepened to violet. "I know his hands." She looked down at the thick fingers, the spatulate nails, the yellow cigarette stains, the raised, angry scars that ran in welts along the knuckles. There was a moment's exhilaration—a quick flash of joy—to see those hands forever stilled, doomed to pass through every stage of mortification. But the joy was quickly countered by dread. The man she had married in Padre Bernardo's church—the father of two innocent children—lay butchered, like a savaged animal. Of that there was no question, and she quickly confirmed it: "It is true what the general claims," she said, with a steadiness in her voice that surprised her. "That is my husband, Nestor Sotomarino. Those are his hands."

Belén was waiting for her when she returned. She stood in the doorway of the schoolroom, with the children playing quietly behind. Downstairs, the padre's voice rumbled like prophetical thunder.

Graciela was pale, ashen. Belén rushed to her instinctively, but Silvia and Pablito reached her first. They flew into her arms, and it was then that they saw the tears—trickling at first, then flowing in long rivers of sorrow, flooding her neckline, staining her bodice with a dark trail of penitence.

Their mother's tears coursed like a silent rain, covering her body with the salt of long-stinted regret. She cried all day long and for three days thereafter, even as her fate was being written. The rains of Graciela fell and fell, mirroring the torrents, mystifying her children. They streamed with a pluvial force, endless flow, so that her clothes were drenched, her pillows soaked, and all the rags the amas could bring would be carried away in wet piles, filling one basket after another. It was as if a river imp had imposed a curse. As if the two purple rings Nestor Sotomarino had inflicted so long ago were tightening their hold, squeezing her eyes—making them mourn his departure.

18

In his youth at the police academy, the general had learned an old Inca dictum, which he later incorporated into the curriculum at the Center for Advanced Military Studies: During an inquest, a magistrate should always face the sun, despite the glare or the prospect of a wicked headache, for the illusion of power is strengthened by a sunlit face. He learned, too, that the person under interrogation should be made to see his release—if indoors, he should face an exit; if outdoors, a road or a river—so he might contemplate what a right answer could win him.

There were other, more subtle factors: the placement of the official table, for instance. The soldiers of the Fifth Region moved it numerous times before the general was satisfied. He insisted that it be placed on the concrete platform in front of the factory, which would give him desirable elevation. But he wanted the natives standing on soil when they testified, so they would know their place. He wanted the table angled a certain way, allowing him to face not only the sun but the Sobrevilla mansion. That way, he could both monitor the household's movements and satisfy Elsa's wish to see him mete out justice. It also occurred to him—brilliantly, he thought on reflection—that the people would be more inclined to speak out against their master if that master's house was not right there in front of them, staring back.

After much shouting and pointing, the general had the table where he wanted it. He instructed his men to place his chair in the exact center, facing out, with a chair at either end for the scribes. One scribe was to list the name of each witness, along with a date of birth and tribe or birthplace. The other was to document the claims and enter the evidence. After the chairs were established to his satisfaction, he sent out a squad of soldiers to summon every adult in the hacienda to report in an orderly fashion. They would be called household by household, according to the general's wishes, with Don Victor Sobrevilla's family as the very last.

The result of the inquest had to be nothing less than total humiliation of Don Victor Sobrevilla Paniagua, whose insolent ways were intolerable. In all his years as an army man, General López had never encountered anyone like him: that insufferable self-assurance; the lack of respect for the sovereign power of a military government; the brazen confidence that, because he was the lord of a distant backwater, he could escape the laws of the land. López didn't care whether or not Don Victor had killed Nestor Sotomarino—the coca runner was no more than a pig anyhow. He wanted to establish the Army of the Republic's dominion over that arrogant son of a bitch. He would teach him a lesson. He would show him who was who.

Before long the laborers and their wives began trudging down the road toward the general's table. They came shack by shack, as soldiers banged on their roofs and ordered them to the hearing. As the sun reached its high point and began its descent to exactly the place where the general wanted it, the people of Floralinda gathered on the dirt before the concrete platform. There was not much else to do. The factory was silent. The hemp had been planted. The cotton and coca wouldn't be harvested again for another month.

The general's inquisition could not have come at a more convenient time. The residents of Floralinda, having lived through a plague of truth and graduated to a plague of desire, now slid almost imperceptibly to another rung in the spiral of human appetites: the hunger for power. They could see that authority had shifted from the big house to the big boat, from cellophane to official parchment, and they wanted to be sure they would be on the safe side, display all the right allegiances. But so much they were encountering now was unexpected: To begin with, they had never experienced an inquest for a murder. Humans were often found mangled along the river—by one animal species or another; it was a fact of life in the jungle. The surprise was not that the army had come upon a headless body; the surprise was that it cared to know why.

One by one, the general called on the witnesses, pointing to each one, directing each to come forth and stand on the stretch of dirt before him. The first testifier alerted the general to the fact that this would be no ordinary polemic. He was one of the hacienda's amputees, an armless man who identified himself as Juan Gonzalez. "With all due respect to your generalship," he said, "a lot of rain has fallen on Floralinda! How do we know that an alligator didn't just swim up to that coca field and bite that man's head off? My own limb was lost to an animal. I wish that the army had been around to care!"

The general's spine stiffened, but Gonzalez went on. "Now, sir, if your inquest looks less at that corpse and more at the alligator, you might actually learn something! Such as: Why, in this particular one-thousand-nine-hundred-and-fifty-second year of the Lord, would an alligator be able to swim up to the coca? Why has there been so much rain in Floralinda? Why has it come in such torrents that it would drive a water creature to pasture? What curse produced such an unnatural thing? In my view, and in the view of my companions who have discussed this at some length over at Chincho's, it's the shapechanger's paper that is responsible! Have you looked at it closely, sir? Have you looked at that shine? Since we started making it, all manner of strange things have happened. My wife's tongue wags endlessly! My neighbors are lusting after their friends' wives! And Don Victor has gotten so rich on this new stuff that he bought us each a goat! And then a pig! I'm telling you—I think there's something going on there. *That's* where you should be looking!"

So many heads nodded in agreement that Gonzalez was moved to continue, but the general put up a hand. He scratched his chin, wondering how to push the man's testimony where he wanted it to go. "So, Juan Gonzalez of the Huitoto tribe, what you are saying is that Don Victor Sobrevilla Paniagua, the owner of this hacienda and engineer of the factory behind me, killed Nestor Sotomarino?"

Gonzalez was momentarily bewildered. He rubbed his stump with the palm of his good hand and contemplated the general's logic. "*Ay, ya!*" he said finally. "I see now, your excellency, how you are figuring the matter: Don Victor made the paper. The paper brought the magic. The magic raised the river. The river pushed out the alligator. And the alligator bit off the head of Nestor Sotomarino! *Sí, señor!* That is exactly what I mean to say."

"Write that down!" the general barked, slapping his hand on the wooden table. "Next!"

Felisberto Díaz, one of the machinists—the most educated and philosophical of the workers—stepped forward and identified himself as someone who could speak about the origins of the magic. "I remember, your excellency, when this hacienda was an ordinary place. We made ordinary brown paper. We had ordinary lives. Day followed upon day, crop followed crop, and nothing very remarkable happened. Don Victor, of course, was always inventing things."

"Things?" the general said. "Things! Señor Díaz. We are here to nail down evidence! Give us examples!"

The machinist gripped the hem of his scruffy shirt, glanced briefly at the bright blue sky, then back at his interrogator's sunlit countenance. "He invented a conveyor belt from discarded old motors, for instance! A wind machine that scared off the birds when the hemp seeds were newly planted! A water mill out of rusted ten-gallon cans! Chewing gum from the rubber trees! But none of those things really affected our lives, your excellency. We went on the same as we had before. But there came a day when all of it changed—it began with the death of Miguelito."

"Miguelito?"

"The grandson of Boruba the cook, God love her. That was when strange things began to happen. It was the first day I ever saw cellophane, although I didn't know at the time that that was what I was seeing." The man went on to explain at great length that the boy had expired on the patio next to Don Victor's dog—in the very same spot, by the way, that the general's soldiers had chained the family's black mastiff. . . .

"What does all this have to do with the murder of Nestor Sotomarino?" the general snapped.

"I'm getting to that, your excellency," said Felisberto Díaz. "The day that the family put Miguelito on a bier and burned him to ashes was the day I mark as the beginning of Don Victor's enchantment. I saw evidence of it myself. I was standing in the fields near the house when the shapechanger walked up to the table where the body lay. The magic had already started—the boy was as blue as the tail feathers of a parrot. Don Victor dropped something very light, very bright onto his belly. Of course, I know now that it was the magic paper. I thought that he must have put a spell on it, or on the boy. I don't know. But why else would you do such a thing? I thought, too, that the paper was like those knots of wood or hunks of stone curanderos snatch out of the bellies of the diseased. That once the boy's body surrendered it, he would come back to life—he would sit up and be well again. But that never happened. Don Victor took the shine from his little belly, held it high above the table so that it winked with a hundred eyes, then brought it down, pressed it into the boy's palm, and closed his blue fingers into a fist. After that, there was a loud sound, like air rushing up to the sky. And then the crow of the cock. That was all."

"And?" the general said, drumming his fingers on the table. "So?"

"Your excellency! That was the day the cellophane started. Don't you see? We first saw it on the belly of the boy! And then within months the factory was making it! What's more, General López, the day something killed Nestor Sotomarino was the day the factory *stopped* making cellophane. How much clearer can the connection be? The shiny paper rises and falls on the dead!"

"Are you saying that Victor Sobrevilla Paniagua killed the boy *and* Nestor Sotomarino?"

"Oh, for God's sake!" Jaime had arrived just as Felisberto Díaz had started and was listening to the machinist's testimony with mounting disbelief. He had worked alongside the man for as long as he could remember and never heard him say a word against Don Victor. Not a word against the cellophane.

"Who are you?" boomed the general.

"Jaime Sobrevilla Francisco," he answered. "I've known Felisberto Díaz for many years, and what he says strikes me as a bunch of nonsense! I've never heard him say those things before."

"That's the whole point, boy," the general said, scowling at him. "I'm giving him the opportunity to speak out. We are finally getting at the truth here! Now stand back. I'll have you arrested and put in my ship's hold if you interrupt again."

"It seems only fair, General, that my father hear what is being said about him. With your permission, I will go bring him now."

The general seemed to pay that no attention. He whispered furiously into one of his captain's ears as he watched Jaime work his way through the crowd and walk briskly away. Felisberto Díaz seemed visibly shaken. "Mr. Díaz," the general said gently. "Collect yourself, please. I'll repeat my question: Are you saying that Victor Sobrevilla Paniagua killed the boy too?"

The machinist glanced over his shoulder cautiously, then continued. "Not with his own hands, mind you. And not willfully. But his paper moves with death, señor. His paper rode in on a boy, rode out on a man. It's what the people of my tribe call a *pishtaco:* a ghoul that lives in white people's factories, kills innocents, and feeds blood to the machines."

Pishtacos!—the ravenous ghosts brought to Peru by white people. The word began to travel in whispers through the crowd. The conquistadors had brought the *pishtacos* to Cajamarca. The English had hammered them into the railroads. The Americans stored them in Coca-Cola vats. The city folk churned them into cement. Were they here, prowling the factory?

The machinist looked around with confidence now, pleased with the effect of his testimony.

"So," the general said, rapping the table with his pencil. "Don Victor's *pishtaco* killed two people?"

"The *pishtaco* in Don Victor's factory did. Yes, your excellency. It happens all the time. Ask anyone here who has worked in a white man's hacienda. Not long ago, I heard of a *pishtaco* that did terrible things in a rubber factory in Iquitos. It ate workers by the dozens—in its rolling jaws!—tore them to pieces one by one. Pishtacos come and go—some big, some small, some weak, some strong. In this case, it is a particularly nasty one. And smart."

"Two victims, not one! Write that down, *capitán*!" the general shouted to the record keeper.

The wife of a pulp carrier, a diminutive woman quite obviously pregnant, stepped up and identified herself as Gloria Huamán. "*Pishtacos,* yes," she said simply and authoritatively. "And yes to the business about the dead man, the dead boy, the rain, and the alligator—yes, yes, yes! But has it occurred to no one but me that the cellophane has brought some blessings? After so many years of barrenness, look at my belly— it is filled with a child! Does anybody doubt that the paper has brought us good fortune? And the fruit trees, the fields! Everything was in bloom in those early days of the shining paper, all ripe for the picking, ready to grab, as if God, the *ápus,* and Pachamama herself were offering us their blessings. The cellophane has brought much happiness, señor."

"And how, my good woman, do you propose we connect all that happiness to the murder of Nestor Sotomarino?"

"With all respect, *Señor Comandante,* Nestor Sotomarino was a very bad man. And, even though Padre Bernardo tells us never to judge a child, Miguelito was bad too. I pray that Boruba's baby will be balm for that misery. She suffered so much with Miguelito."

"Señora, you still haven't told me how it relates—"

"I'm saying, your excellency, that the magic kills the bad and grows the good."

"Ah, I begin to see your logic. You are saying that Don Victor's cellophane kills what it wants to kill and grows what it wants to grow. You are saying, in other words, that the paper is ruling the question of life itself."

"Well, yes. I suppose so."

"Put that down!" the general yelled. "That's blasphemy! Victor Sobrevilla Paniagua thinks he is God Incarnate!"

It was at that very point in the inquest that one of the record keepers tapped the general on his arm and pointed behind them. Don Victor was striding forward from the door of the factory, with Jaime at his side. The engineer was angry, that much was evident. There was a scowl on his face and the unmistakable twitch of ire in his elbows. He planted himself directly before the general.

"I've heard enough!" Don Victor bellowed, shaking Yorumbo's rod over his head like a nettled prophet. The pregnant Gloria Huamán stepped back with a gasp. The crowd swayed in consternation.

"This is an official inquest, señor!" the general said, rising. "I have not yet called you forward." The two soldiers at the table shot to their feet at attention.

"So you harvest my coca on one day and thresh the entire hacienda on the next, eh?"

"Yesterday I took what lawfully belongs to the army. Today I am continuing to mete out the law. I am investigating the murder of Sotomarino."

"Have you located the dead man's head?"

"No."

"Then, how in God's name can you be sure it's that son of a whore?"

"Because only one son of a whore is missing from my boat," the general thundered, "and no son of a whore is missing from anywhere else. It can only be Nestor Sotomarino. Even your daughter says so. Accept it, Señor Sobrevilla. The people of Floralinda have."

"People of Floralinda!" Don Victor said grandly, turning to face them. "Do you answer to the occupying army? Or do you answer to the hacienda that has housed and protected your children?"

There was a rustling as feet shuffled to find new purchase. The people of Floralinda looked down to see whether Pachamama was still there beneath them—or whether the earth mother would now open her arms and pull them down into her bosom, where these masters no longer held sway. How had this happened? Weren't the military and the landowners one and the same? Wasn't one there to protect the other? Why were they being asked whether they answered to one lord or another? They had never had a choice in these matters; never would. The silence was so acute that a flock of papagayos could be heard cawing merrily in the banana trees. Don Victor looked about at the puzzled faces.

His arms dropped to his sides. The general and his two record keepers sat down. Jaime could almost feel Don Victor's will dissipate. He realized all at once how deeply human his father was—how much he relied on the approval of these people. "Don't stop there!" Jaime whispered. "Don't let that son of a bitch cow your workers into saying things they don't mean!" He turned to glean some encouragement from the familiar faces, but the people only looked down, showing no sympathy for the shapechanger. Their change of loyalty was transparent now. Jaime looked from worker to worker, wondering if he'd ever known them. He put a hand on his father's shoulder, but Don Victor shrugged it off.

The papermaker understood now that his only hope was a witchman's miracle. He turned and walked back alone toward the factory. General López pointed sharply for a soldier to follow. The uniformed man did as he was told and tailed Don Victor to the door, but when he peered inside, he saw no one there but a naked old curandero and a worried girl in a yellow dress. They seemed so harmless, so incapable of making trouble, that he hurried back to the table, eager to hear more.

The witchman stared up at the hulking machines, studying each as if it were a rock in an enchanted cavern. He touched the metal tentatively with his fingers. It seemed sullen, mute, hardly capable of making the dread rumble he had heard long ago, before the rains. The cement floor was pocked and stained by sulfates; green pools collected under the steam pipes; an acrid stench filled the air. A chain ladder hung from the spooling dryers and clattered against the drainage siphons, making a hollow sound. High up along the walls was a row of windows that looked out onto the river. Monkeys lounged on those sills, gazed at the water, preening and flicking their tails.

Suraya set down the witchman's tinder, her thin shoulders hunched against the sights around her. She glanced about at the metal ganglia, the heavy cylinders, the seemingly infinite tangle of tubing. The surfaces had a quality she'd never seen before: a dull gray of porcupine quills, denser than stone, smoother than shell—in angles that did not occur in nature.

Don Victor found Yorumbo and the girl at the front of the factory, near the acid baths. They were building a fire. He set Yorumbo's rod on the floor with the other relics—a pot, two gourds, a length of vine. Seeing the witchman at ease, moving through the factory as if he belonged there, the shapechanger was relieved. He tore a wide length of cellophane from a bolt and approached him. It thrummed against his hips like the wings of a dragonfly.

"*Niwi,*" Suraya said, and the word was so like the Shipibo that the two men understood it. "*Nihue,*" said Yorumbo. So light. So clear. Like air.

Suraya took her knife from her belt and cut the vines into pieces, then dropped them into the water and hung the pot over the fire. As the vines began to simmer, Yorumbo hummed the *icaro.* His song echoed through the high chambers of the factory, resonating against the metal, building to such a crescendo that the witchman was lost in its thrall, spinning slowly, around and around, his arms stretched like wings, his head thrown back in ecstasy. Don Victor looked around expectantly, thrilled to see the witchman alive with his magic. It didn't matter what the Army of the Republic was doing outside. That cocky little tyrant was river flotsam—he would soon tire of his game, float out as he had floated in. Here, in the heart of Don Victor's temple, the real work was being done.

Suraya, too, felt the power of the witchman's *icaro.* Rocking from foot to foot, she shook the beads that hung from her neck, then, lured by the rhythms, spun about slowly and broke into a whirl. Yorumbo's voice climbed even higher, daring the evil to show itself, and the two moved across the floor, spinning and singing.

Up in the rafters, the monkeys braced themselves on their knuckles. Chittering, they leapt from their aerial heights, landed on the cool metal of the machines, and clambered down for a closer look.

Now the witchman took his *mapacho* pipe and lit it with a reed from the fire. Blowing smoke under the headbox, he goaded the eye to fly out and gaze on him. He challenged it to rise from the iron, put its feet on the floor, face its enemy. But apart from the leaping monkeys and the burbling brew, the factory remained deathly still. The spirit did not respond. Don Victor glanced about, waiting for the rush of air, the sound of the *mal ojo*'s sharp hooves. But as minutes passed, fear began to tug at his heart. The curandero took his rod, thrust it into the air, and yelled the incantation of belligerence, taunting the spirit for its cowardice. Still there was nothing. No rumble from the machinery, no eerie growl to suggest that the spirit had seized on the provocation. Finally, the curandero filled his gourds with the liquid of cooked vines and ran alongside the length of the iron entrails, sprinkling the brew on the vats, the mesh, the calenders and spoolers. He banged all the parts with his rod as he ran, yelling threats and commanding the evil spirit to answer to a higher power. But this only succeeded in alarming the monkeys, who leapt about, baring their teeth. Don Victor knew now that the evil was too deep, that the future of all he had built was in peril. He felt his knees buckle.

Yorumbo dropped the pipe onto the cement with a rattle of resignation. "It will not come," he said. "I know it is here. But it will not rise to meet me." He lifted the sheet of cellophane from the floor and it unfurled over his nakedness. Through it, Don Victor could see the wrinkled brown skin, the red paint, the tufts of straw on the knees. "Your magic is clear as air, pacu, fluid as water, but it is also stubborn."

Don Victor was stung with alarm. "You can't rid me of the eye, Father?"

"No," Yorumbo said sadly. "Too powerful. Too cunning." He shook the paper in his hand. "Your magic doesn't lie, pacu, but look—it is full of guile. It draws the eye through. It beckons the heart. But it is shut as stone."

"You can do more, sumiruna!"

Yorumbo studied the shapechanger's face. It was no longer yellow, pinched with desire. It was gray. Bled of all vigor. For the first time, Yorumbo realized he could not give his friend what he needed. The evil in this tomb was too fierce. He could not nod and fetch another vine, as he always had. He could not force fate's hand.

"I have tried to ride the angry animal. Now I will stand back and let it pass. It is time to stop, pacu. I am old. The eye is strong. You, too, are not fit for this battle. It is best that you let go."

"Let go?" Don Victor said, remembering the phrase from his childhood prediction. Let go? What did that mean? The witchman's words pushed into his tired brain. Did it mean that he now must surrender Floralinda to bad fortune? Let the machinery of rude fate reel on, his family crumble, the hacienda fall into the hands of a uniformed cretin? Impossible! He had created a miracle here. He had built a civilized house, conquered the jungle, bested the geniuses of Lima's School of Engineers. "Let go?" he whispered.

"Let go, pacu. Before it pulls you under."

* * *

The people of Floralinda felt a rush of pity for the teacher when they saw her mount the concrete and make her way toward the general's table. She was small, thin, gaunt. Gone was the round little rump that had won so much attention at Chincho's.

"What?" the general shouted. "I didn't ask you to stand up here with us! Stand down on the dirt like the others!"

But the teacher refused. "Forgive me, *Comandante,*" she said in the prim, preceptorial voice she had been taught to use in the Iquitos School for Teachers, "but I am trained in this sort of thing. I learned early in my career that those who are being asked questions should stand before the class. Everyone gains that way—the teacher hears, the class learns, the student understands the seriousness of the responsibility. I prefer to stand right here, if you don't mind, and face these people. It will make everything much easier for all of us."

General López did indeed mind—he was the ruler of the Fifth Military Region, she was an insolent upstart, and who did she think she was? But the crowd obviously approved of the plucky young woman. They began clapping and nodding, murmuring words of praise. The general's mouth opened and closed. He picked up his pencil and clacked it down again. "All right," he said finally. "As you wish. You want to play school, señorita? The Army of the Republic is nothing if not flexible. We can play school, if you like."

She smoothed her skirt and folded her hands before her. The people could see she was in a state: She seemed wolf-lean and feverish. But there was determination in her face and the confidence that she was anyone's equal. Marcela had tasted humiliation. She had witnessed a priest's struggle against the dark angel. She had watched a woman identify her husband's butchered body. She was as prepared as she ever would be for the general's interrogation.

"State your name."

"Marcela Isabel Zevallos Barrientos."

"State your tribe."

"Vertebrate. Capable of reason."

"Don't be impertinent, woman. Where are you from?"

"Iquitos."

"Where do you live?"

"With the Sobrevillas. On the third floor."

"Ah. I see. Well, señorita, I must admit that you interest me. You live in that big house yet are no blood relation to its owners. I assume you will answer my questions with some perspective and detachment."

"I will tell the truth, so far as I am able."

"What do you do in that house?"

"I teach the children—three boys, two girls."

"How long have you taught them and how much are you paid?"

"I've been in this hacienda for a little more than two years, since the eldest was eight and the youngest was one. They are now ten and three, respectively. I have a room, which is spacious and comfortable. I am given food, which, until the onset of a recent affliction, I have taken at the table with the others. And at the end of each month, I am paid fifty soles in cash."

"What is the affliction you speak of?"

"*Susto,* General. A touch of panic is all, and a chronic, high temperature in the innards."

"Hmm. *Ya-a.* And what is your overall estimation of the Sobrevilla family?"

"Quite good, I would say. The children are alert, quick learners."

"And what do you think of the señora?"

"She is like a mother to me."

"What about Don Victor?"

The teacher did not hesitate. She pointed to the house, unafraid. "That man is a menace to society. A hedonist and a moral reprobate."

A gasp went up from the crowd and the general sat straight in his chair, more alert now. "In what way has he shown himself to be immoral?" he said, his face brightening. "Explain what you mean."

"He preys on innocent women."

"Ahhh," the general exclaimed, leaning back, eyeing her with new comprehension. "And you have seen this for yourself?"

"More than seen it."

"He has preyed on you, then, has he?"

"Yes."

Again the crowd gasped. Marcela looked out on the people of Floralinda. There were few faces she recognized—she seldom mixed with the workers. And yet the people were showing solidarity. She gave them a wan little smile.

The general whispered something to the record taker, then turned again to the teacher. The tone of his next question was almost tender. "And what has he subjected you to, señorita, exactly?"

The teacher took a deep breath and put a hand on the table to steady herself. "I was going down to the dock to gather the mail as I always do. I was walking down that dirt road over there, minding my own business. Suddenly, there was a dreadful noise—like an animal panting. When I turned around, there he was. Don Victor was running toward me, hanging on to his hat, pulling it down over his head. I could see he was sweating profusely . . ."

"And?"

"And when he reached me, General—I'd swear it on the Bible, but I don't see one here—he got down on one knee, tore off his hat, and a whole flock of yellow butterflies flew out from under it."

The people murmured their approval, remembering the moment. Many who had seen it happen had been baffled by their master's behavior, and they commented on it now, seconding the teacher's memory. The general placed an elbow on the table. "What is so immoral, if I may ask, about a hat with a few butterflies under it?" He raised an eyebrow, punctuating the interrogative.

"Well. That's not the end of it, *Comandante.* There is more."

"More!" someone shouted from the crowd, anxious as a schoolchild.

"Shush!" the general waved at him. "Go on, Marcela Isabel Zevallos Barrientos. Finish your story."

"The next time he came with a big heavy basket. It was rough, round: the sort of thing one would use for freshly caught fish."

"He struck you with it?"

"No, señor! First, he held it in front of me; then he whisked off the lid, and—whoosh!—a parrot rose into the sky."

"With all due respect, *Profesora,*" the general said, defeated now, "a few yellow butterflies and a parrot may have cause to complain. Not you." He peered out from under his frown. "Is that all?"

"One more thing."

"Make it quick," he barked. "We don't have time for more bird stories."

"He brought me a straw skirt."

"Let me guess. With a hen on top. Laying eggs."

The crowd tittered, pleasantly surprised to learn that the general had a sense of humor. Exasperated, he waved a hand for her to continue.

"No. There was no hen. No eggs. He made me put the skirt on."

"Oh?"

"And then take everything off under it."

The general was perfectly still now. The two scribes glanced up, their pencils in the air, envisioning the old, whiskered engineer, the young teacher, the grass skirt. "And then he put his fingers up high, between my legs."

The crowd grew so quiet that Marcela could hear a cloud of parakeets flap in from the river and bank swiftly away. Her eyes followed their arc, up, back, as the bright birds flew over them, into the trees.

"Go on," the general's voice commanded.

"He came up to my room a night later and did it again. Except this time there was no skirt."

A loud exhalation—like the sigh of a great leviathan—came from Floralinda, and then a frenzy of conversation, as people weighed in on the reprehensibility of Don Victor's conduct.

"So!" the general shouted, banging his fist on the table. "*Capitán!* Let's get this straight for the record! Write down every word I say! The man who lives in that house, who built the factory behind me, who makes fancy paper in this jungle—I am talking about Don Victor Sobrevilla Paniagua—is a degenerate!"

"Yes, sir," the teacher said firmly. "That is exactly what I mean to tell you."

"And if such a man is capable of defiling an honest woman—a young teacher like you, in his employ!—he is capable of murdering his son-in-law."

"Pardon me, General," a pulp shoveler volunteered, "but putting your hands on a woman is not the same as killing a man in cold blood. If it is, Peru is a nation of criminals and you'll have to make jailbirds of us all!" At this, the people laughed long and hard.

"Who says?" General López roared, leaping to his feet. The speaker slithered back into anonymity. "Don't forget this is a court of law!" The general puffed out his chest, and the brass decorations glinted in the sun. "We mean to show a pattern of behavior. Now, *Capitán*, stand at attention and read out the charges so far."

The man to his left sprang up and sang out, "Conjurer!"

"Conjurer!" the general confirmed it, rapping his knuckles on wood.

"Murderer, either by hand or by proxy."

"Yes! One or the other!"

"Blasphemer."

"Correct! We have it right here, on paper."

"And now, General, by this latest testimony: Pervert."

"Well, then, good people of Floralinda, there you have it. That, in four words, describes what we have established so far about your eminent leader. Conjurer, murderer, blasphemer, and pervert. There you are." The general sat back in his chair.

"He's not *my* leader!" one of the field hands shouted. "Nor mine!" someone else seconded. "Nor mine!" "Nor mine!" others agreed, until they were all chanting it. "We have only one chief in this hacienda," a woman's voice sang over the shouting. "And you, *líder máximo*, are he."

Jaime could contain himself no longer. "Lies!" he shouted, pushing his way through the crowd. "That teacher tells lies! You *all* tell lies."

"Quiet!" the general yelled. "Young man, I told you that if you interrupted me for a second time I'd have you arrested. I could arrest all of you Sobrevillas now, if I wanted to. I certainly have the evidence to do it. But to show these good people how fair their *líder máximo* can be, I will allow everyone to take the stand and say their piece. Even rude upstarts like you. Approach the table! State your full name for the record."

"Jaime Porfirio Sobrevilla Francisco. I am, as everyone here well knows, the proud son of Don Victor."

"Mm-hm," the general said. "Proud, eh? Well, well. That's certainly a peculiar way to describe it."

"What do you mean?" Jaime responded, taken aback.

"What I mean, Señor Sobrevilla, is very simple: Why should anyone here believe a deviant like you?"

"Deviant?"

"*Sí, hombre.*" The general fixed Jaime with a hard look. "A man who fucks his sister."

"More lies!" Jaime erupted. "First you believe that ridiculous teacher, who, by the way, threw herself at me like an ordinary whore when no one was looking. Not for a minute do I accept her stories about my father. And now," he said, pointing a finger back at the house, "you say you believe that raving *loca*! Don't tell me you think that woman's obscene accusations are true!"

"If by '*loca*' you refer to your wife, Elsa Márquez y Márquez de Sobrevilla," the general answered calmly, "I believe her completely. I think you say she is mad because it is in your interest and in the interest of your entire family to do so: She tells the absolute truth about all of you, and the absolute truth is abhorrent. Your family disgusts me, Señor Sobrevilla. It makes me ill to think what depths you Amazon lords can sink to out here in the jungle. You're worse than animals." The general took a deep breath and thrust his chin toward the river, signaling the way to freedom. "Citizens of Floralinda!" he said at last, pausing for effect. He pointed to the house. "Behold that unfortunate creature in the window, trapped like a bird under a fiend's hat!" Three hundred heads turned on three hundred necks, like cogs in a giant wheelwork. When their eyes found Elsa's window, however, they saw not a bird—nor even the *loca*—but their priest, and he was brandishing a crucifix, arms over his head. The people looked on in a silent stupor. The general sprang to his feet and the soldiers beside him followed. "*Capitán!*" López barked at his record taker. "The Army of the Republic summons that priest!"

"The priest! The priest!" the people murmured, and their voices rose like a spiral of angry bees.

Jaime burst into the cathedral silence of the factory. His father was there—the very picture of defeat. Suraya was behind him. And the curandero.

"*Chukri,*" Jaime said to Suraya, "sweet."

"Kai-me," she answered.

"*Mal ojo*," Don Victor added. The evil eye. He gave the headbox a whack with Yorumbo's rod. "The old man can't root it out."

"If you ask me," Jaime said, "it's because it's not there. If there's evil anywhere in this hacienda, it's outside answering to the name of López."

"No, son. It's not just him. It's a deeper thing—a curse I can't get rid of."

"Ha! Don't tell me you believe in that rubbish! The evil eye? In all the years you've been bringing the sumiruna here to do his rituals, you've done it to please your workers! Those rituals are not for us. Not for you!"

Don Victor shook his head, hardly listening. "I don't know . . . I don't know much anymore, son. Everything seems suddenly built on sand."

"Not as long as I'm here, Father. We'll ride this out together. In a few weeks, we'll be laughing about it down at Chincho's."

Don Victor searched his son's eyes and drew strength there.

"Go back to the house," Jaime told him. "They need you. I'll lock up the factory and follow. But if you hurry, the three of you can slip out through the fruit trees. Now! While the general and his men are distracted."

"Never!" Don Victor said, drawing up to his full height. "May God strike me dead before I slink through my own hacienda like a frightened animal. I'll walk back the way I came."

He was as good as his word. The three marched past the digesters openly, crossed the very center of the concrete platform, and walked down the main road. Jaime had been right. In all the confusion of the priest being carried by his elbows to the table, Don Victor and the two Indians were hardly noticed at all.

Jaime clamped the lock on the main doors and buttressed them with a bag of cement. He patrolled the west wall, checking the Fourdrinier, keeping an eye on the monkeys as they scampered back to their perches in the windows. The noise from the general's inquest seemed muted now, like the gentle chirr of night locusts. The factory lay unnaturally still, and, except for a fugitive breeze that rattled the loose metal parts, a cavernous silence reigned. As he walked the length of the plant, spinning each roller to see whether its joints were free of rust, he worried about his father. In all his years, he had never seen Don Victor so vulnerable. He had looked old, his cellophane dreams behind him: old, defeated, and spent.

Jaime walked past the dryers, considering that change in his father, but when he bent over to inspect their underside, he froze. Something was there, moving quickly in the opposite direction. Feeling the hair on his neck rise against his collar, he squatted down for a better look. It took a few seconds to factor what he was seeing: human feet, bare, running noiselessly through the far side of the factory.

He stood and tried to get his bearings. Were they workers? If so, why hadn't they identified themselves? Surely they had seen him. Why were they running? Why were they mute? And how could so many be so silent? He calculated the distance to the rear doors: no more than thirty meters. Could he sprint? Would the sound of his boots give him away? His mind raced as he weighed his choices. Finally, deciding that his only option was to engage them, he raised his head and called—*"Chipi! Huni! Mim hana!"*—Brothers! Men! Speak to me! He stood on his toes, straining to see through the murky light. He was beginning to wonder where they had gone, when two hands shot out from under the machinery and shackled his ankles like iron. As he tumbled forward, he saw a face, domed with red and blue feathers, the dry *urucú* markings in bold chevrons under the eyes. Suspended from a string around the Indian's neck, wobbling on the floor like a puckered fruit, was the head of Nestor Sotomarino.

19

Nonsense!" the general's voice exploded, the fading sun in his eyes fierce now. "The devil, you say? In Elsa Márquez y Márquez? Not in that fine specimen of a woman, Padre. You'd have better luck searching for him in her father-in-law!" But the people began to murmur, "The loca! The loca!" They had always suspected her skin was too white, her dress too strange, her wild-eyed, solitary vigil too frightening to be anything but evil.

"Listen," the priest said, gathering his wits. "And I mean all of you. This won't be the first I've said it: You muddle your minds with rubbish! The general has a point. Don Victor has been playing with witchery for a long time, and now it has had its effect." The crowd squirmed at that but, eager to hear more, quieted quickly. Padre Bernardo took silence as consent, gripped his rope belt, and continued.

"Here are the facts, General López. The devil has found a purchase in the fragile mind of Elsa Márquez y Márquez. The woman is not to blame! She's a perfect innocent! It was Don Victor's hoodoo that invited the devil's attention, and when the devil surveyed potential bases of operation in the Sobrevilla house, she was the easiest target. It's run-of-the-mill Satanic strategy, used time and again since man's days in the Garden: Offer a little temptation, identify the weak link, then move in with a vengeance. Elsa is possessed by dark forces, General—of that there is no question. But there is also no question that God will prevail. If only I can go back to her. If only you'll let me finish what I've begun!"

The general put a palm to his forehead. He was sick of this silly man. All of a sudden he longed to be in Iquitos, away from this infernal hacienda. "We have already proven, Padre Bernardo," he said bloodlessly, "that Don Victor Sobrevilla is a conjurer, a murderer, a blasphemer, and a pervert. It will surprise no one here to learn that he is also in service of the devil."

The padre was taken aback. "Murderer?" he said. "Pervert? No, no, General, there must be some mistake." He shook his head brusquely. "Perhaps at some point in Don Victor's life he may have killed in self-defense, or hurt someone in error. Perhaps even strayed from his vows. We are all sinners. But he is not what you say he is. He simply needs to return to the good grace of our Virgin. When the serpent is expelled from his daughter-in-law and the poison is driven from his house, he will come around to his good old self. Of that I am sure."

The general yawned. Everything in this place was suddenly tiresome. The priest was too tolerant of bad behavior. The coca fields measured a fraction of what he first thought. The factory, when it wasn't producing paper, was just a stinking canker on the river. And, what's more, the people seemed unsurprised—even grateful—that, after so many years, Nestor Sotomarino should turn up without his head. The general was weary of the game, weary of Don Victor, weary of the ignorant Indians and their easily won loyalties. Now that the rains were over and the river was navigable, he longed for a soft bed and a warm dish of his wife's carapulcra. Why not slap Sobrevilla up against a wall and execute him? No, no. He didn't want that blood on his hands. Who knew who his cronies might be? Better go by the rules. At the close of the priest's testimony, he would end the inquest, arrest the engineer, take him to Iquitos, and throw him in the dungeon. But for the moment, he tried to focus his mind on the priest's phrase, "good old self."

He was formulating his objection when he heard a whoosh—then the thwick, thwick of two arrows meeting their mark, followed by odd, gurgling noises. He looked to his right and saw a line of dark foam gather along his soldier's lips; the man's eyes rolled up into his head and he pitched forward onto the table. A loud thwack came from the other side and his other man doubled over. Now both record takers were slumped on the wood, arrows jutting from their backs. General López dove under the table.

"Up there!" a worker yelled. "Up in the vents!" The people of Floralinda staggered back and strained to see the roofline of the factory, but all they could see in those high, narrow windows were the sharp, slanted shadows of the sun. Even the monkeys were gone. "The factory!" a woman's voice screeched. "The shapechanger's factory! Don't you see? It's the *pishtacos* in his machines!"

The people turned and fled, thundering along the road like a herd of bulls, kicking up dust so that it swirled high into their noses and clogged any possibility of reason. Padre Bernardo stood his ground and pleaded with them to come to their senses: "*Pishtacos?* Those arrows don't come from phantoms!" he shouted. "They come from the bows of *men!*" But before he could get any of the workers to listen, he found himself being shuffled into the hold of the *Augusto Leguía* alongside the general, in a tight little cluster of armed guards.

So. These were Suraya's people. Arms caked with animal blood, hair smeared with grease, they smelled foul. Fear darted through Jaime, freezing the chambers of his heart.

All his life he had heard his father speak in dread tones about the Jivaro—in awe of their terrible truculence. But in his dreams Jaime could never have imagined these men: lean, muscled, limber as macaques. They leapt from the high slits in the wall and clambered down the exhaust pipes. They were naked, feathered, their chests painted with a thick layer of red paste. Human heads dangled from their reed belts, bounced against their thighs, tiny and lifeless as dolls. They chattered incomprehensibly, sliding from the machinery as if they were dismounting great beasts.

Even the old headman seemed vigorous. He vaulted from metal to cement, gesturing his warriors to gather around him. The strong, chiseled face barely moved as it spoke, but the feathers that circled his head trembled with agitation. He looked from his men to the prisoner and back again. They were talking about him.

Jaime had been so stunned to see his brother-in-law's head in its strange, abbreviated state that the warriors had overpowered him easily. Nestor's face was completely recognizable in spite of its tiny size: the heavy brow, aquiline nose, wide mouth. Even the hair was as Jaime remembered it—tawny brown, wavy, with sun-bronzed streaks. But it was the grotesque exaggeration of the facial features that was so terrifying. In shrunken form, the unexpected grew larger: The bristling nose hairs. The leathery pores. Seeing the ghoulish orb wobble on the floor, Jaime had been momentarily paralyzed.

They had wrestled him across the cement floor, lashed him to the wood scaffolding, thrust wads of green cellophane into his mouth. When the fierce one wearing the head of Sotomarino put an arrow to his throat, the headman had stopped his hand. The old man had shouted, pounding his spear on the floor, jabbering as he pointed his weapon, first at Jaime's forehead and then at his shoulders. Jaime felt the sweat run down his face and a wave of nausea rise in his stomach. What would they do with him now?

All afternoon they watched him. He counted forty of them. Two scrambled back up the wall to squat on the windowsills and keep watch. Three spent the better part of an hour puzzling over the giant lock he had clamped to the front doors. Five more were deployed to far corners of the factory. One warrior dragged a spare roller from under the dryers; it clanked on the floor and rolled languidly away. The rest of them sat in a circle on the floor, talking quietly, glancing about in awe at the machinery as dusk came, the heat lifted, and a fickle breeze rattled the metal.

That evening, when darkness enveloped them, two men pulled him to his feet and marched him to the rear of the factory. They shoved him through the door, out into the still black night. He could see the glow from his father's house. He could see the shadows of men moving along the deck of the army boat. He tried to call for help, but, gagged by paper, all he could issue was a moan. One of the Jivaro gave him a sharp slap to the back of his head. As they strapped him to a leg of the towering ball digester and tied long leather strips around his ankles and wrists, he could hear the sounds of men running—a hard, rapping rhythm of boots. The Jivaro worked quickly, then slipped back to the factory, taking cover behind the boilers as they went. Three shots rang out—one after another in quick succession. Jaime looked up and watched the bullets ping off the iron like pebbles against a rock.

"Dead soldiers!" Don Victor sang out. "Two of President Odría's sons of bitches!" His voice was shrill with excitement. "Finally! The people have come to their senses!" He climbed down from the patio chair. "It's our son!" he told Doña Mariana. "Leading the insurrection!"

"What?"

"Yes! Out there in the factory!"

"No!" she cried. "Dear God, no!"

"*Querida,* you don't understand!" Don Victor said. "That's why he left us to live with the workers, don't you see? I knew he had a bit of his old man in him!" He paced the patio tiles like a frustrated marshal, cursing the army for confiscating his firearms, and then, gradually, as if light were gathering on the rim of comprehension, he concluded that his own son had appropriated the guns. "His plan is masterful! Masterful!" His voice was filled with so much enthusiasm that the dog lifted his head with hope.

Doña Mariana was desperate now. Not only was her son in mortal danger, her husband was losing his mind. Don Victor saw that flicker of panic. He took her firmly by the shoulders and told her that though Jaime could well be in peril, they should take heart, be grateful that he was so brave. At last, someone had the courage to go up against that tin prick of a general! "Oh, Lord!" he shouted, wheeling around spiritedly, "I wonder which of my workers drove those two arrows? A Huitoto surely! Or maybe a Bora! By God, they're great marksmen!"

"Señores!" A soldier was striding toward them from the kitchen. "Inside! Both of you! My men are securing this house."

"*Ay, por Dios!*" Doña Mariana cried. "What for?"

"The army is under attack, señora. We're not taking any chances."

Once inside, they could see that the soldiers were dead serious. A scar-faced lieutenant was marching Ignacio and Louis Miller in from the dining room—a rifle jabbing their backs. "Stay here!" he snarled. "One step outside and we shoot." He whirled around and reprimanded two soldiers as they grabbed food from Boruba's counter. Ordering them to man the doors, he ran out the back of the house.

"Children, children!" Don Victor shouted, flinging his arms as he crossed the foyer to the sala. "The tables have turned! The general will now see what he's up against!"

Belén, who was fumbling with the library key, looked up, aghast. What in God's earth was he talking about? Her father seemed completely disoriented, unaware of the peril that had just descended.

In the sala, Graciela was thrusting the family silver into the lowest drawer of the sideboard. She slammed it shut and rose, brought to her feet by the sight of Louis Miller. Before she could stop herself, she was in his arms. "Luis!" she cried, clutching him fast. "Thank God you're safe!" Then she drew back, searching his face. "Where is my brother, *mi amor?* What have they done with him? I have a terrible feeling..." She stood like a child before the American, twisting his shirt in her fingers, looking at him expectantly. But Doña Mariana was so filled with worry that she didn't notice. She stood in the middle of the room, wringing her hands.

As daylight dimmed, the family huddled in the living room, fretting about Jaime's whereabouts. Don Victor clung to the hope that he was still in the factory, surrounded by armed collaborators. Doña Mariana preferred to think he was out in the shacks, safe from harm. They drank Boruba's mint tea infusions, considering the possibilities. With two soldiers dead, Louis Miller ventured, the general might cut his losses, slip away. If so, Ignacio countered, he'd only be back, with more men and more ammunition. Distraught now, the women went upstairs to see about the children. As darkness stole over the house and the hum of crickets mounted to an angry whine, the three men imagined the ways a cruel army might retaliate. They talked on into the shadows until dusk settled over Floralinda and night swallowed it whole.

Rising to light the lanterns, Don Victor railed on against the general's impertinence—who was he to accuse anyone of perversions?—and the way the priest had played into the general's hand with his rant about rain forest shamans! It was high time, he said finally, that the ass in the uniform got his comeuppance. An insurrection was just the tonic to set the little prick straight.

"If it's an insurrection, Don Victor," Ignacio said quietly, "what makes you think it's not against you?"

"Not me, boy!" Don Victor balked. "I'm talking about the green jackets—against *them*! You think the people of Floralinda would dare raise up against me? Ha! Not in a million years. I give them a little bread, a little circus, and they eat from my hand. I've always known how to handle my workers."

A crack of gunfire resounded through the night. It was a faraway shot, followed quickly by two more. The men scrambled to the front door. Ignacio had just enough time to look out the doorway before the guard shoved him away. But Don Victor was able to push his way onto the patio. Out in the night, he blinked into the vastness. It was dank, inky, impenetrable. He reeled around, his arms out like two useless rudders. He felt strangely unmoored in the night air. There was nothing to hold on to. Nothing to see. Nothing at all but black sky and stars.

A large hand clamped him on the shoulder. "Jesus, God!" Don Victor rasped, as the soldier jerked back his thin frame, then hurled him headlong into his own foyer. He staggered across the tiles. "Just you wait! They'll come after you pigs!" he bellowed. He moved unsteadily, grasping at walls. He wanted to call out to Boruba, tell her to bring out the knives. But all at once he felt dizzy, helpless—too tired to talk or think. He wove his way through the sala, clutching at furniture as he went. And then, at long last, he dropped into his chair with a groan. Like a small stone in a huayco, his spirit began to sink.

"There's nothing we can do, *Ingeniero*. It's best that you sit for now," Ignacio offered, as if he'd read his mind.

"They've got four soldiers guarding the house," Louis Miller told them. "I've counted them. There may be more, but that's all I see."

"Four, eh? Not many, but they have guns," said Ignacio. He thought briefly, then put forward a plan. "Luis, the next time those soldiers are distracted—I don't care what it is: gunfire, shouts, any commotion whatsoever—we'll slip out a window into the dark. We'll make a run from the house, crawl if we have to, and circle around until we reach the shacks. We'll gather some men then. Try to find Jaime. We can be back here before morning."

Don Victor was fighting exhaustion now. He closed his eyes. Surrendering his head to the sturdy rattan, he let the crippling fatigue overtake him. Ignacio was right. There was nothing to do but wait. He sank his spine into the pillow, took a deep breath, and released all the air with a long sigh. Blessed rest! It was the only thing he wanted now. As he drifted in and out of consciousness, he imagined his son inside the magnificent bastion of his factory, devising a strategy, drawing a grand plan on the floor.

Ignacio and Louis Miller stayed awake all night long, listening for more sounds, more shots, some evidence of rebellion. When none came, they could only pace the room, drum the windowsills with their fingers, bristle in frustration. In the darkest hours of morning, Doña Mariana descended the staircase like a ghost from the afterworld—her long, gray mane floating behind her—and coaxed her weary husband upstairs.

Suraya had slinked past the guards easily. In her childhood, her father had taught her to run silently, from cover to cover, so she could fool even a watchful animal. She stole through the servants' quarters, sped through the black, and made her way noiselessly to the gramalote, where she nestled against the tall grass. She waited there, eyes hard with purpose. When daylight revealed the sprawled figure of Kai-me, she stood swiftly. The guards saw her. They fired two shots into the air—bringing Ignacio and Louis Miller to the window. And then she began to run. The soldiers tried to call her back, but she wouldn't listen. She raced through the ferns like a deer through an open field.

Louis Miller threw open the window, leapt out, and he, too, began running. Years later he would not be able to say what made him do it. Was it the sight of his friend, in the full light of day, bound and gagged like an animal? Or was it Graciela? She had already been subjected to so much—the corpse of a husband, the corpse of a child, the corpse of a dog. He thought of her fingers twisting his shirt, her lovely face wrung by worry. "*Mi amor!*" she had said, begging for news of her brother. There was only so much the woman could be made to see. Or perhaps it was the sight of that tiny girl in yellow, flying so bravely into danger. He didn't know. But he followed Suraya toward the unseen aggressor, as if destiny offered no choice. "Luis!" Ignacio called, clutching the frame of the open window, reckoning instantly his own responsibilities. His brother-in-law was in shackles. The American was headed for clear danger. Off to the right, a soldier was darting through the bushes. Who knew what state Don Victor was in upstairs? He had no choice but to stay and protect the women and children.

Suraya fell to her knees when she reached Jaime. Tied to his hair were three yellow cock-of-the-rock feathers—her father's mark. Everything came into focus now: Mwambr had followed her upriver, over jungle, through the rains, just as she feared he would. He had smelled her blood. Gasping for breath, her heart pounding in her ears, she scanned the distance. Seeing no one, she glanced behind. No soldiers there; only the maize-haired man, racing like the wind toward her. Quickly, she plucked the cellophane from Jaime's mouth, pulled the feathers from his hair. And then she took measure of his condition. He was covered with perspiration. His eyes were puffed red, but he was awake and alert, pushing against his bonds, struggling to speak. "Kai-me," she whispered.

She assessed the situation quickly. They hadn't killed him outright. They had put him here, unharmed, alive. It was not like her people to do this. In war, they would have taken the man's head. They would have rushed the house, butchered everyone, including the daughter betrayer. Something else was at work here. Her father was taking no risks. She reached for the knife in her belt.

"Atsá! Nung-ka!" A loud voice came from inside the factory.

She froze. The sound of her own language was terrifying—it had been so long since she'd heard it.

"Suraya!" the man called again, and she knew then that it was her father.

"Ápa?" she said, in as strong a voice as she could muster.

Louis Miller came to a sudden halt, frozen between Suraya's private drama and Jaime's desperate predicament.

Jaime licked his lips, his head struggling against confusion. He had

not learned much of her language, but he understood that one word—
ápa. He had known instinctively his captors were her tribesmen. But
was the old headman her father? The men with him her brothers?
Feeling a frail hope rise in his heart, he prayed she might make peace
with them now.

Louis Miller needed more time to gauge the situation. He was surprised, bewildered, uncertain of what he should do. He had heard
Suraya's name called from behind those large doors. He had heard her
answer. He had been sure she was a feckless girl, flying from love to
peril. Now he could see that he had been a fool to think so. The bravery
was all illusion. She was one of *them*. He launched himself forward again.

"No!" Jaime choked out hoarsely. And then, with all the strength he
could muster: "For God's sake, no, Luis! The factory is full of them!
Don't move!"

Doña Mariana paced the room, swatting her stick against the brass orbs
of her bed. "What do we do now, Victor?" she wailed. "Our boy! Out
there like a goat for carving!"

"For God's sake, woman, calm down. Can't you see he's there for a
reason? Can't you see he's alive? Be quiet and let me think." Don Victor
willed himself to concentrate. He put his hands on the windowsill and
felt a knot travel up his chest to his throat. His son, the very man on
whom he had placed all his hopes, whose imagined rebelliousness had
allowed him to sleep, was in grave danger now.

Time was playing games with Don Victor. He was reeling suddenly
through the years, whirling into the past with increased velocity. It was
as if he were a boy again, standing before Señor Urrutia's shop, watching the parts move, seeing balls fly, knowing there was a missing piece
to the puzzle, doubting the trick was as it appeared. Before him lay
something like an intricate machine, yet all of its parts were inert,
clogged, stuck in time like a rusted relic. There was his son, still as
stone, lashed to his own machinery. There was the Jivaro girl, sitting on
her haunches, gazing at the factory, transfixed. There was the American
cartographer, as rigid as the statue in Trujillo's Plaza de Armas—one

heel raised, so that the thick sole of his boot was clearly visible. Why was nobody moving? What unseen force—what hidden contrivance—was in the wings, preventing the motion?

Suddenly the entire universe seemed to stand still, poised on a trembling fulcrum. It seemed to him that nothing had changed for years; nothing had happened, in point of fact, since the day he last looked through a window on Garcilaso de la Vega. His entire existence was spooling somewhere between Señor Urrutia's wheelwork and the poster of the Amazon Indian on the wall. There she was, a Jivaro girl, squatting before his cellophane factory, as illogical a picture as any he might have imagined forty years earlier—before he had traveled the Andes, before he had slipped down the river with a wife and two daughters, scoured Pucallpa for a witchman to bless his son. Don Victor pressed his head to the window frame. Was his beloved boy there like one of Señor Urrutia's displays, a show for the eye—an illusion? Had Don Victor traveled the circuit of life only to rattle back to the starting point? Here he was, as he had been in the beginning and ever would be, standing before a window, witnessing a spectacle that strained credulity. Or perhaps life hadn't stopped at all. Perhaps it was simply a phenomenon of gravity. An aberration of starlight. The imperceptible circling of heavenly bodies. Perhaps he was moving so quickly he couldn't factor it, swinging through galaxies in perpetual orbit—a cog in an infinite ambit, meant to travel the loop until he came back again. Could it be, Don Victor wondered, clutching his head now as if demons were swirling in it, that he had always been destined to stand before windows? Always destined to dream through glass?

"Kill him!" the *kakaram* yelled, pointing to the man with the yellow hair.

Mwambr peered through the doors. The gap was the width of two fingers and gave him ample view of the termite clearing. He watched the mythical creature come to a halt. He remembered the sky-filled eyes, sun-filled hair, but now the face was different—not as pleasing as it had been out in the fields, mating with the *tsunki* woman. And yet the golden man had just spurred his daughter toward him like a benevolent spirit. Hadn't the ancestors always said that a man with such hair had special powers? Harming a golden head could bring lifetimes of bad fortune. But now, there it was, carrying its benevolence too far. It was poised over the captive, eyes on the leather rope.

"Suraya," the old headman called again.

"*Ápa,*" she answered dutifully.

"Do not set the prisoner free."

"The prisoner is my husband, Father."

Mwambr tried to slow his breathing, calm the pain in his head. "She is as sly as a snake, *ápu,*" the *kakaram* whispered. "Give the order. She has betrayed you. She has dishonored us all. Say it, and I will kill her for you."

Mwambr jerked his head sharply, signaling the warrior to be silent. Suraya was looking back toward him, eyes filled with expectation. It was true: She had betrayed them. But there was something else in those eyes. Something else.

He pressed his forehead into the door and listened to the sounds behind him. A few of his men were wielding stones, smashing the hinges on the hulking beast, pulling the great rollers free and lining them up on the floor like so many canoes. The hollow cylinders were heavy, long—as thick and straight as the trunks of strong trees. They fell to the floor with the loud ring of armor.

"*Ápu, ápu!*" the *kakaram* insisted. "Give the killing order! It is time. We will kill them all." Two of Mwambr's warriors prepared to signal the ten shooters squatting in the windows with arrows pulled taut against their bows. "Sssss!" Mwambr hissed. He felt the weariness pull through his chest and drag his heart along with it.

Four guards sprang from the trees and ran, shoulder to shoulder, toward the factory. It was a natural movement, easy as a spider's across bark, but that single-minded scurry—practiced over and over again at military school and rendered now in perfect unison—made Suraya twirl around, mouth open, wrist limp in surprise. Louis Miller dashed forward and snatched the knife from her hand.

"What in God's name are you doing?" Jaime yelled.

"She's one of them!" the cartographer yelled back, pointing the knife at the factory. "She's with those people!"

"I know!" Jaime said. "But she's also with me. She came here to cut me free!"

Louis Miller looked down at the knife. Its handle was polished mahogany, in the shape of a leaping cat. But before he could spin it in his palm to get a good grip on it, a piercing howl went up and reverberated to the far corners of the hacienda. The American whirled around: The soldiers were no longer in formation. They were staggering back, struggling to pull arrows from their chests. He watched in astonishment as they dropped to their knees, squalling like wounded chickens. They bellowed, coughed blood, begged God, and wept, as if they were mourning their own passing. As if tears could buy back their lives.

"Good God!" he whispered. But before he could tear his eyes from the writhing bodies, the voice came again. *"Wi jau."* It was reedy, high, insistent—and when it spoke, he saw the girl tense.

The voice raddled on—the call of some incomprehensible intelligence—as the wounded men wailed and shouts came from the boat, commanding the soldiers to stand ground, hold their positions. With brisk motions now, the American began cutting the leather that bound Jaime's legs.

"Atsá!" Suraya said unequivocally. *"Atsá!"*

"Stop!" Jaime told him, translating what little he had learned of her language. "She says to stop."

"Stop saving your life?" Louis Miller said, astounded.

"She must have a reason. Something her tribesman said. She would not risk losing my life, Luis. Believe me."

The sun was over his factory now, and all he could do was stand there and squint into its brilliance. A flicker of light was dancing along the far wall. Then two. Then three.

Eventually there was no mistaking them: They were parts from his factory, metal rollers he had installed himself between the Fourdrinier and the reelers. He watched them wobble over the dirt toward the concrete platform—long silver cylinders, moving on human legs.

Don Victor lunged toward his dresser to reach for his field glasses, but, as he did, his eyes landed on a silent apparition. It was a gaunt man, cadaverous—a walking skeleton—with hair as white and flocculent as new cotton. The intruder stood staring at Don Victor, bewildered, as if he had walked into that bedroom expecting to find it empty, and now here he was, confronting the master of the house.

Don Victor's first instinct was to cry out, but there was something arresting about the face before him. The skin was pale, near jaundice. The eyes were cavernous and tormented. Just as Don Victor was about to say something to him, the man's lips moved to speak in return. Don Victor held his breath, taking the stranger's measure, registering his proximity with a mounting sense of alarm.

Gradually, it came to him that he was in the presence of the devil incarnate. Here was the beast himself, summoned by the priest, prowling the house freely. Doña Mariana's deepest fears had been realized. The face was inhuman—there was glassiness in the stare, cruelty about the jaw. The more he looked at it, the more demonic it seemed, and the more it appeared to understand that Don Victor had reckoned its identity correctly. It looked back warily, its shoulders drawn up, as if ready to strike.

"Satan!" Don Victor cried, and the demon spat back at him soundlessly. The scowl was monstrous, evil. Don Victor danced away, horrified.

"Mariana!" he yelled. "Mariana!" And then he looked about in consternation, unable to locate the face again. The intruder had vanished as quickly as he had come.

"Darling, what is it?" his wife said. She was running toward him now, fearing the look in his eyes.

"He was here! In this room! Over there!" gasped Don Victor. "I saw him!"

But when she looked, she saw only her faded mirror.

Marcela took every opportunity to peer out into the humid day. Seeing the events unfold, she was filled with worry, but she spoke to the children with a cool head and a level voice—as she had been taught to do at the teachers' academy.

Having been raised in the great jungle city of Iquitos, aware of how crucial it is to stay calm in the face of tribal hostilities, Marcela applied herself busily to the effort of distracting her charges. The younger ones had been easy to divert with games and rhymes; they had no sense of the seriousness of the circumstances. But Pablito, being ten years old, knew better. When she had released them all to Graciela and Belén, he had descended the staircase blanched and nervous, clutching his mother's skirt.

Now that she was alone, she realized how frightened she, too, was. She went about tidying her schoolroom, flitting back and forth from the windows to monitor events outside. It was during one of those quick interludes that she looked out and spied a dark prow on the river. At first, it seemed no more than a squared-off wood nose, but then she saw—with a little twitch of her heart—that it was the barge from Pucallpa. It lurched over the water, riding the current, and then, quite precipitously, swiveled toward the dock.

The barge looked unnaturally empty. There was little it seemed to be transporting apart from a few barrels and trunks. The vast expanse of greased wood, usually laden with cargo, was bare—its weight light, so that the vessel sat up on the water and tossed spiritedly from side to side. In the back, by the engine, was the unmistakable figure of the Australian, holding his hand against the sun. In the middle, sitting primly on a barrel, was a stout woman in a jade dress, under an ornately painted parasol. Marcela could not see her face, since the parasol blocked everything above her shoulders, but it was clear the woman was not accustomed to the rain forest. Her sleeves reached for her wrists, her skirt to her ankles, and a long, richly hung necklace swung back and forth, striking her ample bosom.

Marcela was struck by that unexpected vision just beyond the drama, and she raised one hand to chew thoughtfully on a finger, puzzling over who the woman might be. But even as she contemplated the possibilities, she saw the people of Floralinda emerge from their shacks and gather in front of Chincho's. They were looking toward the factory, pointing and talking animatedly. Their faces flickered in awe as three huge paper rollers advanced along the walls, scampering on human legs. The cylinders looked larger than they had in the mill: They were shining, perforated with tiny holes, skimming above the ground like specters.

Guns suddenly bristled from the flank of the army boat and fired a

round at the cylinders. But the bullets only pinged off the metal, rico-
cheted from the wall, and clattered about on concrete. The cylinders
rolled forward, the human legs running and squatting, pressing on in a
gradual offensive until they came to a stop behind the great metal cookers. As the shapechanger's machines rose up with a mind of their own,
the people of Floralinda grew bolder. They began to edge down the
road, whispering to one another. They looked back over their shoulders
toward the house, where they had seen Don Victor stand like a boy at
a window, his face in a permanent state of surprise. Now all they could
see was the teacher, and they marveled at the meaning of that. How
strange were the white people! How firm their alliances! After such a
resounding denunciation before God and the army—after her scathing
account of his perversions—there was the teacher, back in her master's
house again, safe in his tower, surveying the world from his domain.

Suraya scanned the two men's faces. Kai-me and the yellow-haired man
were arguing feverishly now, punching the air with their hands. The
loud cracks behind her sounded like nothing so much as the sharp little hooves of an evil spirit. As rifles fired and hard metal flew off hard
metal, she cringed, drawing her shoulders to her ears. She began to
wonder what had made her think she could live on scarred ground, in
the deafening world of these men. "*Wi jau,*" her father had said—I am
ailing—and suddenly she wanted to see his face, feel his hands, beg the
old man's forgiveness.

  She could see that the shining tubes, wide enough to shield a man's
head and body, were bulwarks for her tribesmen. They scuttled over the
dirt like clumsy beetles, then crouched down, repelling the gunfire. Just
as Suraya was losing her nerve to the flying bullets, just as she was
about to scramble away on her knees, a Jivaro darted from behind a
roller and sped over the concrete from vat to vat, toward the *Augusto
Leguía.* He was lunging for the pier when a shot rent the air and drove
a bullet into his foot. There was an agonizing cry as he fell, and when
he turned to look at her, Suraya saw that it was the *kakaram,* struggling
to stand, clutching one leg.

"Wi!" he yelled out—and hobbled closer, brazen in red paint and wrath. "Kawau nuwa!" Evil woman! "Shuwin ji!" Spittle flew from his mouth. He was moving toward her more quickly now, and Nestor Sotomarino's diminutive head bounced from his chest—a shriveled bauble with bright, black eyes. Louis Miller stood abruptly and the gesture had the effect of paralyzing the warrior. The Jivaro's eyes ranged over the golden man. Slowly, he reached for the quiver on his shoulder.

Louis Miller read the danger instantly. He pulled Suraya to the floor just as a fusillade of gunshot rang out and pounded the kakaram's back. There was a moment when the whole body danced forward—arms flung overhead, arrows in hand, bounding through a halo of blood— and then it plummeted in one swift motion, stiff as a felled tree.

"God!" an imperious voice shouted. An elderly woman in a green dress tottered across the dock toward the Augusto Leguía. "Phantasmagoria!" the woman called, waving her parasol in the air. "What nightmare have I wandered into?"

No one answered, stunned as they were by the flying blood and the old lady in shimmering brocade descending to their hell like a vaporous creature. "This is the home of Victor Sobrevilla Paniagua, is it not?" she asked, bustling toward them, wielding her umbrella with no thought to the danger. She dabbed her brow as she went, with a handkerchief pinned to her bracelet.

"Stand back!" an army man's voice commanded from somewhere inside the boat. She scanned the impressive vessel, but seeing no one there, continued her trajectory toward the concrete.

"Halt!" the voice resounded once more.

"I will not!" she barked back. "I will not obey someone I cannot see. I'm too old and I've traveled too far to play games with ghosts!" She toddled toward the stairs that led from the dock to the factory, shading her eyes with her hand. The handkerchief drooped along one side of her face, limp in the windless morning.

"Señora!" the man yelled again. "If you do not stand back, you are in contravention of the command of the Army of the Republic! Identify yourself!"

At this, the old woman stopped. She glanced back at the boat, which still bore no sign of life save its bristling gun barrels. She took in the naked Indian in a pool of blood. His *tsantsa* trophy, no larger than a chicken's head, lay staring at him in mockery. She turned to study the corpses of the four soldiers, curled side by side like dead centipedes, hands clutching the arrows that had claimed them. And then she surveyed what she could of the living population: three figures—two white males, one Indian female. "You want me to identify myself?" she called out. "I am Esther Paniagua, daughter of Homero and Catalina Paniagua. Granddaughter of Wong Hsing Tao!"

"Tía Esther!" Jaime rasped.

"Who are you?" she asked, eyes widening with surprise.

"Jaime," he answered. "Sobrevilla. Son of Victor Sobrevilla Paniagua."

"Jaime!" she said indignantly. "And what in God's name are you doing there, trussed like some pigeon for dinner?"

"How on earth . . . ?" Jaime asked.

"On a barge," she replied. "With John Gibbs."

"I beg you, señora," Louis Miller said, stepping toward her briskly now. "You are in danger. As you can see, this is no game."

"Game! Ha!" Esther said, snatching the pendant cloth and wiping the perspiration from her forehead. "That's exactly what this looks like to me, señor. Cut my grandnephew free. What are you doing there with a knife in your hand and that silly expression on your face? Cut those ropes from his hands and feet this very instant!" She climbed down the stairs to the platform and hobbled forward, using the folded parasol as a cane. Behind her, the guns lowered into position. Suraya, still trembling from her encounter with the fallen warrior, scrambled to her feet. She could not tell the sex of the person before her; the breasts and genitals were covered; the voice was deep as a man's. But there was no question about the necklace. It was a glittering chain with polished stones of many colors. On the bottom was the shrunken head of a cougar, a *tsantsa* such as she'd only seen in tribal ceremonies around the necks of the ancients. Had her father seen it?

"*Ápa!*" she called out.

"Who is that girl, Jaime? What is that '*ápa*'? What is she saying to me?" Esther Paniagua asked.

Suraya called again, "*Ápa,* do not kill this ancient! He is an *iwishin!* He carries the head of a cougar!"

Mwambr had seen the magnificent cat face right away. It had loomed into view like an answer out of a drug dream. He had never seen a *tsantsa* around the neck of a woman—and a woman she surely was. It seemed odd, wrong to see a cat head banging against those draped teats. Yet there was something more: A woman had appeared now, in the thick of things, with that symbol of undisputable power. She had materialized on the dock just as his *kakaram* had struck the ground, just as his men intended to take back his daughter. What did it mean?

"Cut those ropes! Cut them!" the old lady ordered, shaking her finger at the American. "I can see that this girl is harmless. Why are you standing there like a perfect idiot?"

Suraya understood the ancient's commands by his gestures, which were elaborate and expressive. "He wants my husband free!" she pleaded with her father.

There was a long moment of silence as each reckoned his position. The Jivaro men shifted the rollers in their hands with a new understanding: A powerful force had joined them on the battlefield, but what it was and whether it was friend or foe they had yet to find out. Mwambr rubbed his temples with his fingers. The feathered string that circled his head had shrunk in the rains. It felt like a vise around his throbbing skull. He felt his patience wane, like the river in a dry season. Why was his daughter negotiating with him as if she were an agent of the termite tribe? And how many more moons of bad fortune would he bring on his people if he ignored the priestess with the cougar head? With a flick of his wrist he called down the shooters from their high vigil.

"Daughter!" he bellowed. "Listen to the *iwishin!* Do her bidding! Cut free the termite man. Let him go!"

20

Don Victor did not recognize Tía Esther immediately. It had been forty-two years since he had last seen her, and the stocky figure with the bobbed white hair no longer bore any resemblance to the lithe young aunt he had kissed good-bye on the doorstep of the Trujillo house. He snatched up his field glasses again and peered through the cracked lenses at the old woman who, like the fly in Señor Urrutia's contraption, had soared into view, interrupted the flow, and, in the process, clarified things. All the gears in the wheelwork of events shifted and trundled off in a new direction. He watched—through his tears— as his son was cut free. He watched eleven naked Jivaro, streaked with red dye, appear from behind the cellophane rollers and retreat, quick as dragonflies, along the far wall of the factory. He watched the boat's guns flip up and point to the sky.

"What the hell?" he muttered. "Who *is* that crone?" But Doña Mariana did not reply. She was on her knees, pulling out one drawer after another in their massive chest, rifling through the contents, in search of her prayer cards of the saints.

The answer burst through the door with Belén. "It's Tía Esther," she gasped, as if she had just witnessed a miracle.

"Tía Esther?" he said, in disbelief. "How in God's name would you know? You've never laid eyes on her!"

"There's no doubt in my mind," Belén answered, her voice trembling between joy and alarm. "It's Esther. She promised me she would come."

Belén's simple declaration, uttered with juridical authority, moved like a ship's prow through the frozen sea of Don Victor's heart. He lowered the field glasses, his mind flooding with unbidden memories: His aunt marching purposefully toward the monkey Negrita and his puzzling fortune. Her lessons about brokenhearted coolies, trees that pushed their way through churches, paper that was portable life. He summoned the image of his little Chinese sister hugging her knees, rapt in those fabulous stories. He called forth the memory of his aunt standing in the front hall with her brown suitcase and birdcage. He remembered the shiny long dresses, the jacket with the leaping dragons. "Tía Esther," he said, in a whisper. "Of all people. Here."

John Gibbs secured the ropes and sprang onto the dock. He had turned his back for a moment and, when he turned around again, the señora was no longer there. Where had she gone?

She was a hard old bird. He had found her on the ramshackle pier at San Jeronimo, not far from Tiruntán. She had waved her handkerchief at him as his barge sped a fast route downriver. The sight of her there struck him as a mirage, a river captain's hallucination—the cloud of white hair, the green brocade, the ridiculous little suitcase. Not fifty feet away, a riverboat was taking on water, sinking fast. A cluster of men scrambled from it, struggling under the weight of its cargo. He swung the barge east, toward them.

The old woman had called out that she was stranded, trying to make her way to her family north on the Ucayali. When she said her destination was the hacienda in Floralinda, he carried her suitcase onboard.

Where was she now? The gunshots had filled him with mounting trepidation. Soldiers were swarming the *Augusto Leguía*, battening down the deck. He broke into a trot. He could hear men's voices as he passed: a string of loud orders followed by the reverberations of slamming wood.

He ran past the nose of the boat, past a cluster of abandoned barrels, past the long railing of the dock, before he could get a clear look ahead. The old woman was there, at the foot of the dock, making her way across a ramp with the help of the American mapmaker. Don Victor's son was sitting by the iron behemoth, unraveling twine from his ankles. A flock of naked Indians was racing toward the forest. There was nothing immediately alarming in this. But what he saw next made his gut twist with fear: A mob of workers was coming up the road. There was a considerable mass of them—one hundred or more angry faces— and he was reminded, with jarring clarity, of the butchery he had witnessed on the Indian continent not five years before: the raised knives, the surging crowd, the impending threat of revolution.

Suddenly, he no longer cared about his own safety. With a new stab of apprehension, he feared for the teacher now.

Don Victor rushed from the bedroom, exhorting Belén to mind her mother. Doña Mariana had found her prayer cards and was arranging them carefully on the furniture. As he sped past Graciela's doorway, he could see the children nestled on her bed, leafing through a great pile of books, blissfully innocent of the chaos around them. Descending the stairs eagerly, he headed for his workshop.

He swung open the door and scanned the room. The massive table seemed a rock of stability. Evidence of his labors lined the walls: metal canisters brimming with nails and screws; a row of clamps from which the cellophane had first hung; long wooden shelves filled with tools in calibrated sizes. He breathed in the ferric air. It had been months since he'd spent time in that sanctuary, and it welcomed him back like a long-lost prodigal.

Pawing through his inventions, he found what he needed: A vest made of coconut skins lashed tightly to steel mesh, designed to repulse the sharpest of arrows. A helmet of metal—half a globe of the world, inherited from Alejandro—with one hole in Guyana, another in Brunei, a movable visor, and a strap that tied under the chin. A spring-loaded dart shooter, carved from bamboo, so light it could hang on a belt alongside a pouch of ammunition. A lance, soldered together from old spindles—with a hatchet on one end and a knife on the other. He dressed in that improvised armor, checked his reflection in the tin of his goosenecked lamp, and, as a finishing touch, twirled his mustache with paraffin from a little pot under the stuffed condor. Feeling as ready as he could be, he hastened out to bring Esther home.

As he rushed past the house, he heard Ignacio and Pedro arguing at the door of the kitchen. Yorumbo was there too, muttering to himself. It was remarkable: Don Victor could hear each of them clearly, as if his helmet amplified sound. "The church!" Ignacio was saying. "Someone should go to the church—the padre's not there to protect it."

"Get someone else!" Pedro snapped. "I don't give a damn about that church, or that priest, or that wooden woman!" and then Pedro shouted the whole thing to the witchman in Shipibo, including a description of the carved idol and how the Sobrevillas got on their knees to talk to it.

Don Victor pulled the Northern Hemisphere more securely around his ears, amazed at its listening properties. He aligned the visor so that it was squarely over his brow, shading his eyes and allowing him to look out into the distance. Were Jaime and Esther still there? All he could see was a crowd of workers, teeming onto the platform, rushing toward the factory with sticks in their hands. He felt oddly detached, indifferent toward them now. They had not mounted an insurrection against General López. They had not rescued his elderly aunt. Since Tía Esther had set foot on the dock, there had been no gunfire, no show of arrows—but who knew what a capricious general might do? Don Victor pressed on, the dart shooter flapping against his hip, the lance resting heavily on his shoulder. Wafting up into his nostrils was the sweet scent of coconut, invading his senses, reminding him of his wife's skin.

Before long, a resonant noise began to vibrate his helmet—loud as a clamor of monkeys. A good number of the hacienda's citizens—fifty or more—were swarming up the road, elbows churning in the air.

Little by little, he recognized the faces. There was Antonito, the shoveler; Juan, the one-armed Huitoto; Gloria, the pregnant wife of a pulp carrier; Felisberto, the machinist. And there, too, was the seamstress; the *chicha*-maker. Their voices were clear, sharp as bells, reechoing in his head like the chimes of the Trujillo belfry. The moment they saw who was in the ludicrous armor, wielding the cockeyed lance, they cried out. "*Oye, mira!* The shapechanger! In his machines!"

He pushed on ahead, hearing each word with increased clarity.

"Conjurer! Murderer! Blasphemer! Pervert!" "He's a factory on legs!" one woman screeched. "Don Victor's *pishtacos* have gone too far!" someone else shouted. "They're everywhere. In his workshop! His living room! His head!"

The mob was almost upon him now, screaming incomprehensibly—he was sure his helmet would explode. Perspiration trickled under the tin and ran in rivulets down his neck.

He came to a halt, afraid for the first time of his people, many of whom he had brought to that bend in the river—workers who had built his house, grown his hemp, cooked his pulp, spun his paper. They had always been temperate folk, obedient and grateful. What had happened to their gentle natures? Did they really mean to frighten him? Or hurt him? Or kill him?

"Antonito?" he called out softly, but he could hardly hear his own voice for the din. Their eyes were narrowed, their nostrils flared, their mouths curled back in hideous rage. The mob surged toward him like a wave on an angry sea. And then it broke and parted, slipping past like an army of ghosts. Incredibly, improbably, they hurtled by, hardly looking at him; and when they were behind him, he heard them break into a run. He whirled around to see them spill down the road, then up, like a dark plague of insects, toward the house. He could make out the small, square figure of Ignacio—dark as a boroshuda fly—standing solidly, with his arms folded, watching the horde approach.

Reassured by the sight of Ignacio, Don Victor scanned the shore. There was Tía Esther, talking to Louis Miller—two little figures against a large canvas of confusion. But then his eyes fell on the scene behind: A line of workers was moving like an army of ants, carrying dead soldiers over their heads, dropping them into the river. One by one, the corpses splashed into the water and bobbed to the surface like buoys. Others were doing the same with the metal rollers. "Stop!" Don Victor called out. "What the hell are you doing?" But they were too far away to hear.

Just as he was deliberating what to do, he saw Jaime, racing toward the cast-off rollers, his face tight with purpose.

"Sainted Jesus!" Don Victor whispered to himself. He pulled off his helmet, tucked it under one arm, and forced himself into a trot.

* * *

The apparition was loping toward her, an old man with flying white hair and a stiff mustache. His torso was covered in what appeared to be a garment of matted monkey fur and he labored under it mightily, a crooked pole waving from his hand. Under one arm was a ramshackle globe of the world. On the opposite hip swung a device that looked like a small birdcage. "Would you look at that! It's Don Victor," Louis Miller said.

"Victor?" Tía Esther said, disbelieving her eyes, unable to square the vision before her with the straight young boy she remembered. But his face broke into a smile every bit as beatific as the one he'd beamed up at her when she'd told him of gypsies and magic. It was her nephew for sure—as bizarrely as God was now offering him. "*Ay, por Dios,* Victor," she cried, "it's been so long!" and she hobbled out to embrace him.

They greeted each other tenderly, then stood back to study how time had marked itself on their faces. "You've grown old, Victor," Tía Esther said. "God knows there was a time I thought you never would!"

Despite the urgency, they spoke of old times: the Trujillo house; the massive desk, which his brother had sent across town to his law offices. But even as she was relaying greetings from Alejandro, fate interceded in the form of General José Antonio López. The belligerent was suddenly there, thrusting his chest like a bull inviting hostilities. Just as quickly, three soldiers appeared, the butts of their rifles held high, like clubs. Don Victor stepped back, one hand on his coconut breastplate. Tía Esther eyed the guns, trying to absorb the gravity of this new horror.

"Señor Sobrevilla," the general declared, "listen closely. I have no reason to talk to you, really. I am standing here only because I am a fair man, an honorable soldier. I have issued an order for the *Augusto Leguía* to depart your hacienda. I am suspending the inquest. We are leaving you to the mercies of your Indian raiders. We are surrendering you to the justice of your own people." He nodded toward the factory, whose main doors were open now, and from which Floralinda's workers— barefoot and shirtless—were lugging steel mesh, bags of caustic soda, iron hinges, sheets of metal, out to the creaking dock. Don Victor opened his mouth to speak, but he closed it just as quickly. Jaime was striding alongside the looters, shouting.

"It seems you are your own punishment, señor!" López barked. "I leave you to face your little nightmare. You are as good as dead, as I see it, and I will not waste precious bullets on a corpse." The general crossed his arms, savoring the moment. He saw a flicker of bewilderment in the papermaker's eyes. "Ah, yes. There is something more," he added. "Something I want you to understand perfectly. I am holding your priest onboard my ship. I intend to release him in exchange for Elsa Márquez y Márquez. The lady has been promised safe passage. I have already sent my men to fetch her. I tell you this only because I want it clear: Your priest will not go free until she is in my hold."

Don Victor's hands moved to his darts instinctively.

"No, Victor!" Tía Esther grabbed at her nephew's arm. "No more arrows! No more bullets!" She turned back to the general. "Did you say Elsa Márquez?" she asked him. She couldn't quite picture the young woman Jaime had married so many years before, but she knew the Márquez y Márquez family—their priceless collection of pre-Colombian artifacts, their endless sugar fields, their towering mansions, which clustered around the main square and glittered, like Moorish palaces, along the shoreline. She recalled the stooped figure of Doña Aldoña Márquez, in her Paris satins, limping from the door of her Packard to the Hotel de Turistas for tea with the ladies.

"Yes, Elsa Márquez," the general confirmed, clicking his heels. "Precisely." His gaze dropped to the grizzled little head resting on the old lady's bosom. His lips curled in disgust.

"Ah. I see," Tía Esther said with perfect comprehension, patting her nephew on the hand. She was thinking of another soldier, pushing his way through Trujillo during the insurrection, closing her sister's eyes for all eternity with a prodigal swing of his gun. "I see it all now, Victor. The Army of the Republic is meting out its brand of justice. It has come to the aid of those with all the power. To the people who least need it. Even here, in the heart of the jungle."

* * *

Although Jaime was trembling with hunger, weak from his night in bondage, he limped back and forth from the factory to the river, begging the men to come to their senses: There were no phantoms in the machinery, he shouted, no evil eyes in the paper, no bloodthirsty imps in the spindles and chemicals.

"Cover your ears!" Pedro cried, as he scaled the bamboo scaffolding.

Jaime, misunderstanding, turned to the gardener with hope. "Pedro! Help me! Tell them to stop!"

But Pedro only glared at him and the workers did as they were told: They put their hands over their ears as they hurried back from the water's edge, ordering one another not to listen to the shapechanger's son. He was a bewitcher, they said, a fountain of lies, a bringer of curses—like his father. The men carried on, wrenching the metal from the machines. They labored under that burden to the river, warbling in high-pitched voices so that they wouldn't succumb to the white man's enchantments. One by one, they dropped Mr. Meiggs's treasures—forged in the steel mills of Hamburg, brought to life on the shores of Pucallpa, reworked on the anvils of Floralinda—into the great, bronze river, where they plunged into the muddied turbulence and sprang up, like exuberant dolphins. A troop of capuchin monkeys, seeing the spirited action, ran from the trees, screeching with joy.

Two soldiers dragged Padre Bernardo from the hold of the *Augusto Leguía* and thrust him into the sun. The first image he saw as his eyes adjusted was a blur of green rushing toward him. He blinked rapidly, trying to focus. The lines quickly sharpened: There was a shapely bodice, a burst of folds, a beautiful, fierce-eyed woman. "Didn't I tell you?" she snarled at him. "I'm off!" It was Elsa, flanked by a phalanx of six soldiers, headed toward the ship's staircase. God was giving him another chance.

He reached out, like a sinner toward salvation. "Elsa! Come back! Don't let that fiend rule you!"

"Miserable cur!" she snapped. "How dare you? *You* are the fiend! *You* are the curse!" And then she was gone, belowdecks—her emerald train slithering into the captain's quarters.

The soldiers shoved the priest across the deck, toward the plank, and he made his way over it gingerly. As he stepped onto the dock, he saw a cluster of figures in the distance and recognized one as Don Victor. There was another man too, it seemed, holding a third's elbows.

The priest looked about to reassure himself that he wasn't dreaming: To his left, men reeled from the factory, toting machinery, ululating in high voices. To his right, a pregnant woman dragged a carved chair through the grass. Ahead, field workers with sticks and hoes were racing to the house. He heard the cough of a motor, caught a whiff of the sharp stench of kerosene, and then the army boat's engine rumbled to life behind him. He swung around to see Elsa Márquez y Márquez looming in a porthole—smiling, laughing—her pointy little chin looking for all the world like the spiked beard of Satan.

His heart heavy with remorse, he turned toward his church, longing for its comforts, but all he could see were fruit trees. As his eyes swept the crop fields, he saw the Jivaro girl in her bright yellow tunic, wandering toward the very end of the dirt road. She seemed lost in thought—a solitary figure against a dark wall of forest. Something else was hovering there too. For a fleeting moment, from a corner of his vision, an orange tongue flew up and licked the sky. But his eyes were playing tricks now.

"Bloody hell!" the Australian bellowed. Flames sprang from the workers' shacks, wriggling like snakes, casting a methyl glow on the pale straw beneath them. A black plume coiled up into the heavy air. "They're burning their own huts! Better say ah-dios to this place, old man!"

Don Victor gaped at the brute with the monkey arms. "*Loco porfiado!*" he barked. "I'm not going anywhere! My wife is still in the house, *comprende?* With my daughters and grandchildren!"

"I know," the Australian growled back. "And Señorita Marcela too. Don't you recognize this for what this is, man? A goddamn uprising! If you go up to that place, who knows what they'll do to you!" He opened his black shirt to reveal a revolver and a bow knife strapped to his chest. "I'm prepared to save your wife and everyone else in your household. Go to my barge, señor," he said. "I'll bring them."

"Victor," Tía Esther said in a voice that brooked no argument, "the man makes sense. He and I have traveled far together. I trust him."

"You trust this—"

"Stop this very minute. I didn't come all this way to see your corpse dumped into the river. Look at yourself. You are as old and decrepit as I am. And you're twenty years younger! You can't fight this many people. Don't test your fate. Do as the captain says!"

Powerless, with no more than his coconut skins to protect him, Don Victor glanced toward his mansion just as his worktable—that crucible of his imagination, birthplace of his inventions—peeked tentatively from his workshop. He watched it edge its way into the sunlight on the backs of four men. It was stripped bare, freed from its clamps and grappling hooks, all of its years in a butcher shop still evident in the wood, which gleamed a deep red even from that distance. The men walked it around, fanning it slowly, so that he could see every inch of its ruby grandeur. Then, willy-nilly, they ran it to the river, its legs up and jiggling, like an upended cockroach carried by ants.

Panting with effort, Jaime half-ran, half-stumbled his way toward his father. The old woman was there, as was the priest, looking wild-eyed and confused. Don Victor threw down his lance when he saw him. "My boy!" he said, and embraced him with feeling. "You foiled the Jivaro. Not many can claim it."

"They came for Suraya, Father. Just as you said they would. And now look what's happened! Our own men—stripping the factory. I can't stop them! They won't listen!"

"Look over there!" said Tía Esther, pointing toward the house. Fire had consumed the crests of the casuarina trees, and their long branches plummeted to earth like great flaming arrows, crackling as they fell. Through the black smoke they saw movement. They strained to make out what was coming through that blur of inferno. It was indistinguishable at first—a mere shadow, cloud white, dancing through the reeking fumes. They heard it before they saw it—a sharp cough, a gentle murmur, a high, ringing sound—and suddenly life itself emerged from the

oblivion: The Australian was walking with Ignacio. Behind them followed the rest: Doña Mariana, Graciela, Belén, the five children, and
the black dog, trailing a chain and laughing.

"Praise be!" Doña Mariana cried when Jaime rushed forward to kiss
his children.

"The house!" Jaime said, as he gathered the littlest ones in his arms.
"What are they doing to it?"

"Destroying it," Belén answered.

The people of Floralinda didn't seem to want to hurt the family, she
told him, after she caught her breath. They weren't interested in the living.
They were looking for ghosts trapped in the physical matter—*pishtacos*,
evil eye, shine. They had shouted at her to move back as they tore down
the portraits, thrusting bare feet through the canvases. They had called
for the spirits in the furniture to stand forth and show themselves. They
had wrenched the legs from the piano and marveled when its great
black breast struck the floor and howled at them. They had thrown the
silver against walls until it snarled back with twisted maws. They had
gone through the shelves, crashing through china, pulling out linens,
ripping their way room to room. They had freed the dog, freed the parrot,
freed the plants from their pots, but little else met with mercy. No matter how much Belén begged them to spare the Sobrevilla's possessions,
the people would not listen. They would not stop. "They will finish
with all we own," she told them. "Everything."

Belén looked down at her own hands. Not everything. She was holding Sor Juana's *Dream*. From its pages dangled a bright yellow tassel.

"The Virgin of Copacabana!" the priest cried when he realized they
were talking about the material world. "I must go to the church! I must
save her!"

"Stand back!" the Australian's face was dark with fury. "I'm the only
one going anywhere, *comprende*? The teacher is in the house, waiting for
me. And the cook is in there with her. What are you people, *loco*? Don't
you understand anything? This is revolution! If you're in one piece now,
you won't be when they've done with the furniture. Get out! All of you!
Get yourselves on the barge!"

They backed away, slowly at first, but the gruff man's fear was all the impetus Don Victor needed. He pulled the priest, took his wife by the arm, and began herding them toward the river. "Do as the man says!" he shouted. "Go!"

Suraya heard a drum, its rhythm as insistent as a frenzied heart. All at once she saw her father, a tiny figure at the margin of jungle, stone-still among the towering matapalo. He raised a hand, but she couldn't tell whether he was beckoning her forward or bidding her farewell. Even as the drum intensified, he stepped back into the shadow, and his form—once vivid in reds and yellows—faded precipitously to black. Suraya tensed, every sinew in her body taut now. She strained to find him again, but though she could feel his eyes, she could see him no longer.

The people of Floralinda were shouting at one another, streaming from the long flat structure to the water with heavy machinery on their backs. At the end of the road, she could see Kai-me and his people. The *iwishin* was there too now, and the priest. They were talking intensely, like a gathering of elders. Behind them, the gray boat was skimming away—a bloated river creature. Fire had overtaken the shacks, and a wall of smoke wafted from them, carrying its black stench into the forest. Suraya turned back to Kai-me again. He was talking animatedly, holding the little children. A sting of regret pierced her heart: She loved him—she was sure of it. But she did not love his world. She did not love its chewed land, loud life, bewildering ways. The drums were calling her clearly now. Come now, they seemed to say: back, to the stillness of the forest. She spun and broke into a sprint, over the bare earth, toward the place where her father had been standing.

The knife with the carved cat fell away easily when she untied the string. It had brought Jaime to her; it had cut him free; now it plunged to the ground with a clean motion. She ran on, calling her father's name. As she reached the strip between field and jungle, she grabbed her dress and flung it over her head. It caught a breeze, sailed up high, floating like an airborne chrysalis. Then it shot back to earth and tumbled along the shoots, a fugitive streak of yellow. Freed from the garish cloth, she seemed a fleet creature of nature. Her skin was barely distinguishable from the earth beneath. Her hair rose like wings; her legs gleamed in the sunlight. As she dove into the labyrinth of trees, the drum ceased, the dress rolled to a sullen stop, and the girl was gone—swallowed by an immensity of green.

Jaime watched as her agile body disappeared behind the dense wall of jungle. "Suraya!" he called. "Come back!"

How could she leave? Why had she run? Didn't she realize that her tribe had released her? From the instant the Jivaro had raced toward the forest, he had ceased to worry about her safety. So much else had gone wrong. He wanted to race after her now, pull her back into the sunlight, shield her from harm. But she was no longer visible—he could see only the smoke and the great stillness of a forbidding forest. A lancing pain shot through his wrists and ankles, summoning the misery of his last twenty-four hours. He looked down and saw he was holding his children's hands.

Don Victor patted his shoulder. "Come on, boy. Come with us now." He could see the pain in his son's eyes.

Jaime had no other choice. With lightning comprehension, he understood that he would live on with a shattered heart now; she was gone forever. He looked down at the three little faces. They looked back with reflected sorrow. The one thing he could do now was save them. Mustering his strength, he led them toward the barge.

The family moved like a jittery flock now. The air was thick with smoke and the river was filled with refuse. Shrill screams came from the house, but Don Victor could not know whether they were calls of joy or of desperation. The flow had reversed, the undertow was here: The ball was reeling in another direction. He curled his thumbs into his belt. "Ignacio!" he yelled. "Make sure my wife doesn't slip on the moss! The wood on the dock is slick with it! Belén! Hold on to your old aunt's elbow! Jaime, see about the children. Hurry!"

A troop of tittering capuchin monkeys followed them as they filed down the dock and crossed the plank onto the flatboat. The creatures bounded along, swinging from clothes, dodging the hands as the family swatted them away distractedly. One by one, the people stepped onto the barge, while the monkeys lined up on the dock like monks in a pew—chattering prayers, rolling their eyes. A great crash resounded from the house and Don Victor pointed at a shroud of dust that billowed up and circled the walls. Their home, the wellspring of all their dreams, was disappearing. The leader of the monkeys, a large dun male, pointed a finger too. His companions turned to look. There was a hoot, a clacking of teeth, and then the entire gathering of simian onlookers was pointing, jabbing the air, curling their black lips, chirring at the wonder of their abilities. Soon they were loping along on their knuckles, swarming onto the barge, then out to where the water beckoned. From there, they leapt onto whatever bobbed by providentially—steel drums: hard, hollow, perforated by drainage holes. Copper boxes: pried back, the metal curled open like flowers. Clinging to fortune's vessels, at once prisoners and potentates, the monkeys skimmed downriver, shrieking for dear life.

Boruba climbed the trembling mahogany staircase, carrying the great orb of her belly. The people of Floralinda were moving from room to room, flinging furniture, yanking Don Victor's emergency cords so that bells trilled endlessly in the servants' quarters. The walls shuddered with the rumble of falling debris. The witchman had fled the house, down the path, toward the fires, as if he were on an urgent mission. The barge captain, haggard and fierce, had pushed the family out the door; Graciela had pleaded for Boruba to come with them, but the cook had seen her husband dash by—across the foyer, up the stairs. She lumbered up the mahogany after him, one step at a time.

Boruba wasn't halfway up the staircase when Filomena crossed the landing in one of Elsa's dresses. Her bare teats dangled like ripe figs over the diminutive bodice. The skirt was so long that it fanned on the floor and she tripped as she walked, chortling at the game of it. "*Ei,* Boruba!" she called when she saw the cook laboring up the steps. "Look!" She squatted at the top of the staircase with her bald vulva in view. "Do I look like *La Loca*? Do you think I'm crazy?" She danced away, flicking her tongue. There was a loud whoop and a round of shrieks as more women tumbled from Elsa's room, some naked in hats and gloves, others trussed in chiffon or charmeuse. A toothless old hag, mother of Antonito the pulp shoveler, trooped by in nothing more than an olive green hat, its brown feathers quivering.

Boruba grabbed the banister to steady herself. She felt queasy, as if all the matter in her gut were suddenly roiling in rebellion. She forced herself up the last few steps. She reached the top just as her friends Maria, Carmen, and Yarua flew past like magnificent birds of paradise, trailing bright scarves and ribbons. The fabrics, like plumes, licked her arms. But just as she stepped onto the landing, a boom shook the side-wall, as if something heavy had struck it, and the force of the reverberations caused her to fall forward, onto her knees. A fine plaster dust crawled languidly across the ceiling. She rested there momentarily, catching her breath as Antonito's daughters wobbled out in high heels. So absorbed were they in the absurdity of their feet that they didn't see the large woman panting in the murky hallway, struggling to stand. They clomped away, giggling. A pulp shoveler rushed by in a dress of clear cellophane; through the yoke Boruba could see his buttocks. For so many years she had known these people, and now, as they searched high and low for *pishtacos,* they struck her as nothing so much as those ghouls—vile and fearsome—flying hungrily through her masters' house.

She peered into Elsa's room. The night table and reading chair were dismembered. The paintings lay mangled on the floor, the jungle scenes punched and torn. Elsa had never been kind, but seeing the violence done to those worldly treasures, Boruba was suddenly filled with pity. She leaned against the door frame.

"You!" a voice shouted. "Don't just stand there!" Pedro staggered into view, his wiry form straining under the weight of a mattress. An iron crucifix was thrust into his back pocket and it stood straight, resting against his belt. But he did not wait for Boruba's help. With a grunt, he heaved the mattress out the window, onto the dirt below.

"What are you doing?" she yelled.

He wheeled around, his brow wet with perspiration. "You can see for yourself, woman."

"You're destroying your master's property!"

"The *loca* is not my master."

"The bed belongs to Don Victor!"

"I don't work for him anymore. I don't work for any white man. We are all our own masters now."

She studied the face as if it were a stranger's. He was no longer her gentle husband; no longer the tight-lipped son of the curandero; no longer the gardener who worked the soil and nudged out its fruits, who wrapped lilies in parcels of cellophane. His eyes seemed flint-hard and lusterless. "Don't give me that face," he spat at her. "I know what I'm doing. I've sweated for years—for *their* cashews, *their* rubber, *their* stinking cargo. And then a shapechanger comes along and thinks he can buy my soul with his flimsy paper? Look at what's going on here, woman! Don't you know anything? That white family is done! Through! This hacienda is ours. The land in it belongs to us and the people who work it." Two faces appeared from behind the screen, looking out in mute wonder.

It was too much for Boruba. She crossed the room, holding her belly with one arm, waving the other like a scourge. "Give me that crucifix!" she yelled.

"What for?"

"Because it doesn't belong to you! Because you have no respect for it!"

"You're a Shipibo, *chukri*. The corpse on this cross has nothing to do with you." He pulled the crucifix out from behind him.

"I am a believer. Give it to me."

"You, a believer! You can't even read that thing you call a holy book! You don't even know the meaning of your prayers! You made me dress up that wooden doll, but you don't know who she is!"

"Yes I do. She is Christ's mother."

"Ha! The mother of a dead man! She means nothing to me. This iron means nothing to me!" He shook the cross over his head. "Don't you see? It's over! No more bullies! No more threats from that priest! No more orders from the señora! We can raise that baby in your belly as a Nahua, as a proud creature of this forest, as our fathers raised us to be!"

Boruba lunged at her husband and seized his arm, trying to wrench the metal from his hand, but he raised it beyond her reach. "That cross belongs to the padre!" she panted. "Give it to me!" She stretched on her toes, her hands grasping at air, her considerable heft against him. Finally her fingers closed around his wrist, and the heavy crucifix, with its image of Jesus—eyes on the sky, mouth gaping in agony—flew from his hand, out the door, just as Señorita Marcela was flying down the hall into the arms of the Australian. It struck the teacher on the head and knocked her to the floor.

Perhaps it was the sight of that towering colossus—the very antithesis of a rain forest Indian, with his hirsute arms and stubbled chin—bellowing with rage and lifting the limp woman high, that rendered Pedro immobile. Boruba stumbled out, grabbed the fallen crucifix, and raced downstairs after the barge captain. The people of Floralinda didn't notice. They poured through the corridors of the house, leaping and shouting, ferrying loot on their heads.

"Follow me!" the Australian roared to Boruba. But she was too distracted. Through the dust, she could see men staggering down the knoll, under a hulk of metal. Little by little, she made out the spheres in graduated sizes, ranging in rows, glinting in the sun. It was her masters' brass bed, like a great skeleton, parting its way through grass. She pressed the priest's heavy relic to her breast and made the sign of the cross—forehead to lips, shoulder to shoulder.

Boruba closed the kitchen door, fastened the hook behind her, and set the crucifix on the table. Gently, she lowered herself onto her stool. The room seemed a bastion of calm. Everything was in its place, just as it had been that morning. Yet all the order in her universe had buckled in the course of a day. She looked around at her knives, still hanging from hooks, shiny and clean. There was squash to pare, yuca to peel, papaya to chop. She reached out and felt the mesh dome Don Victor had constructed to keep the insects from devouring her delicacies. She glanced at the sink he had brought from Pucallpa; the counter he had built of huacapu; the tidy little pile of cellophane squares, cut and ready to wrap candy. So much life was crowded into this room. She had spent twenty-two years within the sanctuary of these walls, ever since the day Doña Mariana had marched to the river and lured her away from a riverboat galley. She had been fourteen years old.

This was the room where she had grown up: The room where the padre had taught her about Jesus. The room where she had fed three generations of Sobrevillas. The room where she had learned that the man she loved had been killed by a panther. The room in which their daughter saw first light, slipping from her like a fish, wet and tiny. The room in which her grandson ate, grinning like a cat over his sweet potatoes. These were the walls through which she had overheard the family gossip; the place in which she had come to know Pedro loved her; the room in which the two of them had opened their eyes that very morning. How could he have changed so much from one day to another? What insanity had he contracted at Chincho's? Why was he renouncing the masters she loved?

There was little recognizable beyond the boundaries of her kitchen. The people of Floralinda had destroyed everything else. She peered through the door and saw the disorder in the dining room: the contorted silver; the crippled table; the chairs upended, their elegantly turned legs shorn into ragged stumps. There were gashes in the wall, broken dishes on the floor, glass shards strewn into the foyer. Boruba felt Pedro's child roll heavily inside her. She sighed. It was time to go. Back in the kitchen, she took the crucifix and tucked it into a burlap sack. Then three papayas, two knives, the dried lily swaddled in cellophane. Hoisting the bag over her shoulder, she headed out to join her people.

She exited the rear door, squinting through the thick haze. They were there—small as dolls in the distance—standing on the barge. She could see Doña Mariana, her long hair tumbling to her shoulders; Don Victor scanning the shore. The Australian leapt on, holding the lifeless teacher. Gently, he carried her to where the engines hunched like insolent creatures. He laid her out on a folded tarp.

So it was that the Sobrevillas prepared to depart Floralinda on the very waters that, for years, had been their umbilical to a world beyond the hacienda. Just as the teacher blinked to consciousness, just as the Australian was about to untie the ropes and release the barge from its moorings, they caught sight of the witchman limping along the dock with what looked like an armful of driftwood. Wordlessly, Yorumbo held out the bundle for the shapechanger. "Come with us!" Don Victor yelled in Shipibo. But Yorumbo shook his head vigorously.

"Sweet Lord," Padre Bernardo whispered when he saw what the curandero was offering. It had been years since he had seen the Virgin of Copacabana unadorned. He rushed in and took her gently from the pagan's arms, awed by the wonder of that deliverance. A witchman had answered his prayers, produced a miracle. He bowed his head in gratitude. No sooner did the priest have the Virgin in his grasp than the Australian untied the ropes and the barge drifted off with the current. Yorumbo put a hand in the air and chanted an incantation. The south engines sputtered to life.

So it was that Esther Paniagua, too, departed Floralinda. Welcomed in by an army general, waved good-bye by a jungle shaman—on the very day of her arrival, on the barge that had brought her there. She stood with a hand on her nephew's arm and looked out at the flaming spectacle of his hacienda. The factory doors were agape, revealing the men who, like maggots, wriggled over iron carcasses. Where shacks once stood, there were but smoke and embers. Flames leapt from trees, through the tall grass, and rippled toward the mansion. All at once, the church collapsed, surrendering a black funnel of smoke, which slid out the door like the tongue of a dying animal. The priest gasped while the others hurriedly crossed themselves. Tía Esther's hand reached for her cougar necklace. "In the face of magnificent creation . . ." she whispered.

". . . our symbols are paltry things," her nephew added.

She turned and looked into his grizzled face—a cathedral of skin on bone. "Those words, Victor! You remember the words!"

"I've never forgotten them, Tía."

She smiled at the thought of the boy, his mouth hanging open as she spun her tales. "And do you remember a little black monkey with an orange beret? Do you remember her on that tiny church?"

He reached under his vest and drew something from his pocket: a child's wallet, rubbed dull by time and use. He pulled out a scrap of paper, pink and delicate as a butterfly wing. "My God." Esther Paniagua drew back, and the cat head swayed under her face. "You have it? After all these years?"

"Listen to what it says," he began, his voice filled with derision: *"There are those who think you a dreamer. Pay them no mind."* He snorted bitterly and looked out at his factory, watching his dreams course to the river and bob in the water like toys.

"Go on. Go on."

"You will encounter many things during your time on earth . . . but there will come a day when you face something dire, for which you cannot prepare." He stopped abruptly, his fingers marking his place on the old paper, as if it were a rosary.

The workers, he could see now, had spilled down to the dock and were applying their axes to the pilasters. He felt a great emptiness in the core of his chest. All along he had worried that he would encounter the dire in a wrong turn, an impossible venture. He'd never expected it would come like this. In the destruction of all he had built.

"It says more, Victor. Read it." Her face was filled with light now—suffused with the warmth of love and wisdom.

His eyes skimmed the faded lines until they came to the part he knew she meant him to see. And suddenly there they were: the words Yorumbo had spoken, words he had puzzled over much of his life. *Let go.* "*Let go,*" he read aloud. It was as much as he could manage. Tears sprang to his eyes.

"Let go," Tía Esther said. "Let go of this." She swept out an arm to indicate the hacienda. "The people you love are here on this barge. You are a fortunate man. Let the rest go. Find victories in things no one can take from you. Strange, isn't it?" She held up the cat head. "Lars went back to Norway so many years ago—half a century!—and yet he was with me today. I let go, and he stayed forever."

An animal squawked. A spool of cellophane floated by, ferrying a monkey along the rushing water. It was slipping and sliding, trying to dig its fingers into the paper. The cellophane unraveled as it went, and the shine swayed under the surface like the tail of a mythical fish.

"Is that cellophane, Victor?"

He nodded.

"It's very beautiful."

"Yes."

"You know why you love it so?"

"Because it is of this world. Because it grows from the earth," he said as if he were reciting catechism. "Because it puts roots in the dark, rises toward the sun. Because it is life transformed. You taught me that long ago, Esther."

The man and his aunt stood silent, watching the paper go. If she had traveled one thousand weary kilometers over desert, mountain, and jungle in the eighty-second year of her mortality, it was all worth it now. He had remembered her words, learned from them—even now, after so many years. It was remarkable, she thought, how the boy's fetish had grown into a swarming empire. She had appeared when he was a boy to witness its beginning, and she had appeared again almost fifty years later to witness its terrible end. The only evidence of his triumph was in a drawer in Trujillo—in a box of letters, recorded on brown paper, in Belén's elegant hand. But she had left all of that behind now, in another world. She turned and moved slowly, a hand to her tired back, using her parasol to buttress herself, leaving him to his thoughts.

The barge sailed on, parting the debris that littered the water: The silver dome that had followed the Sobrevilla progenitors from Spain— that had survived a war with Chile, served at Don Carlos's garden parties, been polished for Don Victor's baptism, then polished again for every family celebration thereafter—floated by, hopelessly mangled. The big bed, with its hundred lustrous brass balls, swayed languidly against the riverbank, dragging the river moss as it went. Belen's books—Ricardo Palma's stylish tales, Turgenev's letters, Blake's poetry in admirable translation, Jose Martí's recollections of Manhattan, all of Chekhov's plays—swirled by in every stage of despoliation: some with their covers intact, others torn back and swollen, many reduced to pages that swooped in the waves like schools of freak fish at play. Overhead, a king vulture wheeled slowly, watching.

"Boruba!" Graciela called out, and suddenly all of them looked up to see their beloved cook, running toward the water, gesturing frantically.

"I told her to come," the Australian said. "She didn't want to."

"Look at my loyal girl!" Doña Mariana murmured. "Look how she waves good-bye!" They waved back at her wistfully.

And so their lives moved on, like the endlessly moving river. They would see life whirl by as any mortal might—dimly and imperfectly, but they would never see Floralinda again. Within days it would be razed to a charred field. Within weeks worms would breathe new life into it. Within months, the matapalo trees would begin to inch back toward the water. Wise men would gather to shake their heads and shiver their nose rings. They would sprinkle the hard ground with river water, cluck their tongues about the plague of tongues, plague of hearts, plague of rebellion. And then they would puff smoke over the empty hacienda and bemoan a termite's inability to see. The virus had done its work: The people had stumbled on truth, thirsted for love, lusted for more, and then ravaged the world they inhabited.

Don Victor took one last look at Floralinda as it slid out of view. He had taken this turn in the river a thousand times, in search of Yorumbo. He had sailed it, motored it, rowed it, flown it—high—with the wings of a condor. But this time, he knew he would never return. The evil had pushed him out, but the Virgin had spared their lives. Now he was adrift on this river, a mite in the hands of God. A swift pulse of heat traveled his spine, mounted his neck, and slipped imperceptibly into the air. Now his head was clear, his body light, as if he were floating against gravity.

His family was huddled at the center of the barge—a tableau of humanity against the scrolling water. Tía Esther had been right. Everything he truly loved was on that expanse of wood with him. There was Doña Mariana, her head proudly in the air, like a bird scanning the horizon. There was Jaime, staring intently into the trees, tears coursing down his face—his children stroking them away with small fingers. There was Esther, holding the cougar head, telling its story to Ignacio. There was Belén, gazing at them, as if her heart would burst. There was Graciela, eyes sparkling like garnets, watching Louis Miller adjust a cartographer's device and place it carefully into her son's hands.

Don Victor considered his own hands, barely able to see them for tears. He was holding something—fragile, pellucid, a tissue as beguiling as glass: It was Negrita's fortune, entwined in his fingers. He brought the pink scrap to his face, smelled its sweet age, pressed its soft wrinkles against his lips. What tree had it come from—Amazon or Andes? What field—sugar or rattan? What rag? What bog of rice? What portable life traveled deep in its tiny pores? He himself had lived in that rose-colored universe, studied its lessons, struggled to measure its meaning.

It was different from any other talisman he could think of—different from Belén's hat or Tía Esther's cat head. Different from Yorumbo's rod.

It was a string of words, scribbled by chance, plucked from the dark by a monkey, tendered out of a carnival of possibility to nourish a hungry heart. It was paper.

He raised it up; it fluttered against his fingers. He brought it back and its ends opened like eager wings. He opened his hand, let go, and the fortune flew out like a restless bird, riding the wind until it was high above him. Suddenly a breeze swept it away, and it grew smaller and smaller, until it was a delicate petal against a vast army of trees. It danced wildly and, for a fleeting moment, he wished it back again. But by then it had banked away. Suddenly the paper was indistinguishable against the curtain of jungle. It was transparent. It was elusive. It was ingenious.

It was gone.

About the Author

Marie Arana is editor of *The Washington Post Book World*. She is also the author of a memoir, *American Chica: Two Worlds, One Childhood*, a finalist for the National Book Award; and the editor of an anthology, *The Writing Life: Writers on How They Think and Work*. Born in Lima, Peru, she now lives in Washington, D.C.